Son of a
beautiful sla...
courag... ...ough his veins.

FLAVIUS

Correus's half brother, their father's rightful
heir, a Roman possessing every advantage
except self-confidence and his father's respect.

APPIUS JULIANUS

A relentless general with a glorious past, he
expects his sons to carry on the family legacy
of military triumph—and burdens Correus
with a devastating oath.

AEMELIA

A senator's daughter and promised in marriage
to Flavius, she falls desperately in love—with
Correus.

FREITA

The proud German girl whom three Roman
soldiers could not subdue—Correus is
compelled to make her his slave.

THE CENTURIONS SERIES
VOLUME I

THE CENTURIONS

DAMION HUNTER

Library of Congress Catalog Card Number: 81-66173

ISBN 0-345-29691-5

Produced by BOOK CREATIONS, INC.
Executive Producer: Lyle Kenyon Engel

Manufactured in the United States of America

First Edition: December 1981

For Mouse and D.B.

Contents

MARE
GERMANICUS
(GERMAN SEA)

MARE
SUEBICUM

AVIONES

ANGLU

NUITONES

REUDIGNI

SUARINES

Albis (Elbe)

LANGOBARDI

Amisia (Ems)

SEMNONES

Visurgis (Weser)

Rhenus

Castra Vetera

GERM ANIA

GERMANIA
INFERIOR
(LOWER
GERMANY)

Colonia Agrippina

Bonna

Moguntiacum

(Main)

Mosa (Meuse)

Moenus

HERMANDURI

Mosella (Moselle)

Augusta
Treverorum

Rhenus (Rhine)

Nicer (Neckar)

NICRETES

BELGICA

Aquae

Danubius (Danube)

Augusta
Vindelicorum

Argentoratum

AGRI
DECUMATES

RHAETIA

GERMANIA SUPERIOR
(UPPER GERMANY)

Vindonissa

Aenus (Inn)

NORICUM

Augusta Raurica

Rhenus

GERMANY AD 72
.... Provincial boundaries
- - - The frontiers

ITALIA

· THE ROMAN EMPIRE ·
DURING THE REIGN OF
VESPASIAN AD 70

—— The frontiers
········ Provincial bounda[ries]

The Roman Emperors

AUGUSTUS	27 B.C.–14 A.D.
TIBERIUS	14–37 A.D.
CALIGULA	37–41 A.D.
CLAUDIUS	41–54 A.D.
NERO	54–68 A.D.
GALBA, OTHO, VITELLIUS	68–69 A.D. (the Civil Wars)
VESPASIAN	69–79 A.D.

WHEN THE EMPEROR CLAUDIUS DIED SUDDENLY IN 54 A.D. (it was suspected, probably with good reason, that he had been poisoned) he was succeeded by his nephew, Nero. Nero proved to be hopelessly inept and capricious, and finally, in 68 A.D., open revolt broke out. The leader of the revolt did not survive, but one of his supporters, Galba, the governor of Nearer Spain, was proclaimed emperor by his troops. The Senate confirmed this, and Nero, by now abandoned even by the Praetorian Guard, committed suicide in June. Galba, who was seventy-one at this time, began to march on Rome when he learned that Nero was dead. His arrival in the City was not without problems, and on New Year's Day, 69 A.D., the army in Upper Germany revolted and called on the Senate and the Roman people to choose a successor. The following day the Lower German forces saluted an emperor of their own, Vitellius, the governor of Lower Germany. Galba, hearing what had happened and having no son of his own, decided he should adopt an heir as quickly as possible. His choice earned the lethal objections of Otho, who had been one of Galba's supporters and had expected the succession for himself. On January 15 Otho had Galba put to death along with his heir. Vitellius then marched on Rome, and after a severe defeat, Otho committed suicide on April 16. The Senate promptly confirmed Vitellius as emperor. However, in the meantime the eastern legions and the troops of the Danube had

transferred their allegiance to Vespasian, governor of
Judaea. Vespasian's Danube supporters arrived ahead of
him, overwhelmed the army of Vitellius, dragged the
short-lived emperor from his hiding place, and lynched
him. The Senate hastily declared Vespasian his successor.

With Vespasian began a relatively stable succession,
but the memory of the Civil Wars, the Year of Four
Emperors, remained as a horror in the minds of most
Romans.

Cast of Characters

ROME

APPIUS	Flavius Appius Julianus the elder, a retired general
FLAVIUS	Flavius Appius Julianus the younger, his son
CORREUS	Appius's son by a slave, later given the name Correus Appius Julianus
JULIA	Appia Julia, daughter of Appius and his wife
ANTONIA	Wife of Appius and mother of Flavius and Julia
HELVA	A slave, Appius's mistress and Correus's mother
ALAN	Ex-cavalryman, a Briton, master of the cavalry remounts raised on Appius's estate
DIULIUS	Freed slave and former chariot driver, master of the chariot horses raised by Appius
SABINUS	Former centurion and staff aide to Appius, now weapons master to Appius's sons
FORST	A German slave
PHILIPPOS	Steward of Appius's estate
NIARCHOS	In charge of the indoor servants in Appius's household
EMER	A kitchen maid
THAIS	Former nurse of Flavius and Correus
AEMELIUS	A senator and neighbor of Appius
AEMELIA	His daughter
VALERIA LUCILLA	His wife
PERTINAX AQUILA	Camp prefect at the training camp of the Centuriate
MUCIUS	Drillmaster at the training camp

xiv

GENTILIUS PAULINUS   A senator and an old comrade of
                      Appius

ARGENTORATUM

PROBUS   Camp prefect at Argentoratum
PAULINUS   Lucius Paulinus, a historian, ne-
                      phew of Gentilius Paulinus
TULLIUS   Ex-legionary, servant of Paulinus
SILVANUS   Centurion in the Eighth Legion
                      Augusta
VERUS   Silvanus's body servant
BERICUS   Flavius's body servant
CALPURNIUS RUFINUS   Legate of the Eighth Augusta
MESSALA COMINIUS   Commander of the Eighth Cohort
                      of the Eighth Augusta
LABIENUS   Senior surgeon of the Eighth Au-
                      gusta
LUCANUS   Labienus's junior surgeon
ANSET   An Egyptian wineshop keeper
RHODOPE   A madam
JULIUS   A slave
BEORN   A German trader
QUINTUS   A man of Correus's century

GERMANY

NYALL   Nyall Sigmundson, chieftain of
                      the Semnones
MORGIAN   Nyall's mother
LYTING   Nyall's nephew
KARI   Son of a Roman woman and a
                      warrior of the Semnones
GEIR   A Semnone warrior, Nyall's envoy
HALLGERD   A Semnone woman
GILLI   Called Gilli the Lame, Hallgerd's
                      brother
ASUIN   A priest of the Semnones
ARNGUNN   Chieftain of the Nicretes
GUDRUN   His wife
FIORGYN   His daughter
SAEUNN   One of Fiorgyn's waiting women
VALGERD   A priest of the Nicretes

ARNI
INGALD }   Warriors of the Nicretes
RANVIG

HOSKULD   Chieftain of the Suarines

JORUNN   One of the ten chieftains of the Agri Decumates

FREITA   A woman of Jorunn's tribe

Prologue

HE WAS CALLED CORREUS, AFTER A CHIEFTAIN OF HIS
mother's people in the old days, and he was conceived in
a tent in a marching camp between Syria and Rome. His
father was a professional soldier, Appius Julianus,
legate of the Tenth Legion Fretensis, urgently recalled
to Rome by the Emperor Claudius in that ruler's last days.
His mother's name was Helva and she was seventeen,
bought as a slave after a minor rebellion in Gallia Belgica
some two years before. As a mistress she was entirely
satisfactory. As a companion to a man who suddenly
found himself up to his ears in the Emperor's business,
she became a liability, and he installed her among his
young wife's waiting women. Before he returned to the
Emperor his wife had also conceived.

Appius Julianus did his best for the aging Emperor,
but in the end it did little good. Claudius died, amid whis-
pers of poison, and Appius Julianus wisely made his
peace with Nero, the Emperor's great-nephew and successor. He then returned to his legion in Syria, which was
about as far away from that unstable prince as he could
get, and resumed his career with his beloved army.

Behind him he left two sons, half-brothers, born
within an hour of each other, and each a dark-side
shadow image of the other.

1

I

The Gods of New Ventures

BY THE TIME THEY WERE SEVENTEEN THE PHYSICAL LIKE-
ness between them was uncanny, but the likeness in the
soul was a dark, dimly sensed bond, and more often than
not a tie that chafed where it was felt.

Correus, feet braced against the chariot floor behind
a team of his father's ponies, sought to shake off the feeling that had clung to him all day and wondered if
Flavius felt it too. The sensation had grown even
stronger in the two years since their famous father had
come home to retirement. And today there was something more than that in the wind.

The gray ponies came into the turn, heads high, tails
frisking in impatience against the tight rein. The light
training chariot swung into the straight and he leaned
forward. "Now—fly, you devils!"

The ponies lengthened their stride, and his dark eyes
narrowed against the wind and sunlight under the rim of
his helmet. The helmet was ancient army-issue, stripped
of its crest and insignia, and he had balked at wearing it
four years ago when he had first begun to drive, protest-
ing indignantly that it made his ears hot.

"I'll make your backside hot if I catch you with it off
again!" old Diulius had said, jamming the helmet down
over Correus's brown hair. "Little good it'll do you to
split your head open like a melon before you've learned
not to overturn yourself on a curve!" Diulius had driven
a chariot himself once, in the Circus Maximus at Rome,
and his word was law on the training track, even for the
sons of the master. So Correus had worn his helmet, and
now it seemed as much a part of him as the bones of his
skull, although he still pulled it off occasionally—when

2

Diulius's watchful eyes were turned elsewhere—for the sheer pleasure of the wind in his hair.

The ponies swept past the painted arm of the starting pole, and Diulius dropped the hand with which he had been methodically beating time on the fence rail. "The best yet! That is a team! Tomorrow we'll try them against young Flavius and see how his blacks like being passed!"

"Nay then, hold off a day or two, and don't go stirring the waters just yet," the man beside him said. He nodded toward the far ring where Flavius was putting a bay horse through its paces, weaving in and out through a line of upright poles.

Diulius spat through the gap left after one of his teeth had remained behind, with a broken chariot, in the sands of the Circus. "Typhon take it! They aren't a pair of fighting cocks. I can't keep 'em apart forever. You let 'em train together yourself. It's natural."

The other man, Alan, was a time-expired veteran of the cavalry auxiliaries and master of the horses that the estate sold to the army as remounts. "And when they *do* work together, nine times out of ten young Correus shows the better, and the young master looks fit to split his gut. I'm telling ye, Diulius, let it bide for now. Don't race them."

"That's pure spite, and young master would do well to unlearn it. He doesn't want to be a charioteer anyway. He'll follow the old general's road and be a commander. Correus, now, he could have all Rome throwin' him posies in the Circus. It's a good way for a lad with no inheritance to make his way in the world."

"Aye, and he could take his shield in the cavalry," Alan said, looking sideways at his old friend, "and do a job that's fit for a man, not peacocking about in a fancy tunic to give some fat old hens a bit of excitement."

This disagreement was obviously of long standing. "Show me the man who ever got rich in the cavalry," Diulius snorted, holding up his hand in salute as Correus pulled the grays up at the gate. "The best yet, lad! Now go and walk 'em dry before Sabinus gets here, or he'll chew my tail for keeping you from your swordplay."

Correus pulled his helmet off and shook his head in

the light breeze, brown hair clinging in damp waves about his sharp-angled face. "The gods forbid," he said piously, and flicked the reins, grinning over his shoulder at the two trainers.

Alan raised his arm and whistled, and the boy in the far ring turned his mount toward them.

Flavius Appius Julianus the younger, called Flavius, also drew rein before the horsemasters. He was an inch or two shorter than Correus, with the same dark eyes and aquiline features, and dark curling hair like a faun's. He ran a hand down the bay's neck and gave an approving pat. "He's shaping up well, Alan. All of this year's lot are. I think it's the best crop yet."

"Early days, young master," Alan said. "But I'm thinking you may be right. Your father'll give the army its money's worth with this batch. Now off with you and get your shield."

Flavius nodded and trotted toward the horse barns while the two men watched. Alan sighed. "He'd be making a good man if he didn't have a father like Julianus to live up to."

"That's not the old general's fault," Diulius said.

"It's not anyone's fault," Alan said. "When your father's a famous general, you're expected to take up your sword with the Eagles, and he knows that." The trainer looked at the straight, slim back astride the bay horse. "I wonder if he wants to."

"That's like asking if young Correus wanted to be born a slave woman's bastard," Diulius said, exasperated. "Life turns out the way the Fates weave it for you, and you make the best of it. *You* ought to know that, you old fool." Alan was a Briton and had first joined the Roman auxiliaries at spear point, part of a group of young warriors conscripted into the service after the conquest of their tribe. "And in any case," Diulius said, "the general will hand him his manumission soon. He wouldn't have wasted an expensive education on him if he wasn't going to. Then we'll see whose training sticks the best, yours or mine."

Alan was silent, running one hand through his gray hair. It was cut short in the Roman fashion, although he still affected the drooping mustache of his countrymen.

Beneath his tunic his thighs were crisscrossed with scars, the occupational hazard of the cavalryman; and his feet, in soft leather boots, stood wide apart as if he still straddled an invisible mount.

"You look like a broody hen," Diulius said. "You know something I don't, I suppose. I hope you've got sense enough to keep your fool nose out of it."

"Oh, aye," Alan said finally. "There'll be enough other noses stuck in."

At the horse barns the two boys tossed their reins to the grooms who came running to take them and turned off together to the shed where the training weapons were stored. Side by side they looked more alike than ever, a mirror reflection marred only by Correus's advantage in height and by the fact that in him their father's dark curling hair was softened to light brown waves by his mother's blond north-country origins. They had their father's straight-backed military carriage—a bearing beaten into them young by Sabinus, the weapons master —and the confident, slightly arrogant stride of the privileged class. They were marked by their aquiline features and sharp-angled brows as their father's sons, and they had been raised together from birth. When they were five, Correus had become his half-brother's personal attendant, understanding even at that early age the boundaries of their relationship. They studied together, played together, and often enough got into trouble together.

The old general had acknowledged Correus as his son, stamping him as a privileged person, set above the other slaves. But he was still a slave, of course, never a son at Flavius's level. Correus learned well to keep the careful balance between his dual standing as son of the master and slave of the household. And if walking that fine line pricked at him occasionally . . . well, he had learned long ago that he had best stifle that as well.

Correus pulled the laces free of his leather wrist braces and pitched them in the corner where Flavius had thrown his riding boots. They ducked their heads in the water bucket and shook like puppies. "That was a good ride," Correus said. "Some cavalry commander's going to thank you for that horse."

Flavius smiled. "Yes, that one's too good for a trooper's mount. I'll tell Father to be sure he gets a fair price for him. That is, if he can spare the time from his grand plans for annoying his family," he added with a grim twist to his mouth as he slipped on his sandals and put his foot up on the wooden bench to lace them.

Correus heard a faint warning note at the back of his mind. There had been rumors lately, and he wondered if Flavius had heard them too. If they were true, he would have to tread lightly. "What iron has the general got in the fire these days?" he asked carefully, buckling on his sword belt and worn leather scabbard.

Flavius slipped on his own belt and took a pair of battered military swords from the rack in the corner. "He's taken a notion to find me a wife," he said disgustedly. He shoved one sword home in his scabbard and handed over the other as Correus breathed a careful sigh of relief.

"Well, that doesn't sound so dreadful," he said, grinning, as he took their shields from the wall. They were rectangular, overlaid with iron wings and jagged bolts of lightning barbed at the ends, and once they had borne their owners' name, rank, and legion. Someday the sons of Appius would carry their like as officers in their own legion. Or Flavius would. A post in the Centuriate was Correus's heart's desire; but it was something he didn't let himself think much on, because he might never get it. "I shouldn't mind that so much if I were you," he said, turning back to Flavius. (*If I were you . . . If I were Flavius, I would take it all for granted just as he does,* Correus thought bitterly.) Aloud he said, "You'll be going into the Centuriate in a month. You won't have to actually marry the girl for years yet, and you can go a-wooing where you will with no worries of a spear-point wedding." A betrothal was considered as binding as a marriage in Roman eyes. "Unless—I mean . . . the girl's not an absolute horror, is she? No warts or anything?"

"She could be as ugly as Hephaestus for all I know," Flavius said. "I've never laid eyes on her. As far as I can tell, her beauty in my father's eyes consists of the fact that her father, whose name is Aemelius, has bought the estate to the north of ours and has no chick but this one girl child to leave it to. I doubt that Father would mind if she had two heads. Look at poor Junius. *His* father just married him off to a girl who's only eight and already has a bottom like a hippopotamus. Can you imagine what she'll look like when she's old enough to bed?"

"Well, if she's only eight, he won't have to bed her yet," Correus replied.

"For which he was thanking the gods, drinking, the last time I saw him!" They both laughed. "Come along. I'll decide whether to cut my wrists or not after I've seen her. We'd better get our tails out to the practice ground. Sabinus'll be chewing on his sword by this time."

They picked up shields and pilums and a pair of wooden sparring swords as well, then headed for the practice ground where the weapons master was indeed awaiting them, hopping mad, the more so as Appius Julianus had taken it into his head to come to observe his sons' weapons drill that day. The older men fixed flinty eyes on the boys as they made their tardy appearance.

They were lifelong soldiers both, cast in much the same mold, differing only by the circumstances of birth that had made one man a general, the other his twenty-year staff officer. Sabinus had risen from the ranks to centurion, and men who did that rarely went as far as cohort command, and never further. Sabinus had made his place instead on Appius's headquarters staff in the days of the old general's first command, and stayed with him into retirement.

"And where in the name of Atalanta's apples have you been?" Sabinus inquired, glowering.

"We were sweaty and smelled of horse," Correus apologized. He liked Sabinus and had no desire to embarrass him in front of Appius. "We stayed to wash."

"A waste of time," Sabinus said, "since I'm going to make you sweat like you were in Egypt in midsummer. And if the general doesn't like what he sees, you'll do it all again."

Both boys groaned, since the general *never* liked what he saw, at least not publicly. "Go warm up," Sabinus said, pointing to the stuffed straw dummies affixed to

poles in the center of the practice ground. Both boys
started to protest on the grounds that they were *already*
warm, but then shrugged and headed for the straw men.
They knew well enough what Sabinus's retort would be
—you didn't use the same muscles to handle a horse that
you needed to fight a man.

They approached the straw men, shields up and
swords in hand, in the lockstep formation—stab and
take a step, stab and take a step—that was the core of
the Roman fighting discipline. "The short sword and iron
formation—that is the heart of the Eagles," was a favorite maxim of Appius. Positioning their shields perfectly
as they reached the straw men, they pierced them
through, slicing quickly from below, under the straw
men's imaginary defenses. As always, each wondered
briefly with the first thrust what it would be like when
the sword bit into flesh and bone instead of the chaff of
an autumn harvest: Flavius trying to feel how it would
be when a man stabbed *back,* Correus how it would feel
to kill a man he had never met.

Sabinus watched, nodding with a certain amount of
pride. "Blood will tell, sir," he said to Appius. "Blood
will tell, any way it's mixed. You've bred a fine pair." He
pitched his voice low enough so his charges shouldn't
hear and get a swelled head. Then he called, "All right!
Enough! Pilum drill, if you please, gentlemen!"

The boys brought fist to chest in mock salute and
sheathed their swords. Shields still on their arms, they
backed away from the straw men, drew their pilums
from the slings across their shoulders, and stood, each
hefting in his hand the pilum shaft—the deadly javelin
whose iron head went halfway down its length. The
pilum tip was tempered but the mid-length of iron head
was not, so that it bent as it pierced its target—whether
the target was the solid bulk of flesh or an enemy shield
—and could not easily be withdrawn. Thrown, it could
pierce a man at ninety feet.

"At the ready!" Sabinus shouted. The pilums drew
back. "Throw!" The pilums sang forward, with a deadly
whistle, and Flavius's pierced the straw man and shrilled
out beyond it to skid into the dirt. Correus's hit square

on, driving into the support post and buckling at the center.

"Good lad!" Sabinus shouted as Correus went up to wrestle the pilum point out of the post. "Flavius, aim for the post, not only the chest—it will hone your aim." He took up another pilum from a stack at his feet and tossed it broadside to Correus as Correus pitched the bent one aside, to be straightened later by the smith. "Again, please. Mark your target."

Watching, the two old soldiers stood straight-backed against the fence—the habit of lounging had been beaten out of them in their own youth, forty years down the road. "Hafed is bringing a man today I may buy," Appius said, nodding to another shield and sword propped against the fence post. "I want you to work with him, Sabinus, and give me your opinion."

"Hafed!" Sabinus snorted. "That swindling devil worshipper!"

"I am not sure exactly what Arabs worship," Appius said, "but I'm fairly certain it isn't a devil. In Hafed's case, I think it's the genie of greed."

"He'll sell you some broken-down wreck that he's spruced for the occasion, or a troublemaker you won't be able to trust with a blade in his hand. I expect you want him for a weapons trainer?"

"Mmm. This one's a German. The gods know how Hafed got his hands on him—"

"Hit him over the head with a brick in some alley, most likely," Sabinus said.

"At any rate, there's trouble brewing on the Rhenus frontier, and that makes this man useful. The soldier who has already fought an enemy has the advantage. I want my sons to know how to meet the unexpected. This German can show them how his kind fight."

"A most farseeing plan, noble one," a fruity voice behind them said, and Hafed swam forward bundled in voluminous robes of dubious cleanliness; he was followed by two of his men with a third between them. "And knowing as I do Your Honor's most worthy ideas on the training of the young, see: I have brought you the best warrior ever to wreak havoc in the Barbarian North."

"If he's all that good, Hafed, how'd he get himself captured?" Flavius called out. He and Correus had seized the slave merchant's arrival as a good excuse to stop throwing pilums at the straw men.

Hafed beamed genially but ignored the comment, turning his attention back to Appius. "See, noble lord, how strong he is, and young. Please, inspect him if you wish. Hafed sells no substandard merchandise." He clasped his hands placidly across his ample stomach, but the eyes beneath the flowing head covering were bright and beady.

Appius approached the German and nodded at Hafed's men to stand back. The German stood a good head taller than Appius, his long pale hair pulled back and tied in a knot at the side of his head. He wore a pair of breeches, much tattered, but nothing else save a heavy iron collar locked about his throat. He returned Appius's stare with an expression that might have been carved from granite. "Do you speak Latin?" Appius asked him gently.

Hafed answered, "Alas, Your Honor, I fear he has no tongue but the barbarian speech of his birth, but I am certain that he will learn, if he knows what is good for him." He glared at the German and his expression read plainly: "Botch this sale, and you will be sorry to be still in my hands."

"No matter," Appius said. "As you say, he can learn. And he can teach my sons his own tongue, which may prove useful."

Correus pricked up his ears at this—he had a liking for languages and the prospect of a new one intrigued him—while his brother groaned: "Merciful Athena, I have enough trouble learning Greek from a tutor. Now my father wants me to learn German from a barbarian."

"I want you to learn *anything* important that comes your way," Appius said over his shoulder. "The man who is educated has the advantage of the man who is not. As you will see." He turned back to the German and spoke to him carefully in the harsh, guttural speech of the North.

"What is your name, man?"

"Forst, lord."

"Forst. I have heard that an oath means much among your people. Is this true?"

"An oath is that-which-cannot-be-broken, lord."

"Indeed. Then Forst, if I should buy you from that fat thief yonder, would you give me your oath that you would bide by the rules of my household and render loyal service?"

"Do I have a choice, lord?" The German's voice was bitter.

"Certainly. A forced oath cannot bind a man. I won't buy you without your free oath. Refuse and I will tell Hafed I find you unsuitable."

The German cast a hunted glance at Hafed. "In that case, lord, I will give you my word . . . freely. I do not know how you may be as master, but I do know that one. I am thinking you could not be much worse."

"A dubious distinction," Appius murmured, "but honest enough. Very well, Forst, you will show your skill at arms with my weapons master, and then I will decide." He nodded at Sabinus, who picked up a long sword and an oval shield capped with a bronze ornament at the center. He handed them to the German, who raised his eyebrows faintly in surprise.

"I fought a campaign or two along the Rhenus in my own day," Appius said in German, and noted that Forst had begun to eye him with a certain grudging respect.

"Come along, then," Sabinus said, jerking his head toward the practice ground by way of translation. He picked up his own shield and sword.

The German stood bemused, hefting the heavy oval shield and the long blade. It had not occurred to him that he would ever again carry the weapons he had been born to, the war gear of his homeland.

"Get a move on!"

Sabinus's voice pulled him back from whatever north-country trail his mind wandered on, and he moved out cautiously to meet him. Sabinus carried a rectangular legionary shield and a short sword, and had many years of service with the Eagles to lend him good sense; he also wore a much-battered centurion's helmet and breastplate.

They circled each other warily. Neither intended to

THE CENTURIONS

kill the other, of course, although accidents were not unknown on a training ground. But for Forst, much rode on
this sparring, and Sabinus had instructions to push the
German as hard as he could. Appius wanted no weak
fighters to breed bad habits in his sons.

The German pushed forward suddenly and struck, a
high blow swinging down toward the neck, and Sabinus
caught it on his shield and dropped back a pace, maneuvering to get in under the guard. He thrust his own
sword up and in toward the rib cage, and the German
caught it with his shield edge. They circled once more,
then clashed in a flurry of blows that left Sabinus with a
scrape down his thigh where the German's sword had
come in low and stopped only a split second too late as
Sabinus twisted away.

"Did I not tell you, lord, that this one is a warrior
without match?" Hafed said. "The finest fighter of his
tribe, and they are a people of the sword." He embroidered at will on his charge's pedigree. In truth, although
he saw no reason to mention it, he had bought the German cheaply enough from another slave merchant who
had branded him an incorrigible with no discernible
skills and a taste for picking fights with any of the other
slaves who came his way. Hafed had thought of Appius
immediately, deciding that no man who wasn't any good
at it would pick fights so freely. If Appius didn't buy him,
the German was of no use to anyone except an overseer
in the mines, and Hafed had managed to make that
plain to him even without benefit of an interpreter.

The German swung his sword again, and Sabinus
jumped into the blow, catching it on his shield, and continued forward, pushing hard against Forst's shield. The
German steadied himself and took another step back just
in time to block the thrust of Sabinus's sword. He knew
well enough the danger of letting a man with a short
sword too close—as the short sword came within range,
it also came in under the effective range of the slashing
longer blade, and frequently up under its enemy's shield
as well. Indeed, a man with a dagger could kill a man
with a long sword if he could once dodge past its shining
deadly arc and in too close for the long blade to have
effect.

The German pulled back and raised his shield, his long sword well out. Thus, he could keep Sabinus at bay indefinitely. It was when he drew back to strike that his defenses were in danger. The German feinted a blow at his opponent's leg and then brought his blade in high, catching Sabinus's shield at the same time with the edge of his own and jerking it out and down. There was a clang as Forst's blade struck the side of the trainer's helmet, but Sabinus had caught the feint in time and the blow was glancing. They pulled back from each other again, breathing heavily now, sweat running down their faces. The German brushed his forearm briefly across his brow, shield well up and one eye on his opponent. Correus thought grimly that that was another good reason for keeping your head under a helmet—the padded lining kept you from being blinded by your own sweat. But the German armies were metal-poor. Most fighters did not even own a sword, but fought only with the long spear. If this warrior had been trained to the sword, he was undoubtedly of some rank or wealth in his tribe, as Hafed had claimed. But Sabinus was an old soldier and he knew a trick or two, and one of them was fighting long swords.

He began to push Forst hard, keeping the barbarian's shield up and his sword busy, while his own blade probed relentlessly, seeking the split-second opening that would let the vicious, short-stabbing blade slip through. And then with a final push and a quick little quarter-turn that made the German swing around with his eyes to the sun, he found it. As the short sword slipped in under Forst's guard there was an explosion of sound as the German brought his own shield hard into the Roman's, knocking him backward with the sheer strength of one arm. Sabinus's blade slipped up across the German's chest, opening a quarter-inch gash from abdomen to armpit as Sabinus reeled back, one foot sliding from under him with the force of Forst's shield blow. Sabinus stumbled back three steps before he could right himself, while the German stood panting, blood streaming from the gash in his chest.

"Enough!" Appius shouted.

Sabinus raised his sword and dropped it again as Ap-

pius came forward. "That oily thief is right," the old
soldier told Appius, panting. "That one can fight."

Appius nodded. "Ask my lady to have one of her
women see to him." His eye fell on the heavy iron band
around the slave's neck. "And get the key to that thing
from Hafed. No slave of mine wears a dog's collar. Tell
the steward to send him to me tonight after dinner. And
get that scrape on your leg seen to as well," he added.

"It's little enough," Sabinus said. "Time for that when
I've put the lads through their paces."

"See to your leg, man. I'm not yet so old I can't play
at wooden swords with my own sons," Appius informed
him, "and you don't need an infection in that leg at *your*
age." His voice softened. "I've a decision to make, old
friend, and this seems as good a way as any to come by
it."

They were backlit shadows in the gold of the late-
afternoon sun, each with a wooden sparring sword in his
hand, weighted and balanced to respond like the steel
it mimicked. The ridges of their helmets shone with a
parade-armor glow in the dimming light. Behind them
on the gentle curve of a hill sat the house of their birth,
its windowless walls blind under the red tiles of the roof,
all life turned inward to the courtyards and gardens en-
closed within. A ring of fir trees encircled the walls and
swept in stately march down the long drive that opened
out onto the road to Rome. At the base of the hill stood
whitewashed horse barns near hay fields and the brood
mares' pastures, filled now with this spring's foals careen-
ing in the sunlight like a flight of birds. A gaggle of white
geese emerged honking from under the frisking hooves
and retreated in indignation to forage for weeds among
the new green growth of the fields. A fine retirement,
Appius thought. A good enough way for a man used to
the long march to spend his aging years. A retirement
. . . and an inheritance. His eyes went back to the sil-
houetted figures of his sons, almost indistinguishable in
this light—a likeness to tear the heart. Appius raised his
sword and nodded at them. You could tell a lot about a
man when you had fought him. That was another maxim
of Appius's.

Flavius came forward, sword and shield at the ready, and as they made a half-turn so that the sun would shine in neither man's eyes, Appius saw that the boy had bitten down hard on his lower lip and there were taut, strained lines about his mouth.

Father and son came together with a clatter of wooden sword on shield, each seeking the advantage, eyes watchful. A wooden sword was the greatest teacher of all. It hurt like Hades on bare skin and could make your head ring, even under a helmet. And with a wooden sword you fought in earnest, seeking a killing blow. Practice with live steel defeated its own purpose. Appius did not want his sons learning to pull their blows, as steel required, slackening up on their force at the last moment. It was a habit too hard to unlearn, and one that could cost a life. There was no conditioned reflex to slow the arm of the man who had trained with wood.

Nor was there any such reflex in Appius, who could count almost forty years with the Eagles—forty years of fighting in deadly earnest. He feinted low, at the leg, and as Flavius dropped his shield, Appius brought the sword up high and down across the collarbone in a blow that would have severed it. Flavius gritted his teeth in pain, and Appius said to him, behind his shield, "Watch my eyes. And watch my feet. An enemy who swings a sword and doesn't follow by adjusting his feet has no such blow in mind."

Flavius lunged forward and stabbed with his sword, and Appius caught it on the face of his shield. "And never stick your sword point-first into another man's shield," he added. "You may not get it out again."

"I assure you, sir, it was *not* intentional," Flavius said between his teeth. He caught his father's next blow on his shield and flung up his sword blade to block the next thrust.

"Good!" Appius said.

Flavius smiled grimly. He hated this—dear gods, how he hated it!—sparring with his father, never quite measuring up to the old man, while Correus leaned on his shield and watched them. It would be something, perhaps, to be the son of a slave, to have no standard to meet—again he gritted his teeth and blocked a short,

stabbing stroke from his father's sword. A slave never
had to worry that he might not measure up.

"Enough!" Appius said suddenly, watching Flavius's
face across his shield rim. "Go and get cleaned up for
dinner. I'll send Correus to you when I'm through with
him."

Flavius opened his mouth and then closed it again. He
touched his fist to his breast in salute and turned and
stalked up the hill to the faceless house, while Appius
watched him go, his face unreadable. He saw that Correus was also watching Flavius. "All right, you young
layabout, you've had enough of a rest."

Correus lifted his sword and saluted smartly. "Yes,
sir!" Appius saw the flicker of a grin under the shadow
of his helmet and grinned back. He couldn't help it.

Correus came forward warily, but his eyes were bright
and the light breeze had caught a strand of brown hair
and ruffled it under his helmet rim. He had the look of
someone about to enjoy himself immensely, the coiled-
steel exuberance of the born fighter. Appius knew that
look. It had looked back at him from a mirror often
enough. "A little more humility would be in order," he
called across the field as Correus walked toward him.

"I'm sure you'll beat it into me soon enough, sir!" Correus called back, and they both laughed. It seemed to
Flavius, halfway up the hill to the house, that there was
a mocking note to the laughter that pursued him, long
after the sound had faded in the wind.

Correus came at Appius hard, tucked tight in behind
his shield, sword held close and tipped slightly upward
for the stab from below which was the deadliest of all.
As they closed, Appius stabbed first, and Correus's
shield slid out with smooth practice, enough to turn the
blow, no more. The youth's sword flashed out under Appius's guard, and the older man blocked with the same
swift economy of movement. They struck and blocked,
feinted and dodged, and Appius felt the swift exhilaration that came with meeting skill that matched his own.
Appius seldom allowed himself to fight with his second
son. He took too much pleasure in it, and he knew that
such pleasure could cloud his judgment as a father; and
it might be dangerously apparent to anyone who watched.

Ten minutes later they broke apart, panting, hot, sweaty, and entirely pleased with themselves. Each had yet to make the slightest dent in the other's defenses. It was like fighting a mirror, the more so as Correus was left-handed. When this had first become apparent as a toddler, the women of the house had tried to force it out of him, considering left-handedness unlucky, a sign that the gods had some peculiar malice in mind. Appius had come home on leave to find the boy screaming in frustration, his left arm bound firmly to his side. He had put his foot down; it was the first time he had taken much notice of the child, but the boy's furious determination had made an impression on him. And as it had occurred to him that he had never yet seen a right-handed soldier who had once been left-handed show any natural balance at all, he had shaken the women's protests into the wind. Correus, allowed to go his own unorthodox way, had proved his father right; trained all his life by right-handed swordsmen, he was used to fighting a mirror image, while his opponents generally were not. It gave him the advantage, and he had learned to make the most of it.

"You've improved," Appius said, and Correus felt a surge of pride. His father rarely bestowed even that much praise. Appius set his shield down, and Correus dropped his own, uncertainly. There *was* something in the wind. . . .

Appius motioned to him, and they walked in silence out the gate and down to the edge of the horse pasture. Appius was silent for a long while, gazing at the horses and the newly mown hay and the house on the hill where the red sun, Apollo's chariot, was beginning to drop down to the darkness beyond the world. "The future comes upon us, my son," Appius said quietly at last, and Correus found his hands clenching the fence rail tightly. His father rarely called him by those words.

"You know that I intended to free you," Appius went on, "when you were grown."

"I thought it was in your mind, sir, yes," Correus said.

"All this . . ." Appius nodded at the sunset-shadowed acres of the great estate. "I can't give you any of this. It is Flavius's, and I wouldn't give it to you if I could. It is his by birthright, and that is a thing that the gods decide —I think. But you—Alan and Diulius tell me that you have the skill to make a way for yourself in the cavalry, or even in the Circus. Although the Circus is not what I would choose for you myself, despite the fact that a great many drivers have grown rich there. Tell me—is that what you want?"

"Of the two, sir, I think I would choose the cavalry. It's closer to—" He stopped. The cavalry was closer to what he really wanted; and what he wanted was as far beyond him—even as a freedman—as the ownership of Appius's estate.

Appius studied his son's face. "It's closer to the Centuriate, you were going to say. You want the Centuriate, don't you?"

"Yes, sir." Correus held his voice steady. The Centuriate . . . an officer's post in the legions, the Eagles, the elite of the army . . . his father's own road. It was the road that Flavius was entitled—expected by birth—to follow. "Would they take me, sir?"

"The Centuriate will take any *son* of mine," Appius said, with subtle emphasis on the word. "Correus, my son, listen to me. You are in my mind perhaps more than you know. What a man leaves behind him is important to him—you will feel that way also when you grow older, I think. I can't give you what belongs only to Flavius. But there is enough of my name to share. I can give you that to leave behind you in your turn, and with it appointment to the Centuriate."

Appius caught the sudden light in the boy's eyes, the paling of the bleak shadow he had seen there so often when their talk turned to the army. *It is little enough I do for him,* he thought. *Little enough for a part of my bone and blood.*

"If my master could keep his feet still, the laces would arrange themselves more smoothly." There was an exasperated edge to the slave's voice, and Appius stopped fidgeting and stood docilely while his attendant arranged the intricate crossings of his sandal laces to his satisfaction. The sandals were of soft, supple leather, dyed a plain unpretentious brown, but they were a gentleman's

foot covering, a house sandal, and his feet would never look
at home in them, Appius thought ruefully, no matter what
his body servant did to them. His feet had worn heavy
marching sandals for too long, and they had left their
mark in knobs and calluses from heel to toe. Neverthe-
less he studied the floor patiently while his servant secured the last knot. The floor tile was inlaid with a bright
mosaic of a fish-tailed Triton who calmed the waves
about him with a conch-shell trumpet. The surrounding
walls, rising as the land does from the sea, continued this
soothing theme with scenes of Flora in a blooming garden and small Pan-children in a sun-dappled wood, piping to some unseen deity.

The windows looked out onto a rose garden. At its
center was a pool where the kitchen cat lingered in rapt
contemplation of the fish that lurked among the water
lilies; and beyond could be glimpsed a graceful marble
court dedicated to the goddess Athena. An adjoining
room contained a private bath; beyond that was the bedchamber. Appius had adopted the Triton room as his
private dressing chamber, but like most old-fashioned
Romans, he shared a bedchamber with his wife.

The bustle of a household making ready for the dinner hour drifted through the far doors opening onto the
atrium. This was the central chamber of the house, built
around its own small pool with a skylight above and
small altars to the household gods along the walls. A
smell of fish and herbs drifted from the kitchen, and a
serving girl scampered by along the colonnade with a
bowl of fruit, followed by the cook's small daughter importantly carrying a tray. There was a shout of indignation and then laughter from the rose garden. Flavius and
Correus, scrubbed and brushed and wearing clean tunics,
were playing latrunculi at a stone table by the pool and
trying to cheat each other as usual. Since neither one had
the slightest skill at the game, cheating rarely affected the
outcome. They were fond of each other, Appius thought.
Maybe that would be enough. Enough to take the sting
of slave birth from one, and of being always outshone
from the other?

Appius put up his arms and let his servant drop the
white woolen tunic over his head. The plain garment

was proper civilian attire for dining, but it made him slightly uncomfortable, as if he had come out in his undertunic by mistake. Scarlet was a centurion's color, purple for a general, a legate, as he had been. But retired military men who peacocked in their uniforms on country estates had always irritated him. There would be scarlet uniforms around the table again soon enough.

There were no guests that night, and as usual when the family dined alone, they gathered together for their meal: Appius on the main couch, with his wife, Antonia, across from him and their pretty daughter, Julia, beside her, both in pale gowns of blue and yellow silk and the diaphanous scarves which were all the warmth that fashion permitted; Flavius on the third side shared a couch with Correus, in his dual position of attendant to Flavius and unorthodox son to the household. Correus's mother, Helva, did not dine with the family. In spite of the fact that Appius still visited her chamber occasionally, it would never have occurred to him that she should dine with his wife.

The dining room also opened onto the garden in a vista of vine-covered trellises that led to a fountain of marble dolphins balanced on their tails and spouting streams of water. The floor was inlaid with mosaics of baskets of fruit at the corners and lobsters that Julia said always made her feel they were snapping at her ankles. The walls, as in most Roman rooms, were brightly painted over every available inch of plaster with scenes supposedly conducive to good digestion: waving palm trees, garlands of flowers, and cavorting nymphs with bells around their ankles, as well as a banquet table spread with wine flasks and dead game. Appius had his doubts about this last one. One of these days he was going to have something more appetizing painted over it. The dining room of Aemelius had a lifelike depiction of the infant Hercules strangling a serpent.

Appius waited until the first two courses had been served—a light selection of shellfish and salads with honeyed wine; and a rack of roast pork and pheasants cooked in cream—before raising his goblet, which he did just as the fruit and honeycakes came in. The wine

steward bent over him with an amphora, and Appius
shook his head, murmuring something in the man's ear.
He bustled out again and presently reappeared with
another amphora, from which a wisp of cobweb trailed.
The steward gave it a hasty brush with his sleeve as he
bent to fill Appius's goblet. Antonia raised her eyebrows.

"The best wine?"

"Falernian," Appius said firmly. "My father always
maintained that Falernian wine was for serious an-
nouncements and special occasions, and since this is
both, I see no reason to differ with him."

"What is it, Papa?" Julia looked up from her goblet,
interested. She was only fifteen and not often allowed to
drink her wine unwatered. This promised to be an evening of excitement.

Appius splashed a little of the Falernian on the tiled
floor for the gods that guard new ventures. "We will
drink to my son, Flavius Appius Julianus the younger,
who will be eighteen in one month, and of an age for the
Centuriate."

Everyone knew that. Julia made a disappointed face.
"But Papa—" Her mother reached out an admonishing
hand and Julia subsided.

"And to my second son," Appius went on, and there
was a silence like a caught breath. "Correus Appius
Julianus." He paused. "Adopted son of Appius, who will
enter the Centuriate with his brother."

II

The City in Festival

"To serve and obey, lord. By my gods and by your
own." Forst knelt awkwardly with his hands in Appius's
in the master's study. The bedraggled trousers were gone
(probably to be burned, Appius thought with an inward
chuckle) and he looked uncomfortable enough in a

slave's plain tunic of brown wool. Indeed, Forst had
fought desperately at the removal of those trousers, but
the steward, unyielding, had informed him tartly that
when he played at swords with the young master, he
could wear any outlandish garment he chose, but about
the house he would dress like the servant of a civilized
man. That Forst could not understand a word of this had
troubled the steward not at all. He had his standards.
But the iron slave collar was also gone, and when Antonia's women had finished cleaning and bandaging the
gash in Forst's chest, the steward had smeared the gall
marks on the German's throat with salve, and when he
muttered to himself about barbarians, he was not speaking of Forst.

"Very well," Appius said. "Stand up and attend to
me. It is my wish that my sons know and understand the
warfare of the nations they may in time have to fight
themselves. And in view of the trouble your kin are making along the Rhenus, Germany is very high on my
list. I want them instructed in how to fight a man carrying either a long sword or a spear, specifically a German
so armed. If your loyalty to your people will not permit
you to do this fairly, then say so now and I will set you
to work in the fields instead. It will not be as comfortable
a life, but I won't send you back to Hafed, either."

"I will teach them, lord. I swore it."

"Good. I also wish that you teach them your own
language. Though I speak it somewhat myself, I know
not enough to instruct anyone else. There is no point in
their learning bad German from me, when they can
learn it properly from you."

"Yes, lord." His mouth moved in what might have been
a faint smile. "They will have to if I am to teach them my
people's way with a sword, since I do not speak their language."

"As to that," Appius said drily, "you will pick it up. *You*
will have to, since no one else in this household speaks
German but myself. You have one month before they
leave for their service in our army, and I give their
weapon training entirely to you for that time."

Another flicker, this time of something like fear,

crossed the German's face. "And after that, lord . . . you will no longer need me?"

"After that you can help Alan with the cavalry mounts. I do not buy a slave with the intention of reselling him, unless he gives me cause. Now take yourself back to my steward Philippos and he will find you a bed in the slaves' wing."

Forst nodded and, uncertain as to what etiquette demanded, dropped briefly to one knee before turning to go. He would give good service in exchange for decent treatment, Appius thought. As Forst left, Appius noted that his steward's efforts at a civilized appearance had not extended to cutting the German's hair. It was just as well. That long hair was as much a part of a German's soul as his manhood; the coiled knot on the side of his head meant he had killed his man in battle. Forst would not have parted with his hair without attempting to part Philippos's skull in exchange. He must remember to tell his steward to continue to let well enough alone in that respect. You could take so much from a man and no more, before you pushed him to the brink, and Forst had come very close already with Hafed, he thought.

This train of thought was interrupted by the light patter of sandals at the door, and Appius raised his eyebrows in surprise. He knew his wife's step well enough, but she rarely came to him in his study, an entirely masculine room of his own devising that bore more resemblance to a commandant's headquarters than a gentleman's fashionable retreat. The severity of the black marble floor and the shelves of books and scrolls which extended almost to the ceiling against buff-colored walls always made her slightly uncomfortable. She preferred her husband's company in the bright cheerfulness of the atrium or, if the matter were private, in the airy surroundings of their sunny bedchamber with its blue and yellow walls and well-cushioned wicker chairs. Antonia was, however, a lady of much determination, and tonight she had taken all she could stand.

After Appius had disappeared into his study, the atmosphere at the table had been enough to provoke a Vestal Virgin. Julia had been loudly curious, Flavius congratulatory but tight-lipped. After Correus had gone off somewhere, the gods knew where (eyes shining, he was turning handsprings in the marble courtyard by the statue of Athena), Helva had drifted in, blond hair immaculately coiffed and smugness written on every inch of her lovely, stupid face.

How could Appius have done this without even consulting her, Antonia thought furiously. She practically slammed the door open.

Appius, after a glance at his wife's expression, put down the stable accounts he had been inspecting and gave her a bland look. "I think we're spending far too much on grain." He flicked a hand at the sheaf of figures beside him. "I'm thinking of putting that lower field into pasture. It doesn't seem to grow anything else successfully."

Antonia ignored this conversational gambit and drew up a chair before her husband's massive oak desk. She moved a bronze lamp on a stand slightly to one side so she could look him in the eye. Antonia had never been considered a beauty, even in her youth, but she was slender and straight-backed, with gray eyes and dark hair arranged to suit her face, in a lightly curled style elaborate enough to mark her as a lady of position, but avoiding the frivolity of crimped sausage curls and false topknots. She came of the family of Marcus Antonius, and the great man's strength of character had been inherited in full measure. She had been a famous man's faithful and hardworking wife for twenty years and had in the long run grown fond of him. But her deepest feelings were reserved for her children. Now she fixed their father with a steely eye and prepared to do battle. "Appius, you should have consulted me."

"My dear Antonia, I have every right to adopt Correus if I wish to. And since I knew you to be fond of him, it did not occur to me that you might object."

"Of course I'm fond of him!" she snapped. "I've been more of a mother to him than that nitwit that bore him!"

"Well, then—" Appius let the reference to Helva pass, knowing that it sprang not from jealousy but from impatience with a woman Antonia considered to be of very little use. Theirs had been an arranged marriage, as were most unions among the privileged, and Appius had provided his wife with every consideration and courtesy.

Antonia had no real reason to object to his bedding a mistress among the slave women as long as that mistress didn't step out of her place.

"I have *never* objected to your acknowledging Correus!" Antonia slapped one slender, ringed hand down flat on the desk for emphasis. "I have *always* said that you should free him when he was grown, help him to a post in a good auxiliary unit, or anything else his taste ran to! But adopt him—give him *my* son's name—no!"

"It's not Flavius's name I'm giving him," Appius said. "It's my own. His taste runs to the Centuriate, and you know as well as I do that nothing short of formal adoption will take him there."

"I fail to see the need for Correus to join the Centuriate," Antonia said icily. "Many other men have lived very happy lives without joining the Centuriate."

"Correus won't," Appius said quietly. "*I* wouldn't have. Antonia, the Eagles are bred into that boy—my family goes back six generations in that service—and he's too good to waste. Correus could go to the top."

"And rise to be emperor, I suppose."

"I doubt that would appeal to him," Appius said. "It never did to me, though my troops wanted to try it once —did I never tell you?"

"You'd have more likely ended with a knife in your belly, like Vitellius," Antonia said. "I have no patience with sword-made emperors. Now that Vespasian is wearing the purple, there will be no more of that."

"How do you think Vespasian got it?" Appius inquired. "Still, he is a good man, and may hold on to it. I shouldn't expect Correus to go much higher than . . . oh, say a military governorship," he teased.

"At the expense of *our* son! Appius, you are not going to divert me from this!"

"I'm not trying to," Appius said. He was beginning to get exasperated. "I have no intention of leaving Correus any part of what belongs to Flavius. He will make his own way."

"By giving him your *name*, you take away from Flavius. It is an old name and I was proud to marry into your line. It is not something to give away indiscriminately."

She was very serious about this, Appius realized. Hades consign all women to his own domain! He couldn't simply ride roughshod over her. He owed her that much at least. He ran a hand through his hair. "Giving my name to my own son is hardly indiscriminate."

"If every man gave his name to every son he'd ever fathered, the patrician families would have some very odd blood indeed!" Antonia snapped.

"I expect I've fathered more sons than Correus," Appius said mildly. "I assure you I have no intention of rounding them all up for a wholesale adoption."

Antonia's eyes blazed. "You've fathered one other son you'd do well to remember! Your own son, by your *wife*! If I were you, Appius, I'd think carefully before I did this to him!"

When she had gone, Appius sat for a long while with his head in his hands. He was not the kind of household tyrant who would tell his wife to shut her mouth and mind her spinning. But he had not expected this. He wondered uncomfortably if Antonia suspected that her own child was no match for his slave-born brother. He had once thought her devotion too single-minded to allow that thought, but perhaps he was wrong. She obviously feared some ill effect on Flavius by setting his brother as an equal to him. The gods knew Appius feared it himself, he thought unhappily, and he loved his first son. But Correus had to have his chance. It was all Appius had to give him.

When he came to bed that night, Antonia was already asleep (rather ostentatiously, he thought), and she rose early and bustled off to see to the household as soon as her maids had dressed her hair. Usually they made their plans together in the morning, and he knew she was giving him time to think on what she had said the previous night. Appius sighed and felt on the cool floor for his sandals. Antonia had learned to handle him very well after twenty years.

The inner workings of the great house were in full swing by the time he had dressed. The slaves had been up before first light and their mistress not long after them. Flavius and Correus were with their tutor, ploughing through the intricacies of Roman law and history, and

Homer in the original Greek. Julia, who had already received as much education in the grammar school as was considered necessary for a girl, was with her mother, learning firsthand the skills of a thrifty housewife and the management of a staff that numbered in the hundreds. Appius could hear their voices in the kitchen concocting the evening's menu (a company dinner with the family of Aemelius) and settling some squabble between Philippos and the cook, who was an artist and prone to temperament. Outside the walls, the field slaves would be at work and the gooseboy would be driving his fat white charges out to search for weeds in the young growth.

Appius made a frugal breakfast of bread and honey in the courtyard of Athena and had just laid down his napkin when Helva appeared, shooing a kitchen slave to take away the master's tray. Her blond hair was curled and stuck about with gold pins, and she wore a pretty, trailing gown of yellow, with sandals to match. A spindle hung idly from one hand and a basket of carded wool from the other, but she appeared to be making little use of it. Antonia's estimate of Helva's usefulness was fairly correct, but there was little point in bestirring the woman to any task. Work simply was not in Helva's vocabulary, or at any rate no more than it needed to be. Sold into slavery as a girl of fifteen, Helva had spent years building her position in the household on the only advantages left to her, her attraction for its master and his affection for the son she had borne him. Even now Helva's sea-blue eyes and buttermilk skin, and the inviting curve of her hips, could stir his blood. Appius would have freed her if she had ever asked him, but he suspected that Helva didn't want freedom. Not now. She had made her life and was content with it. She had servants of her own and pretty things to wear and a position of some privilege in the household. She was some years younger than he, and Appius suspected that she had every intention of seeing this pleasant life continued after his death. With a son adopted into the family of Appius, the prospects for this would be infinitely brighter.

Personally, Appius wished Helva well. He had provided in his will for her freedom and a small income, although Helva knew the latter was not such as would enable her to lead the life she enjoyed now. Her master's love for Correus was based entirely on the boy himself and on the reflection of his own lost youth that Appius saw in him. For Helva he had the same amused and tolerant affection he would have accorded a lovely and temperamental chariot horse.

She brushed a white hand lightly over his hair and settled herself comfortably on the marble at his feet, making vague gestures toward work with her spindle.

"You look very bright today," Appius said. "Like a buttercup."

"I feel bright," she said, her Latin still retaining a slight exotic accent. "Correus has told me, and the news is all over the house as well, of course. I am so proud that you find our son worthy." She studied her spindle, and then looked up through a gold fringe of lashes. "How did the lady Antonia receive it?"

"I expect you know that, too," Appius said drily, "or you wouldn't be out here in the sun, ruining your complexion."

Helva's hands fluttered gracefully in her lap and then she laid one lightly on his knee. "You know I never interfere in what passes between you and your lady. But, for my son . . ." The hand crept slightly higher. "Come where we can talk without the servants goggling from behind every pillar."

Appius detached her firmly. "I have appointments to keep in half an hour, so you can put that gambit away. I am not going to make love to you in broad daylight, and if I did, it would not change my mind."

Helva giggled. "You did once, remember? In a tent. It was raining."

"I was a lot younger, and all you wanted from me then was a new bracelet."

She had got it, too. Helva's eyes were shrewd, flirtation abandoned. "Appius, you wouldn't change your mind?"

"I'm not changing my mind about Correus. Or about being badgered by you. But I can't simply ride over my wife's objections, and it may take time before the ceremony is officially done. In the meantime, if you say one word on the subject of Antonia to Correus, I will strangle you with my bare hands."

"Never! It would break his heart."

"How did you find out? Were you listening at doors? If you heard it from one of the servants you had best tell him to keep his tongue between his teeth."

"Certainly," Helva said primly, and Appius suspected, with relief, that his first suggestion had been correct.

"Good. Now take yourself off and do whatever it is that you do when you're trying to look industrious."

Helva departed with a flounce, leaving Appius wishing for the second time in two days that the lord of the Underworld would obligingly remove all women from his vicinity.

Antonia, seeing her go, nodded in satisfaction from the pantry window and set off briskly to other work with her maids behind her.

The house of Appius pursued its usual course for the remainder of the day, albeit with a bit more bustle than usual. They kept country hours on the estate, rising with the sun and going to bed at its setting, and a company banquet was a rarer event here than in the fashionable houses of the City. Appius kept his business appointments while Antonia took charge of preparations for the evening. In the kitchen, the cook continued to create, and threw a pastry mold at the scullery maid.

Correus and Flavius had their first workout with Forst and acquired several promising bruises and a healthy respect for the barbarian long spear. They also learned two good German swear words. After they had scraped themselves clean and soaked their bruises in the hot pool in the baths, Correus went to pay his respects to his mother in her chamber before dining.

He kissed her cheek and she patted the couch beside her. "Sit down. You have a few minutes yet." She inspected him. "You look very fine. You do your father proud." His resemblance to Appius was really uncanny, she thought, and was briefly grateful to the gods for having put this advantage to his hand.

"Flavius is the star of tonight's performance," he said lightly. "Old Aemelius has a girl child, it seems, and the general has a match in mind."

"Oh, that," Helva brushed the subject of the girl child away. "I knew that. But what is important now is that your father know how grateful you are for the opportunity he has given *you*. You must make sure of a chance to tell him publicly tonight, so that everyone else knows, too. You mustn't let yourself be slighted."

"My father is well aware of my gratitude," Correus said. "I'm not going to lick his sandals at dinner. And I'm not going to stand in Flavius's light. This has been a bit much for him to take already, I think, though he said he was glad for me. And he won't let me attend him anymore. He said it wasn't fitting."

"Well, of course he was glad about it. You've been friends since you were babes together. Why shouldn't he be?"

Correus had long grown accustomed to letting his mother's schemes and advice wash over him like so much sea spray, and to taking his own road afterward, but tonight she grated on already overtired nerves. "Because he's not, and I know it and he knows it, and neither one of us says anything about it, because we can't, that's why! He has always had what I would have given my soul for, and I am an interloper, and that twists him up!" Correus took a deep breath and got a grip on himself. "Don't worry, Mother, it will all work itself out, especially after we're posted to our legions and aren't kept as close as two sticks to chafe on each other. But I am *not* going to make a spectacle of myself at dinner."

He kissed her cheek and departed, saying that it would be rude to be late, and Helva flung herself back on her couch in exasperation.

The family of Aemelius was arriving as Correus made his appearance, and Appius presented him simply as "my son, Correus," a somewhat ambiguous definition duly noted by Antonia.

Aemelius was a round, pleasant-faced man with pink cheeks and mild blue eyes and a gray fringe of hair encircling his head. His toga bore the broad purple stripe of a senator. Trailing in his wake were his wife and daughter, the one plump and motherly, the other a delicate child of about fourteen with dark eyes and a pretty face. "My wife, Valeria Lucilla. My daughter, Aemelia."

Appius greeted them and brought his own family forth

to be presented. He was formally attired in a toga bearing the narrow purple banding of a knight, the equestrian class that ranked only slightly below the senatorial families. Flavius was similarly dressed, while Correus wore the plain white toga of the free citizen, the formal adoption ceremony having not yet taken place. And as he was unused to it, he found himself spending much of his time keeping the accursed thing properly draped.

Introductions performed, Appius escorted his guests into the dining room, where a larger table had been placed and extra couches brought in. Aemelia and Julia shared a couch and soon fell to giggling between themselves, while the adults made conversation over the first course. The cook had done himself proud, Correus thought, inspecting the table laden with cracked lobsters and fish in pastry baskets made to look like conch shells. The best glass goblets were in use, and the centerpiece was a triumph of pastry columns supporting a melon carved like a ship and laden with dates and olives.

"What does he stiffen the dough with to make it take that weight?" Correus murmured.

"I don't know," Flavius whispered back. "Plaster, probably. At any rate, I wouldn't eat it."

"Jupiter, no! I remember tucking into one of his concoctions that was all tarted up to look like honey cake with little mint-leaf birds on top and discovering that the old devil had made it out of fish and cheese sauce. I don't know why party food always has to look like something else," he added irritably, inspecting a lobster claw for any unsuspected contents. The folds of his toga slithered away as he moved, and he made a grab at them.

"Relax," Flavius whispered. "You look like someone caught in a net. Just remember to keep your left arm clamped against your side, and it won't go anywhere."

"How the hell can I eat with my left arm clamped against my side?" Correus demanded.

"Very carefully," Flavius suggested with a wicked grin. "That damned left arm of yours gives you enough of an advantage with a sword. Serves you right to have a few minor inconveniences."

"I don't call losing my clothes while trying to eat a minor inconvenience," Correus said, cautiously picking at a pastry basket with his right hand. "I'm going to have Paulus drape the damn thing the other way around next time and the hell with fashion. Anyway, you look elegant enough for both of us." He eyed the crisp, immaculate folds of Flavius's toga and the careful curls that crowned his dark head. Correus's own hair grew over the left brow in a spiral cowlick that no hair oil could persuade to lie flat.

"I feel just like a bull dressed up for market," Flavius shot back.

"Maybe the Senator will come and look at your teeth after dinner," Correus said unsympathetically. "You're getting off easy, you know. She's a pretty little thing and she has a nice voice. Julia seems to like her."

"Julia's just starved for someone her own age and a little gossip to giggle over," Flavius said. "Julia doesn't have to marry her."

"Oh, Julia already knows whom she's going to marry," Correus said. "He's going to be as tall as the Colossus at Rhodes and twice as handsome as Phoebus Apollo, and one day he'll rise to be emperor and give her enough jewels to weigh down an elephant. She told me so."

"I suppose you mean that I'm being just as impractical," Flavius said.

"Not at all. But I don't see why you *couldn't* get starry-eyed over little Aemelia. I think she's pretty. And she seems to like *you*."

"Dear Correus. *Always* practical."

"I've had to be," Correus said grimly. "It gets bred into you."

"Sorry," Flavius said. "I expect it does. It's just that I wanted to have some *fun* before I get respectable."

"Oh, I don't know," Correus said thoughtfully, "I suspect you could have quite a lot of fun with Aemelia."

Flavius gave the girl another glance. She *was* lovely . . . and she was looking at them. He smiled tentatively, and the girl smiled back.

The second course appeared, its high point a roast peacock encased in a pastry shell to which its bright plumage had been reattached in a triumphant fan. It was borne by two slaves in pristine tunics under the watchful eyes of Niarchos, the elderly Greek majordomo who ruled over the indoor servants. They were followed by three younger boys with trays of other delicacies, and the wine steward's boy with a gleaming jug of the best of the best wine. He poured carefully, holding the jug just high enough above the goblets so that the light would properly display the richness of the wine. He looked nervous, and as he came to Aemelia she gave him a friendly smile that lit up her face like a dark rose. The boy, staring in open admiration, slopped some of his burden onto the table and then departed in haste while Niarchos followed, fire in his eye.

Appius chuckled. "Even my servants do you homage, little mistress," he said, with a smile at Aemelia, and the girl blushed. Flavius, he noted with satisfaction, was rapidly developing an expression not much less admiring than that of the wine steward's boy.

"This is excellent," Aemelius said, contentedly nibbling at a dish of veal cooked with nuts. "Most delightful. Appius, your house could match any in Rome, you know. Tell me, my friend, why have you never requested senatorial rank? I'm sure the Emperor would grant it. In fact I'm surprised it has not been offered without the asking, especially with *your* military record."

"It was offered," Appius smiled. "By the late Emperor Nero. In fact it took all the influence I possessed to persuade him *not* to grant it to me. You see, country life suits me very well. Evenings such as this"—he gestured at the extravagantly laden table—"are pleasant with neighbors and friends. But a steady diet of it and a constant stream of clients underfoot—no, it's just not in my line." The display of wealth necessary to keep up a senator's position, especially under so capricious an emperor as the late and unlamented Nero, could also bankrupt a man.

Aemelius nodded. "Perhaps you were wise, my friend. I must confess I sleep better myself out here away from the noise and filth of the City. And country living certainly can't be faulted when it counts fresh asparagus among its blessings!" He selected a young shoot from the dish before him. "Your chef has a light hand with vegetables. I wish he could teach mine that there are other ways to cook an asparagus than boiling it into submission."

"He is an excellent chef," Antonia said proudly, "if a touch temperamental. He is at war with our steward at the moment, and as for the rest of the staff, they go daily in terror of him."

"Genius is always allowed temperament, Mother," Flavius said. He reached across the table. "Lady Aemelia, if you'll try the sweet, I'm sure it will attest to his abilities." The girl smiled and took the tidbit from his hand, while Julia grinned impudently at Flavius and received a furious glare in return.

"Behave yourself, Julia," Correus said, "or I'll tell who put glue in Philippos's inkpot."

Aemelia had been modestly brought up and had no brothers to squabble with; she ignored these exchanges, but when she felt the company's attention turned away from her, she let her dark, curious eyes stray to the two brothers across the table.

As the last course was removed, three flute girls, barefoot and with roses in their hair, came in to play while a fourth performed a slow, grave dance in accompaniment. Appius and Aemelius congratulated themselves that they had made a promising match, while their wives conversed together of housekeeping and servants. The following week was the Ludi Ceriales, held each April to honor the Corn Mother Ceres, who quickens the land again in spring. Aemelia expressed a desire to spend the holiday in Rome, enjoying such of the celebration as her mother considered suitable.

"I'm afraid not, my dear," her father said. "I have an appointment which I simply cannot break, and I don't want you in the City on festival day with no better escort than your slaves."

"Why not let my sons escort your ladies?" Appius offered. "I'm sure they'd trade their studies for a festival with no complaints." A private look directed at Flavius and Correus indicated that they had better. "It will give Aemelia and Flavius a chance to get acquainted without being thrown together entirely alone," he murmured to Aemelius. "Julia, you may go with them," he added, seeing his daughter on the verge of protest.

"Excellent," Aemelius said. "Well, my dear, you are to have your treat after all."

Aemelia and Julia bounced happily on their couch
while Correus and Flavius exchanged rueful glances. Es-
corting their little sister, Flavius's prospective bride, and
the bride's mother about the City was not their idea of
how best to enjoy a rollicking festival day, but since their
chances of going at all were otherwise slim, they might
as well make the most of it. Now that it was within a
month of their departure for the army, Appius had been
little inclined to allow them to neglect their training, and
in any case he disapproved of the games at the Arena,
holding that being a spectator to bloodshed in the presence of a mob was a bad pastime for a soldier. Missing
the games (Valeria Lucilla would most certainly not allow her daughter to visit the Arena) would be little dis-
appointment to Correus, who didn't care for them. And
for Flavius, who did enjoy them, the presence of Aemelia
was beginning to be a strong counterattraction.

They saw the girl several times again during the following week. Aemelia and Julia became immediate
friends, and if Aemelius suspected that it wasn't entirely
Julia his daughter was so eager to see, that also suited
him very well.

Several times Correus caught sight of the girls giggling
and watching his and Flavius's swordplay from a distance. He was fond of his little sister and he raised his
sword to them in a friendly salute. Flavius had seen them
too, he noted, and looked pleased. They walked the girls
through the rose garden later and made plans for the
coming excursion.

The day of the Ludi Ceriales was a green and golden
example of the perfect Italian spring, and they made the
ride into the City early, the ladies in a curtained carriage,
their male escort on horseback so that they could ride
close enough to converse on the road. An entourage of
slaves from both households accompanied them, clearing
a path through the holiday throng that choked the road.

All Rome came into the City for a festival day, and
they threaded their way through crowds of merrymakers
peasant and patrician, shepherds herding their charges to
market or sacrifice in the temples, pastry vendors, and
troupes of dancers jingling with bells. A flock of chickens
from someone's overturned cart ran squawking under

their horses' hooves, and "the girl in the cloak" and her sisterhood were out in full force, smirking slyly at any passing male who might have money in his purse. Julia and Aemelia eyed the prostitutes curiously until Valeria Lucilla reached out and drew the curtains with a firm hand.

On the outskirts of the City, they exchanged their carriage for a slave-carried litter for the ladies, while Flavius and Correus elected to walk. Aemelia surveyed the boisterous scene, eyes shining. As they ate pears bought from a man with a tray of iced fruit, they paused to watch a dancing bear that cavorted solemnly to its master's piping, for coins thrown into the box at its feet.

The streets became more closely packed the farther they progressed into the City, where multistoried buildings sprouted balconies that leaned inward over the street, so that the wary pedestrian kept an upward eye for falling roof tiles and, occasionally, the contents of a slop jar.

"Well," Correus said, trying to make himself heard over the din, "are you enjoying yourself in this madhouse?"

"Oh, yes," Aemelia said. "I love it—the color and the excitement. You see," she added naively, "it's all new to me. My father doesn't have the time to escort me to festivals very often."

Correus smiled. "Perhaps he doesn't find them entirely suitable for little maids."

"I am not a little maid!" Aemelia said indignantly.

"No, I suppose you're not." He swept the folds of his toga (now arranged in mirror image to the usual fashion, so that his left arm rather than his right was free) out of the way of an old woman trundling a grimy cart behind her.

Flavius, somehow maintaining his usual pristine appearance despite the dirt and the crowd, came up beside them and presented Aemelia with violets done up in a straw holder threaded with sweet herbs. "If the . . . uh, flavor of the City gets to be too much for you just hold this to your nose," he said, and she smiled and thanked him.

"How lovely. My father would never have thought of

that. What bliss to have a *young* man for an escort, who doesn't keep pointing out a moral just when I'm having fun."

"We're enjoying ourselves too, you know," Flavius said. "It's likely to be our last chance for a while. I foresee a long stretch of muddy tents and no such charming companions as yourself before they see my face in Rome again."

Correus whistled a little snatch from a popular marching song and she laughed. "Don't you want to be a soldier?"

"What we want and what we get to be generally don't bear much resemblance to each other," Flavius said seriously. "Yes, I suppose I do, but even if I didn't, I wouldn't be given much choice. My family goes back six generations in the Eagles," he added with a touch of pride that was tinged, Correus thought, with a certain wistfulness.

"And what about you?" Aemelia asked Correus.

"Oh, Correus," Flavius said. "Correus is going to be a great man in the army and slay barbarians by the thousands. He's happiest in a muck sweat with a sword in his hand."

"Won't *you* miss Rome?" she said to Correus.

"Not particularly," he said. "It's best to do what you're suited for, and fighting seems to be my only talent. I can't compose poetry, and I'm told that my singing voice is enough to drive the crows off."

"You can whistle," she said, teasing.

"True, but you'll find it isn't in great demand at dinner parties."

As they approached the gates of the Arena, the road was almost impassable, the crowd overflowing into the street and arguing and jostling.

"What a mob," Valeria Lucilla said. "They say the Emperor Vespasian is planning to build a new arena as soon as these games are over. He has given a great deal of money to the City for it. You would think he could find a more civilized way to entertain the masses," she added primly.

"The people like it," Flavius said. "Keeps 'em quiet. But I agree, it's no place for young ladies. Would you let

us take you to the races in the Circus instead?" he asked,
seeing the girls' disappointed faces. "No good for them to
come to Rome and not catch some of the fun."

Valeria Lucilla nodded and they began threading their
way around the Palatine Hill to the gates of the Circus
Maximus. The crowd outside the Circus was only slightly
smaller and no better mannered than that thronging the
gates of the Arena, but the slaves managed to force a
path through and the ladies descended from their litter.
On the opposite side of the street was the Emperor's pal-
ace, tier on tier of white marble; Correus, although he
had seen it enough times, still had to restrain himself
from gawking like a peasant.

As they made their way under the aegis of Valeria
Lucilla to the boxes reserved for senators' families, the
Circus itself seemed almost equally grand: row on row of
seats surmounting a track two hundred meters wide by six
hundred long, large enough to contain more than two
hundred thousand racegoers. Rome took her chariot-
racing seriously, and argument over the prospects of the
four competing factions was deafening. The spina, the
central divider, was embellished with columns, temples,
and memorials, including the great Egyptian obelisk do-
nated by the deified Emperor Augustus. At one end a
standard held seven bronze dolphins dancing on their
tails, which could be upended to mark each lap of the
race.

Dodging the food vendors and the scurrying pages sent
by their owners to fetch refreshments or take messages to
friends in neighboring boxes, they took their seats just
as the trumpets signaled the start of the next race.

The Emperor himself was present today, in his own
garlanded and decorated box, and the four young people, none of whom had ever seen him, studied him
curiously. Vespasian was a soldier, as most emperors were
these days, but the first whose bloodline came exclusively
from equestrian rank. He was a stocky, bull-necked figure in a purple toga, with a wreath of laurel on his graying hair. Beside him stood his son Titus, the Praetorian
Prefect, supreme commander of the Praetorian Guard,
resplendent in gilded parade uniform.

"He looks so fierce," Aemelia whispered, nodding at Vespasian.

"He *is* fierce," Julia said. "Papa says he's one of the best generals Rome ever had."

"It's the army that gives a man that charging-bull expression," Flavius said. "That's how we're supposed to end up, sweet—all horns and gritted teeth."

"He's a good commander," Correus said. "A good man to follow, and Zeus know we need one."

The purple-togaed figure in the imperial box raised his hand and trumpets sang out again. The chariots swept through the lower gates, six teams for this race, all four-horse quadrigae. The Blue and Green factions were fielding two teams each, and the Red and White, one. The chariots, gaudily painted with their factions' colors, took their places in the starting boxes, the horses dancing with impatience while the drivers exchanged insults with great meaning. A Circus Maximus race was a do-or-die affair, and a team was as likely to come to grief from a rival driver's treachery as from a bad turn around the spina. Each faction's supporters were equally violent in their enthusiasms, and a popular winner was the hero of the day. If he lived that long, a good charioteer could earn enough to retire in comfort, but most spent such fortune as came their way as soon as they got it—they well knew their chances of living into retirement weren't promising.

The Emperor raised his handkerchief, and as it fell from his hand the chariots sprang forward, each fighting for the position nearest the spina. The chariots were built as lightly as possible and their drivers wore only a short tunic and helmet. Reins were lashed about their waists, and they carried, besides a whip, a dagger to cut themselves free if necessary. Attendants stood by along the track to pull wrecked chariots away before the race swept around for the next lap. Others held buckets of water to douse the chariot wheels—there was always a danger of friction-sparked fire.

As the chariots careened out of the straight and thundered into the second turn, the first of the bronze dolphins tipped down, indicating an end to the opening lap. A Green chariot had taken the lead, hard pressed by the

White, with the rest of the field strung out behind. In
the third turn, the Green maneuvered the White into the
spina, and it went down in a crash of screaming horses
and broken wheels. The driver emerged cursing from
the wreckage as the attendants ran up to untangle the
traces. The horses, all miraculously unhurt, were led
away to the boos of the crowd, and the attendants began
to tow the broken chariot across the track. They had
dragged it nearly to one of the inner gates when the five
remaining teams bore down on them again. Abandoning
the chariot, they dove for their lives through the gate,
leaving the oncoming drivers to steer around the wreckage as best they might. As the flying end of the pack
passed them, the attendants emerged sheepishly to the
catcalls of nearby spectators and pulled the wrecked
chariot back in after them.

The fourth and then the fifth dolphins went down and
Aemelia bounced in her seat excitedly. "If I were a man,
that is what I would be. I can't imagine anything to match
it!"

"It's exciting enough," Correus said, "but Diulius tells
me that the thrill wears off somewhat after your first accident."

"Do you mean you have actually driven?" She looked
up at him wide-eyed. "Not here in the Circus?"

"No, not in the Circus. But I've driven the general's
teams in country races often enough, to show off to buy-
ers. I can live without it," he added. "It seems a silly way
to get killed, having some horse put his hoof through your
head for the public's amusement."

Aemelia looked up at him, hero worship writ large on
her face. His last remark had clearly gone unheeded.

The last dolphin came down, and the race ended with
no more accidents, the popular driver, the first Green,
winning by almost a half-lap. They stayed for four more
races and enjoyed themselves immensely, Julia and Aemelia watching the spectacle enthralled while Flavius explained the ins and outs of the four factions, and why the
Green-Blue rivalry was the most important at the moment. (The Red and White backers were not of the political standing of the other two, nor could they afford to buy
teams as expensive.) Valeria Lucilla sat under her sun-

shade and chatted with friends who paused on their way to or from their own boxes, each giving a critical eye to the other's attire. She noted with satisfaction that her own gown was fully as stylish as any to be seen, although in more subdued taste than those sported by several ladies of less proper reputation.

Correus watched the spectacle through half-closed eyes, his mind wandering dreamily through pleasant scenarios of success and promotion in the Centuriate, the achievement of much distinction, and the eventual raising of the name of Appius to heights that even the old general had never scaled. He was brought back to earth abruptly as Aemelia became faint with the heat and it was decided that it was time to leave. They made their way back to the street with Aemelia supported by two slaves and a third shielding her with a sunshade. Flavius hovered solicitously at her side, leaving Correus to bring up the rear clutching a collection of pillows, shawls, and half-eaten boxes of sweets. So much for dreams of military glory, he thought ruefully, dodging an enormous senator who was holding forth on experimental farming to a trapped-looking client who bounced up and down in a vain attempt to follow the race over his patron's shoulder.

Once installed in the curtained litter and restored with cool water, Aemelia revived, and by the time they reached their carriage she was chattering happily about the day's events.

At her father's gates, she pressed her escorts' hands affectionately and lifted her flushed face to them. "Thank you so much. This has been the most wonderful day! I shall never forget it."

Then she went home to her father and made an announcement that caused that mild and venerable man to throw an onyx paperweight across the library.

III

Spring Leave-taking

THE NEXT DAY AEMELIUS PACKED HIS DAUGHTER INTO his carriage and paid a morning call on the family of Appius Julianus.

"All right, miss, take yourself off into the garden until I send for you," he said sternly, after Appius had greeted them in the atrium.

Aemelia gave him a stubborn look, then turned and marched through the double doors into the courtyard while Aemelius regarded her with the air of a man whose lap dog has suddenly turned into a slavering hyena. Appius raised his eyebrows and motioned Aemelius into his study.

Outside, Aemelia looked around her rebelliously. Her eyes were red and she had obviously been weeping. The rose garden gave off a heady scent and she wandered in that direction, unexpectedly encountering Correus lounging on a stone bench by the pool. He had a wax tablet in his hand and a book of Virgil that he was translating into Greek at his tutor's direction.

He looked up and gave her a friendly smile. "Hello, little maid. What's amiss?" he asked, seeing her stricken face.

"My father is inside speaking to your father." She gave him a tragic look. "He wants me to marry your brother."

"And you don't want to?" Correus asked gently. Maybe he could change the child's mind for her. Flavius would make her a good husband—he had obviously begun to dote on the girl. "My brother is a good man," he began tentatively.

"I think you must be the most noble man I have ever met," Aemelia whispered. She sat beside him in a flutter of draperies and tucked one little hand into his.

Correus began to get an uneasy feeling in the pit of his stomach. "I hardly think I'm . . . that," he began.

"Oh, yes," she breathed, "but it doesn't matter." She raised dark, confiding eyes to his. "I have told my father that I won't marry your brother no matter what. I won't marry *anyone* but you!"

"My daughter has always been the most biddable girl you can imagine," Aemelius was spluttering exasperatedly in his host's study, "and now—now she begins mooning over your second son—or whatever the hell he is—"

" 'My second son' will do well enough," Appius said.

"And swears she wants to marry him!" Aemelius said.

Antonia, who had joined them, shot Appius a scathing look, which he ignored. "I assure you, my friend, Correus knows I would not permit that."

"*You* wouldn't permit it! I have reasoned with her, scolded her, threatened her with a beating—something I've never done before—and all she will say is that she *loves* him. She seems quite certain that *he* loves *her*!" He glared at Appius.

"*I'm* quite certain Correus has no ideas of the sort." Appius's voice was soothing. "He's hardly known her."

"She's been practically living over here, with that girl of yours. *I* thought it was Flavius she was looking at! Anyway, it seems to have been time enough for Aemelia. Daresay it's enough for him, too. She's a pretty little thing, and I'm a wealthy man!"

"I doubt that would influence Correus right now," Appius said with the ghost of a grin. "He's army-mad. It would take more than a pretty face. And as for the financial considerations," he added drily, "he has more sense."

"He didn't have enough sense not to let my daughter go mooning about after him!" Aemelius snapped.

"Knowing Correus," Antonia said, "I have to agree with my husband. It probably never occurred to him." She rose. "I'll go have a talk with the girl. I take it your wife has already tried?"

"My wife has gone to bed sick with a headache," Aemelius said gloomily.

"How helpful. Well, I shall see what I can do." She nodded briskly and left the men.

"*In love,* by all the gods!" Aemelius said. "*I* wasn't in love when I got married. Were you?"

Appius shook his head. "We'd . . . uh, met twice," he said. "But it didn't seem to have the same effect."

"Well, I can't *force* her to marry young Flavius," Aemelius said. "She'd hate me for it, and I won't have that. She's my only child. But if that young bastard of yours so much as winks at her, Appius, I'll cut his throat!"

"I'm quite certain Correus has both eyes wide open," Appius said. "He may well do more to discourage your daughter than anyone."

"He had better," Aemelius said. He stopped pacing and glared at Appius again. "Well, what now?"

"Have a drink," Appius said.

Correus sat with his arm around Aemelia while she wept into the shoulder of his tunic with all the desperation of fourteen years. He cast a brief, hunted look at the skies, wondering why the Lady Aphrodite should choose him to amuse herself with. "Little maid, you mustn't marry anyone you don't want to, but—they'll never let you marry me!"

She raised a tear-stained face to his, her eyes overflowing, and she looked so miserable that he hugged her to him. "You do like me?" she whispered.

She was young and warm and she felt good in his arms. Through tears, her face had a wet-lily quality that caught at his heart. Correus realized that some part of him did like her very much, and he shifted uncomfortably. "Yes," he whispered back, "I like you very much, but it won't do, and it's best not to think of what won't do. I've learned that well enough," he added grimly.

"Correus . . ." She pushed her tangled dark curls back into some semblance of order and dried her eyes on the embroidered hem of her stole. "Correus . . . if you were Flavius, would you want to marry me?"

If he were Flavius . . . if he were Flavius he would be away from here on his father's business today, spending a pleasant lunch with the officer in charge of remounts at the cavalry training barracks outside the City.

But Aemelia . . . with everything a man could want wrapped up in the soft yielding body cuddled in his arms . . . "If I were Flavius, I'd marry you in a minute."

Aemelia smiled, happy now, and he realized with regret he shouldn't have said that. "Then we must wait, and when they see that we mean it . . . Julia says that your father is going to adopt you."

I hope he still is, after this, Correus thought bitterly. Aloud he said, "My father will give me his name, Aemelia. Only his name. He won't give me Flavius's inheritance, *or* his wife, and I wouldn't take them. I am *not* Flavius."

"I know," she said quietly. "You look like him, but you aren't him. That's why I love you, not him." She touched his cheek with her hand. "Kiss me, Correus."

Like a fool he kissed her, feeling her mouth soft against his and her eager young body in his arms, and by the time he released her, he was shaking.

Aemelia sighed and nestled into his shoulder. "It will be all right," she said with quiet certainty, and there was no way on earth that he could explain to the innocence of fourteen the difference between love and desire.

Antonia, coming out into the colonnade, found a most unsettling tableau in the rose garden and sent a servant to inform Correus that his tutor required his presence— immediately.

Correus received this summons with fervent gratitude, and fled. Antonia took his place.

"Well, child," she said, not without sympathy. "This is all very impossible, you know."

Aemelia sniffled but straightened up and bit back her tears with determination. She looked absurdly young— too young to have any sense, and Antonia said as much.

"I am old enough to know what I want," Aemelia said with dignity.

"What we want, child, and what we owe our families and our position are very frequently not the same. You are a senator's daughter. Your father would never let you throw yourself away on a slave-born man. And I may as well tell you right now that Appius will not permit it, either."

"That is what Correus said," Aemelia began, "but—"

"Correus is showing a great deal more sense than you. You may think that he is only being noble, but I think Correus knows very well what the circumstances are."

"He wants to marry me."

"I don't doubt it," Antonia said with some asperity. "He'd be a fool if he didn't. But he also knows he isn't going to, and you can't tell me he told you it was possible."

"N-no."

"Very well then, be sensible. Correus's army pay would not be enough to provide you with even a proper house, and if you think either your father or his would part with a denarius to do so, you've been out in the sun too long."

"I can go with him. Plenty of women follow the army."

"Respectable ones don't, not unless they're senior officers' wives; and I can tell you from experience that you wouldn't like it even under those circumstances. What you'd face as the wife of a penniless soldier doesn't even bear thinking about."

"I wouldn't mind," Aemelia said. "I wouldn't care *where* I lived as long as it was with him."

"You'd care, child," Antonia said, looking at her delicate face and thinking of the dirt and heat and backbreaking weariness of travel on a provincial frontier. "And it would be far too late to change your mind. Now dry your eyes and come along to your father. You needn't become betrothed to Flavius just yet, you know. Give it some time. But *he* is very fond of you, child. Indeed, I think you could wrap him about your finger, and that is more than most girls can expect when first they're wed. You'll find that affection grows slowly, from living together. And affection and respect last longer than romantic nonsense."

"But I don't want to live with him," Aemelia wailed. "How could I marry Flavius and see Correus all the time, knowing—" She stopped, hiccuping miserably, and Antonia looked thoughtful.

When she had restored the unwilling Aemelia to her father, Antonia informed Appius that she wished to speak with him before the evening meal and then set out to assure her servants that so much as an allusion to the recent upheaval would bring instant banishment to the copper mines.

But Helva had already wormed enough information out of the slave who had interrupted her son's interview with Aemelia to fill her mind with visions of future comfort far beyond anything she had previously imagined. She found Correus in his own room with Forst, gloomily memorizing German verbs; she would set about bringing him around to the same view.

"You may go," she nodded to Forst, who looked inquiringly at Correus.

"Forst, wait for me on the practice ground. I won't be long." The German shrugged and left. Correus gave his mother a harassed look. "If Philippos sees him idling about, it'll get him in trouble with my father."

Helva found Forst of small importance and said so. "My dear one, things could not have come out better. Of course, you mustn't say anything to your father until after the adoption, but if you can persuade little Aemelia to be patient—"

"I imagine my father will have a great deal to say to *me*," Correus said sarcastically.

"Correus, how can you be so blind? This could mean everything for you."

"It could get me thrown out of this house!" Correus practically shouted. "I want you to keep your hands out of this, Mother. I mean it."

"Someone has to be clever for you," Helva said, smiling, "since you won't do it for yourself."

"You're too damn clever to have good sense," Correus said.

"I've managed very well so far, thank you," Helva snapped. "People in our position must play the dice as they fall, or get nothing. That child would drop into your arms if you so much as looked at her."

Correus snatched his good tunic off over his head and picked up the ragged one he used for practice. "I'm well aware of that," he said, his voice muffled in its folds. "So I'm *not* going to look at her!" He stalked out the door.

Behind him his mother's voice said sweetly, like honeyed ice, "Don't tell me you wouldn't *like* to look at her!"

In the garden Correus picked up a fallen apricot and flung it viciously against the wall. His mother was right, he thought, sickened. It would be so easy to let Aemelia fall in his lap and claim, truthfully enough, that it hadn't been his fault: Aemelia and everything that went with her, he added, for honesty's sake . . . all the things that were Flavius's by birthright.

He took out his temper on the practice ground until Forst informed him that berserkers, while a useful force, were generally only useful once.

Correus flung his practice sword down and looked as if he would like to stamp on it. Forst put on his granite face and just stood there until Correus began to feel sheepish. "I'm sorry," he said. "I've stuck a pitchfork into a hornets' nest, although I didn't mean to, and now I'm pursued by the consequences." Forst looked as if he had understood one word in ten of Correus's Latin, and Correus rephrased his explanation: "I'm in trouble."

"Ah. Not of your own making?"

"No."

"Then you must . . ." Forst groped for a phrase, and then lapsed into German, "ride the waves."

Correus nodded to signify his understanding, and Forst gave him one of his infrequent smiles. "Good." He clapped him on the shoulder. "And your German is improving."

Ride the waves. Forst had managed to ride the waves of his own circumstances, Correus thought as he watched the blond man pick up his shield and sparring sword and walk up the hill to the house, shield slung over his shoulder and back straight as if he were striding into his own hall. To have it all and then have it wrenched away was worse than having an ancient name and a post in the Centuriate handed to you on a gold plate. He could forgo Aemelia, he thought, and if he felt he couldn't, he would talk to Forst again.

He picked up his practice sword and worked the rest of his temper off on the straw men. On his way to the baths, he met the green-eyed kitchen maid Emer with a clean tunic draped over one freckled arm, and realized that it was still the women's hour in the baths. He had once spent a pleasant evening in her arms in the hay fields at harvest time, and now she giggled and beckoned to him.

"They've all bathed and gone," Emer whispered. "Little mistress, and your mother, and the rest. I'm the only one left. I stayed late to help cook—I dropped a whole crock of cream and he was in a foul mood." She gave him a mischievous smile. "The men won't be coming to bathe for another half-hour."

The memory of Aemelia was still singing in his blood, overlaid with a memory of the kitchen maid's tanned bare legs in the moonlight, and he caught the girl by the waist and pulled her into the bathhouse with him. A moment later he was pursuing her giggling form across the stone floor. Emer shucked off her tunic as she ran and he caught a flash of round bottom and flying red hair as she dived into the warm pool.

"I'm not even clean yet," he laughed, splashing in after her. Etiquette demanded that bathers rinse and scrape themselves clean with the wooden strigils hanging from hooks in the wall before entering the baths.

The girl just laughed and dived under the water, pulling his legs out from under him so that he fell with a splash into her arms. Minutes later, they were rolling entwined on a towel on the edge of the pool, and the tension that Aemelia had left in him washed away.

Correus was drying himself when Appius came in, followed by his body servant bearing towels and rubbing oil. Ordinarily he bathed in the private pool adjoining his bedchamber, but Antonia was using it at the moment, and after the upheavals of the morning he had decided to leave her in peace. Appius heard bare wet feet pattering away down the corridor and eyed his son speculatively but made no comment. If Correus was tumbling a servant girl in the bath, it seemed unlikely that he was eating his heart out for Aemelius's daughter.

"Good evening, sir." Correus rubbed himself briskly with the towel and reached for his clean tunic, while the attendant divested Appius of his. The older man was still hard and muscular, his olive skin crisscrossed with the white scars of nearly forty years' service with the Eagles. He sniffed the rubbing oil dubiously.

"Damn it, you've got my wife's. I'll smell like a Syrian page boy if you rub me with that."

"Here, sir." Correus held out his own unscented flask.

"Thank you." When the servant had rubbed and scraped him clean with the ivory strigil that hung from his waist, Appius nodded his dismissal. He dipped a toe gingerly into the hot pool and then sank contentedly into its steaming depths. "Ah . . . my bones ache like an old gladiator," he said. "Too many miles on the march. Too many years behind a shield." He watched as Correus knotted the girdle of his tunic. "Well, Aemelius's child has stirred up the domestic waters," he said. "As I have infinite faith in your good sense, I presume you did not help her come to this unfortunate notion."

"No, sir," Correus said shortly.

"As I said, I didn't think so. All the same, you'll have to tread carefully for a few weeks. I think it's high time *you* took up a shield in the army."

Correus relaxed and gave his father a half-smile. "The moment you can arrange it, sir," he said fervently.

Appius smiled back, and affection lightened his usual sardonic expression. He made a shooing motion with his hand. "Go and get ready for dinner. I'm going to enjoy a soak before the rest come stampeding in. And Correus—" His son turned toward him inquiringly. "Tell your . . . uh, companion that she left her hairpins."

Correus snatched up the bronze pins and went away laughing. At the door he turned, fist to breast, to give his father a mock salute.

The boy had an unnerving charm when he relaxed and let it show, Appius thought, his eyes still on the empty doorway. It was just as well that he was unlikely to be around Aemelia from now on.

He soaked like a crocodile, eyes and nose barely above the water, while the kinks worked themselves out of his muscles. Then he gritted his teeth and took a dive for health's sake in the cold pool.

When he had dressed and strolled through the late-afternoon sunlight to the outer door of his study, he found his wife waiting for him, as he had expected.

"I don't blame Correus," she said, "but he must be got

away from Aemelia immediately." Antonia beat around
no bushes.

Appius settled himself at his desk without comment.
"Appius—"

"I heard you, my dear, but I don't know how you expect me to achieve that."

"The army, of course. The sooner you arrange a suitable posting, the better it will be. I've talked to the child,
and I think that if she has a few weeks to get to know
Flavius better without Correus under her nose, she may
come around before Flavius leaves for his own posting."

"Let me make one thing crystal clear to you, my
dear," Appius said pleasantly. "I have not yet formally
adopted Correus, because of your objections. But I have
promised him the Centuriate. I am not suddenly going to
hustle him off to the auxiliaries instead. If Correus is not
to have the Centuriate, he stays here."

Antonia clenched her fists in irritation, but she didn't
reply. She knew her husband's calm, pleasant look, and
the flinty light in his eyes that went with it. In this mood
Appius was as immovable as the Palatine Hill. And with
Flavius in the Centuriate, posted to the gods knew where,
and Correus idling about the estate under her feet, Aemelia would never show any sense. Antonia made a decision.

"Very well, Appius," she said abruptly, "you have
won. I think you will regret it, but you have won."

The gardens of the house of Appius blazed with light
from an extravagant display of lamps on pillars along the
walkways and suspended by chains from the vine-
covered trellises. Each servant on the estate had been
given a new set of clothes, and the statue of Athena wore
a garland of roses in her hair. It was the eighteenth birthday of both young men and the formal adoption of Correus into the house of Appius Julianus.

The garden was thronged with guests, the purple-
bordered togas of the men setting off the bright finery of
their wives and daughters. Carriages filled the drive between the fir trees, and servants bustled back and forth
among them trying to keep the roadway clear. Plank tables had been set up on packing crates at the foot of the

hill for the field slaves to share in the holiday, and Appius had sent enough wine for their merrymaking to guarantee that each man would wield his hoe with a headache the next day. In the gardens, the house servants circulated with trays of hot food and iced fruit and saw that no guest's wine cup remained empty.

The air was heady with the scent of roses and jasmine, and a full moon rode low in the sky, mingling its light with the gold of the lamp glow. Correus stood apart, his back to a fig tree near the far wall, his face hidden in its shadows. He had already played his part, and his hands were still shaking from the moment when he had placed them between Appius's and heard his father claim him and call him by the name Julianus.

"You're a bit too big to lift," Appius had said, smiling—a Roman child was accounted legitimate only when its father had picked it up and held it. Instead, he put his arms around his son and kissed him. And then a slave had come forward with a toga edged with the purple of a knightly house, and Appius had taken it from him and draped it around Correus with his own hands.

A cheer went up and someone handed Correus a silver beaker of wine. He drained it down amid shouts of "Vivat!" and "Salve!" and an enormous senator with a wreath over one eye hiccuped loudly and slapped him on the back. After that the party got into full swing. Appius was drawn off to talk politics with two of his cronies, and Correus drifted, bemused, through the throng until he fetched up under the fig tree. He was more than half-drunk, he thought. He had been too nervous to eat, and the wine had been unwatered. He shook his head and things came into focus somewhat.

Under the statue of Athena, the poet Martial was declaiming a work in honor of the event to anyone who would listen. Martial could exhibit a biting wit, but tonight his efforts were entirely laudatory, and Correus thought that even the Lady of Wisdom looked bored. He suspected the poet was hoping for some largesse from Appius, for like many writers, Martial lived a good day's march beyond his means and hovered permanently on the brink of debtor's court.

"Our loud friend is wasting his time." There was a

footstep on the grass and Flavius drifted up, goblet in hand. "My father . . . *our* father," he corrected himself carefully, "is solving the problems of the Empire with Julius Agricola. Or arguing tactics. They couldn't seem to make up their minds about which one when I left." He peered into his wine cup. "Empty," he said with sorrow. "Good stuff, this."

He was obviously very drunk indeed, and Correus put out a steadying hand. "Here, sit down a minute, or you won't last the evening."

"'S all right," Flavius said. "'S *your* evening. Welcome, brother." He raised his goblet. "Think I'll find some more of this. Drink your health some more. I wanted to talk to Aemelia," he added, "but I couldn't find her." He eyed Correus.

"That's odd," Correus said. "I haven't seen her either," he added deliberately.

Flavius nodded and wandered away, and Correus leaned back against his tree. He saw Antonia on the walkway and decided that he ought to go and make his peace with her. He straightened his toga and hoped he didn't look as drunk as Flavius. As he approached, Helva tripped by in a flutter of pale silk. She bowed politely to Antonia, but satisfaction radiated from every pore and she was dripping with half the contents of her jewel box.

"I've spoken to the cook about more pastries," Helva said complacently, "and we've almost run out of wine. Philippos should have the steward bring some more up from the cellars, I think."

"By all means," Antonia said.

"I'll tell him," Helva said. "It would be such a pity to run short tonight of all nights." She gave Correus a fond smile and trotted off down the walk, pausing as she went to greet Appius's guests in proprietary fashion.

Correus winced and wished he had stayed under his fig tree, but it was too late.

Antonia regarded Helva's retreating figure with compressed lips. To have that doxy whipped would be beneath Antonia's dignity, but Cybele! she would enjoy it. Still, she turned to Correus with a friendly face. The adoption being done, Antonia would make the best of it. The truth was she liked the boy and wished him well in every way, insofar as his well-being took nothing from Flavius.

Correus bowed, a tall grave figure in a toga. *Grown,* she thought; *they are grown up. Mother-of-All, they are men now!*

"I hope I'm restored to your good graces."

"My dear, you were never out of them. But you must realize that this nonsense of Aemelia's cannot be permitted."

"I wouldn't try," he said, and she smiled and patted his arm. *Put firmly in my place,* he thought when she had gone. His adoption by Appius had extended the boundaries of that place somewhat, but not to the extent that he might tread on Flavius's land.

A servant passed by with a wine jug and a tray of cups, and Correus exchanged the silver beaker for a shallower cup of red-brown Samian ware. If he let them keep refilling that beaker he'd be as drunk as a maenad. He looked up and was unnerved to see Aemelia with Julia, some ten paces away. Julia had found the recent to-do over Aemelia's marriage most exciting and was entirely in sympathy with her friend. Aemelia looked quickly over her shoulder for her mother, and then at Correus. Feeling like a beast, he pretended he hadn't seen her. By the far wall near the niche which housed the statue of Priapus, caretaker of the garden, his father was talking with a younger man in the parade uniform of a legionary legate, and Correus took refuge with them. The fertility god, guardian of all growing things, Priapus stood saucily with member erect and seemed to wink at him. "Mind your own business," Correus murmured respectfully to the little god. It was always unwise to upset Priapus, but Correus felt he could do without his intervention just now.

His father presented him to the other man, Julius Agricola, legate of the Twentieth Legion in Britain, and recently returned to Rome on the Emperor's business. Agricola was barely into his thirties, but he already had the reputation of a man who got things done, a commander who could be sent where there was trouble. He came of a senatorial family and had succeeded to his present command through a course of political offices, rather than a series of lesser commands as Appius had done, but his love was for the army. He had played a part in putting Vespasian on the throne, and had been sent to Britain to take over a legion that was reported to be bordering on rebellion. Agricola, by means best known to himself, had straightened out his mutinous troops in record time and then preserved the honor of his legion by reporting to the Emperor that he had found them loyal from the first. Vespasian didn't believe him, of course, but he was more than happy to have the appearance of unity preserved.

Agricola greeted Correus with genuine interest and nodded approvingly when Appius told him that he was shortly to take a post in the Centuriate.

"I can think of no better career for a son of Appius," he said. "I have long been an admirer of your father, even if we don't see eye to eye on the uses of cavalry."

Appius laughed. "New wars beget new strategy, but I prefer arguing tactics to talking politics with old Quintilius, from whom we are hiding now, or listening to Martial hiccup his way through an endless paean to my family name."

"All the same, sir," Agricola said, "you're really going to have to go and listen to him or he'll never shut up. With all due respect to your family name, I prefer his satires to his tributes."

"So do I," Appius sighed. "Very well, I shall steel myself. Correus, there's no reason you should share this dread fate unless you wish to."

"Thank you, sir. I don't at all wish to," Correus said. "Perhaps you'll recite it to me later," he added with a sadistic grin.

"Insolent puppy." Appius put a hand on his son's shoulder. "Go and enjoy yourself. This is a night for the young."

Correus watched them walk away, the legate's uniform a spot of martial color among the white togas of the guests; then he looked about for some company. He could see Flavius under the lamplit trellis in raucous conversation with a trio of friends. An ivy wreath hung precariously over one ear and he was reciting a bawdy verse about the quaestor from Paestum. It would probably be wise to avoid Flavius this evening, and Correus couldn't

think of anyone else he really wanted to talk to. The
sound of pipes and a cithara drifted up from the hay
fields. They were his people too, Correus thought, as
much as the patrician gathering in the gardens, and he
felt the need to make a leave-taking with them. He returned to his fig tree, where he had hung his own wreath
among the branches. Most of the older generation had
scorned wreaths as a frivolous adornment best suited to
young people, and Correus had soon taken his own off;
it had made him feel silly. Now he retrieved it and set it
carefully on his hair. He winked back at Priapus as he
passed, and slipped out through the back gate.

A path of stair-stepped stones led around the walls and
through the terraced kitchen gardens that were fragrant
with herbs and new onions. At the edge of the hay fields,
a line of dancers swayed within a torch ring to the lively
sound of the pipes. A dark-haired girl accompanied them
on the cithara, and Correus could see Forst sitting cross-
legged on the edge of the circle, slapping out the beat on
a leather drum. Wine cups of the cheap African pottery
ware used in the slaves' hall circulated freely, as did the
beer brewed on the estate by the Gaulish and German
slaves for their own use. Someone put a mug of beer in
his hand, a heady dark brew for which Correus admitted
an unpatrician fondness, and he took a deep gulp. Another man slapped him on the back and kissed him heart-
ily on both cheeks. A number of the house servants had
joined in the merrymaking by this time, and Correus
had played among the field slaves in his childhood, learning to speak to most of them in their own tongue by the
time he was ten. Now they made him welcome without
question. He was one of their own, and they rejoiced in
his good fortune with a pride and affection that suddenly
felt very dear to him.

The dancers, seeing his face in the torchlight, called
out to him, and Correus laughed and ran out to join
them, catching on to the flying tail of the dance, beer mug
still in hand.

The leader was a burly Greek of peasant birth who had
first educated Correus in the colorful distinctions between
the Greek of tutors and the Greek of the slave hall. As
Correus joined the dance, he laughed and stepped up the

pace, sending the dancers' feet leaping and flying, to spill the young master's beer for him. Correus laughed back and handed the mug to a girl among the spectators. He kicked off his sandals between steps, then unwound his toga with his free hand, dropping it behind him in the trampled grass. Dancing in his tunic as the line flew past the girl again, he retrieved his beer mug, raising it defiantly above his head. There were shouts of encouragement as the music rose to a crescendo and the dance ended with a stamp and a flourish, and Correus stood panting with his wreath over one eye, making a show of finishing the beer.

A plump, graying woman who had been Flavius's nurse and his own in their childhood was shaking out his discarded toga and folding it, and he dropped a kiss on the back of her neck.

"I'll just put this where you won't be ruining it your first night to wear it, Master Correus," she said severely.

"Thank you, Thais," he said, hugging her, and her expression softened.

"You never did have any sense," she said lovingly. "Well, go on then and enjoy yourself, but you mustn't stay too long. Your place is up at the house now."

Correus took a deep breath of the warm night air and watched the moon, riding fat and contented above the hill. "Not tonight," he said. "Tonight I'm going to dance in the hay."

Thais snorted. "Roll in the hay, more likely, you young scapegrace. Well, you'll have little enough chance to play the fool in the army. I suppose you might as well do it tonight."

Correus laughed and refilled his beer mug from a cask on the table, nodding at Alan and Diulius as he passed. They had no real place among the gathering at the great house and had come to the hay fields to drink among their own kind. Of the upper staff of the household, only Sabinus felt comfortable mingling with the guests, but he was a Roman and freeborn, and that made a difference.

The dark-haired girl picked up the cithara once more and began to sing. It was a haunting, plaintive melody of a people who once were kings in their land and now were gone forever, and the shouting and laughter died down as the servants of Appius gathered about her to listen. Correus picked up his beer and went with them. For tonight, these were his people. And if red-haired Emer were to come and smile at him, he thought, watching the moon sink down over the hill, he might well make Thais's prediction come true. She danced past him, laughing over her shoulder, because the thought was so plain on his face.

Two days later, with the few personal belongings he would need in the training barracks at Rome slung in saddlebags behind him, Correus sat astride a sorrel named Antaeus. The color of a new-minted gold piece, the horse was his father's parting gift to him. Flavius sat beside him on the fine bay he had put through its paces on the day, which now seemed so far distant, when Appius had first told them they would go together into the Centuriate.

A light breeze ruffled the horses' manes, and the two brothers looked at each other and smiled. It was a new adventure, the end of childhood, and they faced it with more warmth between them than they had felt since that long-ago time when they first knew that each possessed the thing the other yearned for.

Not even the memory of the last interview with his father could dim Correus's excitement, although it gnawed at the back of his mind like an oracle dimly understood, a feeling of something wrong that had no words.

Appius had called Correus into his study on their last evening at home, kissed him, given him a sum of money for his first six months' allowance and the promise of the horse Antaeus; then he sat down behind his desk and looked across it at Correus with eyes dark and serious.

"I have given you my name," Appius said, "and a place in the Centuriate, because you are worthy of them, and because I love you greatly. And now there is one thing I want from you in return."

"Of course," Correus said. He would have promised Appius the moon just then.

"I love both my sons," Appius said, and there was a faint note of sadness in his voice. "I have watched you both as you grew to manhood, and it is in my heart, although I have never said this, that of the two, you are the stronger. Perhaps it is as well. Flavius's place is made for him in the world, and you will have to fight for yours. I don't know. I do know that he needs you, and that it will be bad for him to know that. But it is necessary that *you* know it."

"What would you have me do?" Correus asked.

"I want you to stay by him, give him the love you would give me, forgive him when . . . he finds it hard to love you. You are the stronger and you must promise me."

And in the end Correus had promised, because it was Appius who asked it. He wondered whether he had the strength to keep that promise.

Now Appius stood at the gates with Antonia beside him and Helva two paces away, to bid their sons farewell and the gods' speed. The household staff had turned out as well and lined the carriage road under the fir trees. They, too, called their farewells as the horses passed, and Emer, when Philippos's back was turned, blew a kiss to Correus.

It was early morning but the sun was already white and hot against the sky. With Flavius beside him, Correus heeled the sorrel's flank and put his horse's head east, on the road that ran arrow-straight toward the heart of the world: Rome.

IV

Centurion

THE MAIN CAMP OF THE PRAETORIAN GUARD—THE HOME guard of Rome and the Emperor's personal troops—was an imposing compound located outside the northeast wall of the City. It was here that Correus, Flavius, and forty-five other hopeful candidates for the Centuriate took their military oath, said brief prayers to any gods handy, and listened to a burly centurion with a voice like a crocodile

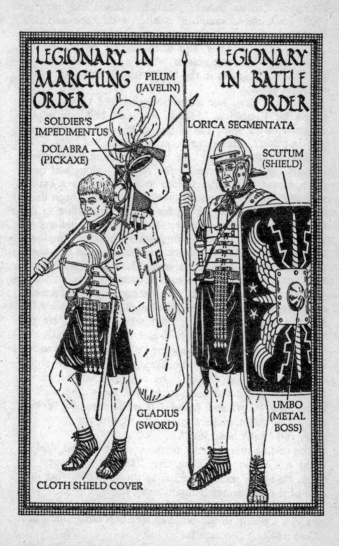

LEGIONARY IN MARCHING ORDER

LEGIONARY IN BATTLE ORDER

PILUM (JAVELIN)

SOLDIER'S IMPEDIMENTUS

DOLABRA (PICKAXE)

LORICA SEGMENTATA

SCUTUM (SHIELD)

GLADIUS (SWORD)

UMBO (METAL BOSS)

CLOTH SHIELD COVER

inform them sadistically that their young lives were now in his hands. "In six months you'll be officers and men, or you'll go home to mama in a litter. I do hope as that's clear?"

"Yes, sir!" the ones who were quicker on the uptake responded with enthusiasm, while a junior drillmaster prodded the laggards in the back with his vine staff to get the point across.

"All right now. My name's Mucius, and to you that's gonna be Centurion Mucius, *sir*. And bein' as you're all gentlemen's sons, I'm gonna call *you* 'Centurion, sir' too, but don't you get to takin' it serious."

Mucius, they learned later, had risen from the ranks to become centurion in one of the regular legions and been given a post in the Praetorians as a reward for a career that was still legendary. For ten years, he had been drillmaster to candidates hoping for direct commission to the Centuriate, and there were senior officers in a number of legions who still recalled him with a shudder. Final authority over the Centuriate candidates lay with the camp prefect, Pertinax Aquila, but it was Mucius who made his hand felt through the six months of their training.

They were paraded first past the camp surgeon, an elderly man with a beady and intelligent eye that belied his habit of conversing with himself when annoyed. He ordered them to strip, inspected each for any obvious deformities, and marked every man's height on a wooden slate, turning away one who came in an inch too short.

"I'm sorry about it, lad," he said, not unsympathetically, "but you could have come by a measuring stick at home, you know, and found out without taking up our time. You might make a good soldier, but you know the rules, and I can't bend 'em."

The rest he marched out to the exercise ground, and he stood while, five at a time, they ran briskly around its track, clad only in their tunics, to the accompanying catcalls of the guardsmen lounging nearby.

"Hai, Ogulnius, did you ever see such a sorry lot? I'll give you a penny to the commander's best horse not a one of 'em makes it two months!"

"Aye for sure," his companion drawled lazily, "the

Emperor must be hard up for spear fodder when he starts in recruitin' babes off their mammies' laps."

"Nah then," a third man put in. "They're a present to the king of the Germans. To play with, like."

Two of the much-tried candidates turned with raised fists to dispute the point. *"Get back in line!"* the surgeon bellowed. "You will have to put up with a lot worse, so get used to it!" As the panting runners finished their lap, he put his ear to the chest of each and made notations next to their names on his slate. One man he dismissed immediately, and one he sent back for another lap, accepting him grudgingly at the end of it.

"You'll do, I think, but I want you to check in with me once a week while you're training. If you make it through this, I daresay you'll make it through anything else the army hands you."

The candidate nodded and the surgeon turned to the other man. "It gives me no pleasure to certify a good man unfit for service," he said gently, seeing the boy's downcast face. "Somebody thinks a fair amount of you or you wouldn't have been recommended here. But if you still want the army, you might consider the medical corps. We've always a need for good officers there, and you're not at death's door, you know. I'm just not sure you'd hold up on a forced march and a battle at the end of it, and that makes you a danger to yourself *and* your men."

"I—I don't know, sir. I'll think about it." The boy turned and walked off, disconsolate.

"Mucius!" the old surgeon yelled, and the other candidates blinked in surprise as the drillmaster stepped up and saluted with a flourish. "Go and talk to him, and put a little tact into it. I want that one for my corps. All right, next!"

Part of the last group circling the track, Flavius stared straight ahead as he ran, ignoring the comments of their unwelcome audience. Correus followed suit until, halfway around, he realized that in six months he would outrank his tormentor. *Begin as you mean to go on.* He could almost hear Appius say it. Catching a German accent, he gave the man a leering smile and shouted something back. The guardsman started for him with a bellow, but was pulled back to his place by two of his fellows. Correus ran on, chuckling. Flavius dropped back until he was abreast of him.

"What did you say to him?"

"I called him the son of six fathers," Correus said mildly. "I *thought* he mightn't like it. Forst tells me the Germans are *very* one-way about their women." Germans from the Roman side of the Rhenus frontier had often been recruited into the City guard, especially during the anarchy of the Civil Wars three years earlier. Those who had walked carefully had managed to remain there when Vespasian took the purple.

"Well, that was stupid," Flavius said. "Now he'll try to take your head off."

"He can try," Correus said.

They halted, sweating but breathing lightly, before the camp surgeon. "Well, you two are in better shape than most," he said approvingly as he came to them. He studied their faces. "Brothers, I think."

"Uh . . . yes," Flavius said.

The surgeon made two marks on his slate, lifting an eyebrow as he came to their names. Appius Julianus— that explained it. "I met your father once. Fine man. Hell of a reputation to have to drag around after you, though. Don't make too much of it or they'll run you ragged just to see if they can."

His inspection completed, the surgeon turned back those he had passed to Centurion Mucius, who marched them at a fast trot back to the training barracks. There the camp barber awaited them to deal with any man whose hair, in the opinion of Centurion Mucius, exceeded regulation length. Most did. Correus and Flavius soon found themselves shorn like a pair of sheep, their hair reduced to the army standard of one inch.

"I'd tell you how funny you look," Flavius said moodily, "except that I expect I look the same."

The next stop was the supply shed, where they were unceremoniously stripped again and issued standard army tunics of lightweight scarlet wool, a heavier tunic for cold weather, neck scarf, hobnailed sandals, and a heavy military cloak, also in scarlet as befitted their theoretical rank. Clad in light tunic and sandals, they were lined up and trooped off to the armorer, where they were loaded down

with an unwieldy collection of pilum, sword, dagger, sword
belt, shield, and, finally, armor: iron greaves for the lower
legs, helmet with the red fanwise crest of a centurion, and
leather harness tunic with skirt and sleeves of red-dyed
leather strips, over which went the body armor—a lorica
of segmented plates. Parade armor, Mucius informed
them, would be issued at such time as they could be paraded as a unit without embarrassing him.

Carrying their acquisitions, the candidates trooped back
to barracks again, praying fervently not to drop anything.
Beds were assigned, rules were explained ("Anything you
ain't been ordered to do is against orders!"), and they
were promptly hustled into full kit, which, it seemed to
Correus, never came off again for the next week. In full
gear, they ran, marched, drilled, climbed ropes, walls, and
ladders; they saluted each other, they saluted the prefect
and the junior drillmaster, they saluted everything in
sight, and once, out of habit, they saluted a red-cloaked
wagon driver, who fell off his seat laughing.

They memorized the organization of a legion above
and below their own rank, from the lowliest enlisted legionary up through the extra-pay men—trumpeters, ar-
morers, and the standard-bearers who carried the cohort
and century standards and the great gilded Eagle that
was each legion's pride. Above these were the numerous
optios, a combination of clerk, second-in-command, and
general aide; one was assigned to assist each officer from
the rank of junior centurion up. In their hands the daily
routine of the camp rolled smoothly on, and a headquarters optio was a force to be reckoned with.

Next was the rank of centurion, the backbone of the
army at every level, from junior centurions with a century of eighty men in their command, through the cohort
commanders with six centuries in their charge and five
junior centurions below them, to the primus pilus, commander of the First Cohort and second-in-command of
the legion. On his way to the exalted post of primus pilus
a centurion could expect to receive command of several
cohorts, from the lowest, the Tenth, on up. He might also
find himself in command of smaller outpost forts or be
posted with the fleet or the auxiliaries. Beyond the rank
of primus pilus he might be named camp prefect of a

legionary fort under the legion's commander, the legate. Legates and military governors were generally senatorial posts, but an exceptional career officer could aspire to those as well. Appius Julianus had done it. Most direct-commissioned centurions never went beyond cohort or frontier-fort command, and men promoted to centurion from the ranks never got that far. But greater things were possible and each candidate, studying the table of ranks and striving to remember whether a junior surgeon out-ranked a senior optio or vice versa, paused to picture himself in the gilded breastplate and eagle-crested helmet of a legionary legate, commander of ten cohorts and all he surveyed.

The tribune, although technically superior in rank to any centurion, was regarded with mild scorn. The trib-unes were young men of senatorial rank, doing their re-quired short term with the army before embarking on a political career. The Centuriate candidates considered themselves career men, doing the real work while former tribunes argued about that work in the Senate back in Rome.

These lordly visions ceased abruptly with the end of the brief study time allotted them, and Centurion Mucius returned the candidates to reality with a rag and a jar of metal polish.

They polished lorica, helmet, greaves, pilum points, and, as mounted officers and gentlemen, their horses' ac-coutrements as well. A single speck of rust brought pun-ishment drill, the offending candidate forced to run three times around the training track, holding the substandard object at arm's length (no easy task if it happened to be his lorica) and yelling "Rust!" at the top of his voice with every step.

The riding instructor, an ex-cavalry commander named Rufus, proved only slightly more benign than Centurion Mucius. The legions were infantry, but an officer and a gentleman rode a horse. And if he didn't, he did by the time Decurion Rufus was through with him. On their first day they found their mounts led out fitted up with a light bridle and nothing else.

"All right, gentlemen, knot your reins, cross your arms on your chest, and hit those jumps!"

They made a terrifying circuit of the training ring, most flying off at the first jump. Only Correus, Flavius, and six others made it all the way around, whereupon for their pains, Decurion Rufus had them do it again so the rest could watch. It was a drastic method, but by the end of two weeks each man could take the jumps bareback, arms crossed and praying, and come around still on his horse.

They learned to vault onto horseback and to mount and dismount fully armed, with shield, from either side. And the man whose horse wouldn't stand for that got to spend his off-duty hours retraining him.

They attacked posts with wooden swords from behind wicker shields, both of twice the standard weight, and learned to shoot a bow and use a sling on the theory that an officer should be able to do anything that anyone under his command could—and better. They learned to build a marching camp in one day, complete with ditch and wall, and then tear it down again; and twice a week Mucius trotted them through the streets of Rome to the icy waters of the Tiber for a swimming lesson. They ate ravenously anything that was put before them—standard army fare of dried meat or fish, eggs, bread, olives, and a routine-issue wine that Flavius said would make a wonderful bronze polish. At night they fell into bed like so many corpses and slept until a bugler blew unwelcome reveille at first light of dawn.

As the camp surgeon had predicted, Mucius ran the sons of Appius Julianus harder than most, but for all the candidates the first two months were undiluted hell. Generally at the top of the class—their father's training had stood them in good stead—the brothers slogged through it. But Correus could tell by looking at Flavius that he loathed those training months with a silent hatred that went bone deep. As for Correus, he loved it. Even through the aching muscles and blistered feet, and the occasional comments of fellow candidates who counted him a lowborn upstart and made it known, he loved it.

This was home, he thought, standing on the parade ground at evening worship in the long shadow of the cohort standards. He saluted the standards and felt the same tug of loyalty that he knew Appius had felt when

he had first stood there. This was the real Rome, the
Army of the Eagles who had built their roads across half
the world and taken Rome with them as they went. And
in the shadow of those standards, Correus found more
sense of belonging than he had ever achieved in his father's house. Had Appius known that, he wondered, when
he had given him the Centuriate?

After two months Mucius presented them with their
parade uniforms ("Terrific," someone murmured, "something else to polish"), marking them for the envious eyes
of newer recruits as candidates who had successfully
passed the first stage of their training. They numbered
only thirty-four now, having lost ten more who resigned
in the first weeks, and an eleventh who had been pulled
by the surgeon for a bad knee that showed up on a march.
They learned that the boy who had been dropped on the
first day had indeed gone to the medical corps and
passed the tests for apprentice surgeon.

For the successful, the training was now no less rig-
orous, but it did grow more interesting, as the interminable drills and marches slackened off to make way for
classes in organization and administration, in military law,
tactics, and the command of men. An officer from the
corps of engineers instructed them in bridge and road construction, and they learned how to build siege towers
and ramps, and how to take down, reassemble, and fire
the catapults—from the light bolt-shooting scorpions to
the great stone-throwers. Their instructor for this last
was a wiry artilleryman with three fingers missing who informed them solemnly that catapults "was tricksy," and
then set his terrified novices to practice on them.

They held their first full-scale parade under the stern
eye of the camp prefect, Pertinax Aquila. Parade armor
consisted of a cuirass of bronze scale over skirt and
sleeves of white leather strips fringed in gold. The greaves
were silvered and embossed with a vine pattern, and over
the cuirass they wore a leather harness with a silver
roundel bearing the V-shaped centurion's insigne. The
parade harness would also carry military decorations if
and as they were won; and the candidates looked en-
viously at the tall figure of Pertinax Aquila, resplendent

with three rows of awards and two silver-and-gold Valorous Conduct torques gleaming above them. In place of a helmet he wore a gilded wreath of oak leaves which Correus realized with awe was a *corona civica,* awarded only to a man who had saved the life of a fellow citizen under the most dangerous of circumstances.

The prefect lifted his hand to Mucius, who signaled a trumpeter. The horn sang out and the ranks of candidates parted with precision to pass in review, their scarlet pennant snapping in the breeze before them and every bronze scale gleaming. The quick parade step and the intricate maneuvers were almost second nature now, and they completed the drill perfectly while Mucius held his breath.

That night they were considerably startled by the appearance of an optio, a staff aide, delivering a ration of good wine "with Prefect Aquila's compliments, gentlemen. And Centurion Mucius says don't let it go to your heads."

"We're in!" someone shouted. "We're gonna make it!" He raised his cup and took a deep drink.

A black-haired boy jumped up on a clothes chest, his mailed sandals stamping out a little dance step. "To the Centuriate, brothers," he said, laughing. "May we all live through it!"

Flavius raised his own cup, his dark angular face losing some of the tension of the parade. "To the Centuriate," he said, and drank.

The wine went around again and they filled their cups happily. Correus stood up as if to say something when another man, with a pale, blue-eyed face that was beginning to get flushed, glared at him belligerently. "Hey you, Julianus Minor, why aren't you drinking?"

"Pipe down and I'll tell you," Correus said mildly.

"Don't use that tone to me—freedman!"

"You're drunk, Marcus," Flavius said. "Stop it."

The other turned to Flavius with an unpleasant smile. "Fuckin' adopted freedman. You said it yourself. No business in the Centuriate," he added.

The others sat in uncomfortable silence while Flavius reddened. "Marcus, be quiet," he said again.

Correus slammed his empty cup down on a bench. "I can defend myself—brother!" he snapped. "As for you,

Marcus, drink up and keep quiet or I'll put a pilum down your throat!" He went to his cot and lay down, face up.

Someone dragged Marcus away to the far end of the barracks, and the others returned self-consciously to their wine. After a moment Flavius got up and went over to Correus.

"I'm sorry," he said. "What I said to Marcus . . . I—I didn't mean it the way he said it."

"I know how you meant it," Correus said, his lips tight. "So don't worry about it."

"I'm sorry," Flavius said again, embarrassed. "I—" He looked desperately for some change of subject, cursing the devils that had prompted him to spout off about his half-brother to Marcus—and those devils that had let Correus find out about it. "Uh, why weren't you drinking?" he asked finally.

"I don't like being seasick," Correus said obscurely, and turned on his side, his back to the room.

The literal and figurative meanings of Mucius's warning, as well as the wisdom of Correus's abstinence, were brought home to all of them the next morning as Mucius informed them with ill-suppressed amusement that a training ship of the fleet was in port and they would be marines for the next few days.

The training ship was a trireme, the *Tyche,* and for this expedition she had been given a slightly shorthanded crew of mixed seamen and marines. The Centuriate candidates discovered to their horror that they were to fill the empty oar slots on the first day out.

The *Tyche* bobbed like a water bug next to the grain ships, her deadly underwater ram barely visible below the surface and her oars drawn in. Correus and the others marched up the boarding ramp in full kit to be met by a bored-looking naval officer who gave them a casual salute and told them to strip down to their tunics.

"You can't command a warship, gentlemen, until you know what makes her move, and when there's any maneuvering to be done, it's done by the strength of some sailor's arm, as you'll discover." He nodded at a seaman beside him. "Take 'em below, but spread 'em out, mind, so they can get the hang of it from the lads next to 'em.

And have 'em sit tight till we're clear in the river. I don't want a lot of broken oars."

They followed the seaman unsteadily. The ship was hardly moving, but there was a queer unstable feel to the deck as if it might suddenly lurch out from under them. Most had done enough traveling to have taken ship from time to time, but their expressions said plainly that they had not enjoyed it. Below, the oars were arranged on three levels, one man to each oar, and their escort indicated to each seaman whose place he would take. Flavius shot Correus a furious glance as he climbed past him to the mid-level and sat next to a blond young seaman in a green naval tunic. The previous night, with Correus firmly pretending to be asleep, Flavius had drowned his irritation and embarrassment in a wine jug and now his head pounded like an anvil and the gentle rocking of the ship set his stomach crawling up his rib cage.

Most of the others looked as if they felt much the same, and a seaman near the bow of the galley could be heard telling the pale-faced boy, Marcus, who had baited Correus, "Heave up your breakfast on *my* oar bench, and I'll heave you overboard!"

"*Tyche*, hah!" someone else grumbled, and then made a little gesture of apology to the goddess of good fortune, the galley's namesake.

At a signal from the commander, the hortator in the stern tapped his mallet twice and the oars were run out through the oarlocks. The hortator set a slow, steady beat on the sounding block and the rowers bent to their oars. Those on the port side gave way, while the starboard oars backed, and the *Tyche* came about into the river. She turned her nose seaward, toward the port of Ostia, twenty miles downstream, growing livelier and more buoyant as the sail was sheeted home. Correus could see the wind-filled crimson curve of it above him, marked with the great black eagle of the fleet. After the ship had made its way clear of the heaviest of the river traffic that put in daily to the Tiber docks, the thirty-four seamen picked for tutors slid over on their oar benches and showed their reluctant pupils how to grip the oars and pull in unison so that one hundred seventy oars dipped as one to the hortator's mallet.

The clean, spacious oar benches of a naval galley were a far cry from the cramped and stinking quarters occupied by the slaves of a merchant ship (rowers in a fighting galley were also soldiers and proud of it). But it was back-breaking work, and the great oars were heavy and unwieldy so that a mistake could easily cost a broken rib. As the galley slid past the marshy coastal plains below the City, the newcomers felt the strain in their arms, even while heading downstream, and long before they reached the salt pans along the shore above Ostia harbor, their muscles ached like fire and their hands were blistered raw.

The seamen regarded them tolerantly enough, with only an occasional smirk to show their amusement at the sight of thirty-four fledgling centurions sweating like oxen at the oars and often catching a handle in the teeth on the upstroke.

"Try to hear the beat with your back and arms, not just in your head," the seaman beside Correus advised. "The rhythm's got to get *into* you, like."

Correus nodded and ducked his head to wipe his brow on his tunic sleeve, almost catching himself in the eye with the oar as he did so.

"And *don't* do *that*," the seaman added with a grin. "Here." He wore a strip of linen tied around his head to keep sweat from his eyes, and he unknotted Correus's scarf and tied it for him in a similar fashion.

"Thanks. And you do this for a living? You have my admiration."

"It's none so bad when you're used to it," the seaman said. He pulled one foot up on the oar bench and braced it comfortably against an upright beam. "This is just a sightseeing excursion, mind you. The real work comes when you're trying to outmaneuver another ship, or keep your head above water in a storm."

"Thank you, this trip will do me very well," Correus said. He could feel the blisters swelling on his palms and winced as one burst.

The seaman leaned comfortably against the back brace. "Nice to have a bit of a holiday, though," he said.

They made it from the port of Rome to Ostia harbor with only two broken oars, which the *Tyche*'s commander said with some resignation was better than he had expected. As they neared Ostia harbor he pulled the novices off the oar benches, and they slunk wearily up on deck to drop in their tracks. There was a great deal of traffic in the harbor, including ships too large for convenient docking at Rome, and he wanted no accidents resulting from a Centuriate candidate's mistake.

They stood out well into the harbor and dropped anchor while the naval commander and an officer of marines eyed their blistered charges thoughtfully. Riding on the swell in the harbor, those who hadn't been seasick at the oars promptly made up for lost time.

"Damn you, Julianus," one of them said, lowering himself to the deck beside Correus and putting his head to the cool metal of a catapult brace. "You knew, didn't you? How did you find out?" He had bright dark eyes and a sleek cap of black hair like a seal; he was Vindex, the one who had toasted the Centuriate the night before from the top of his clothes chest.

Correus leaned his back against the deck railing. "Believe it or not, Mucius told me. I think he was just being evil-minded because the parade had gone so well and he thought he looked smug. And that way we couldn't say he hadn't warned us about the wine."

The dark boy laughed weakly. "Marcus is as sick as a pig and serves him right. But why didn't you tell the rest of us?"

"I should have," Correus said. "I meant to. I got mad."

Vindex nodded. "I can't say as I blame you. We should have stifled Marcus right off, and not left it to Flavius."

"It wouldn't have mattered," Correus said. "It was Flavius I was mad at."

Vindex regarded Correus's angular face and grim mouth thoughtfully.

"I'm sorry," Correus added.

"Well, we won't die of it," Vindex said. "And *I'm* not going to tell that you knew. But the sooner you're posted apart from your brother, the better, I think."

Correus didn't answer, and he let it go, turning to watch a Greek merchantman come into port, her great banks of oars rising and falling to the hammer beat. She was a big ship and slid by close enough to hear the overseer's voice below deck and the crack of a whip, followed by a cry of pain from one of the rowers chained to his bench. The seaman who had sat on Correus's bench stopped beside them.

"I wouldn't have the life of those poor bastards for anything," he said with pity. "It's a filthy way to move a ship, with no pride left to you."

Correus turned to watch the merchantman move past. The barbarity of a leg shackle had never touched his own life, but his slave days had marked him strongly enough that he winced and turned back again. Vindex was right. He would never outrun those days with Flavius like a shadow on his heels.

With the seamen at their accustomed benches, the *Tyche* put out to sea the next day. The Centuriate candidates were chased ruthlessly up and down the rigging by the mate, learning to let out the black-and-crimson sail and sheet it home, and then to furl it again.

"Tyche grant us she keeps an eye on her namesake!" Flavius shouted over the wind and the flapping of the sail as they clung side by side in the rigging, struggling to secure the crimson canvas; and Correus knew Flavius wanted to make peace.

He smiled and Flavius smiled back, but it did little to dispel the uncertainty in Correus's mind. He had seen Flavius's tight-faced look as they climbed the rigging and knew that Flavius was terrified. Flavius did well enough with Correus beside him—he would have followed his half-brother through the gates of Tartarus just to prove he wouldn't back down. Alone, Correus wasn't so sure what Flavius would do. And if he did back down, he would carry the mark with him for life, if only in his mind. Damn the promise Appius had made him give!

When the mate had run them through their paces, they were given a brief course in the use of signal flags and then turned over to the decurion of marines. They spent the rest of their cruise in full armor, being drilled on deck and learning the fine points of disabling an enemy ship. They also learned how to swing out the "raven," a wicked little boarding ramp with a long iron spike like a bird's beak at the end that could punch through the deck-

ing of an enemy vessel and hold it alongside the galley to
be boarded.

"Don't get to thinking you know it all now," the marine
decurion told them as the *Tyche* made her way back up
the Tiber three days later, "because you damn well
don't. But you know enough not to fall overboard the first
time you find yourself at sea, and to know what the crew's
doing. The legions are a dry-land army—if you're shipped
somewhere, you won't need much more than you know.
And good luck to you; I'm sure your drillmaster's eager to
have you back."

Vindex groaned. "I'd almost rather stay on board."

They had only three months left in their training, and
time passed with surprising speed—two new classes of
candidates had come in behind them, and Correus's group
watched with hardened amusement as the newcomers
were put through their paces. As senior candidates, they
were allowed a little leave time in the City, and once in a
wineshop Correus encountered the German guardsman
he had insulted on his first day in camp. The man came
forward belligerently, ready to fight, but he had waited
too long—Correus had begun to think like a centurion.
He fixed the German with a blazing eye and ordered him
back to quarters, and the guardsman went, while Centurion Mucius, unnoticed in the far corner, bent over his
wine cup in laughter.

At the start of their last month, Correus was named
commander of his group and from then on led them at
drill and parade. Flavius offered tight-lipped congratulations, and Marcus kept up a snide commentary on his
lack of qualifications. Finally Vindex angrily took Marcus
by the collar and told him to stow it.

"He can't punch your face in now because he's the
commander, but if you don't shut up, Marcus, I'll do it
for him!"

This was seconded by most of the group and Marcus
retired in silence. Thereafter he simply ignored Correus's
existence except to obey a direct order, and Correus
breathed a sigh of relief and let him. There wasn't much
use in trying to change Marcus's mind, and Correus saw
no reason to try.

Mucius, on the other hand, startled Correus considerably. From his first day in camp, Mucius had run him harder than all the rest. Now he had handed him command of the group. The old crocodile had even smiled. It was highly unnerving, and Correus adjusted with difficulty to the idea that Centurion Mucius, whom he had learned to loathe in the first week, actually had decent moments after all.

For Mucius, of course, it was quite simple. He knew a good commander when he saw one and he didn't care if his mother had been a baboon.

With two weeks to go, Pertinax Aquila began to summon the candidates to his office in the Principia, the camp headquarters, for private interviews. They went with considerable trepidation, which was not lessened when he sat each one down and proceeded to go over his record. (This appeared to contain every rusty pilum point and wrong turn on the drill field; Centurion Mucius was thorough.) They were then allowed to request the posting of their choice. There was no guarantee that they would get it, of course, but the army graciously allowed them to request.

Correus went for his interview with a reluctance in no way connected with his performance as a candidate. He assumed reasonably enough that if there was much wrong with that he would not have been given the command. Rather, it had to do with the dark shadow of Flavius, recently returned from his own session with the prefect.

It was evening, warm and slightly humid, and the wind was in the west, bringing with it the fishy and decaying odor of the Tiber dockyards. The cooking smells of the City lingered in the air, and it made for a heady mixture. The cohort standards had been taken down for the night, but the windows of the Principia glowed with lamplight. Correus caught a faint whiff of incense in the air.

"The City is particularly ripe tonight," the prefect said, adjusting the incense burner. "The older I get the more attractive the frontier becomes again." He was of provincial birth, a Spaniard, with light hair going gray at the temples and a lean, lined face tanned from years in the field. He sat idly rubbing his thumb over the rough-ened spot under his chin, the callus of a legionary helmet strap that was as good as a brand.

"Sit down, Centurion Julianus, please." He took a records folder from his desk and thumbed it through. "You have an admirable record, except for a tendency to squabble with your mates, which Centurion Mucius is more inclined to lay at their door than yours. All in all, it's obvious your father was right to send you to us. You have justified his faith in you admirably."

"Thank you, sir," Correus said. He made it sound sincere, but apparently Pertinax Aquila was not deceived.

"That wasn't very tactful of me, was it?" the prefect said. "Look you, young one, you're going to have to get used to remarks about your birth, until it slides off your back and doesn't bother you. The Centuriate is crammed with fools like young Marcus."

"Yes, sir."

"Very well. Now then, Centurion Mucius speaks very highly of you, and I'm inclined to give you your choice of posting—subject to availability, of course. Is there any legion you particularly want?"

Correus pulled at the leather fringes of his harness tunic and then his hand clenched tightly. He looked up. "Yes, sir. I understand that my brother has asked for the Rhenus frontier."

"He has," Pertinax Aquila said.

"May I ask, sir, if he's going to get it?"

"I rather expect he will," the prefect replied. "There's no great surplus of officers wanting to serve on the Rhenus just now." The cold climate made it an unpleasant posting, and the current upheaval one of the most dangerous. "Am I to infer that you also wish to be in on this campaign?"

"As to that, sir, yes," Correus said slowly. "But—also, I would like a posting in the same legion as Flavius."

Pertinax Aquila was silent a moment. "I know I said I'd give you what you wanted," he said finally, "but are you quite sure of this?"

Correus looked back at him steadily. "Yes, sir."

Pertinax Aquila regarded him narrowly, trying to read some answer in that dark, level gaze. Did Julianus realize what that posting could cost him? Seeing the grim line about the youth's mouth, the prefect decided that he probably did. "Very well," he said reluctantly. "I will try to arrange it."

"Thank you, sir." Correus stood up and saluted.

With sympathy, Pertinax Aquila watched him go. Young fool, to be throwing himself a fixed roll of the dice deliberately! And Aquila doubted if he was doing Flavius much of a favor, either. Of course, he could always claim the requested posting had proved impossible to arrange. . . . He shook his head. No, he had given the boy his word. Let him have it.

Thirty-four fully commissioned centurions, of an entering class of forty-seven, stood on the parade ground in full dress kit. There was a wind blowing and the sky was pale blue behind light, scurrying clouds. The sunlight shifted constantly, dancing off bronze scale and scabbard tips, and turning scarlet helmet crests to fire. Prefect Aquila stood on the reviewing platform with the Praetorian Prefect Titus beside him, while the junior candidates were paraded behind them to receive inspiration.

Centurion Mucius growled at the newcomers: "All right, you slovenly babes, dress up that line and take a good look at what you're shooting for!" There was an undignified ripple of laughter from the graduates.

One by one as their names were called, they marched in solitary glory to the reviewing stand to receive their posting and the vine staff of their office.

"Silvius Vindex," the optio called. "Sixth century, Eighth Cohort, Sixth Legion Victrix."

Vindex saluted and turned at parade quickstep back down the stairs of the reviewing platform, his vine staff tucked proudly under his arm and his eyes shining. The Sixth Victrix was a good legion, one of the Emperor's pets.

"Sulpicius Silanus, sixth century, Tenth Cohort, Third Legion Cyrenaica."

"Marcus Fulminatus, sixth century, Ninth Cohort, Seventh Legion Gemina."

"Flavius Appius Julianus . . ." Flavius stood parade-straight on the platform, the bright, blood-red crest of his helmet a gaudy splash against the purple cloaks of the prefects. Correus watched with caught breath as Aquila handed him his staff and the wax tablet with his orders. "Sixth century, Ninth Cohort, Eighth Legion Augusta."

The Eighth Augusta . . . a Rhenus legion and one of the best. The Emperor had brought the Eighth to Germany two years earlier to straighten out the mess left by rebellion and the Civil Wars when he had cashiered four of the seven existing frontier legions. So Flavius at least had gotten his wish. The Eighth had come from Moesia, and Pannonia before that, Correus remembered, and Prefect Aquila had served in it himself in the old days. Correus could almost feel Aquila's eyes, shadowed by the gold leaves of the *corona civica,* watching him.

"Correus Appius Julianus," the optio called out. As commander, his was the last posting given, and all watched him curiously, knowing that he could have had his pick.

Correus touched fist to breast and accepted the vine staff and the congratulations of the prefects. *It's done,* he thought. He had asked to have Flavius tied around his neck. If Aquila had given it to him, there was no taking the request back again.

Pertinax Aquila seemed to hesitate, and then he touched Correus lightly on the shoulder and handed him his orders. A post in the Legions, a post in the Centuriate. His heart's desire, and yet . . . Correus studied the scarlet Imperial Seal, official and unchangeable, as the optio called out the posting: "Sixth century, Eighth Cohort, Eighth Legion Augusta."

Correus saluted, the prefects saluted, and he strode back down the steps while Flavius watched with something unreadable in his eyes.

V

The Agri Decumates

THE GRAY STONE RIVER GATE AND JETTIES OF ARGEN-toratum came into view as the *Melpomene,* a patrol gal-ley of the Rhenus fleet, nosed her way downriver past the fields and vineyards of the civil colony that clustered on the western bank in the shadow of the fort.

"Well, there you are, lads!" The captain gave a signal and the single bank of starboard oars backed in the wa-ter. The *Melpomene* swung around to the jetty. "The place is still being rebuilt so you may find it somewhat lacking in the soft touches," he said as the sentries on the rampart above the gate called out to him for identifi-cation, "but the Emperor's got a nice little war on to keep us all busy. *Melpomene,* you fools!" he shouted to the sentries. "Do I *look* like a German?"

The frontier fortress of Argentoratum, newly recom-missioned, stood on an island finger of land between the Rhenus and a smaller tributary at the meeting of the old river road that ran north and south, and the new road that the army was pushing eastward into the mist-shrouded forests across the river.

The rebuilding of the fort was part of a campaign that sought to remedy an old mistake: three years earlier, in the grim days of the Civil Wars, the Batavian tribes of the northern Rhenus had been invited by one of the Emperor Vespasian's adherents to make a little trouble that would keep the troops loyal to Vitellius too busy to march on Rome. Instead the Batavians had called in Gaulish allies from the Roman side of the frontier and begun a major rebellion that had set the whole Rhenus road in flames. It had taken the better part of a year for the avenging Roman army to hunt the rebels down. In the meantime, the tribes of the Agri Decumates, a triangle of German

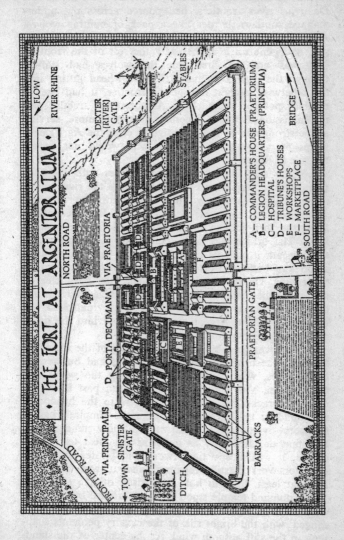

THE FORT AT ARGENTORATUM

RIVER RHINE

FLOW

NORTH ROAD

DEXTER
(RIVER)
GATE

STABLES

VIA PRAETORIA

BRIDGE

VIA PRINCIPALIS

TOWN SINISTER
GATE

D PORTA DECUMANA

FRONTIER ROAD

DITCH

BARRACKS

PRAETORIAN GATE

SOUTH ROAD

A— COMMANDER'S HOUSE (PRAETORIUM)
B— LEGION HEADQUARTERS (PRINCIPIA)
C— HOSPITAL
D— TRIBUNE'S HOUSES
E— WORKSHOPS
F— MARKETPLACE

forestland bordered on its long edges by the Rhenus and Danuvius river frontiers, had poured across the under-manned southern border like a pack of hunting wolves. Argentoratum, staffed with only a small auxiliary garri-son, had gone up in flames with the rest of the frontier.

It was not the first time the wolves had stalked through the Agri Decumates. An arrowhead jutting into the otherwise straight line of the frontier, it had been a trouble spot for years. Now Argentoratum, rebuilt and recommissioned, was a legionary base once more, serving as the stronghold of the campaign to clear the Agri Decu-mates permanently of Germans who would not accept the rule of Rome.

Correus and Flavius exchanged salutes with the cap-tain, and the *Melpomene* came about into the river again, maneuvering cautiously past Argentoratum Bridge, which spanned the wide waters of the Rhenus upriver from the fort, joining the frontier road on the western bank. The bridge was high enough for patrol galleys to slip beneath it, and its upstream pilings were guarded by a series of buffers to catch any rams sent downstream by the enemy. On the far bank the land had been cleared and its timber incorporated into the bridge and the re-built fortress; a new, log-paved road, patrolled by detachments from Argentoratum, stretched into the dark-ness of the German forest.

At the river gate, built upon the stones of the old forti-fications, the brothers stated their names and business to the sentries, who passed them in along the swept dirt track of the Via Principalis where it ran past the bath-house, barracks, and tribunes' quarters to the headquar-ters building in the Principia. Like the Empire's camps the world over, Argentoratum was built to a standard pat-tern that deviated only as much as the local terrain re-quired. It was mostly timberwork and plaster and some old stonework hastily repaired, and it was big—fifty acres at least, built to hold a garrison of five thousand.

A columned temple stood in the courtyard of the Prin-cipia, and in it the cohort and century standards were ranged, with the bright silk of the cavalry pennants snap-ping in the stiff autumn wind. At the center of the stand-ards stood the great gilded Eagle of the legion, perched on crossed thunderbolts with its silvered wings swept back as if to lift in flight. Its staff was thick with honors and bore a plaque where Correus read its name and number: LEGIO VIII AUGUSTA. There was a newly added honorific from the Emperor Vespasian: PIA FIDELIS. With a catch in his throat, Correus saluted the outspread wings. This was his legion, his Eagle, the start of a service for which he had truthfully told his mother he would have sold his soul.

In the Principia a bored optio informed them that the legate of the Eighth was up at the Emperor's front line with the bulk of the legion, and he passed them on to the camp prefect, remarking that he'd be glad enough to see new centurions.

"They've been losing junior officers faster'n they can train 'em up there."

"How delightful," Flavius murmured, and Correus laughed. Very junior centurions like them were almost beneath the notice of a headquarters optio.

The camp prefect, a middle-aged centurion with close-cut but thick graying hair and the no-nonsense expression of a career officer, welcomed them somewhat more gently.

"I'm Centurion Probus," he said. "And you'll be . . ." He matched their orders against a roster from among the clutter on his desk. "Ah, yes, Julianus and Julianus. Well, Mithras knows we can use you. I'll have the optio show you to your quarters, and you might as well relax and enjoy them because you'll be going out with the patrol in the morning to catch up to your troops." He consulted the roster again. "Eighth and Ninth Cohorts. Good. That puts us damn near up to strength in those two at least. I don't suppose any more were posted out with you?"

"No, sir," Correus said. "Two of our class were posted to the Tenth Gemina and the Sixth Victrix, and a dozen more to the Twenty-second and the Fifth."

"Frankly, Centurion," Probus said with a faint grim smile, "I am not at the moment interested in any legion but the Eighth. Although the gods know those last two could use officers, too," he added. He studied the roster again and then shoved it under a stack of requisition slips. "Damn! Well, the legate's going to have to promote from the ranks whether he likes it or not. We can't go on this short of officers." He looked up to find them still standing at attention, faces correctly expressionless, but curiosity fairly radiating from them.

"Sorry," he said brusquely. "Dismissed."

"Well!" Correus said. They had stowed away Flavius's kit in the officer's quarters at the end of the Ninth Cohort's sixth-century barracks, and were sorting through his own in the Eighth Cohort building. "It looks like we've walked right into it."

"We asked for it, if you'll recall," Flavius said, stretching out on the bed while Correus shed his lorica and harness tunic and hung them on a T-shaped stand in the corner. "Damn it, Correus, what possessed you to ask for the same legion?"

"I didn't," Correus lied, folding his spare tunics into the clothes chest, his back to his brother. He had known this was coming. "I just asked for the Rhenus, same as you did. I suppose they thought we'd like it." He closed the lid gently and turned to Flavius with a slightly fixed smile. "Frankly, I do like it. It's less lonesome this way."

Flavius sat up and gripped Correus by the forearm as he knelt to stow his shield under the bed. "I like it, too," he said, catching Correus's eyes with his own. "It isn't that—"

He means it, Correus thought. *Or at least he wants to.* "It's just that you don't like being thought of as half of a pair, like matched ponies," he said lightly. "No more do I, but that'll wear off when we've been here awhile. Come on, let's go and have a soak in the baths while we still can."

They took their dinner in the officers' mess—standard army fare of the sort best eaten quickly and not thought of—with Centurion Probus and such of the other legionary officers and auxiliary commanders as remained with the skeleton garrison at Argentoratum. They made up no more than one long table—Correus, Flavius, the commander of the Third Cohort (the garrison cohort) and his five junior centurions, a junior surgeon with the staff of Aesculapius on his belt buckle, a scattering of cavalry decurions, and another junior centurion, named Silvanus, of the Ninth Cohort, newly released from the hospital and heading back to the front lines in the morning.

Silvanus had a healing scar on his shield arm, thick hair the pale color of ripe barley, and light brown eyes flecked with amber. His skin, tanned bronze by a hotter sun than Germany's, was startling against his hair, which was cut somewhat longer than the army training barracks at Rome had allowed. Correus, looking at him, decided with relief that apparently he was not expected to spend his entire career with his head mowed like a temple lawn.

Next to Silvanus sat a thin, sandy-haired youth in a civilian tunic, perhaps a year or two older than Correus, but still very young. His homely freckled face was eager and alert as he talked with Centurion Silvanus of the current campaign. Centurion Probus gave him a look of disgust as he took his own seat at the head of the table.

"Damn it, Paulinus, you're not even supposed to be inside the camp, much less sponging at my officers' mess."

A legionary with a wine flask moved down the table and the sandy-haired boy held his cup out. "Why, Prefect," he said innocently, "you invited me to dine yourself, if you remember."

"I invited you to dine in my quarters next week, not to come gathering secret information from my officers for that seditious journal you keep."

"I think 'seditious' is a bit strong." Paulinus appeared undeterred and applied himself to a plate of fish and cured olives. "I'm a historian. I deal in facts. And unlike my predecessors' tomes, my *History of Modern Rome* will be written by a man who saw it, not by some self-serving retired magistrate with time on his hands and a pack of inaccurate old scrolls to steal from. I want to give my readers a true picture of our frontiers." He picked up an olive, mottled black and brown, and regarded it dubiously. "And if I'm willing to poison myself at your appalling table to get it, you ought to be grateful."

"Well, I'm not," Probus said shortly. "Most generals don't want your 'facts' going crosswise to their own reports, much less getting into the Germans' hands. After that last ambush, the legate's looking over his shoulder for spies and wood-elves every three paces as it is."

"I keep my notes in Greek," Paulinus said mildly. "I doubt that Nyall and his Germans would find much use for them."

"I don't care if they're in Egyptian hieroglyphics, you're not going to run tame in *my* camp." Probus cracked open an egg and glared at his uninvited guest. "You may finish your dinner and then I want you *out* of here. Understood?"

Paulinus sighed reluctantly. "Very well. Would it make you any happier if I told you I was leaving Argentoratum in the morning?"

"Infinitely," Centurion Probus said. "Go and annoy the garrison at Moguntiacum if you must." He turned to Silvanus. "And as for you, Centurion Silvanus, you had no business letting him in here in the first place."

"Yes, sir. I'm sorry, sir." Silvanus looked as repentant as possible. Unless it occurred to the prefect to forbid it directly, in the morning Silvanus was going to take Paulinus into the Agri Decumates. He turned to Flavius on his other side, and learning that he was posted to his own cohort, struck up a conversation with him. Meanwhile, Paulinus, whose curiosity appeared to be boundless, drew the young surgeon into a discussion of the best treatment for infected wounds.

"Rumor has it that the Germans poison their spears," Paulinus said, sliding the topic carefully back to the current campaign. "Have you seen any evidence of it?"

"Nothing to which a good copper verdigris dressing doesn't prove an antidote," the junior surgeon said with a trace of sarcasm. "If you want my opinion, that's a tale in the wind—probably spread by a surgeon who didn't like admitting he'd lost a patient."

Paulinus chuckled and resumed his meal. Correus sat quietly, occasionally joining in Flavius's conversation with Centurion Silvanus but mostly just watching, taking stock of his companions and his new legion, pondering the service that would be home to him for the better part of his life. If the "spies and wood-elves" didn't get him, of course. That was always a possibility, but tonight, in the still heady excitement of his new commission, it seemed remote.

Most of the junior officers were young, of mixed races

and accents; soldiers' sons, most of them, many from the provinces, where their fathers had settled and married. They were all tall—the Centuriate had a height standard —but for the rest, they were blond and dark, Roman, Gaulish, and Egyptian, and they made their prayers as frequently to Mithras or Isis as to Jupiter Thunderer or Phoebus Apollo. But they had one thing in common that was a closer tie than blood: the look that marked them for soldiers—the look that was born in the training camps of the Centuriate. It was a look Correus had seen often enough in his father, and on the faces of Pertinax Aquila and Centurion Probus. He hadn't before realized that by now it must mark him as well.

When they had eaten, Correus and Flavius strolled with Centurion Silvanus to escort Paulinus to the landward gate. The ground was wreathed in mist and the air was wet.

"There's good hunting in these parts," Silvanus said, "when we aren't out hunting Germans instead. Did you bring your own mounts with you? If you didn't, I warn you that what you'll get assigned is what the cavalry doesn't want, and they're mostly enough to make you think someone had lopped the ears off a mule and tried to make him do."

"My body servant is bringing them," Flavius said easily, "at a somewhat slower pace than the army wanted from us. I've no desire to ruin my Nestor before I get him here, and he doesn't think much of riverboats. We tried."

Silvanus laughed. "Yes, my mount had to come by land also. They ship the cavalry horses by river in transports, but even in ships that are built special for 'em, it's a nightmare. Is your body servant coming along also?" he inquired of Correus. "You'll be glad of your own. There's precious little that's of much use in the slave markets out here."

"Horse, yes; servant, no," Correus said. "I find that I'm happier doing for myself," he added, feeling it unnecessary to explain that he had flatly refused to buy a body servant. He had found the slave market a somewhat too pointed reminder of other days.

"My brother has a few egalitarian thoughts on the subject of slavery," Flavius said, and Silvanus looked

amused, remarking that for himself, he disliked polishing armor. Paulinus gave Correus an interested look, but
he made no comment.

Feeling irritable at this talk, Correus parted from them
at the gate while they were still making plans for the
morning. He knew that Flavius was unable to resist the
temptation to dig at him in that fashion and that he did
not consciously mean him any harm, but it set his teeth
on edge all the same. He decided to walk off his temper
and turned down past the barracks rows toward the
southern wall. It was full dark and the ramparts were
illuminated at intervals by torchlight; he could just catch
the red crests of the sentries as they passed from one circle of light to the next. A knife-sharp wind came up,
bringing with it a cold, dank smell from the river. Correus wished he had brought his cloak and decided that he
was too pigheaded to go to his quarters and get it.

He stalked on, past more barracks rows, parade ground
and drill shed, armorer's shop and the pottery works,
where a stack of roof tiles lay on a wheeled wooden pal-
let. Farther still was an open-air marketplace, its stalls
shrouded for the night; here, such vendors as the prefect approved were permitted to offer their wares to the
garrison. It had a swept and regimented air to it and
would probably prove far less interesting than the jumbled market square of the nearby civil colony.

Argentoratum felt empty. There was something odd
about it that nagged at the back of Correus's mind, but he
could not pin it down. He turned into the broad cleared
stretch along the river wall where the squat bulk of the
granaries rose on his left, well out of firing range from
enemy ships. An owl floated by on silent wings, intent
on mice. Then it came to him. The Eagle. If the Eighth
Legion was in the field, why was its Eagle standard still
standing in the Temple of the Standards before the
Principia? The Eagle—heart and soul of a legion—went
with it always.

He was still wondering about that when they rode out
the next morning to the Argentoratum Bridge. Their
horses had not arrived, and he and Flavius had been
given a pair of mounts from the cavalry barracks that

bore out Silvanus's prophecy all too well. Silvanus rode
his own horse, a white gelding with a strain of Arab
blood that showed in the bright, intelligent eyes and
small, pricked-up ears. Correus, applying his heel to a
dun nag whose father had apparently had his way with a
cart horse, wished fervently for Antaeus, while Flavius
was astride a hammerheaded hack with a mouth like an
iron bar.

The sandy-haired historian, Lucius Paulinus, rode beside them, along with a man who was apparently his
body servant. They were muffled in gray, army-issue
cloaks, and Silvanus had provided them legionary helmets
apparently acquired in some devious fashion.

"Here, put these on," he said, laughing. "I've squared
it with the sentries on the bridge, but you never know
when Probus'll take it in his mind to trot by. He'll have
my head if he finds out I have anything to do with you."

Paulinus, who practically disappeared into his helmet,
could not have been mistaken for a soldier at a distance
of less than a hundred paces, but his servant, settling the
helmet on his head and twisting his cloak into a military
fold, had the look of the legions about him. The set of his
shoulders fairly screamed of the drill field.

They trotted across the wooden planks of Argentoratum Bridge, which seemed to float in midair above the
mist-shrouded river, and Correus saw Silvanus slip something into the hand of the sentry as they passed by onto
the log road on the other side. "Keep tucked in yet
awhile," he said to Paulinus, a look of mischief on his
tanned face. "Once we're clear of the first patrol, you can
take that thing off. You look like a kid with a pot on his
head."

"I couldn't say," Paulinus replied austerely. "I have
never put a pot on my head."

"What, never as a youngster, to play soldier?"

"I am a writer," Paulinus said, and Correus saw that
his mouth was twitching with amusement under the out-
sized helmet. "Primarily a historian, and an occasional
poet. When I'm feeling nasty I write a satire. If I want
someone hacked to pieces with a sword, I ask Tullius to
do it."

His attendant, a barrel-chested man with arms like

an ape, nodded solemnly as an expression of pure devotion played across his broad features.

"He sounds a most useful sort of slave to possess," Flavius said.

Paulinus chuckled. "Tullius is no slave. He followed the Eagles himself once and took up with me quite voluntarily. But as to his usefulness, I grant you I have little fear of robbers in the streets at night."

The ground was rocky now, dotted with tree stumps, and the log road was too narrow to ride all abreast. Flavius and Silvanus trotted on ahead, with Correus and Lucius Paulinus behind, leaving Tullius to bring up the rear with Centurion Silvanus's servant. The road was of oak planking laid over brushwood and pegged to the ground; a steep drainage ditch to either side kept it reasonably dry.

"Half this accursed country is mountains and the other half's bog," Silvanus grumbled. "The legate's staff is crawling with engineers. He consults 'em like oracles before we move a foot. I've dug enough drainage ditch since I've been out here to circle the Capitoline."

"That reminds me," Correus said to Paulinus. "Why are the Eagle and the cohort standards in Argentoratum if the legion's in the field?"

"Noticed that, did you? Well, you see we're not at war out here, not officially. The legate's playing at cat-and-mouse with Nyall, who's the king or lord high what-have-you of the strongest German tribe in these parts. The legate doesn't want it to come to a pitched battle if he can help it, not while he's still undermanned. What he wants is for Nyall to have a nice long think and come to terms. So he leaves the Eagle at home and sets out as if he's engineering; but he takes every man he's got available. Nyall knows what an Eagle is, all right—the northern tribes have still got the three they took from Varus in Augustus's reign. And Calpurnius Rufinus—that's our legate—figures that if Nyall doesn't see the Eagle he'll figure this isn't the whole army marching about and be so impressed that he'll come bounding in hung all about with green branches and surrender to us."

There was a note of blatant skepticism in Paulinus's

voice. "I take it *you* don't think he'll surrender," Correus said.

"I am not, praise Athena, a general. But no, I don't think so. I think Rufinus is underestimating Nyall. I'm not so sure who's the cat and who's the mouse."

"What's he like? Nyall, I mean."

"I've never met him face to face, and I'd give quite a lot to. He's from the Semnones, one of the tribes of the Suevi, whose lands are just outside the Agri Decumates. He doesn't fancy having Rome's soldiers on his border, so he's worked up the local tribes to resist, and he's put more sense of unity in them than anyone else ever has. The German's a funny beast. They live to fight, and they don't seem to care much *who* they fight. When they're at peace with us, they fight each other, just for something to do, apparently. This Nyall seems to have got them into a fairly cohesive unit, and they have the advantage of knowing the land. They practically rise up out of the bog under your feet—that's what Probus meant by wood-elves. We may not be at war, but we're mounting double patrols, and often enough the Germans manage to pick off a man or two, anyway."

The road was angling uphill now, and at the crest the cleared land widened around a fortified tower surrounded by two rings of ditch-and-wall. After the guards had passed them through, Paulinus dragged off his helmet with relief. It was cool in the forest, but the air was murky and oppressive, and the black woods that rose on either side of the cleared road bank were as inviting as a rat-hole.

"Nice spot for an ambush," Correus commented to Paulinus.

"Oh, we're safe enough this far back, but I expect we'll have to go the last distance with one of the patrols."

"You're damn right we will," Silvanus called over his shoulder. "The German bastards come and go like water snakes, sometimes just three or four at a time. One minute everything's lovely, and the next minute you notice that the last man in line isn't there anymore. And they have a liking for officers' crests!"

Correus raised an eyebrow at Paulinus, who explained. "They have a tendency to pick off officers, I'm

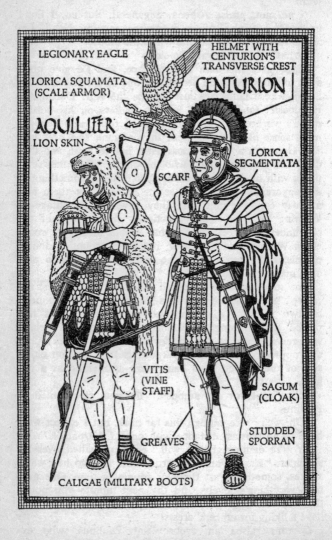

LEGIONARY EAGLE

HELMET WITH
CENTURION'S
TRANSVERSE CREST

CENTURION

LORICA SQUAMATA
(SCALE ARMOR)

AQUILIFER

LION SKIN

LORICA
SEGMENTATA

SCARF

VITIS
(VINE
STAFF)

SAGUM
(CLOAK)

STUDDED
SPORRAN

GREAVES

CALIGAE (MILITARY BOOTS)

told. Most of them can't tell one legionary uniform from another, so they look for the man whose helmet crest is set sideways. Highly dishonorable, of course."

"Highly effective, I should think," Correus said, running a hand over his own helmet crest. "What in hell are you doing in the middle of this, may I ask?"

"I want to be the first man to write the history of a major campaign from the battlefields, without having his own military reputation to consider. Having a military reputation clouds one's veracity somewhat, I should think. Mine will be unquestionable."

"That's more than I can say for your chances of survival," Correus said frankly. "This expedition could cost you more than you bargain for."

"Perhaps," Paulinus said. "It's certainly costing me a great deal of money. But then I happen to have a great deal of money and my father is no longer alive to quarrel about how I choose to spend it. An admirable man in many ways, but we never did quite see eye to eye."

"I don't doubt it," Correus said, and gave up. He had taken a liking to Paulinus and, after all, it was his own hide. "I take it you think it will come to an outright war in the end?" he said, after a minute or two.

"If Nyall can keep a firm grip on these tribes, yes," Paulinus said. "His mother was Gaulish and that gives him the perfect stick to beat the Germans into line with."

"So was mine," Correus said. "I don't see the connection."

"You wouldn't. You're Roman. Think about it. Years ago, when Julius Caesar got there, Gaul was pretty much in the same state Barbarian Germany is now. That is: divided. If the Gauls could have united instead of trying to play Caesar's army off against their neighbors, they might have stopped him."

"Gaul's been a Roman province for more than a hundred years," Correus said thoughtfully.

"Nine-tenths of the Gaulish tribes think like Romans, act like Romans, dress like Romans. They *are* Romans. Even when some of them joined in Civilis's rebellion, they were trying to set up a Gallic Empire fashioned after Rome. There's nothing left of the people the Gauls used to be. The Germans know it could happen to them.

Nyall's got conquered Gaul to point to when his German allies start to waver."

They caught up with the legion a full day's ride from Argentoratum, covering the last stretch with an incoming foot patrol: a century of the Fourth Cohort, which they picked up at the last guard post. The centurion in charge gave them a friendly nod and salute, and pointed them toward the command tent inside the turf-and-timber camp. Paulinus had quietly disappeared and Correus suspected that he had slipped in among the confusion of the baggage train, where one body more or less would go unnoticed. The chronicler was taking no chances of being thrown out of camp by a suspicious commander.

The marching camp was laid out in the usual pattern and heavily fortified; two steep V-shaped ditches surrounded its walls, one of them filled with dark, unhealthy-looking water—probably runoff from the drained land. Beyond the ditches was a field of "lilies" —small, sharpened stakes set in holes and camouflaged with brushwood. The walls were timber on a turf bank with tri-level towers at intervals, and the land had been cleared of trees for some distance in all directions. A small stream, a tributary of the Rhenus, ran past the northern wall, and a centurion of engineers was supervising the digging of a water-intake channel to the camp.

In the command tent, a palatial six-roomed affair with a plank floor, the legate was studying a map and a sheaf of engineers' projections simultaneously. Calpurnius Rufinus was a stocky, balding figure in field uniform. His helmet was on the desk beside him, its eagle-feather crest dusty and disheveled in the fading light. Rufinus had a cold in the head and a harassed expression, and he gave them a cursory inspection before signaling to an optio to present them to their respective commanders.

They found Correus's century and most of the rest of the Eighth Cohort at work on the log road that the legion was pushing westward from the camp. The cohort commander, Messala Cominius, was a career officer in his mid-twenties, and at the moment he was standing in a ditch, mired to the knees in black mud. His discarded greaves and vine staff lay some distance away on a tree stump, along with his helmet. As Correus approached, he wiped his face with a grimy hand.

"First posting?" he inquired pleasantly. The sixth century was the lowest in a cohort and the standard spot for a new man. "Well, they pitched you right into it. The sixth century is down along that way with the fifth, redigging a channel because the sacred oracle of our infallible engineers has changed his damned mind again. Their centurion will show you around. They're a good lot, only keep your eyes open at first—they'll push a new man a bit just to see how far they can get with it." He picked up an entrenching tool and hefted it. "Glad to have you with us, Centurion." He turned to the sweating legionary beside him. "Look you, Porcus, if you swing thus"—the blade came down and bit into the black earth—"you get a clean stroke at the right angle, and you don't waste your time smoothing out the sides afterward."

Correus headed off in the direction Cominius had pointed and found his new command and another young centurion, who looked relieved to see him. The other man, no more than two months out of his own training, had been moved from the sixth to the fifth century when the fifth centurion had broken a leg working in the drainage ditch.

"Two centuries is one more than I really want on my hands," he said frankly.

Correus nodded and touched the optio of the century on the shoulder. He had him call the rest up out of the ditch, and they stood on the bank, black as river rats, while Correus told them that they would look to him for orders now. Then, having decided that Messala Cominius was a commander to emulate, he stripped off his own greaves and helmet and set to work beside them.

The rest of that day and the days and weeks that followed were back-breaking work, digging drainage ditches and piling the turned-up earth on the roadbed to make a causeway, or cutting brushwood to throw in the ditches to check flooding or to tie in sheaves to form the foundation of the log road. When the planks were laid and skewered into the roadbed at each end, the men moved ahead to clear the next stretch of forest, while the engineers argued with each other over the proper course. At intervals in the cleared land, a fort would be built and a patrol garrison installed. When the road reached a full day's march from the legion's base, the entire camp was dismantled and moved up, leaving a patrol tower in its place. Two other legions from Moguntiacum in the north and Vindonissa in the south were doing the same, slowly cutting the Agri Decumates into thirds; and couriers came and went daily between their generals.

The German villages were quiet enough as the army passed by, although the inhabitants were somewhat less then helpful. The engineers made use of the Germans' tracks through the forest and laid their road over them when possible. One aged headman assured them with such transparent deviousness that the track ahead ran into bogland and had been abandoned by his village for that reason, that the centurion of engineers called him a liar to his face and ordered the road run over it anyway. Midway through the work the engineer discovered to his chagrin that the headman had been quite truthful. The route was redrawn and the headman went cackling back to his hut.

There was a noticeable lack of fighting-age men in the villages, but they were an unseen presence manifested in sabotaged roadwork and ambushed patrols. Correus, taking his century on a sweep from the leading edge of the road to a village at the end of the cleared land beyond, eyed the forest with suspicion, and marched his men in full battle gear.

"Did you ever have the feeling that something had its eye on you?" he asked Paulinus that evening. "The whole way back I had the feeling that someone out there was thinking about jumping us."

"I wouldn't be surprised," Paulinus said. "They generally wait for a good chance. If you don't give 'em one, they may back off. But they're always around—and my bet is there's a war brewing."

Correus laid down the scabbard strap he had been mending and dragged two pottery cups from a chest by his camp bed. "There was a German envoy in camp today, a fierce-looking old boy with one eye and enough scars for a gladiator. Not the sort you send when you want to be diplomatic." He filled the cups from a hoarded crock of native beer and passed one to Paulinus.

"I know," Paulinus said. "I asked the legate about him and he bellowed at me to mind my own business and threatened to revoke my pass, so I gave up." Two days after his arrival in camp, Paulinus had become bored with the baggage train and had presented himself to the legate. There had then ensued a verbal battle which Paulinus had won by sheer stubbornness and by mentioning several influential connections in Rome. He took a drink of beer and made a face of distaste at Correus.

"I like beer," Correus said. "Put it down to my low birth."

"I put it down to its being better than the army's wine," Paulinus said. In the past weeks they had become friends, and Correus had found in him one of the few men with whom he could discuss his slave origins without feeling twitchy and defensive.

Paulinus had returned the compliment by letting Correus read the journal from which his history would be written. Paulinus kept two journals. The one for publication was a bit more honest than a legate would have cared for, but presentable enough. The second, private, one was a highly inflammatory document in which its author cast a ruthlessly honest eye on everything that came to his notice. This one was prudently kept in a locked chest under the constant guardianship of Tullius. Correus had also developed a fondness for Paulinus's hulking servant. Tullius had the loyalty of a watchdog and the fighting technique of a gorilla, and Correus had ceased to wonder that Paulinus was willing to travel in dangerous lands with no other escort.

"Actually, he's a bit of an embarrassment at times," Paulinus said. "He goes too far. I mean, just because an innkeeper's trying to cheat us doesn't necessarily mean I want him turned inside out and tied in sailor's knots."

Tullius had entered his service in a dingy wineshop in Judaea on the day he parted company with the Fifth Legion there. Clutching their discharges, the hard-earned testament to twenty-five years on the march, Tullius and four cronies had repaired to a favorite dive in Emmaus to celebrate. The Bird in the Tree was not renowned for the quality of its clientele, and as happened often enough someone started a brawl, this time with a deadly difference: the wineshop keeper got stabbed. Everyone got away but Tullius. The shopkeeper, who died, was a cousin of the local magistrate, and in those days Judaea was wavering on the edge of rebellion. The officer of the watch was fully prepared to sacrifice Tullius in the cause of maintaining peace. It was then that Paulinus, who had prudently retired to a corner at the start of the excitement, had come forward and testified that Tullius had never come within ten paces of the shopkeeper. Tullius's gratitude proved embarrassing. He figured he owed Paulinus his life and Paulinus found it impossible to get rid of him. Finally, in desperation, he took Tullius back to his lodging, to reason with him when he had sobered him up. Emmaus was a chancy place to go strolling after dark. They were attacked by a pair of back-alley thugs in search of an easy mark. Tullius, even falling-down drunk, had picked them up and smashed their heads against a wall. Then he had hiccuped and told his newfound benefactor that he needed a guardian.

Thereafter Tullius had accompanied Paulinus on all his travels, and Paulinus had long since given up trying to make him go away. Tullius still had a grant of land coming to him for his army service, if he ever wanted to take it up, but the truth was that he needed someone to look to, and he had eagerly transferred his allegiance from the army to Paulinus.

Now he poked his head through the flap of Correus's tent to inform his master that his supper was ready, and there was enough for the centurion too, if he fancied joining them. "Better'n you'll get in the officers' mess," Tullius said proudly, wiping his hands on a disreputable apron. "A nice little chicken and some greens."

Paulinus chuckled. "Don't ask him where he got the chicken," he said.

VI

Red Wolf, Black Wolf

THE NEXT MORNING THE SKY WAS LEADEN AND THE WIND had teeth in it. Correus had never spent a winter this far north, but he had the feeling that they were soon in for bad weather. His cohort commander confirmed it.

"We're going to have to pull into winter quarters pretty soon," Cominius said, "either in Argentoratum or out here. I'm guessing here. We're close to connecting up with Vindonissa's and Moguntiacum's words, and we have a pretty good supply line from Argentoratum."

"It looks like it's going to come down any minute," Correus said, watching the black clouds shifting above the trees.

"I expect so," Cominius said resignedly. "The Germans see the Underworld as a chasm of ice, and once you've spent a winter here you'll know why." Just then the wind came up in a vicious blast, driving a cloud of dirt and debris before it and whipping their cloaks about them. "The legate has finally pushed Nyall's envoys around to a council meeting, so there's a chance we may be able to loll about in Argentoratum this winter without any fighting, but I wouldn't bet on it." He adjusted his cloak. "Centurion Julianus, I'm told you speak passable German."

"Very colloquial German, sir," Correus said. "Enough to deal with the locals."

"Good. I want you at that meeting. The legate has enough interpreters to start a school, but they're nearly all Germans themselves and we never have figured out which ones we can trust. If any," he added in a disgusted voice. "Mostly they interrupt to argue with each other, and half the time they tone down anything that they think we wouldn't like. I don't want you to interpret, just listen, especially when Nyall's talking, and report to me any discrepancies between what he and the interpreters say."

When he heard about Correus's new task, Paulinus was openly envious and spent days concocting schemes to get himself admitted to the conference as well.

"I speak German, too!" he said indignantly.

"Which is precisely why the legate doesn't want you there," Correus said. "So if you've got any notion of hanging around disguised as a tree, with leaves in your hair, forget 'em. And don't come wooing me afterward with any stolen chickens, either," he added. "I've got strict instructions not to give you the time of day."

Paulinus retired thwarted, and Correus laughed and went in search of Flavius, who also spoke some German and had been ordered by his own commander to attend the council. Unable to get information from Correus, the next person Paulinus would try to pump was Flavius. Correus liked Paulinus tremendously, but he didn't trust him when he was after information.

Correus had seen less than usual of his brother since they had joined their legion. After the usual round of Castor-and-Pollux jokes (they looked so much alike it was inevitable), the other officers had ceased to comment on their relationship, and each found himself more involved with his own cohort and century, learning to command the men under him. That was something which in truth could only be learned by doing. All the theory their training had offered did not equal the actual day-to-day responsibility of commanding eighty legionaries. The brothers grappled—hesitantly at first, then more confidently—with homesick recruits and barracks lawyers, malingerers, and jilted lovers who laid their woes on their centurion's desk. Occasionally they spent their off-duty time together, more, Correus thought, from a feeling that they ought to than anything else.

Correus had put up with a certain amount of patrician disdain from the other officers, but Flavius, to give him credit, had added no more fuel to it than he could help. Some officers simply kept their distance from him, regarding his inclusion in the Centuriate as unfortunate but beneath their notice. Correus ignored them in return. He

had learned early in life to keep his own distance, and
in truth Paulinus was the first real friend he had ever
made. The unspoken disapproval of his brother officers
was nothing new to him, and he smothered the dull ache
of loneliness by concentrating on leading his men. At
least he had them, which was more than he had ever had
before.

As for the cohort commander, Messala Cominius was
shrewd enough not to care if his officers were sons of
painted Picts as long as they were capable, and young
Correus Julianus was proving to be one of the best. Correus was a born commander who also cared for his men,
which was more than Cominius could say of his well-
born brother. Correus's men responded by showing a
loyalty and discipline that was rapidly turning the sixth
into the best century in the cohort. Cominius had every
intention of promoting Correus within his own cohort as
soon as he decently could, before he lost him to another
one. His fourth centurion had been hopeless from the
day he was posted, but he was due for promotion for
sheer length of service. Cominius had ruthlessly recommended the man be transferred to the Sixth Cohort,
which needed a third centurion and whose commander
he didn't much care for. That would leave an opening,
and Cominius could shift Correus to the fourth century
and let him straighten it out before it got to be real trouble. Sixth to fourth century was a bit of a jump for a
new centurion, but if Julianus came off well at the legate's treaty council, that would help justify the promotion. Cominius drew a little eagle in the dirt with his vine
staff while he thought. He fully intended to have his own
legion someday, and the performance of his cohort would
decide the next promotion on his path to it. He was quite
prepared to use any halfway honorable means that came
to his hand to ensure that performance.

On the day of the council, it snowed—a light flutter
of white that drifted artistically from the iron-colored
sky and mostly melted as it hit the ground, turning the
dirt streets of the camp to mud. The sentries and the
honor guard posted half a mile out along the log road
regarded the weather gloomily. Boots and trousers pat-

terned after the native garb were their usual cold-climate
uniform. But now they wore parade dress, and its only
concession to the northern climate was a pair of short
cavalry trousers under the tunic; it left a lot of shin ex-
posed.

"Jupiter Thunderer! Will you look at it?" a legionary
muttered, stamping his feet. His breath hung in a cloud
in the cold air.

"Wouldn't you know it?" his companion said. "If that
heathen king of the Germans doesn't show soon, we'll
freeze to the road like milestones and they can chip us
out in the spring."

"Heads up!"

A trumpet sang out from the guard tower ahead and
the soldiers could feel the faint shiver of hoofbeats in the
roadbed. The trumpets sounded again as a cavalcade of
horsemen swung around a curve and the hoofbeats clattered on the wooden planks. The Germans rode at full
gallop, two abreast, and the legionaries stiffened instinc-
tively.

The centurion of the honor guard flung up his hand as
they approached, wondering what he would do if they
didn't stop, but the horsemen obediently slowed to a
walk, allowing the honor guard to fall in ahead and behind them. The legate had specified no more than twenty
in Nyall's escort, and the centurion, eying them with respect, found himself wishing that he had seen fit to cut
the number down still further.

They were tall, heavy-boned men with grim, set
mouths half hidden by mustache and beard; and their
flaxen hair was as long as a woman's, pulled up and
knotted at the side of the head with bright bronze pins.
Their cloaks and trousers were a jumble of color beside
the orderly bronze and scarlet of the legion.

The one-eyed envoy of earlier meetings rode at the
center of the horsemen, and beside him on a roan sat a
flame-haired warrior with the gold arm rings and collar
of a chieftain. This was Nyall Sigmundson, chief of the
Semnones and effective overlord of the Agri Decumates.

Nyall's red hair was braided into a long plait and
knotted like the others. Though he wore a drooping mustache, his square jaw was beardless. He wore a wolfskin

GERMANS AND VILLAGE

cloak, green woolen trousers the color of the forest, and short boots of supple dyed leather. Like some of his hardy followers, he was bare-chested despite the chill, his pale skin crossed with healed scars.

And he was young—so young that Correus stared in surprise as the German strode into the command tent with two of his fair-haired warriors behind him. Nyall was no more than twenty. Correus felt a growing respect for any man who could hold the quarrelsome tribes of Germany under his hand at that age.

Polite introductions were made between Nyall and the legate and the eagle-crested commanders of the other two legions who were present to lend weight to Rome's bargaining power. The cohort commanders and the tribunes of the legion stood at attention behind them, with Correus, Flavius, and such other officers as had been included in the council. At the end of the table were the legate's interpreters, German tribesmen from the Roman province who twitched uncomfortably in their seats while Nyall studied them and found them insignificant. He sat down and returned his attention to the legate.

"Look you, Commander of the Eagles," he said, his voice steady and with some bite in it, "I have come here because I am weary of talking to this messenger and to that one, none of whom can speak of what Rome will do but only badger me with talk of what *I* should do. Therefore if you have something to say to me about why you build your wooden roads in the Free Lands, say it now."

Calpurnius Rufinus gestured to his interpreters and listened thoughtfully as one of them translated. The tribesman didn't change the meaning of the speech, but Nyall in translation was much more polite than Nyall in his own tongue.

The legate folded his hands across his gilded breastplate and toyed with the purple silk of his sash of office. "Very well," he said. "Into those roads Rome builds the peace of her frontier. It is as simple as that."

"Your frontier lies back along the river," Nyall said, "at the fort of the Eagles there."

"That was Rome's first decision," the legate said flatly, "but it changed somewhat when that fort was burned."

Nyall's gray eyes narrowed. "All this I have heard

before, and seen the *peace* that travels your roads. It is your *peace* that burned your fort, Commander of the Eagles."

"I fail to understand your meaning," said the legate. His wry expression said that he understood quite clearly.

Nyall stood up and put his hands on the council table, leaning forward with a swift movement that made the row of centurions rest their hands lightly on their sword hilts. "Then I will make it plain: you come with your Eagles and make a peace of thrall collars and burned huts. You dishonor the groves of the Mother and build forts with her trees. And when she grows angry and calls her children to rise up and fight you, I don't think you are really very surprised at all."

"I would be very surprised," the legate said, "if the Mother-of-All, whom we also worship in our fashion, had anything to do with a provincial rebellion, Nyall of the Semnones. I doubt that the Goddess has much to do with your actions. And in any case, the Semnones don't hunt in the Agri Decumates. Why have *you* come to meddle in Rome's business?"

Nyall sat back down in his chair, spreading his wolf-skin cloak out beneath him, and rested his arms on the low chair back. He stretched his legs out before him, tipped his head back, and regarded the legate from beneath half-closed lids. "I have come here because I don't like having Roman soldiers in my back garden," he said sweetly. "You might decide to make a *peace* with the Semnones while you were at it."

"Rome does not make war on tribes which offer no provocation."

"That, no doubt, is how Rome acquired her empire."

"I can tell you this in all honesty," the legate said. "The Emperor wishes no further frontier than the Agri Decumates. I will swear to that if you like."

"Great kings have often changed their minds," Nyall said. "I would prefer to see to it that yours doesn't have the chance to change his. Pull back to your forts along the river, and *I* will guarantee *you* a peace. Try to take the Free Lands and it may be that you have taken too large a bite."

The legate leaned forward on the council table, his

face amused. "You are very young to come and spit in the eye of the Empire."

Nyall also looked amused as his mouth twitched under his red mustache. "I have been a warrior and a chief of my people since I was younger than your beardless babes yonder." He nodded at the purple-uniformed tribunes of the legion, young patricians marked for senatorial careers, putting in their obligatory year in the army.

The head interpreter, who was not overly fond of the tribunes' lordly ways among the villagers, translated this last remark with ruthless exactness, and the tribunes bristled, while there was a ripple of laughter from the cohort commanders.

The legate fixed his officers with a steely eye and they subsided, assuming an expressionless military stare. Nyall watched the interchange with a small smile. So the Commander of the Eagles also had his troubles hunting his dogs in one pack.

"It may be that the legate is forgetting one thing," he said. "We know the Black Forest, the lands you call the Agri Decumates. You do not. Already it begins to snow and your men stamp their feet and curse the weather and wish themselves warm in their fort on the river.

"In two months, the Black Forest will be as cold as the halls of Hell. Your men will begin to freeze and die of the lung disease, for your warriors were not born to this land and they do not know how to survive in it. How long do you think you can hold them here?"

"My men are not warriors, they are soldiers," the legate said with quiet pride. "They serve loyally where they are posted."

"So. You have much faith."

"I do. And that, since you asked, is how Rome made her empire. As to your Black Forest, we have withstood many winters on the Rhenus, and I do not see that this land differs greatly."

"You will when the forest itself begins to fight you," Nyall said. He was still leaning back in his chair, his cloak thrown off his shoulders, apparently impervious to the chill that clung about them even in the command tent. "When the ice cracks under your feet or the snow falls away and the ground opens up beneath you; when the black mold eats away at your stores and the wolves howl up and down your log roads; when the Old Ones of the Forest come out of their caves to hunt you with the flung spear you cannot see. We make our first prayers to the Sun Lord, my kindred and I, but we have great respect for the Dark Mother, and the forest is hers. If you stay here, her people will hunt you down."

The interpreters translated nervously, and one of them made the Sign of Horns behind his back as he did so. But this time the legate smiled outright at Nyall.

"Those are tales to frighten children," he said. "I know perfectly well that someone has been fouling the water and setting man traps on the trails and harassing my patrols; and I rather doubt that it's the Little Folk, whatever you'd like my men to think. Keep it up, Nyall of the Semnones, and we will hunt *you* down with a cold iron pilum point—one that you can see quite clearly."

At that, Nyall leaned forward, his eyes glinting dangerously. "The head of the last chieftain who thought to war with the Semnones ended on a post in the sacred grove. Look you that your head does not come there also."

The legate snapped his fingers at an optio who handed him a piece of parchment with an Imperial Seal. "I have had enough of this," he said, "and I am beginning to be annoyed. These are the terms which the Emperor offers: the tribes of these lands will behave themselves and they will pay the taxes for the upkeep of the patrol roads. For our part, we will establish civil colonies here and guarantee the protection of the native tribes from any invader. Such as yourself," he added drily. "The Semnones will return to their homes and Rome will push her frontier no farther than the Agri Decumates. That is our offer."

"These are not your lands," Nyall said. His voice was soft and cold, like the snowfall.

"Nor are they yours," the legate replied. "We each claim them and it is plain enough that the lands have little choice in the matter. I fail to see the difference between you and us."

Nyall stood up. The legate bared his teeth a little, and they stared at each other, red wolf and black. A cold wind whistled through the tent flap and snapped at the parchment in the legate's hand. Nyall said, "I am not a Roman tyrant to force my will on my people without council. I will tell your terms to the chiefs of my allies. You will have our answer in a seven-day." He turned on his heel and the sentries at the tent flap drew the leather curtains back. Nyall and his companions strode through to the knot of warriors outside who sat waiting, still mounted, under the watchful gaze of the honor guard. Nyall, the one-eyed envoy, and a third, younger man whose blond hair was braided into its warrior's knot in the same fashion as Nyall's, swung into their saddles. Nyall barked an order, and the warriors fell in behind him, swiftly riding down the muddy track of the Via Praetoria, with the honor guard beside them, trotting to keep up.

They kept their silence until the honor guard left them some distance outside the gate on the log road, and then the one-eyed man turned to Nyall with a fierce, sideways grin.

"So. It is as I told you. The commander of the Eagles will not back off."

Nyall laughed. "It never occurred to me that he would, old friend. But I gave my word to Arngunn of the Nicretes that I would hear the Roman's terms. So now I have kept my word."

The snow was coming down more thickly now, fat white flakes that clung to their beards and powdered the horses' manes. Nyall dropped his reins, pulled his cloak around him, and pinned it. "I have shown off enough for one day," he said, laughing. "Now I want a dry shirt and a warm place at Arngunn's hearth. Also my dinner."

He kicked his horse into a gallop, and they dropped into single file behind him as the roan left the log road where it ended near a watchtower and plunged up a narrow track into the trees. The fallen leaves deadened their hoofbeats, and in a moment they were lost in the snow and the black, haunted woods.

In the Principia tent the three generals sat looking at each other grimly.

"If I were you, I'd dig another ring of ditch-and-wall,"

the legate of the Twenty-second Legion said. He stood up and shouted for his optio while Calpurnius Rufinus nodded in comprehension. Nyall might make a show of consulting with the chieftains of the Agri Decumates, but it was more than obvious that he would do as he damn well pleased afterward.

The legate of the Twenty-second made his departure. He had several days' ride before him and the weather was turning foul. Rufinus looked at the third general, whose own troops were pushing their road northward from Vindonissa.

"How quickly can you hook up with our road?"

"If the weather holds a little longer, we may just do it before the snows," Vindonissa's legate said. The Eighth Legion was catching the worst of the Germans' attacks, and the hookup with Vindonissa was vital. The log roads would be passable long after the forest trails were closed. "We'll do our damnedest," he said, and sneezed. "The son of a bitch was right about these winters."

Rufinus nodded gloomily. "I can't remember when it was that I didn't have a cold. What I'd like now is a nice command in Judaea."

"They've settled *their* rebels," the other man said. "Titus and Vespasian got a nice triumph out of it. What do you suppose they'll give us here?"

Rufinus snorted. "The thanks of a grateful nation. And another tribe of barbarians to cope with somewhere else."

"Well, you have met the enemy," Cominius said. "What did you think?" He swept a tangle of sword belt and spare harness straps off a chair near the camp desk and gestured to Correus to sit.

"I think you were right, sir," Correus said. "The interpreters are scared of us, and they're scared of Nyall. They were toning everything down out of sheer nerves. Also, I suspect they don't want a war because if Nyall wins he might remember them afterward."

"Mmm. That doesn't make them overly reliable in emergencies. They could decide to change sides just to get in his good graces. What did Nyall actually say?"

"Pretty much as translated. Just ruder."

"I'll bet." Cominius chuckled and then his face turned thoughtful. "Just how good *is* your German, Centurion Julianus? Could you have interpreted that meeting?"

"Yes, sir."

"And your brother?"

"His German is not nearly as good as mine, sir. I'd be surprised if he got half of it," Correus said truthfully. There were limits to brotherly loyalty.

Cominius nodded. "In that case, Centurion, I am going to offer your services to our legate, thus calling both you and myself to his favorable attention. A pleasant coincidence."

Correus's mouth twitched as he rose and saluted. "Indeed, sir. Uh, what about Lucius Paulinus? If I know him he'll be lying in wait outside my tent."

"Avoid him like a disease for the next three days," Cominius said. "After that I doubt it will make much difference."

Correus nodded. Paulinus, he knew, sent the work he intended to publish to his senator uncle in Rome, for his critical appraisal. Things were brewing up fast and the legate would have to send his own dispatches soon, but he would be highly irritated if Paulinus's messages to Rome preceded them. He wondered idly why Cominius had said three days, when Nyall had given seven as the term in which he would send his answer, but it was not his place to ask. And it went from his mind quickly enough when Cominius handed him command of the fourth century.

In only two days he had the answer to his unvoiced question, in the form of a newly erected shrine of smooth, sanded timber. Within its circle stood the cohort standards, and at their center the golden Eagle of the legion. It was a declaration of war. The legate had known what Nyall's answer was going to be.

Flavius had seen it too, and he came to Correus's tent that evening when he had finished posting sentries, a task at which the Ninth Cohort was currently taking its turn. Flavius had also heard of his brother's promotion.

"It seems the legate may not need an interpreter after all, but you'll have your new century to console you," he said. "Congratulations!" Flavius managed a smile as he sat down on the bed. "You move up in the world."

Correus looked up from the greave he was polishing. "Thank you. Messala Cominius wasn't overly flattering about the fourth century, so it may be a dubious blessing." He wondered if Flavius had come purely to snipe at him about that, and decided that he hadn't. There was a thin-drawn look to Flavius's face. It occurred to Correus that although neither of them had as yet encountered a single German except across the council table, it was now inevitable that they soon would. Small wonder that everyone's nerves were rubbed raw just now.

"I'll still be able to tell Nyall to go take a dip in the Styx when he comes back," he said lightly. "I've rather a fancy for that."

"It'll be One-Eye more likely," Flavius said. "Nyall wouldn't trust his hide within a mile of us with the answer he's going to give."

"You may be right," Correus said. "What a pity. I would have liked to meet him again," he added seriously.

"What the hell for?"

"He impresses me." Correus put down the greave and picked up the other one.

"What?"

"He impresses me."

"The snow's got in your brain," Flavius said. "He's a dirty half-naked barbarian who thinks he can order Rome around, and you liked him?"

"Not exactly *liked*. I thought he was intelligent, devious, and about as trustworthy as a hungry wolf."

"I fail to see the distinction."

Correus sighed. "No. You wouldn't." He passed Flavius the polished greave. "Here, take this and hand me my lorica—it's right beside you." Flavius did so, looking irritable, and Correus resumed his work. He was *not*, if he could help it, going to pick a quarrel with Flavius tonight.

Paulinus nearly did it for him, arriving a few minutes later to offer loud congratulations on Correus's promotion until Correus changed the subject in exasperation.

"If you want to chase old Broken Hoof anymore this winter, we'd better do it soon," he said to Paulinus. They had taken to spending his off-duty hours hunting in the forests west of the camp, and there was a wild boar—old Broken Hoof—they had tracked and lost twice. Paulinus regarded the failure as a personal insult. "It'll be cold enough to freeze a gorgon in a couple of weeks." Correus looked down at the gray woolen trousers and fur-lined boots that they all wore beneath their tunics. "Jupiter, but I hate these things. I have the feeling that they look a lot better on Nyall than they do on us."

"Where's your national pride?" Paulinus said.

"With my sandals. I'll thaw it out in the spring."

"Be glad we've got this gear," Flavius said. "I damn near froze at that council meeting in parade kit. My shins were turning blue. And then my commander gets a flea in his ear because I couldn't tell him verbatim what the German was saying," he added angrily. "I had warned him I probably couldn't, but no, he has to make a fool of me, trying to one-up Cominius, who was showing him up with my own damn—" He bit the words back in his mouth and stared at the tent wall. Then he turned back again and said carefully, "Why don't we go after this famous boar of yours, the three of us, the next time we both have leave?"

You could almost see him gritting his teeth and being nice, Correus thought dismally. He wished Flavius wouldn't bother. "I thought you hunted with Silvanus?"

"Silvanus, like half the people in this damn, sopping fort, has a cold. The surgeon confined him to quarters with a poultice around his neck that smells like a Tiber dock."

"Actually, I'd thought of passing up my leave day," Correus said. "I'm a little dubious about leaving my century to their own devices this soon."

"But you brought the idea up yourself!"

Correus had grabbed at the first topic that came to hand, to shut Paulinus up, but he couldn't say that. He began to feel cornered.

"Of course, if you'd rather not—" Flavius's voice was flat.

"No, no—"

"For the gods' sake, your precious century isn't going to mutiny if you stop watching it for one day!" Flavius snapped.

Correus knew that leaving them for a day without his eye on them *would* compound the neglect of which their former centurion had been guilty. Still, making his peace with Flavius was more important. He could put the fear of the gods in the fourth century later on.

"Judging by their past performance, they're probably capable of just about anything short of mutiny," he said lightly, "but I doubt they can get organized in one day. All right, then, let's do it." He hung his lorica on its stand and tossed the polishing rag into his cleaning kit.

"Good." Flavius smiled. "Antaeus will be glad you changed your mind. He needs some of the oats run out of him."

Their horses had finally arrived, in the charge of Bericus, Flavius's body servant, and they had gratefully returned their borrowed nags to a decurion of cavalry who had given a hoot of mirth and informed them that those two were kept by the legion's horsemaster for the express purpose of annoying officers.

"I'm going to strangle that bastard when we get back to Argentoratum," Flavius said.

Correus nodded, but was privately planning a subtle and more elaborate revenge on the horsemaster. He hadn't quite worked out all the details yet.

For the next few days Correus had scant attention to spare either for putting the horsemaster in his place or for his dubious relationship with Flavius. Messala Cominius had somewhat understated all the things that were wrong with the fourth century. They were under-trained and underdisciplined, and showed a marked disinclination for physical labor. They also had more budding barracks lawyers than Correus was willing to put up with.

Mentally cursing his predecessor (and the man had been rewarded with a *promotion* for creating this rabble!), he set about shaking them into shape. He spent a frustrating day making heavy use of the vine staff, a necessity that set his teeth on edge, and ended by sending four of the worst offenders to the guardhouse to meditate on their sins. The next morning he paraded them in a snowstorm and made them stand there shivering while he gave them a tongue-lashing that would have done credit to Centurion Mucius. Then he drilled them mercilessly for the rest of the day, informing them curtly that he had no intention of facing the Germans with a century that was as likely as not to stick a pilum in his back out of sheer ineptness.

By the third day they had begun to have second thoughts about the new centurion, and by the fourth they were beginning to come into line. So far it was all on the surface, he knew, but the rest would come with time, and he thought he could now let them out of his sight for a day without inviting disaster.

He heaved a sigh of relief as they trooped off the drill field for an icy splash in the austere bathhouse that the camp afforded, and pulled his helmet off wearily. The fourth century gave him a headache.

Messala Cominius, watching him from the far end of the field, gave a little chuckle of satisfaction and resumed his progress to the east rampart. He had sentries of his own century, the first, on duty on the walls, and they kept a sharper eye out when they knew that *his* eye was on *them*. He pulled the scarlet folds of his cloak closer around him and tipped his helmet forward. It was going to snow again soon, he thought, looking at the leaden sky. The recent snowfalls were nothing compared to what a winter on the Rhenus frontier was like when it really got going. The light was beginning to fade, and from the hills across the cleared land came the long-drawn-out howl of a wolf on the hunt.

Paulinus heard it too and felt the hair on the back of his neck rise. It was the sound of winter hunger to come, he thought. The brindle hound beside him raised his head and gave a low growl. The dog had been acquired by Tullius from a native headman in exchange for two of the army's blankets, which hadn't been missed yet. Paulinus put his hand on the animal's head to quiet him and lit the oil lamp on the folding table that served as his desk, before picking up his pen again. His private journal, a bound book of blank pages, was opened before him; and, thinking perhaps of the wolf, he began a new paragraph.

*   *   *

A hungry land, the Rhenus. Metal-hungry, cattle-hungry, hungry for something to give a shape to their lives. Warriors who die well in battle are taken to Valhalla—Paradise—by Wuotan's daughters for an eternal life of free-flowing beer and other pleasures. Small wonder they fight each other for amusement. Now they make ready to fight us. We come with the orderly precision of a well-oiled machine and roll over their world, exchanging this barbaric way of life for the benefits of civilization. Do they *wish* to be civilized? I do, but I'm not a German. They won't be either after a few decades under our rule. If we can hold them. The Rhenus has been trouble from the start.

Do we need the Agri Decumates? Yes, if we are to hold the Rhenus. Do we need the Rhenus? Augustus thought so. Claudius thought so. Now Vespasian thinks so. Myself, I am not so sure. Nor am I an emperor.

Young Julianus has no such doubts, but he is a soldier, and the army is the heart and soul of his life. Also I suspect that, like the Germans, he rather likes to fight. Maybe that's the Gaul in him—they were kin to the Germans before we made them like us. Although I remember hearing the same said of his Roman father. I am speaking of Julianus Minor, Correus Appius Julianus, not his half-brother Flavius Appius—who doesn't love the army, doesn't love his brother, and feels guilty about both. Flavius should be in Rome, taking in the games and living off his income. Instead he is here, grimly preparing to fight the Germans because he wasn't given a choice. He is trying desperately to become a good soldier, and he probably will, but it seems hard on them both that he has to try.

As for Nyall of the Semnones, I have never talked to Nyall, but I have talked to those who have and mostly they have come away from the experience gibbering. Physically he is tall with a head of hair that's as red as a fox—that's the Gaul in him. The Germans are flaxen-haired mostly. He's extremely young, and I suspect that Calpurnius Rufinus is banking on that youth rather too much. If the gods are with

Rufinus, the shade of General Varus should be fluttering around his head with a timely warning about now. Varus lost three Eagles to the Germans, and for years the deified Augustus frothed at the mouth and chewed the cushions every time he thought about it— and Augustus was a man of some restraint.

There is war coming. It's in the air, like the feeling you get before an earthquake. A sensation of something brooding in the forest that won't go away. We lost a centurion and two men out of a patrol today— another ambush, just to unsettle us, I think. Nyall sent in his reply just afterward—a masterly stroke of reverse diplomacy—and now everyone's nerves are stretched tighter than a catapult. Mine included. And, I suppose, those of the tribes in these parts. We haven't stopped to ask them if they would like a war, and I don't expect Nyall has, either. They'll get what we and the Semnones give them. As for Nyall, he won't be able to launch a full-scale attack until the spring, but he'll make a wonderful nuisance of himself all winter. If my boar has decided to forage eastward of our current camp, I shall leave him to his own devices.

Calpurnius Rufinus, I feel sure, wishes that I would do the same for him. If he ever got his hands on this journal, he would pack me out of here in a mule cart and no number of imperial passes or senatorial uncles would save me. My *History* will content me for now, but I would like to see the unexpurgated version published eventually, for the enlightenment of future governments.

He thought a moment and then added with a smile:

Pompous ass. Still, perhaps I shall will it to my first great-grandchild when everyone who might take exception will be too dead to care.

The brindle hound growled and Paulinus laid down his pen and cocked his head, listening. The wolf howled again. The cavalry horses were having hysterics. Suddenly Paulinus felt the need for lighter company than his own thoughts. He laid the journal back in its chest and locked it as the wolf's mate answered across the valley and the quavering howl dipped and rose.

He would find Correus and drink some appalling beer with him. Perhaps that would chase away the uncomfortable feeling that the hungriest of the wolves were those hunting on two legs.

VII

The Boar

"I used to have a plow,
    Two oxen and a cow—"

The singer sounded depressed about it.

"And it didn't seem too grand to leave behind
    When I signed on with the legions
    For a tour of other regions—
    But now I rather think I've changed my mind!"

The song issued from the latrine, accompanied by the slap and splash of a mop, as the hunting party trotted by in the dawn light. Behind them the voice of a member of the "on report" list continued its lament:

"I've done a tour of Libya,
    Of Britain and Iberia,
    And I know 'em best by barracks and by roads,
    And the aqueducts that fill 'em,
    'Cause I'm the chump that built 'em
    With the thousand tons of granite that we towed!

"From the east to Rhenus Gate
    We've been occupied of late
    With catapults and countin' of our dead;

And when the fightin's done,
And a fellow wants some fun,
There's another flamin' road to build instead!"

The voice rose in a wail of indignation, and Tullius
smiled reminiscently as the singer's mates joined in the
last chorus with enthusiastic harmony.

"That's the truth of it all right," he said. "I saw the
Sphinx by moonlight once. Some silly ass had written
'Glaucus cheats at dice' across the foot, and the centurion
turfed us out of bed at midnight to clean it. But I've built
more road in my day than I've looked at monuments,
that's for sure. *And* mopped out more latrines. Makes
you think, like, doesn't it, sir?"

Flavius, who had never cleaned a latrine in his life,
and certainly couldn't imagine doing so, ignored this, but
Correus laughed.

"Join the army and see the world by log road," he
said. "Freeze your ass off," he added as they rode on,
head down into an icy wind.

It had snowed again in the night, and the road was
thickly covered, only the line of ditches on either side
marking its course. The cleared land was flat and des-
olate and the forested mountains inky black around it.
They were bundled in woolen cloaks and trousers, with
fleece-lined leggings, and they carried heavy hunting
spears. The brindle hound trotted ahead, sniffing at the
forest edge. They turned off where a game trail ran uphill into the wood, and after a moment the hound began
to snuffle excitedly at the base of a clump of wild berry
canes. The ground around them was trampled, and Tullius dismounted to look.

"That's pig all right, sir. He's been rooting around
here."

"Do you think it's the same one?" Paulinus asked.

"It looks like him. He's got that funny bit to his right
front hoof, like it had been damaged. I remember that."

The others, including Flavius's servant, Bericus, gathered around him to look while the brindle hound sat happily fanning his tail in the snow and looking pleased with
himself.

It was easy enough to track in the new snow, but after

a while the trail dived into a thicket of underbrush and fallen trees. The hound circled the thicket, disappeared into it, and in a moment emerged yelping triumphantly on the far side.

They followed him, the horses dancing skittishly in the cold air. The wind had died down and Correus took a deep breath, looking about with satisfaction. It was good to have Antaeus's broad golden back between his legs again; Flavius was laughing and happy, and this was the freshest trail their quarry had left for them yet. It had not been such a bad idea after all, to go hunting with his brother.

A squirrel, perched on a low branch with a nut in his mouth, retreated into a hole in a tree trunk and then popped his head out again to curse them indignantly. The forest grew thicker and shafts of cold sunlight splintered through the branches overhead. In spring, with the trees in full leaf, there would be no sun at all in the heavier stands of forest. The boar's track was crossed again and again with the marks of other forest wayfarers —the small sharp hooves of deer, and the marks of hare and mice. Once they came on the tracks of a pair of wolves, overlying the deer trail, and the hound growled and bristled at the scent.

Tullius called him away sharply, and then, at the hillcrest, they came out of the forest into a stretch of open moor, studded here and there with rocky outcroppings and a few stands of windblown trees. Here the snow had melted into the sodden ground and the boar had stopped to wallow in the mud of a small stream that had its mouth in a spring beneath the rocks. They paused to let the horses drink of the cold, swift-running stream, while the hound cast up and down the far bank for the scent.

From here the water ran westward, winding down among the moors and forest to the Rhenus Valley, where it joined the river in its northward course to the great delta on the edge of the German Ocean. Just a little to the east, every stream became instead a tributary of the Danuvius, running the length of the Roman frontier to empty into the Pontus Euxinus far to the east.

Correus mentioned this to Paulinus and the historian nodded. "I know," he said. "It's like we're standing at the crest of the world." A look of dreamy speculation came over his plain face, and he looked eastward over his shoulder where a still higher hill rose up from the cloud bank. "They say there's a spot where you can stand and actually see the Danuvius rise up from a hole in the ground. I should like to see that."

"Certainly," Flavius said. "We'll just apply to Nyall to send you over as a scientific expedition. Then you can put a cork in the hole and cut off his water supply." He pulled his horse's head up from the stream. "No, you, that is enough."

Paulinus, unruffled, appeared to be considering a search for the source of the Danuvius until, in exasperation, Correus smacked Paulinus's horse on the rump and sent it trotting across the streambed. On the far side, the brindle hound (Tullius said that his name meant Big Gray Dog in German, but he couldn't pronounce it so he simply called him Dog) had picked up the trail in the brown winter grass and was casting back and forth along it, whining in excitement. At a word from Tullius, he set off at a lope, and they put their horses to the gallop to follow.

It was exhilarating, galloping across the spine of the world with the cold wind singing and the distant peaks rising from the cloud bank that obscured their foot.

Far below, Correus could just see a single shining loop of the Rhenus where it wound through the wide flat valley above Argentoratum. The river mist had burned off and the patrol galleys of the Rhenus Fleet showed as scarlet dots on the silvered water; two of them, like a pair of hunting dogs, coursed warily upriver under oar and sail. Beyond the river were terraced vineyard slopes pruned back for the winter and showing black against the snow.

Just ahead, Dog bounded through the frost-killed grass; Correus pulled his horse up sharply as the ground fell away into a rocky slope at the edge of the moor. There was a trodden game trail going down the slope, and they followed Dog along it until the moor ran again into the edge of the upland forest. By the growing excitement of Dog they knew the trail was getting hotter now, and they gripped the heavy boar spears while Dog took care not to

lope too far ahead of the horsemen. The fanged and
tusked wild boar of the Black Forest was a different animal entirely from the tame pigs of the farmyard.

"This time we've got him!" Paulinus shouted. For all his
slightness, Paulinus rode like a centaur, and he guided
his mount easily over the fallen leaves of the forest track,
his spear balanced in his right hand. Tullius was a few
paces behind him, close enough for his nervous mount to
fleck the rump of Paulinus's horse with foam. Correus and
Flavius rode two abreast behind Tullius, with Bericus in
the rear, his young face alight with excitement. Bericus
had been sold out of a City household to pay the estate
taxes, and he was beginning to think that he had gotten
the best of the bargain. Flavius was a pleasant master, if
strict, and certainly the frontier was proving a far more
interesting environment than the orderly household he
had been born to.

The trail took a sharp bend, dived beneath an over-
hanging pine bough, and came up against a steep rise of
rock with moss and small plants clinging precariously to
its face. A thatch of brown grass and a few scrawny pines
crowned the top. At the base of the outcrop a thick tangle
of wild blackberry screened a fissure opening into the
rock itself. There was a strong, rank smell of pig in the
air.

Dog sat panting in front of the blackberry, showing his
teeth in a crocodile grin while he waited for them to
catch up. "All right," he seemed to say. "I found him, you
get him out." Dog was wise in the ways of the hunting
trail and not the fool to worm his way into that fissure
alone.

"Damn!" Flavius said. "He could lie up there all day.
We've got to pry him loose. Bericus, see if you can get up
on the top of that outcrop from the far side and gallop
around a bit. It'll echo like Hades in that cave, and it may
stir him up."

"He'll be in a fiend's temper," Paulinus said.

"I suppose you think you've put him in a pleasant
mood by chasing him all this way," Correus pointed out.
"He'll get more irritated yet when you stick a spear in
him."

"Or he may just go roaring on past without stopping to

fight," Paulinus said. "We've got to be ready for him. Correus, you and Flavius spread out on the right there, and Tullius and I will take the left. Dog can put a tooth in whatever's showing."

They spread into a semicircle outside the rock cave, waiting for any sound from within. There was a shout from above and they looked up to see Bericus on the summit, waving his arms. He dug his heels into his pony's flank and raced him to the far end and back, the iron shoes ringing on the flat rock table that covered most of the summit.

Something stirred inside the rock, and Flavius waved his arm at Bericus to do it again. Dog crouched low in the snow, scrabbling a little with his claws for traction. The snow on the clearing before the rock face was not deep, but the winter sun had melted the top layer so that it was slick and precarious.

The iron shoes rang out on the rock again, and suddenly there was a loud snorting growl and a thrashing in the blackberry canes and the boar erupted into the clearing. He was a huge beast, thick and humpbacked with vicious curving tusks. He halted for only a moment in the circle of horsemen, eyes glowing red and dangerous. Flavius licked his lips and shifted his grip on his spear, and then the boar charged straight at him.

Flavius hesitated only an instant, but it was too long. Nestor caught his nervousness and shied, and as he did so, his right rear hoof came down on a jagged rock half buried in the snow. The horse tried to balance himself, but the ground was icy and unstable and he went down on his flank with a terrified neighing, Flavius half in and half out of the saddle.

There was a horrified cry from Bericus. He pulled his horse's head around and sent him crashing down the steep slope on the far side of the rock face.

Nestor's forelegs were entangled in the reins and Flavius lay with one leg trapped beneath the horse, desperately trying to shorten his grip on the spear shaft as the boar came in. His face was ashen with fright.

Dog sprang, sinking his teeth in the thick muscles of the boar's shoulder, but the boar shook him off like a rat. Paulinus and Tullius kicked their horses forward and

Correus came around the other side to drive the boar off, but their quarry, furious and in pain, saw only that one of its tormentors was down. Flavius's spear slid along the boar's flank, opening up a deep gash, and then he was pinned beneath its weight, the razor-sharp teeth an inch from his face.

Correus flung himself from his horse and stumbled in the snow and rocks to dig his spear into the boar's haunch. There was a howl of rage and the boar turned to face him. Correus yanked the weapon free, backed carefully a few paces, and braced himself, the spear shaft suddenly slippery where the blood had run down it. The boar stood panting and looked from Correus to Flavius, its red eyes stupid with rage. Flavius was bleeding, leaving a bright red pool in the snow. Correus shook his spear at the boar to distract him while Tullius moved around from the other side, and Paulinus, also dismounted now, tried frantically to untangle the reins from the bay's legs before he rolled on his rider in his terror.

Tullius circled around carefully, almost afraid to move for fear of driving the boar on Flavius and Paulinus, or prodding him into a charge at Correus.

To Correus, standing in the snow with nothing but a spear between him and the deadly tusks, it seemed as if everything froze and came sharply into focus. And then the scene exploded. The boar, making up its mind, came at him. He shortened his spear and thrust hard, staggering back as it went in and caught somewhere on a bone and the boar's great weight crashed against him. He could see its red, dripping tusks and caught a choking lungful of its foul breath as he rolled desperately out from under it. The boar stumbled and righted itself. Correus grabbed at his spear, still buried in the boar's forequarters, and drew it back while Dog came limping in again to sink his own dripping fangs in the boar's throat and Tullius drove a spear downward into the humped back. The boar came at Correus, who thrust again, and this time the angle was right and the spear sank almost to his hand into the heart. The boar squealed, and dropped. It thrashed in the snow, then was still.

Correus fell heavily to his knees. His heart was pounding, his mouth dry. He felt light-headed. He rubbed a

handful of snow across his face, and the world came into
focus again. He saw that the horse was on its feet, but the
still form near it in the snow had not moved. Correus
pulled himself up.

Bericus was kneeling beside Flavius, sobbing in fear
and grief while Paulinus methodically tore strips from the
edge of his cloak.

"I should never have gone away from him," Bericus
said, choking.

"Nonsense," Paulinus said. "He ordered you up there
himself. Now help me to lift him while I see how deep
that gash is."

Flavius had a bleeding cut on his cheek and a great,
deep tear in his chest where the boar's tusk had gone in.
He lay perfectly still, as pale as the snow, but Correus saw
almost with relief that he was still bleeding freely. That
meant he was alive.

"I think he hit his head," Paulinus said, his voice
shaking. "And we've got to stop that bleeding." He cut
the tunic away with his knife, then Bericus and Correus
lifted Flavius by the shoulders while Paulinus pressed a
pad of cloth over the wound and wrapped a long strip
tightly around it. Behind them, Dog sat licking a gash in
his own hide while Tullius ran his hands up and down the
bay's legs.

"He'll do," he said to Paulinus. "The leg's not even
strained, more's the mystery. But can we get the centurion
on him?"

"I don't know," Paulinus said.

Flavius stirred and his eyes opened. "I can ride," he
said thickly.

"No," Correus said. "Put him up on Antaeus and I'll
ride behind him."

Flavius shook his head and set his mouth in a stubborn
line. He started to sit up and then slumped backward
against Correus, his eyes closed again.

"Well, he can't argue with us," Paulinus said practically. "Get him up on the other horse," he told Tullius,
"and hold him until Correus can get a grip on him."

"Will he live?" Bericus whispered.

Paulinus scrubbed his hands in the snow and stood up.

"That is for the gods to decide, lad. But I think yes, if we can get him to a surgeon fast enough."

Tullius lifted Flavius into the saddle and held him while Paulinus quieted the sidling horse to let Correus swing on behind. Correus knotted the reins around the saddle horns and put both arms around his brother. "All right, let him go. I can guide him with my knees."

"What about that?" Tullius looked at the gray bulk of the boar, its blood sinking into a pool in the snow.

"Leave it for the wolves," Paulinus said. His face was chalky beneath the freckles. "I don't think I want it much."

Tullius looked up at the sun, now low among the trees. "There was another track we passed, just at the top of that slope of scrub," he said. "It may go down to the road. We've taken it before, I think, and it would be a sight faster. Do we chance it?"

They looked at Correus. He hesitated. If they took the wrong track . . . But it was a long way back if they went the way they had come. He slipped his hand under Flavius's cloak. The bandage felt sticky; he was still losing blood. "We chance it," he said grimly.

They set off, Tullius and Dog in the lead with Paulinus behind them. Bericus was leading Flavius's bay, but showed such a tendency to hover beside Correus, his stricken eyes on Flavius's blood-smeared face, that Paulinus finally took the reins from him in exasperation when they came to where the track led upward to the moor. A second track ran away down from it, sloping at right angles into the trees.

"If you want to be useful, head down there and see if you can find out where in the name of the Mother we're going," Paulinus ordered.

Bericus nodded and put his heels to his horse, and Paulinus sighed with relief. Correus had enough to contend with, he thought, looking back at his friend's grim, set face.

Except for the crunch of the horses' hooves in the snow, the black woods were as silent as a passage to the Underworld. There was precious little any of them could say, and Correus found himself uncomfortably alone with his thoughts. His head still felt vague and cloudy and he was

guiding Antaeus more by instinct than anything else; all
he knew with any certainty was that he did not want
Flavius to die. He was his brother, and in his fashion he
loved him. Telling Appius that Flavius had died for no
better reason than a day's hunting was something he could
not face.

After a while Bericus's pony came slithering back up
the trail. "It . . . it peters out down there. I'm not sure. I
think we're on the right track, but I'm no woodsman."

Tullius whistled up Dog and they trotted off ahead,
while the others plodded on silently. The trail dipped
sharply, and at the base, where Bericus had turned back,
Dog sniffed about, then set off through a gap in the trees.
The snow was unmarked, but he seemed to know where
he was going. The gap opened up into a clearing where
a rabbit track ran across the ground. Dog paused and
whined uncertainly.

Tullius looked worried. "I wish I knew how to say 'Go
home' in German." Dog had been well trained for the
hunting trail, but he was unused to Latin commands.

Correus brought Antaeus up beside Tullius and
snapped his fingers at the hound. Dog looked dubious.

"Go on, you damned fool," Tullius said.

Apparently reading permission in his voice, Dog approached Correus, and Correus let him sniff his hands and
the saddle leather and the warm horse—the scents of
camp. "Home," he said firmly in German. "Take us
home, fellow." He hoped he had used the right command.
It could have been "hearth" or "hut" or the name of
a village that the dog would understand. The forest dark-
ened suddenly as a scudding bank of clouds ran across
the sun. Flavius stirred and Correus felt him shiver under
the cloak. "Home," he said again, then added, "Romans!"
That might be a word the hound knew.

Dog turned away and began to cast about the clearing,
this time ignoring the rabbit tracks. There was something
eerie about this grove of trees—a ring of great oaks with
an open space at the center and a flat table of rock jutting
up from it. It had a feel to it, Correus thought, like a little
cold wind running down the back, and he saw that there
was a sheaf of wild grasses and a handful of withered
berries laid on the rock, half covered with the snow.

Suddenly he wanted to be gone out of there. This was a sacred grove of the Mother, and he had a feeling that they profaned it merely by their presence. Gripping Flavius tightly with one arm, he reached under him into the pouches slung behind the saddle and drew out a crust of bread. He dropped it on the rock altar with a swift prayer asking forgiveness for trespassing.

Bericus gave him a startled look. The mysteries of the Mother were women's business, and in this present guise she was not even of their world.

"It never hurts, lad," Paulinus said quietly. "This is her wood, and we have brought blood and iron into it, which I think is forbidden." He pulled a dried apple from his own saddlebags and dismounted to place it beside the bread.

Dog barked sharply from across the clearing and they circled wide around the altar to follow him. He padded on through the snow, following whatever trail lay beneath it. He seemed more sure of himself now as he ran downhill, the sun low on the right.

With a yelp, Dog dived through an opening in the trees and there was a slithering sound of fallen branches and loose snow. A moment later he reappeared, shaking the snow from his hide. He yelped again and sat down, panting and pleased with himself, while the riders pushed forward to the edge of the trees.

Below them the bank dropped sharply, with a wide, churned-up path where the hound had slid down it on his haunches. And beyond that was the cleared land, with jagged stumps of trees jutting from the snow and the log road running through it, tracked by the passage of a supply train from Argentoratum.

Tullius put his horse down the slope with a shout of relief, beckoning to Bericus to follow him, while Paulinus with the led horse and Correus with his brother inched their way down behind them.

The horses sank to their hocks as they slid through the steep drifts, but the log road had been well cleared by the supply train. A wooden post pounded into the ground beside it showed it was no more than four miles from the camp.

"All right, lad," Tullius said to Bericus. "Here's where

you can help. Ride like the Furies and tell the surgeon to be ready for us."

Bericus nodded and kicked his horse into a gallop, the trampled snow flying up behind him.

Flavius groaned as Antaeus took the jump over the narrow drainage ditch awkwardly because of his double burden. "Soon," Correus whispered. "We'll make camp soon. Hang on, brother!"

Flavius nodded and said something unintelligible. He leaned back again into Correus's shoulder. They made better time on the log road but still dared not push beyond a fast walk for fear of worsening the injury. Blood had already soaked through the makeshift bandage. By the time they turned through the camp gate, it was almost full dark and Correus could feel the warm blood through the folds of Flavius's cloak.

Bericus was waiting at the gate with an orderly who took a look at the blood-soaked cloak and told Correus to take Flavius straight to the hospital. Correus nodded. He swayed slightly and tightened his arms around Flavius, afraid of losing his grip.

Paulinus looked at him in concern. "Here, are you all right?"

"I feel a bit light and stupid," Correus said. "Fuzzy . . ." His voice trailed off.

Paulinus handed the bay's reins to Bericus and took Antaeus by the bridle. "You just hang on. I'll lead him. Did you know you're bleeding?"

Correus looked down to his left where a little trail of blood showed dark on the snow in the torchlight. "I though it was Flavius," he said, but his left leg ached like fire.

"Well, it's not," Paulinus said sharply. "It's you. Your boot's full of blood."

The hospital lay at the center of the camp, behind and to one side of the Principia. It was built of timber, in contrast to the leather tents that served as offices and barracks in a marching camp. Labienus, the senior surgeon of the legion, a lean, plain-faced man in his thirties, met them at the doorway.

"You can let go now," he said gently, and Correus

loosened his grasp as Labienus and a junior surgeon reached up to lift Flavius down.

Correus slid wearily from Antaeus's back and limped into the hospital after the others. He found a bench against the wall in the main surgery and dropped down on it. The surgery was lamplit and a half-dozen iron braziers glowed warmly around the room. He sat, letting the cold ease out of his body until such time as someone had the leisure to see what was wrong with his leg.

Labienus and a junior surgeon had gotten Flavius up on a surgery table and were expertly cutting away the shreds of his tunic. Labienus inspected the wound as the sticky bandages came away. He set about cleaning it with a basin of warm water that had been heating on a grill over one of the braziers. The wound was still seeping redly. Labienus put a pad of clean bandage over the gash and held it. Flavius groaned and opened his eyes.

"I want ephedron powder and a verdigris dressing," Labienus said to the orderly. "And a half-dose of opium. I'm going to have to stitch this."

Correus roused himself at that. "He hit his head," he said, his own head propped wearily against the wall. "He was out off and on most of the way back."

The surgeon ran his hand through Flavius's hair and found the bruised spot at the back. He pulled Flavius's eyelids up and looked closely. "Damnation. No opium then. I'm afraid you'll just have to grit your teeth, son."

Two oil lamps hung from iron arms that swiveled about a central pole, and Labienus fiddled with them for a moment and then sent the orderly for more light. "I can manage well enough here," he said to the junior surgeon as the orderly set up another lamp stand. "Go and see why the centurion over there is bleeding on my floor."

"How is he?" Correus whispered as the junior surgeon, whose name was Lucanus, tugged his boot off gently and began to slit his trousers up the inner seam. At his feet, blood was soaking into the wood of the floor.

"He'll do all right," Lucanus said, "but it's a good thing you got him in as quick as you did. He's lost a lot of blood."

Correus sighed with relief, thinking of the diverging trails in the snow, and then winced as Lucanus pulled the trouser leg back from the inner thigh. The boar's tusk had slashed along the fleshy part, leaving a four-inch cut, and strands of wool were stuck to the edges.

"You'll do all right, too," Lucanus said, inspecting it. "Messy but not serious. Another four inches, though, and you'd never be anyone's dad."

"Comforting," Correus said. "Odd, I didn't know I'd been gored."

"Wounds are like that sometimes," Lucanus said. "They don't start to hurt till the shock wears off. Up with you on the other table and I'll take care of it."

Correus pulled himself off the bench and, lifting himself with his arms, sat on the table edge. He lay back, feeling as if a hot iron had been laid along his thigh. "I'm noticing it," he said with gritted teeth as Lucanus began to swab it out.

"Here, hold this." The surgeon pressed a bandage over the wound and put Correus's hand over it. He trotted off down a corridor and reappeared with a pottery cup of some dark liquid. "Drink this."

Correus sniffed it. "No, I don't need—"

"Don't be an ass!" Lucanus said with an authority far beyond his years. "No man in this hospital stays in pain for no reason. That's a direct quote from Labienus," he added with a smile.

Correus sat up and drank the liquid while Lucanus held the cup for him. Somehow it didn't seem fair while Flavius was having a much worse wound stitched undrugged. The drink left a strong, dark taste in his mouth, and after a moment the thought slid away from him and the room became very strange and unreal, like a reflection in a pool. Lucanus dressed the wound and began to stitch it, and it hurt, but in an odd way, as if it were someone else's leg. He was tired, he thought, tired to the bone, and almost as soon as the stitching was finished he slipped into a gray sleep across which odd little dreams flickered. At one point he was looking into a mirror, in full uniform, the rim of his helmet shadowing his face. It was hot and he took his helmet off, and as the figure in the mirror did the same, he saw that the hair was dark and it wasn't himself at all, but Flavius.

"He's all right," a voice beside him said, and he came

groggily up out of the dream to find Paulinus sitting beside him in his own tent. Everything was slightly fuzzy and his eyes were thick with sleep. He closed them, then opened them again, and things began to sort themselves out.

"He'll be laid up for quite a while," Paulinus was saying. "I am in great disfavor with his commander, but he's going to be fine. There's no sign of infection."

"Infection?" Correus asked. "How can you tell so soon?"

Paulinus looked amused. "Soon? You've been asleep for two days," he said. "You had a bit of a fever, but Labienus said it was exhaustion and doped you up again. Here." He handed a cup of water to Correus, who drank thirstily. "You lost damn near as much blood as Flavius. How in Hades you held on to him and that horse all the way back I'll never know."

"Pigheaded," Correus said. There was a vile taste in his mouth and he reached for the water again.

"I had no idea you were hurt," Paulinus said, and his face was contrite. "I should have taken Flavius myself."

"You couldn't have held on to him."

"Or Tullius could have. I'm sorry."

Correus leaned back against the pillow. "No matter. Where is Flavius?"

"In the hospital. Labienus wanted to keep an eye on him to make sure the wound didn't open up again, but he said you'd do all right in your own tent and I thought you'd rather be here."

"Thank you. I would."

"Messala Cominius says to stay off that leg for a few days and then get your ass back to your century," Paulinus said with a chuckle. "And the legate says that the next officer who gets wounded by anything but a German can recuperate in the guardhouse. I am in no one's good graces at the moment."

"Mine," Correus said. "You're in mine and Flavius's, Lucius. I don't think we'd have made it without you and Tullius." He was tired and his eyes had begun to close again. Paulinus drew the blankets up under his chin and slipped out, and Correus drifted into sleep again, oblivious to the dull ache in his thigh.

*   *   *

When he awoke again it was full daylight and he dragged himself out of bed and dressed, limping first to the latrine and then to the bathhouse. He wasn't sure whether he was allowed to get the wound wet, but he felt as if he hadn't washed in a year. He would bathe first and then ask.

In the wooden bathhouse he stripped and pulled the bandage off. The wound was healing already, but the stitches itched maddeningly. He resisted the temptation to scratch them and slid gingerly over the rough-cut rock ledge into the warm pool. The water stung, but after a moment the itching began to go away. He dived under the surface, scrubbing his hair with his fingers, and came up again as a group of young officers came in to wash off the day's work.

"Well, the walking wounded," one of them said. He came and knelt by the pool, and Correus recognized him as an officer of the Fourth Cohort who had previously been reluctant to acknowledge his existence. "Seriously, old fellow, that was a damn fine thing you did, getting your brother back like that. Uh . . . we're proud of you." He rejoined his mates as they stripped and plunged bravely into the cold pool in the next room, and Correus thought the man had been a little embarrassed.

He lay soaking as other officers crowded in to bathe (the bathhouse was small and they went in shifts, officers first), and then he reluctantly dressed and limped up to the hospital. There he was chewed out by Labienus, who rebandaged his wound.

Flavius lay alone in one of the small four-bed cubicles that lined the outer walls of the hospital, separated from the central surgery room and a dispensary by a roofed corridor. He was awake and looked well enough, although the cut on his cheek was going to leave a scar. Correus drew up a stool by the bed.

"How are you feeling?"

"Fair enough," Flavius said. "They doped me up some after Labienus decided I wasn't going to pass out on my own from that knock on the head. I've been sleeping mostly."

"Me, too. I still feel groggy. The bastard got me in the leg."

"They told me," Flavius said. "On my account. You could have been killed yourself." There were sharp lines about his mouth and he looked unhappy.

"Flavius, don't—"

"I told everyone what you did," he said.

"You didn't have to."

"Yes I did. I'd have been dead if it weren't for you." His head felt hot and he rubbed his hand across it restlessly. "I'm grateful," he said. He wondered miserably if he really was. If Paulinus had not been there also, would he have made such a point of singing his brother's praises? It was not something Correus would have boasted about himself, after all.

"I'm your brother," Correus said. "Forget it." There was an odd look on Flavius's face and Correus wished he had kept away. He had a feeling that Flavius didn't much care for owing him his life. He rose to go. "Get some sleep now. Life will look much better when that wound has healed."

Flavius lay awake after Correus had left, his unwilling gratitude hanging about him, like a suffocating cloud. If it hadn't been for that dark cloud, Flavius would never have painted the picture he did when Silvanus, a smuggled flask of wine under his cloak, came to see him.

VIII

The Mirrors of Memory

FLAVIUS KNEW THE NEXT MORNING THAT HE SHOULDN'T have done it. Knew and would have retracted every word if he could somehow take them back. Remembering Silvanus's shocked, indignant face, he knew that the wine had gone straight to his head and mixed there with the bitterness of owing Correus his life. And so he had painted for Silvanus a black picture, wholly untrue though built of true things twisted. Flavius turned over and buried his face in the pillow. It was too late now.

Correus, for his part, found to his disgust that his command had taken advantage of his enforced absence to make Messala Cominius's life difficult. The cohort commander greeted him with a certain grim pleasure four days later, when Labienus had pronounced him fit for duty.

"Let me make one thing clear, Julianus. I've had those slovenly soldiers in my hair for four days now, and I haven't had time to cope with 'em properly. So I don't want to see 'em again until they're as prim as Vestal Virgins and dressed like lawyers. Got it?"

"Yes, sir," Correus said. "Uh, four days, sir? You mean they came unstuck in just four days?"

"The legionary is a beast of short memory," Cominius said with a sigh.

Correus sighed in return and gave a little chuckle. "I hate to think what my brother's going to find when *he* gets out of the hospital," he said.

"No, you don't," Cominus said. "But I don't think he'll have much trouble. He's had 'em a few months. By the way, when you've knocked yours straight again, come see me and I'll tell you a pet theory. And in any case, your brother's men aren't in my cohort, so unless they actually start a riot, I don't care if they go on parade in their grannies' nightgowns." He gave Correus a level gaze. "*My* cohort, you understand, is another matter."

Correus saluted, Cominius saluted, and Correus went away to see that his men started saluting.

Purely wonderful, he thought at parade that morning. *Only gone four days and they're falling all over their pilums again.* They trooped past him like a drunken centipede and Correus looked wistfully at the well-oiled precision of the sixth century nearby, so recently his own. The fourth century was assigned to work on the log road for the rest of the day, and at the end of it they drew an extra parade.

"*All right!*" His voice snapped like lightning, three lev-

els louder than they were used to, and they eyed him
warily.

"You will proceed with the usual drill, and we are *not*
leaving this field until I see a performance that could not
be achieved by a drunken bath attendant and his eighty-
year-old mother. Now *march*!"

It took a week to straighten them out, and at the end
of it Correus remembered Messala Cominius's mention of
a "pet theory" and asked him about it.

Cominius startled him by smiling and offering him a
cup of wine—very good wine, acquired through channels
of his own. "You've grasped the short-memory princi-
ple," the cohort commander said, and Correus nodded.
"Well then, you know why your men fell apart and your
brother's didn't. Now apply that further. They don't teach
this to Centuriate candidates because it makes them dangerous," Cominius said, "but it's a lesson we pick up on
our own one way or another." His parade harness, thick
with medals, lay jumbled on the desk beside him, and he
fiddled with it thoughtfully as he spoke. He had the hands
of a man who uses them, Correus thought, the callused
palms at odds with the carefully trimmed nails.

"A legionary signs on for twenty-five years," Cominius
said, "same as you and me, but he spends it all in the
same legion, and mostly in the same province, and he
can't resign if he's a mind to. The only things that shape
that soldier's life are the immediate ones: drill or no drill,
holidays or the 'on report' list, a dock in his pay or a
bonus from the Emperor. If his centurion is tough, he'll
shape up and work because the alternative is unpleasant.
If the centurion's lax, he takes advantage while he can. If
the centurion's dishonest enough to take bribes, he'll pay
them for the same reason—a softer berth now. If the centurion's brutal, the officer may even get knifed. You'll get
an occasional bad lot of men, but mostly it's all in the
officer, because the legionary only thinks in terms of *now*."

And that made it no hard thing for a strong commander to turn his troops to his own uses, Correus
thought. Cominius had practically given him a handbook
for civil rebellion.

Cominius saw the way his thoughts lay and nodded.
"It is perilously easy. Promise them a bonus, and if you

have the power to give it to them, they will rise up and call you emperor. Centurions *are* the army, and its stability rises and falls with them."

"That seems . . . shortsighted, sir."

"It is, and we've paid for it before now. It's what makes Vespasian dubious about giving us more men— I'm afraid we may be going into this war undermanned, but he still shies at the thought of too much legion power in Germany. But that power's the price of holding the Empire. In the old days, the armies were disbanded when peace came. Now, the only way to hold the land we've conquered is with a standing army, and that makes the army a power in its own right."

Correus found that frightening and said so.

"It'll scare you worse yet, the higher you rise," his commander said. "In just over a hundred years a whole class has come up for whom the army is an inherited service. You were born to it, and so was I. The days when a general left his plow to lead an army and then went back to his turnip patch are gone for good. The army becomes our life now. You, Julianus—even now, would you be happy if you left it?"

"My circumstances are somewhat different, sir," Correus said.

"I don't think so," Cominius replied. "You're here because it was bred into you. If all you wanted was a chance to shake off a slave birth, there are plenty of other ways to do it."

"I suppose there are." But he had never really thought about them.

"You take my point," Cominius said. "Take off your helmet and relax. I'm not advocating your leading a rebellion, you know. But you should be aware that you may someday have the power to do so, and make up your mind and principles accordingly, so that you don't fall victim to 'here-and-now' thinking yourself when the time comes."

Correus took off his helmet and drank a sip of wine, watching his commander with interest. Cominius fascinated him. Appius had never been so ruthlessly honest. "What about yourself, sir?" he asked. If anyone stood the chance of having to make that decision one day, Cominius was a more likely prospect than most.

"I should do what we did three years ago," Cominius said. "Go with the strongest man who showed the best chance of keeping the Empire—and the army—in line afterward. It wasn't my decision then, but it's the one I would have made. I don't have much desire to be emperor and spend my time looking for a dagger in the back."

"And if the strongest man were you?"

"Mithras forbid!" Cominius said fervently. "But then . . . then I'm rather afraid I would make the same decision. It's what Vespasian did, I've always thought. He was happy enough in Judaea until Otho and Vitellius began squabbling over the purple and tearing the Empire apart in the process."

This was a thought that had never occurred to Correus before, and he let it sink in. "That is not a decision I ever want to make," he said at last.

"Nor I," Cominius said frankly, "but it arises from the same problems you are dealing with now in your men. Your influence over them will be in direct proportion to how well you handle them, and *how long* you have exerted that influence. When good behavior becomes a *habit*, they will still think in terms of *now*, but in ways other than disobeying you. The army as a whole reacts to the Emperor in the same way. The populace may not care much who wears the purple as long as he keeps them amused, but to us it's vital."

And to the eighty men under him, the centurion might as well *be* emperor, Correus thought, for the way he shaped every hour of the legionary's life. Unnerving. "I remember our drillmaster," he said. "Mucius. The only thing that kept me from strangling him with my bare hands a couple of times was the thought that I only had to stand it for six months."

"Precisely," Cominius said. "It is harder to look ahead when the term is twenty-five years." He stood up. "Keep that in mind, Julianus, and if you're unlucky enough, you may rise to be emperor. And now I've got to go and quarrel with the quartermaster about supplies." He settled his helmet on his head and departed, brisk and purposeful.

Correus thought a good deal about the army and Centurion Cominius over the next few days, while he wrestled the demons of the fourth century into line. He imparted Cominius's views to Paulinus and found the historian in agreement.

"All the best leaders since Julius Caesar have learned that," Paulinus said. "If he doesn't get killed, Cominius is going to go somewhere."

"You'd have made a good officer yourself," Correus said idly.

Paulinus looked horrified. "I'd sooner dig latrines in Tartarus. Go and fight your Germans and leave me out of it."

"I haven't fought a German yet," Correus pointed out. "Between them and building road, I'd sooner have the Germans."

"Oh you'll get them," Paulinus said, "but you'll get another chunk of road first. Did you know the legate's pulling the legion off the eastward road and putting it to work on the hookup with Vindonissa?"

Correus blinked. It made sense. The Vindonissa hookup was more important, with Nyall's armies massing for a spring assault, and the legion short-manned. But it hadn't been announced, even to the officers. "And just how did you find that out, O Eyes-and-Ears?" he asked suspiciously.

"It just, uh, occurred to me," Paulinus said, and Correus laughed.

"I take it back," he said. "You should have been a spy."

Paulinus gave him back a blank, pleasant smile and drifted off, leaving Correus wondering if he hadn't hit rather closer to the mark than he had intended. Just what had Paulinus been doing, the night he met Tullius in a dive in Judaea at the start of a rebellion? The Emperor Vespasian seemed inclined to let him wander where he would these days, with an Imperial Post permit at that, and Vespasian had been governor of Judaea at the time. Correus didn't doubt that his friend's literary efforts were

genuine, but still, it had been the old German legions that
had first declared for Vitellius. Vespasian would keep a
sharp eye on legions serving in Germany for some time
to come.

Appius Julianus sat staring at two letters. They had
been presented to him by a much-amused Gentilius
Paulinus, uncle of the man whose signature was scrawled
on the outside of each sealed papyrus sheet.

"They came along with a letter to me from Lucius,"
the senator said, drawing up a chair in Appius's study.
He was an ample man, well-fed and unassuming.

"Ah yes, the aspiring author." Appius raised an eyebrow.

"And don't ask me how he got a permit to use the Imperial Post," Gentilius said. "I don't know and I don't
think I want to."

"Probably did some favor for our Emperor." Appius
shrugged. He would have bet his whole house that
Gentilius did know, but he wasn't going to ask. He and
the senator went a long way back—long enough to know
when to keep quiet. "An enterprising young man, your
nephew," he said in bland tones. "How is his history pro-
gressing?"

"Very well, I think," Gentilius said. "He writes with a
flair, and certainly no one can say he gets his material at
second hand."

"No," Appius said. "I gather from my son's last letter
that he is more than underfoot in Germany at the moment. That one arrived by regular channels, I might add.
Will you forgive me if I find out why both my sons have
now seen fit to abuse the privileges of the Imperial Post?
I assume that is who these letters are from. I can't imagine why your nephew would write me a letter, much less
two."

Gentilius nodded and Appius slit open one of the purple seals. His face clouded as he scanned it, and he
opened the second letter without comment. Gentilius
watched him with patient curiosity, and when he had finished the second letter Appius felt obliged to speak.

"A hunting accident, it seems. They both write to assure me that the other is still in one piece." He stared at the letters thoughtfully.

It was the senator's turn to raise an eyebrow. "By Imperial Post?"

"They are . . . very close." Appius's saturnine face had become guarded, and he rubbed his thumb along the old helmet-strap callus under his chin.

There was more than that, Gentilius thought, but it didn't concern him. He had hoped for more than a family problem, something to confirm or deny his nephew's hints of trouble brewing on the frontier. "If the greatest excitement on the Rhenus is a day's hunting, things must be quiet with the Germans," he murmured.

Appius's eyes snapped open. As long as he had known him, his companion had never pursued a subject without a reason. "No . . . I did have another letter from Correus yesterday, but written some time before this one . . . the civilian post being what it is." He dangled the bait gently.

The Senator bit—carefully. "There has been some talk of a pitched war," he suggested.

"All right, Gentilius. I see no reason not to tell you— it's hardly a military secret. There's going to be trouble when they start to consolidate the Agri Decumates. One of the tribes from beyond the projected frontier is showing every sign of trouble, and it's thought that they were also the force behind the attacks three years ago. Attacks which would never have been made if Romans hadn't been busy fighting each other. Now, *you* tell me why you want to know."

Gentilius smiled, a bland, deceptively innocent smile that Appius would have recognized if he had ever met Gentilius's nephew. "I . . . uh, like to keep my hand in. The Senate can vote more troops to Upper Germany or . . . not. One likes to know if they're needed."

"Uh huh. In a pig's silk dressing gown. No matter what the Senate says, the Emperor will still do what he wants to do. Don't try that on me, Gentilius."

"The Emperor would like it if the Senate did it without his prodding," Gentilius said. "Looks better, you know. And Upper Germany . . . touchy province."

Appius clapped his hands for a slave, ordered a tray of

wine and cakes, and used the interval while he waited to think. Upper Germany was the closest military province to Rome—the closest concentration of troops—and it had been the staging ground for so many bids for power by its commanders that Appius couldn't remember them all. Except for the one that burned the clearest in his memory, of course—Vitellius, the short-lived emperor overthrown by Vespasian. Vespasian would want to be very sure of a number of things before he ordered more troops into Upper Germany. Sure of its commanders, for instance, and sure there was a genuine threat by the Germans. And the Senate, remembering the executions and horrors of civil war, would be even more uneasy than the Emperor about reinforcing legions in Germany.

The slave padded back in, his bare feet politely noiseless on the marble floor. He poured two goblets full of wine and splashed a dollop of water on the top, as befitted a morning refreshment. Appius took a long drink and tapped his fingers on the desk.

"Now listen to me, Gentilius. I am through with all this. Through with the army and the making of emperors, and through with spies and passwords. I did my best for Claudius, poor old man, and I supported Vespasian, but he's going to have to hold the purple without me. I am going to raise horses, and I said so when I retired."

Gentilius studied his goblet, black potteryware with a thin thread design in red—Hercules wrestling a bull. "I presume you want a peaceful retirement?"

"I do. As far as I can tell, the threat from the Germans is genuine. I know there's been talk of cutting our Upper German army down even more, and I would advise against it. I'd be more inclined to step up its strength. But I can't answer for the generals' loyalties other than that I think Calpurnius Rufinus is sound enough. If I didn't, I would have pulled in some favors to keep my sons from being posted to him." He gave Gentilius a sharp look. "Why don't you ask your nephew?"

Gentilius gave a low chuckle. "Now what makes you think *he* would know?"

Because you think so, Appius thought. *And you won't admit it because our Emperor never trusted his men enough to tell one what the other was doing—not even to tell you what your precious nephew is doing.* "Pure speculation," he said, with a look that gave his words the lie.

Gentilius stood up. He had known Appius Julianus well enough in the old days to know that when Appius had spoken all he was willing to, no amount of wine, women, or camaraderie would ever drag another syllable out of him. Gentilius had once even tried himself, in the days when he was thin and handsome, and Appius Julianus, who had a reputation for taking his pleasures as he found them, had taken that one also and volunteered not a single helpful word. But Appius was honest when he could afford to be. When Appius said he had retired, his old comrade could believe him. It was plain enough, as he saw Appius's troubled gaze hark back to the letters on his desk, that affairs of state had taken second place to the affairs of his sons—and that something was wrong there. The only question was, was that *all* that was wrong in Upper Germany? Or merely all that Appius could see?

When Gentilius had gone, Appius sat quietly, staring first at the letters with their purple Imperial Seal and then at a brown spider inching her way up the bookshelf. She let out her line a little every few inches and secured it as she went—Arachne's daughter, hunting flies for breakfast. Appius knew he should call a slave and chew someone out for the presence of spiders in his study, but he didn't bother. It was pleasant to watch a little innocent web-spinning for a change. He looked at the letters again and thought that he had spun a mistake into his own: a burden he should never have placed on Correus.

He picked up a stylus and a sheet of wax in a wooden holder. He didn't know what he could do about the stiff and almost resentful way in which Flavius had informed him that his brother had saved his life and been hurt in the process, or about the equally stilted tones in which Correus had simply said that Flavius would be fine and he wasn't to worry. But he could do what Gentilius had asked, as long as Gentilius didn't know about it and come seeking his alliance in other political matters. When Appius Julianus discussed troop strength, even the Emperor Vespasian knew enough to pay attention.

A light patter of footsteps went by on the colonnade outside as Appius bent his head to the wax tablet. He had claimed to be busy all morning, but in truth he had been playing latrunculi with himself, and allowing his left hand to cheat, until Gentilius had arrived. Aemelius and his brood were coming to dinner, and that had raised the old vexing question of Flavius's marriage. Antonia and Helva had got an early start on their machinations, and Appius had finally fled to his study where they couldn't get at him.

Aemelia showed no signs of weakening in her refusal to agree to the marriage and seemed to regard her father's pursuit of the subject as a persecution to be gloried in. She went about looking pale and brave, and Helva, he knew, was egging her on. There was a tap at the door that opened onto the colonnade, and Appius looked up to see that the footsteps had been Helva's. It was raining outside and she was wrapped in a pale blue cloak, looking as damp and pretty as a sea siren.

"May I come in? Truly you do not look all that busy to me, and I hardly see you these days."

"You would see me if you would keep your fingers out of family business," Appius said.

Helva smiled. "Not a word." She had decided to try another tack anyway, and slipped up to run her fingers through his dark hair.

Appius sighed. "You're a she-cat," he said, "and it's a pity you aren't ugly."

Helva giggled and kissed him.

Antonia, curled with a book on a couch in her sitting room where the heat from the hypocaust ran the warmest in the channels under the floor, heard their voices and slammed the scroll down hard enough to crack the wooden pin it was wound on. She knew Helva wasn't going to change Appius's mind, but it tore at her that Helva could tease him back to a good mood after she had infuriated him.

Antonia picked up a silver-backed mirror from her dressing table and studied her face. She was good-looking enough, but a respectable Roman matron didn't wiggle her behind when she walked and try to seduce her own husband in broad daylight. Helva was troubled by no such reservations.

Antonia laid her mirror down and sighed. Appius was

a hot-blooded man and he lay with her more often than she really wanted him to, if she were to be truthful. Let Helva have him this time. There were more important things to think about. She picked up her mantle and called Julia to come and help in the kitchens, where the slaves were cooking and putting up the fall harvest.

Appius slipped out of Helva's room feeling a little silly at his age, but grinning nonetheless. She had kept her promise and stayed off the subject of Correus, and he had promised her a new bracelet after extracting a promise to continue to stay off it. Helva's promises didn't generally last all that long, but it would buy him a few days' peace. A pity the same technique didn't work with his wife . . .

He had the wax tablet in a fold of his tunic, and seeing Forst turning into the slaves' wing, he called out to him.

"Yes, lord?" Forst inclined his head and stood waiting.

Forst looked much improved, Appius thought; comfortable in a tunic now, and with the gall marks on his neck healed. But there was still a blank, shuttered look in his eyes, and that would never go away.

"Take this to Philippos, and tell him I want it taken into the City. It is to go to the Emperor, and no one else, so he had better take it himself."

"Yes, lord," Forst hesitated. "Lord, your sons—they are serving in my country, are they not?"

"Yes," Appius said. "They are."

"May I ask—how is it with my people?"

"You are of the Semnones, aren't you?" Appius asked.

"Yes, lord."

"Well, Forst, I am afraid that your people are going to bring much trouble on themselves," Appius said, his voice not unkind. "The man who led you into this"—he gestured at the garden and the estate, an alien land—"will come to it himself if he makes a war on the legions."

"Nyall Sigmundson, you mean?" Forst asked quietly. "Do you know him?"

"I . . . rode with him, lord," Forst said. "Give me your letter and I will see that it reaches Rome for you, lord." He turned away quickly so that Appius should not see the bleak look of longing that washed over his face, while the garden and the gentle rain seemed to waver around him and blur into a harsher land of dark woods and snow, with a cavalcade of riders flying down a hillside track with their spears lifted to a winter sun.

Did the Companions remember him? he wondered. Or had they merely said a quick prayer to Wuotan Father that he had found his peace in Valhalla and then forgotten him among the other dead? He stopped and lifted his face to the rain, letting it wash away his visions. It did not matter. He was here on a Roman farm whether he was remembered among the Semnones or not. Forst tucked the tablet into his tunic and went to find Philippos.

It probably would not have eased Forst any if he had known that Nyall remembered every man, alive or dead, who had ever ridden with that tight-knit band. Nyall *had* prayed that Forst found peace—in Valhalla or wherever it was that the Romans had taken him—and knew that it was most likely the latter. They had not found his body, and the Germans searched carefully for their dead.

Nyall watched the sunset burn down behind the trees to the west. So many men gone into that sunset with a Roman thrall ring around their throats. There must be no more. No more of the slow eating away at the Free Lands until a legion stood here on the Semnones' doorstep with a "treaty" that translated as "thralldom" in their hands.

"Nyall." A woman came out of the hall, and Nyall turned and put an arm around her. She had red hair streaked through with gray at the temples, like bird's wings, and a look of him in her face. "Can you not come and eat? They are all afraid to begin without you, and the men are growing drunk."

"They are bored." He smiled. "They have nothing to do but sit in my hall and grow fat and pick feuds with each other. I am taking them back tomorrow."

"So soon?"

"I only came here to make Council with the whole tribe. We'll winter with the chieftains of the Black Forest. They convince more easily at close range."

"Not content with the mastery of your own folk, you

must needs make yourself master of the Black Forest tribes also," she said.

Nyall turned her away from the timbered hall and the cook smoke rising above it, and faced her westward. "Look you, Mother, it is not for the land, or the chieftainship, it is because the Roman-kind are abroad in the Black Forest, and the tribes there haven't the stomach to stop them unless I force them to do it."

She looked troubled, twisting her hands in the green-and-gold folds of her gown. "I followed too many war trails with your father. I am tired of wars and of men coming back broken."

Nyall bent down and kissed her. "I'll bring you a Roman thrall to carry your cushions about for you, and you'll be the envy of all," he said lightly.

"The Roman-kind make dangerous thralls," his mother said, unamused. "And I won't envy us this winter with no men in the holdings."

"I'm only taking the Companions. We'll call up the rest in spring."

"The Companions are the best."

"You'll have no trouble from raiding. The other tribes know we fight their battle for them. Come. We'll eat before they get too full of beer to ride in the morning."

She pulled him back. "Nyall—the Companions. Not all of them? Not Lyting?"

"Lyting has ridden with me all summer," he said, surprised. "He is one of us."

"He's too young. Too young for a hosting, Nyall."

"He came to manhood a full year ago. Lyting is old enough to have killed his man on his first raid. He wouldn't *let* me leave him."

"You could make him! Nyall, he's sister's-son to you. Don't take him, not this war."

"I can't tell him to bide at home like a babe," Nyall said. "He's of the Kindred! He has the right!"

She gave him an angry look. "My daughter died bearing him. You and Lyting are all I have. I won't lose you both in one hosting!"

"If you chain him to the hearth while we take the war trail, you'll lose him more surely," Nyall said. He put his arm around her and led her into the hall. She bit her lip and wouldn't look at him. He watched her move sadly to her place at the table, gathering her women around her as the thralls began to move among the company with plates of hot meat and baskets of bread. The hounds crouched expectantly beneath their masters' benches.

The hall was always full of dogs, and Nyall, watching them scuffling over the bones and crusts on the floor, thought that if he didn't find some exercise for his restive men they would soon be snarling among themselves like the hounds. He would take them west and let them snarl at Arngunn instead, and shake the old man out of indecision. He felt restive and on edge himself, as if they were all only marking time. He fidgeted in his chair at the High Table, scraping it back and forth in the rushes on the floor, eager to be gone—westward to spit in the eye of the legion commander and his Eagles, and in the eye of the eagle-faced centurion who had sent the commander's final message back with Geir the envoy. His German had had the accent of the Semnones, Geir had said, and had been rude enough to have been learned at his mother's knee. That was unlikely. But one of these days Nyall would put a knife to his throat and find out where he *had* learned it.

He fidgeted some more, tearing his bread into little balls and rolling them between his fingers. Kari, a warrior of the Companions with the dark hair and eyes of the half-blood, saw him and smiled, reaching up onto the wall behind him for the deerskin bag that hung there with his harp in it. The Germans did not breed harpers, preferring a harsher music, but Nyall's mother had taught Kari when his own captive mother had died and the boy had needed something to hold to for a while. When he had proved to have the music in him, she had sent to her own people for a Gaulish harp for him.

Kari could fight like a wildcat, and had thrashed those of his playmates who had taunted him by saying his harping was a womanly thing; now it was accepted with a certain pride that Nyall the chieftain had a harper among the Companions.

Kari took out his harp, ran his fingers lovingly along the strings, and began to make something to keep his chieftain amused. Not the lilting, running battle music of the Gauls, or the trumpets of the Romans, but a battle music, harsh as a long sword blade, stirring as the war chants of his father's people—a striding sound with the feel of the high mountains and the crashing, cold ocean in it.

Nyall stopped twitching and leaned forward to listen, and at the end of the High Table, Lyting leaned forward also, the braided knot on his blond head catching the firelight like gold, his blue eyes eager and shining. Kari's song soared into a chant of death and victory, and the red-haired woman looked at each of the three in silence.

IX

The Peace of the Wine Jars

PAULINUS PROVED TO BE RIGHT ABOUT THE VINDONISSA road. The morning after his conversation with Correus, the surveyors were out in force, measuring and arguing with each other. The legate strode about with a map in his hand, the tribunes trotting behind him, making suggestions. He looked as if he wished they'd go away.

By noon they were digging the first ditches in the half-frozen ground, and two full cohorts were set to clearing timber. It was snowing again and Labienus watched it gloomily through the surgery window while he attended to the morning sick parade. Another winter of frostbite and lung disease. Not to mention every ass who tried to cut his foot off with an axe.

But the Vindonissa road was vital, and they knew it. Correus found he had little trouble encouraging the fourth century to put their backs in it, once he had explained the problem.

He drew a map for them in the muddy snow. "See, here is Vindonissa. Their road extends as far as this." He scratched an X with his vine staff. "And we are here." Another X. "And the Germans are here, and here, and anywhere else you care to name including probably hiding under your beds. So. If we don't meet with Vindonissa now, before hard winter, we aren't going to get a chance come spring."

There was no argument. Even the legionaries could see far enough ahead to know that the German wolf pack that was gathering to the east would be out and howling on their trail with the first thaw. They worked like bullocks, hauling dirt and logs, awkwardly muffled in cloaks and trousers, with their breath coming up around them in steam. Correus was down in the roadbed with them, somewhat before Labienus recommended, but as he explained wearily when the surgeon finally took the stitches out, the positive effect his early return would have on his men was more important than an ache in his leg.

"Well, some exercise won't hurt it," Labienus said. "But take it easy and let the muscles heal, or you'll have a limp that won't take a long march."

Correus worked somewhat more carefully after that, but the leg was healing with no problems and he was grateful. Flavius was up and about now, and avoiding him, but there was more than enough work on the road to put that problem at the back of his mind.

As for the other officers, a subtle shift in attitude had begun. Men who once would have been reluctant to give him the correct password were now being civil, and those who had ignored him were suddenly friendly. Correus began to feel a sense of belonging, not only to the legion now, but to his fellow officers and the close-knit brotherhood of the Centuriate. That went a long way toward making up for the ache in his thigh and the dark, brooding look on his brother's face.

The only exception was Centurion Silvanus. While not a friend, Silvanus had never been less than friendly. But lately his attitude had been hostile at worst, and at best one of cold dislike. Even the other centurions noticed it with raised eyebrows, but it did not seem to alter their own new friendliness to Correus; Silvanus had a habit of tacking against any prevailing wind. Correus resolutely ignored him. He could, he thought, put up with *one* jackass. Although he had somehow thought differently of Silvanus . . .

A letter from his father, affectionate and full of praise
for his promotion, reached Correus a few days later, and
the day after that, one from Aemelia—smuggled into the
post through the connivance of Julia, he suspected. Or
worse yet, his mother, Helva. Aemelia's father would
burst if he found out. But the letter was so full of hero
worship and ignorance of what life in a frontier camp
was like, that he couldn't help smiling. A few weeks of
seeing him fall into bed every night blue with cold and
black and stinking with mud, and she'd get over her passion for him in a hurry.

At last, when they were at the limits of their endurance and on the cold knife-edge of winter, the Eighth Legion met with Vindonissa. The legate called a two-day
holiday in reward, and they poured back into the camp,
cheering and exhausted, with the Vindonissa road crew
and its legate.

The generals held a council and sent off another plea
to Rome for more men; the officers wondered if they'd
get them and breathed a sigh of relief over the comple-
tion of the road; and the men of both legions prepared to
take their pleasures as they found them.

The current camp had been in place for several
months, and the usual ragtag clutter had begun to establish itself nearby. The entrepreneurs who followed the
army were a movable business, and a jumble of peddlers' tents and wine stalls and the hardier of the trollops
from Argentoratum did a thriving business.

One of the wine stalls, which bore the dubious title of
The Emperor's Own on a wooden shingle over the door
flap, had somehow acquired a wagonload of Falernian
wine. Judging by the proprietor, a shady-looking Egyptian with a missing ear who carried three knives in his
belt, it was probably stolen. But it was good wine, and
anyone who could afford his prices descended on it thirstily.

The Emperor's Own was a motley structure, half scav-
enged timber, half tent, with tables made of anything the
Egyptian had found lying around. Correus sat leaning
against a tent pole in the corner, nursing a cup of Falernian and trying to keep his temper.

Silvanus sat at the next table with his back to him, somewhat more rigidly than even his lorica demanded, pointedly ignoring Correus. Silvanus was crowded, which was his own fault, since there was room for another at Correus's table; but Silvanus, seeing who the first occupant was, had chosen to teeter instead on the end of another bench, one hand gripping the rough plank for balance. He called to the Egyptian for another cup of wine.

The Emperor's Own was jammed with legionary and auxiliary officers and such of their men as could put down the price of the Egyptian's Falernian. There was a dice game going in one corner, and some cavalry officers were trying to round up a few souls foolhardy enough to stage a horserace on the log road. Across the room someone was singing a plaintive, off-key ballad about a girl named Chloe who hadn't waited for him. Every so often someone would throw something to shut him up, and he would brood in silence for a while before doggedly resuming his song.

Outside, it was cold as the breath of the north wind, but The Emperor's Own was warm with wine in the blood and the press of bodies. It was almost a relief when someone drew the doorflap open and a whistle of cold air came in behind him. Three legionaries ducked in under the flap, shaking the snow from their cloaks, and staggered through the clutter of benches and tables to the makeshift counter that served as the divider between the public space and the storage bins. There were holes cut in the counter top to hold the long conical amphorae, and it swayed precariously as the newcomers leaned on it.

"Hey, you, Ptolemy, give us some wine!" It was plain that this was not the first stop in their celebration.

"The name's Anset," the Egyptian said softly, crossing his brown arms on the counter, the cat-headed hilt of a dagger within easy reach of his fingers. "Let's see your money first."

"I don't think the little weasel trusts us," one of the legionaries said, and his fellows nodded solemnly, glaring at the Egyptian. The speaker seemed about to comment further when he lost his bearings and staggered backward, fetching up with a thump against Correus's table.

"The Egyptian son of a bitch shoved me!" he announced indignantly, staring at the innkeeper.

Correus stood up. "I think you've had enough." He put a firm hand on the legionary's shoulder.

The man heaved himself around and eyed him belligerently. "Who're you?"

"The man with the vine staff," Correus said, hefting it. "Take your friends and get out of here before you end up spending the night in the guardhouse."

There was a crash as Silvanus stood up and spun around also, his cup in pieces on the dirt floor and the wine soaking into the damp ground. "Keep your hands off of my men, Julianus!"

Correus raised an eyebrow. "Oh, are they yours? Well, they're awash. Take care of them yourself."

The legionary peered at Silvanus and seemed to recognize him. He opened his mouth to speak and a stink of sour wine washed over them.

"Get out of here, Glaucus!" Silvanus snapped.

"But, sir—"

"Go!" Silvanus was furious, his face tight under the fading tan, and the legionaries beat a retreat. "And as for you, Julianus, can't you keep your hands off of *any-thing* that isn't yours?"

"Just what does that mean?"

"Ask your brother!" Silvanus spat at him. "No wonder you carried him back so careful! I'd call that about a tenth part of what you owe him!"

Correus had no idea what Silvanus was talking about, but by this point he was too angry to care. Under Silvanus's goading, his temper had totally escaped its guard. He took a step forward and the men at Silvanus's table prudently picked up their cups and retreated. The Egyptian came out from behind his counter and stationed himself in front of his amphorae.

"You've been snapping about my heels like a dog for the last month," Correus said. "Now's your chance!"

"Large talk for a whore-born bastard," Silvanus snarled.

"Outside!" the Egyptian said firmly, touching his dagger. They had enough sense left under their fury to obey him.

Silvanus was hardly through the door when Correus jumped him, and a moment later they were rolling in the snow. Silvanus kicked free and staggered to his feet, and Correus swung. He couldn't see well in the darkness, and he pulled off his helmet and flung it to one side. Silvanus did the same and swung back, connecting at a point just above Correus's lorica, on the collarbone. Correus fell back and then came in again, catching Silvanus on the chin, feeling as he did so the other centurion's fist in his ear.

The customers of The Emperor's Own poured out of the wineshop after them, and a pair of sentries came running up to investigate the commotion. When they saw that the combatants were officers, they hesitated. "Let them be," someone said. "This has been coming; better to settle it."

Correus and Silvanus circled each other in the snow, Silvanus bleeding from a split lip and Correus with an unpleasant ringing in his ear. Silvanus threw another punch and grunted in pain as he caught Correus full on his iron lorica. Correus took advantage of this to punch Silvanus in the face again, and then his feet slid out from under him in the snow and Silvanus was on top of him. He swung again. Silvanus ducked and hit Correus hard in the jaw and then Correus kicked Silvanus off and rolled aside. He came up just in time to send Silvanus crashing back hard against the stump of a tree.

Silvanus started to rise and then subsided again, the wind knocked out of him. One eye was red and swollen and his mouth was bleeding.

Correus stood over him, panting. He spat blood into the snow and was relieved to see that no teeth came with it. His ear hurt but his temper was subsiding with the satisfaction of seeing Silvanus propped against that tree stump. "Maybe next time you won't be in such a hurry to listen to my brother." Correus raised himself on the balls of his feet a little and settled back again. He seemed to be in one piece. He felt good.

Silvanus started to get up and Correus raised a fist. "Don't bother," Silvanus said. "Next time maybe I won't." He struggled to his feet and wiped the blood out of his mouth. His blond hair hung dankly over his brow and his gold-flecked eyes had the look of a man who is rethinking things. "Get lost," he said curtly. "It occurs to me that I may have heard the wrong end of a story."

Correus turned and walked away through the crowd now dispersing toward the lamplit doorway of the wine stall. Somehow he didn't feel as vindicated as he had a moment ago. He turned back abruptly to Silvanus. "Come and have a drink."

Silvanus picked up his helmet, and Correus fetched his. They turned into the wine shop together. The other officers gave them a wide berth, but the Egyptian eyed them thoughtfully, then shrugged, and poured the wine.

Silvanus took a drink and winced as the wine burned his cut lip. He looked at Correus. "Your nose is bleeding."

Correus took off his neck scarf and held it to his nose.

"Tell me your side. About your mother," Silvanus said.

"My mother?" Correus's voice was muffled behind the scarf. "Oh . . ." A certain amount of light was beginning to dawn. "My mother is my father's mistress. Has been for years. He bought her in Gaul when she was about fifteen. She's made a life for herself, I suppose, but it's not one I would want."

"And Flavius's?"

"Lady Antonia?" Correus thought a moment. "She's a good woman. I'm fond of her. To tell the truth, she's been more a mother than mine. Mother's maternal instinct doesn't run very deep. She's . . ." He took a swallow of wine and his face was sad. "She's adapted . . . to suit her circumstances."

"Who holds the reins in the household?" Silvanus prodded.

"Lady Antonia," Correus said flatly. "And my father, in the end. Mother gets what she wants sometimes by sheer determination, when her wishes and my father's ride together, anyway. But . . . I wouldn't want to be her."

Silvanus looked thoughtful. "That's why you won't own a slave."

"Yes." Correus waved his arm at the Egyptian for more wine. "Your turn. Now tell me how my brother explained it all."

"I gave him some wine . . ." Silvanus said, by way of excuse. "And he . . . he was unhappy."

"Never mind," Correus said. "I saw the mood he was in. I should have known."

Silvanus gave him the tale as Flavius, miserable and half drunk, had told it: a wife supplanted from her rightful place in her husband's house by a pretty, conniving tart who had wangled adoption and preferential treatment for her bastard son as the price of her own favors. Silvanus was an unconventional soul, but there was a moralistic streak in him and a strong belief in duty, and the picture that Flavius had painted had left him outraged. Now he felt put upon. He had liked Correus well enough at the start. He peered into his wine cup glumly. "I've been had."

Correus drained his own wine cup and thought it over carefully from all sides. "That you have," he said finally. "Cheer up," he added, perceiving a bright spot. "We had a nice fight."

"Yes, we did, didn't we?" Silvanus looked happier. He waved at the Egyptian for more wine, and they fumbled in their pouches for some coins. They were both getting very drunk. The ache in Correus's ear was beginning to fade. "What in Mithras's name are you doing in the same legion with him?" he heard Silvanus ask.

"I promised my father," Correus said shortly.

"Mistake," Silvanus said.

"Yes."

"I expect Flavius is sorry, now that he's thought about it."

"He's always sorry," Correus said. "Afterward."

"Oh well, when you get your cohort you're bound to be posted somewhere else."

Correus raised his cup. "To the day." It was empty again, so they shouted once more for the Egyptian.

"Still," Silvanus said, "we had a nice fight." He sounded regretful. He liked to fight, and now he couldn't fight with Correus anymore. He explained this in a somewhat convoluted fashion and Correus nodded.

"Seems a pity." There was a certain exhilaration in punching someone's nose in the cause of justice. "Can't fight you, though," he said. "We're friends."

"Blood brothers," Silvanus agreed.

"What we need is a . . . a . . . *non*-friend," Correus explained.

A group of officers from the Vindonissa legion were lounging on the counter, extolling the superior quality of their men over the Eighth Augusta's. Silvanus eyed them thoughtfully. "How 'bout them?"

". . . back my men against these summer soldiers any day in the week," a Vindonissa centurion was saying.

Correus stood up. "Right." His ear didn't ache anymore, and there was a curious sensation in his limbs. He felt invincible. "That's why they had to call in the Eighth to finish their road for them," he said loudly to Silvanus.

"Certainly," Silvanus agreed. Their helmets were on the table between him and the Vindonissa centurions, and he put them on the floor. "They got lost in the big woods and their mamas were looking for them."

"The Eighth Augusta couldn't find its own ass with a German guide to help look," the Vindonissa centurion said. His three companions moved up beside him and glared, weaving slightly. They were very nearly as drunk as Correus and Silvanus.

Anset the Egyptian put the stoppers in the wine jars and started to yell "Outside!" again, but it was too late. Silvanus dove over the table and caught the Vindonissa legion's spokesman around his boots, and he fell with a crash into the next table.

The dice players, who were Vindonissa men, erupted from their corner and jumped on Silvanus, and Correus threw himself happily on top of them. By the next moment, practically every man in the room had joined in the fray. Mostly it was one legion against the other, but two Augusta centurions who had been arguing tactics over a makeshift landscape of pebbles and a wine cup suddenly stood up and punched each other. The Egyptian stood in front of his wine jars and laid about him with a piece of flat board anytime the fray came too close. He knew better than to knife an army officer, but he would have liked to. Only the unknown Chloe's bereft lover seemed oblivious. He sat on the dirt floor in the corner and began to sing again, hiccuping between verses and holding his wine cup carefully over his head as the booted feet rushed past.

Correus and Silvanus stood back to back, grinning and slugging any Vindonissa officer who came within reach.

Probably it would have gone on until they all fell down insensible or the Egyptian lost his temper and stabbed someone, but as a Vindonissa centurion took a flying leap over a table, he slammed into one of the posts which supported the precarious roof of The Emperor's Own and it came down with a crash, bringing half the wine stall with it. An oil lamp that had hung from a crossbeam smashed on the floor and caught the collection of straw and canvas serving that corner as a roof, and the next minute half the shop was in flames.

"Mithras, god—fire!" Silvanus yelled. "Come on!" They dove through the now gaping wall with three of the Vindonissa men behind them, and sprinted for the water channel that ran to the baths. There were buckets beside it—fire was always a danger in a timber fort—and they grabbed them, breaking the film of ice in the channel to fill them.

More men poured coughing from the wreckage, with the Egyptian behind them dancing up and down in a fury. They doused the nearest flames with water and ran back for more. Someone was drunkenly organizing a bucket line and they fell in at the head of it as the sentries came running up to help. The Egyptian, abandoning the rest of his establishment to the flames, was dousing the straw-filled storage bins where his wine was laid.

By the time the fire was out, The Emperor's Own was a wet, smoking shambles, smelling of burnt hides and sodden ash, but the wine bins were intact, and even the charred remains of the counter were still standing, their amphorae smoke-blackened but unbroken. The proprietor stood behind them, cursing in Egyptian. He glared at Correus and Silvanus as they stood among the wreckage, their faces black and their cloaks and leggings charred. Correus pulled his helmet from beneath a half-burnt table and then dropped it again, shaking his hand. It was still hot and the crest was singed off so that only a few charred twigs stuck up from the top like grass.

"I thought you two had worked it off already," the Egyptian said in disgust.

Correus and Silvanus looked at each other. They stumbled out again and sat down in a snowbank. The Vindonissa centurion came and stood over them, thinking. "He was overcharging anyway," he said finally. He adjusted his helmet and staggered off.

The next morning, stiff, aching, and horribly hung over, they plodded along the timber catwalk that skirted the rampart. It was snowing.

For brawling, they had drawn a chewing-out and a week's extra sentry duty from their cohort commanders, but somehow it still seemed worth it. Correus raised a hand in salute to Silvanus as they passed each other on the windy catwalk, and Silvanus grinned back at him. His eye was black and green and nearly swollen shut, and there was a purple bruise on his jaw. Correus's own face was blotched with bruises and his left hand had been scraped raw along the knuckles by someone's teeth.

"You look like a pair of fresh corpses," Labienus had said the night before when they reeled into the surgery office, soaking wet and still drunk. He had dressed Correus's hand and rubbed some salve into Silvanus's lip, then sent an orderly with them, "to make sure the damn fools can find their own tents."

In the end they had found Silvanus's, and that had seemed to them sufficient, so they sent the orderly back to Labienus and Correus had spent the night rolled in his cloak on the floor.

In the morning, as they stumbled out into the gray light to make their penance with their commanders, they had run smack into Flavius.

They stood, still weaving slightly, arms about each other's shoulders, and he stalked past them white-faced, the healing scar on his cheek flaring red. Correus felt a writhing knot in his stomach that was not entirely due to overindulgence, but he pulled Silvanus back when he seemed inclined to pursue the matter.

"Let it go. He's miserable enough."

"He and me." Silvanus groaned. "Oh Mithras, I think I'm still drunk."

Correus had the same feeling, but by the time he had presented a somewhat halting explanation of his night's activities to Cominius and weathered the aftermath, he was feeling remarkably sober. When Correus was out of earshot, Cominius laid his head down on his desk and howled with laughter.

The Egyptian, cursing nonstop, renewed his scavenging, and by noon the motley conglomeration that was The Emperor's Own was standing again. Correus and Silvanus, he let it be known, were henceforth barred, but the edict was rescinded when the culprits agreed to pay for the damage.

"He's got a nerve," Silvanus said indignantly. "That dump is made out of the legion's castoffs, or anything else he can steal. He didn't lose a penny."

"Well, pay him anyway," Correus said practically, "if you want to drink Falernian."

"I suppose so. It's the last we'll see for a while." They had finished their punishment duty and their regular duties, and were engaged in straightening out the mess they had made of Silvanus's tent. *Someone*—they both glared at each other accusingly—had thrown up on the floor, and since neither of them could remember who had done it, they had decided to clean it up together.

"I can't have my slave do it," Silvanus said. "That really would be too much to ask." They fetched a mop and bucket from the supply shed, ignoring the snickered comments that followed, and set about scrubbing down the plank floor.

It was an odd start to a friendship, but over the winter months Correus and Silvanus grew steadily closer together. In the evenings they diced for wild, imaginary stakes, or let Paulinus beat them at latrunculi. They patronized The Emperor's Own with exaggerated decorum and prowled the hodgepodge stalls of the peddlers to buy food or rubbing oils or one of the heavy native rugs to take the winter chill out of a tent floor.

Winter came down like a thick hand about the camp, and rumors as to Nyall's intent flew wildly with the snow. He would attack Vindonissa first. He would strike at the eastern road. He would wait for the legion to move first.

Every soldier and camp follower had a theory, and they changed with each new rumor. Something was coming, but not yet, not until the thaw, and in the meantime the camp grew edgy with the waiting, and the officers devised endless drills and weapons practice to keep their restless soldiers busy. Catapults were taken out, restrung, and tested; the armorer's shed rang with the sound of hammers, the forge fires sending up black clouds into the air. In the forest the howling of wolves had the thin edge of hunger in it, and every native hut sent someone to keep guard around the lambing pens. In the Roman camp, rations grew withered and tasteless and the men were almost unrecognizable as legionaries now: they were bundled in trousers and cross-gartered leggings, their uniform tunics hidden by two and sometimes three cloaks, and their faces were muffled to the eyes against the northern winter.

Correus saw little of Flavius, and his brother's silence nagged at the back of his mind. Flavius was ashamed of himself, he thought, and furious at Correus because of it. When the holy birthday of Mithras, in whose eyes all men were brothers, came at the winter solstice, Correus decided that it was as good a time as any to shake the barrier down. He found Flavius in his tent, sitting alone and brooding.

"This does us no good," Correus said softly, putting his hand on his brother's shoulder.

Flavius's eyes were dark and brittle-looking, like mica. "I hadn't thought you'd be wanting my company." He knelt to lace his boots, his face hidden.

"You're my brother," Correus said stubbornly.

"The more pity for both of us," Flavius said.

"We're stuck with it," Correus said. He wished he could punch him in the nose, like Silvanus, and get it over with. "We must learn to make the best of it, or we'll pull each other apart."

Flavius stood up and managed a half-smile. "All right. Perhaps we can learn not to tread each other's toes so hard. I admit I've been . . . lonely." That was true. Flavius had never faced anything that frightened him without Correus there, too, forcing him in some indefinable way to go on, to go through with it. He knew that, and the knowledge was a black taste in his mouth. But there was war coming, and the desire to let Correus set his mark for him, to show him what it was he must do, was too strong to override.

He held out a hand, slowly, as if it hurt, and just as slowly Correus put his own in it. Together they went out into the gray dawn to make their prayers to the god of soldiers, who was also the Lord of Light, the Unconquered Sun, born on this day when the year turned round and the days began to lengthen once again.

The Eighth Legion's followers of Mithras had raised their altar in a rocky cave in the wall of a hill beyond the cleared land, and the two brothers entered silently, ducking beneath the stone lintel. They had become initiates independently of one another, each seeking, and finding, something different in the face of the god. For Flavius, it was the strength he feared he didn't have; for Correus, it was the duty and the brotherhood that lay at the center of the worship.

They spoke the invocation as the cloaked and hooded figure of the Sun-runner made the sacrifice—a hare, newly caught. Beyond the altars, flanked by the twin torchbearers of light and darkness, a figure was carved into the gray stone of the wall. He sat astride a bull and the animal's head was bent back before his knife— Mithras, the Guide and Mediator, whose word was Light.

"Unconquered Sun, Redeemer, grant us thy aid and intercession, and take our pleas before the Lord of Boundless Time. As you slew the Bull for our sakes, take now our sacrifice, freely given, and grant us strength."

The worshippers went in twos to the altars to dip their forefingers in the blood. "As brother guards his brother, thus is the faith of soldiers. Mithras, Lord of Armies, grant us victory and grant us peace."

Correus, kneeling before the god with Flavius beside him, added his own whispered prayer: "And peace among ourselves."

X

The Horse Mask

THE CHIEF'S HALL AT ARNGUNNSHOLD WAS CROWDED, more crowded than it should be for comfort, and the two parties were growing twitchy with their enforced closeness. On a platform at the far end sat Arngunn of the Nicretes. Above him on the reed-and-clay wall hung his weapons. A design of multicolored clay made an outflung sun spiral behind them. Arngunn's graying blond hair hung over his shoulders in braids, and he was muffled in a thick tunic and trousers and a cloak held with an amber pin. A fire blazed in a stone hearth at the center of the room and he held his hands toward it. They were cold, the hands of a man past his prime.

Two women sat beside him: one, the elder, in a low chair at his side; the other, a girl with a cloak of pale hair like a waterfall, was curled catwise on the platform's edge, leaning forward, chin on hand. She watched the shifting crowd of warriors—her father's and the imperious interlopers of the Semnones with their hair pinned up in outlandish knots at the sides of their heads. The Semnones moved among the Nicretes lordlywise, with arrogance in every stride, and the men of the Nicretes glared back at them and snarled like foxes.

To Arngunn's other side, Nyall sat with the long fingers of his right hand curled loosely around a beer horn and the other hand drumming lightly on the oaken arm of the chair. His wolfskin cloak was thrown back, and he wore a long shirt of deep green sewn with gold sun's-eyes at the hem. The gold collar at his throat caught the firelight and glowed with it, but the gold-tipped pins that held the braided knot on his head almost disappeared into the flaming hair. The gray eyes were watchful and intent, the girl thought, but his body was relaxed almost to

162

the point of insolence. His feet were clothed in light indoor shoes of soft green leather, and he leaned back in
his chair, legs crossed, one ankle resting lightly on the
hard muscles of his thigh.

Beside him, two of his Companions, his household warriors, sat cross-legged on the platform, their dagger hilts
winking in the firelight. The girl recognized them: Geir
the envoy, with more scars than his missing eye to show
for his years on the war trail; and the younger man,
Lyting, younger even than Nyall himself, who was also
of the Kindred, the royal clan of the Semnones. Like all
the people of the Suevi—the loose confederation of tribes
of which the Semnones were the greatest—they looked as
if they were accustomed to being given what they wanted.
At the moment it appeared that Lyting had his eye on
her waiting woman, Saeunn, and she saw that the girl
kept her hand on her knife as she bent to pour from a
pottery pitcher into Lyting's beer horn. It was a pity that
Arngunn hadn't been as cautious, but it was too late now.
Arngunn had swung in the wind between Nyall and the
Roman-kind across the river for too long, and now they
were both threats.

The trestle tables where they had made their meal had
been cleared by Arngunn's thralls and the High Table
was removed; now the dogs were quarreling over bones in
the straw on the floor. The warriors who had risen to
stretch their legs returned to their benches, Arngunn's men
on one side of the long hall and Nyall's Companions on
the other. A thrall kicked the dogs away from the hearth
and swept the bones and debris to one side, clearing a
space on the hearthstone for any man who might choose
to stand and speak his mind.

Nyall passed his beer horn down to Lyting and
stretched his arms, cracking his knuckles backward with
a little snapping sound that made Arngunn jump. "A fine
feast," Nyall said pleasantly. "My thanks to you and to
your house." He smiled at Gudrun, Arngunn's wife, and
she nodded. She was a tall, raw-boned woman with a
shrewd face. The fine red stuff of her gown hung on her
like a silk blanket on a mare, but there was intelligence
in those sharp eyes.

"You are welcome at our hearth," she said. "But if the

time has come for the Council, best to make it now before your hounds and ours begin to quarrel."

The beer had gone around again and the men of the two tribes were eyeing each other restively. It was an uneasy alliance at best.

"Indeed, lady, you show wisdom," Nyall said, and Arngunn nodded and raised his hand. The thing could not be put off.

An old man in a white robe with a small twist of grain stuck through his belt came forward and tapped with his staff on the hearthstone. "We make a Council of the Free People," he said "as it has been done since the old days." The priest rested his hands below the golden sun disk on the top of his staff and looked first to the Companions and then to Arngunn's men for their silence. "Speak, Nyall of the Semnones."

Nyall stood up. He was an imposing figure, decked in a chieftain's gold. He had eyes the color of a storm. "You have heard the terms the Roman-kind would make. Is there any man here who has a wish to wear their thrall ring?"

There was muttering on both sides, and Lyting stepped down from the platform and stood on the hearth by the priest.

"I have seen the lands-across-the-river," he said. "They become a tribe of farmers and watch their cabbages grow. Is that work for a warrior of the Free People?"

A man of the Nicretes rose and the priest nodded at him. "Speak, Ranvig."

The man came forward and stood, hands on hips, to face his own tribe. "We must go with the Roman-kind, or make alliance with the Semnones," he said. "I am no tiller of cabbage patches and I vote for alliance."

"If the Semnones had not come into *our* hunting runs and urged the tribes to fire the Romans' frontier, a year ago, there would be no need for a choice!" another man shouted.

"Then why did you ride with them, Ingald?" Ranvig snapped.

"Silence!" the old priest said. "We are in Council. Brawl with each other and I will put you in the byre with the cows." The two subsided and Ranvig returned to his place. A man of the Semnones stood up. "Speak." The priest nodded at him.

"I am Kari, old father," the man said. He had brown hair and a somewhat darker complexion than his companions. "My father rode with Armin of the Cherusci when he took three of the Romans' eagle-gods in battle, and my mother was a woman that he took from them. I know something of the Roman-kind. They are small men, not fearsome, but once they have set their fortresses in a land, their towns will follow and then it is like trying to hold back the sea. We must burn them out now, or go the way of the lands-across-the-river."

The one called Ingald rose, and this time the priest nodded permission for him to speak.

"We listened to the Semnones once, and made a burning. But the Romans are still here, and the Semnones are walking lordlywise across *our* lands. We, the Nicretes, will decide whether to go to the Romans or stand against them, and we do not need the Semnones to tell us!"

One-eyed Geir rose and looked down at Ingald. "You need us to fight the Romans, little man. And if you bow your heads to them, we will fight them anyway, and it will be over your burned huts."

He sat down again while Ranvig thumped his fist on the table in agreement, and Ingald stared at him, eyes blazing.

Arngunn wavered. He was not fond of having Nyall, a red-haired puppy half his age, as overlord; but Geir had spoken the truth. Arngunn's own men of the Nicretes were divided. Arngunn knew well that a chieftain ruled only so long as the Council voted to let him. If he did not walk carefully, one side or the other would try to put their own man in his place. Ingald himself had ambitions to come after him, and had already asked for Arngunn's daughter as a means of gaining influence. If Arngunn bent to Nyall, Ingald might try for the Council's vote now. Arngunn sighed. And if he refused Nyall, he would be caught between the Semnones and Rome.

Nyall watched the problem chase itself around behind Arngunn's eyes. He could force his will on the old chieftain if necessary, but he wanted to fight Rome, not the

Nicretes, and he needed their warriors. Which meant he needed Arngunn and the Council vote. And he needed Arngunn before Arngunn wavered so much that he lost his power over the Nicretes. Nyall stood up.

Arngunn's warriors were sprawled along the benches or perched on the trestle tables, arguing with each other. He saw Ranvig tap another man emphatically on the chest, and the man shook his head and turned away while Ranvig thumped his fist on the table again. Another man spoke in Ranvig's ear, and then Ranvig laughed, a crooked laugh that showed crooked teeth in a wide mouth, and a little flame in blue eyes set slightly askew. He followed the other man to the table behind him and they began speaking earnestly to three others sitting there. At the next table Ingald stood with his hands flat on the plank, leaning across it, while the bronze rings on the ends of his braids made little clicking sounds on the wood when they touched it. He too was arguing, and a goat-bearded man came up to add his opinions. Across the room the Semnones lounged on their benches against the clay-covered outer wall. They drank Arngunn's beer, and with amused eyes watched his warriors argue.

Nyall stepped down from the platform and picked his way through the bones and crusts and the trampled straw to the cleared place on the hearth. He waited while the priest thumped his staff for silence and the argument subsided. They turned to face him, and the only sound was the crack and hiss of a green log in the fire.

"You bellow like cattle at the summer herding," Nyall said. His voice was disgusted. "And while you squabble with each other and glower and sulk at my warriors, the Romans build their roads over your hunting trails and think up new taxes. Nicretes, the time has come to decide —now! Ride with the Semnones and be acknowledged free people under your own lord!" He glanced at Arngunn and saw that sink in. Gudrun leaned forward and whispered something in her husband's ear. Nyall went on: "Or bow your heads to Rome's yoke and plough your cabbage patches!"

Voices rose around him and the old priest thumped his staff. "Silence!" His eyes were old and pale under bushy brows and he fixed them on the chieftain in the High Seat. "Arngunn of the Nicretes, let you hear me now."

Gudrun whispered insistently in Arngunn's ear again and he nodded. "Speak, Valgerd."

The priest's voice was quiet, as if he were used to being listened to. "You have heard the minds of your warriors, and of Nyall of the Semnones. Now hear the word of Donar Hammerer. It is this: the Semnones' gods are our gods, and the Romans are strangers who trample our groves with iron-shod feet. Go to Rome and our gods also will fall and the priests and wise ones will go the way of the Gauls—into the eternity of night, never to return to you. And then Donar will turn his back and there will be no light on the earth for you."

There was a deathly silence when he ended. It was a curse, Nyall thought, and his back felt cold. Not even Ingald would go against the fury of Donar when his priest spoke thus. As if in response, there was a crack of thunder and a flash of cold lightning that came in through the withy shutters on the windows, dimming even the fire and torch flare and illuminating the room for a ghostly instant like a scene out of Hell.

There was pandemonium. The serving women shrieked and cowered against the walls, and the tables clattered as men on both sides leaped up, hands clutched to their dagger belts. Arngunn sat sweating in his chair. The old priest turned and walked away, back to his place, leaving Nyall alone on the hearth as the cold light faded and the room came up gold-lit and warm again. Nyall gave a silent prayer of thanks to the Thunderer and faced Arngunn. Only the girl on the platform had not moved, he saw, and a quick thought ran across his mind as to how he could hunt his quarreling dogs in one pack when the alliance had been made.

There was no question about it now. Arngunn, forced to speak some decision, would go with the stronger force. The Nicretes' chieftain moved slowly, shaking his gold-and-brown cloak back from his shoulders and rising from the embroidered deerskins in his chair. "Donar has spoken," he said. "Let you come forward, Nyall of the Semnones, and bind the alliance before my Council."

Nyall came up on the platform so that Arngunn would

not have to kneel in the trash on the floor. Arngunn knelt down stiffly, as if his joints ached, and put his hands in Nyall's. "I, Arngunn of the Nicretes, swear to Nyall, lord of the Semnones, that I will keep treaty with him in all things touching war and the battles of men, and give no harm to his house or his cattle, his thralls or his women, while I live. And if I break faith with him may the sun drop from the sky to burn me, and the ocean come up from the shore to swallow me."

Nyall nodded with satisfaction and turned his own hands over so that they covered Arngunn's. "And I for my part swear that save in the matters of war, the Nicretes are a free people and shall have kin-bond with the Semnones so that no man shall give harm or hurt to their people or anything that is theirs. And if I break faith with you, let it be to me as you have said."

Then Valgerd the priest came out of his corner again and touched their clasped hands with the sun-disk, and it was done. Nyall swept his gaze over the warriors of the tribe, seeing Ingald's cold, resentful face, then turned back to Arngunn again.

"And now, that there may be no quarrel with my leadership, give me Fiorgyn your daughter for my wife."

The girl on the platform sat up straight. There was an exclamation from the warriors, and Arngunn hesitated.

"Fiorgyn is . . . is promised," he said.

Gudrun was thinking hard, but before she could speak, the girl said: "I am promised to no man." She knew that Ingald had asked for her, but she didn't want Ingald. And she knew that her father had yet made no promises. She was too important a piece for him to play before he had to. "I am promised to no one," she said again.

Nyall couldn't tell from her voice whether she wanted him, or just didn't want someone else. Except that it might speed Arngunn's approval, he didn't really care, but there was something in her voice that made him turn and look at her all the same. He had inspected her only long enough to see that she wasn't ugly before asking for her to give him some hold on her father's men. Now he looked at her closely.

She was wearing a blue woolen dress embroidered in red and purple at the throat. Her pale hair rippled like

meadow grass down her back and her brows and lashes
were the same wheat color. Her eyes were the blue of
her gown, and something in them moved in the firelight
the way the sky shimmers with heat. Her feet were
tucked under her, and her hands rested in her lap; pale,
strong hands that could no doubt use the knife that hung
in a red leather sheath at her belt. The only real color in
her face was in her eyes and the translucent flush of her
lips, the color of a berry just starting to turn.

She didn't say anything; she just sat looking back at
him out of those sky-colored eyes, and the longer Nyall
watched her, the more reasons he knew of that he should
have her.

"Let you give her to me," he said again to Arngunn.
"She is of an age to take a man, and I want no would-be
chieftains in my war band."

Arngunn swallowed hard. Gudrun leaned forward and
looked sharply at Nyall. She should have thought of it,
but it had never occurred to her that Nyall would take a
wife from a lesser tribe than his own. But his father had
done the same, she remembered now with an irritated
click of her teeth. A Gaulish princess she had been, and
he had rammed his marriage down his own Council's
throat with hardly a chirp from them.

Fiorgyn was Arngunn's only child, and the man she
married would stand a good chance of getting the Council's vote to lead the Nicretes after him. That made her
too important to throw away in haste, but now that Nyall
had broached the matter in open Council and Arngunn
had acknowledged his half-promise to Ingald, the girl
would have to go to one or the other. Until now, Arngunn
had kept Ingald in tow with that half-promise. Now the
matter was different. Ingald would use her to try to break
the alliance, and Arngunn's hold on his tribe would go
with it. Gudrun knew her daughter did not like Ingald,
but a chief's daughter generally had little choice in the
matter of her marriage. It would be pleasant to give
Fiorgyn what she wanted, since it fell in so well with necessity. Arngunn was still wavering, and Gudrun stood
up quickly before he could speak.

There was a silence as she tugged her red gown into
place and stood fingering the little silver moon that hung

from a chain around her neck. Even a chief's wife had
no real authority, but a wise woman was respected, and
it was well known that Gudrun's voice spoke behind
Arngunn's often enough. Gudrun was a priestess of the
Mother also, and a marriage was a matter in which the
Goddess must be heard if she should choose to speak.
Gudrun closed her hands around the silver moon and
shut her eyes. Even Ingald waited in silence, but his
hands were clenched tight on the edge of the table. His
handsome face was taut—a string about to snap, Fiorgyn
thought, looking quickly from him to her mother.
Gudrun's plain face was calm and quite still, as if her
thoughts had gone away.

Gudrun stood motionless, and Nyall watched her with
respect. He couldn't tell if her communion with the Goddess was real or feigned (he gave a quick mental apology to the Dark Mother for that thought) but surely
something important was at work. While Gudrun's hands
were clasped on the silver moon, her lined and bony face
became almost beautiful, the beauty of the seasons and
the harvest, and of the unchanging ebb and flow of the
world. Then Gudrun opened her eyes.

"Let the tribe hear the word of the Mother," she said.
"War is the work of the Sun Lord, and the Mother does
not trouble herself in such matters except that she be
given her due. But marriage is for the Goddess." For a
long moment she looked at Nyall out of those shrewd
blue eyes—the same sky color as her daughter's. The
hall was silent, almost breathless. At last, she said, "The
Goddess has spoken for Nyall of the Semnones."

There was an exclamation from the warriors on both
sides, and Ingald leaped up as if to protest. "Let no man
go against the Goddess," Gudrun said, looking right at
him, and there was a threat in her voice. "It is the wish
of the Mother of All that Nyall of the Semnones shall
take Fiorgyn, Arngunn's-daughter, to wife, that both our
peoples shall be as one, and that the Roman-kind shall
make no more sacrilege in the sacred Forest of the
Mother."

Nyall smiled and inclined his head to Gundrun. "My
thanks to the Mother," he said, and it was hard to tell
whether he meant the Goddess or her spokeswoman. "Let

Arngunn give me his daughter to bind us and it shall be as you have said, Gudrun."

Fiorgyn let out a caught breath and moved her hands in her lap. It was done. Her father would accept what had already been decided for him, as always, and she would go with the red-haired Semnone lord. If in time, as seemed likely, it was he who ruled her tribe, she would rule with him. And . . . he wasn't Ingald.

"It shall be as the Goddess has said," Arngunn said, with some show of taking the decision into his own hands. "There shall be a hand-fasting now before the Council, and if any man has a mind to dispute it, let him come forward or keep his silence forever after."

Ingald was still standing, head up, his tall, muscular body braced against his fury. "For what reason does the Goddess set aside the promise made to me by Arngunn?"

"Do you question the Goddess?" Gudrun said, giving him a level look.

"I question the right of Nyall of the Semnones to take a chief's daughter of the Nicretes!" Ingald said bitterly.

Gudrun started to speak, but Nyall said softly, "This is for me to answer."

Gudrun gave him a startled look and closed her mouth.

Nyall stepped down from the platform and came close to Ingald. "The thing has been done," he said, so quietly that only those close by could hear him. "Make no open war with me."

Ingald glared back. "You think to take what is mine. Look you that you do not find more war than you were seeking." He also spoke softly. To those ten paces away they might have been discussing the sale of a cow. But there was a tension between them that snapped like Donar's lightning.

"Do you want to fight me for it?" Nyall asked. "Do it now if you do. I will agree to a combat."

Ingald looked at Nyall, and then around the room. Now . . . no. If he won he would still need the Council, and he didn't have them with him now, not so soon after Gudrun's meddling. "No. I'll not fight you now," he whispered. "But walk warily."

Nyall nodded and walked away, leaving Ingald staring

after him, a little spear point of light flickering in his eyes.

Ten days later on the night of the winter solstice, as the officers of the legion had made their worship to Mithras under the hill outside their camp, the warriors of the Nicretes and the Semnones together raised their prayers to their own sun lord in his sacred grove, and to his son Donar Thunderer. Nyall, stripped to the skin and gritting his teeth against the cold, stood at the center while Valgerd made the signs that confirmed him in his leadership. His red hair hung loose down his back and it fanned about him like the mane of the white horse that stood tethered to a stake at the center of the grove—the King Horse.

Valgerd put a bronze knife into Nyall's hands and raised his own arms to the sky to begin the high, keening prayer of offering to Wuotan All-Father, lord of the horse herd and hence of the life of the tribe. His face was hidden behind the white horsehide mask, cut from the head of last year's King Horse.

The bronze knife flashed in the moonlight, and the King Horse screamed and went down, its blood spreading in a dark pool into the snow and the earth beneath. A clean kill was a good sign. There was a shout from the warriors in the torchlit circle, and Valgerd stepped forward to dip the shock of grain from his belt in the blood and make the sun sign with it across Nyall's chest. Nyall, shivering, knelt down in the snow and began to cut away the white hide from the horse's head.

As it came free Valgerd lifted the dripping, fresh-cut mask to the night sky and set it on the head of the naked man before him. Nyall could feel the blood soaking into his hair, hot and sticky, and the life in the thing made his skin crawl. The smell of fresh blood was thick in his nostrils, suffocating after the clear cold of the winter air. He felt his stomach rising and fought it down. A circle opened in the ring of torches and two men appeared, Ranvig and Lyting, with the bridle reins of another white horse, the new King Horse, in their hands. He was yoked to a two-wheeled chariot with bronze disks running down its sides—the earthly carriage of the Sun, who was reborn at winter solstice from the sacrificed blood of the King Horse. In the old days when the Mother had held the tribe's worship in herself alone, it had been the king himself who had died to give his people new life. Now it was the King Horse who paid the price instead. Nyall repressed a shudder. Those ways were not as far off here among the Nicretes, the people of her forest, as they were among his own tribe. That was what gave the marriage of a Nicrete chieftain's daughter so much importance.

They put him in the carriage while the King Horse stamped and whinnied at the blood smell of the other white form that lay with its bloody head in the snow. In a year's time, a year of the best grain and the best mares and the lordship of the herd, he would return to the grove. Perhaps he knew it.

Nyall stood bracing his bloodstained hands on the front rim of the chariot with the white mane falling down his back like a streak of snow against his red hair. The blood smell was thick and choking in his face. He had not wanted to go to his wedding this way, but a union between lord and lord's daughter, both of the Kindred of their tribes, became an offering in itself when done in this fashion, and the world's rebirth was mirrored in their coupling. It made a strong thread in the bond between his folk and hers, so in the end he had consented to do it.

Lyting put a strand of grain in Nyall's hand and Ranvig a bronze axe—it had an oaken handle, and an inscription of magic runes ran sideways down the head. They turned the carriage about and moved through the trees with the warriors trailing behind them in the torchlight.

A half-mile away they halted where another trail ran slantwise across theirs. The wood was still. The wild things had disappeared with the first scent of man, and the silence was sharp-edged and shining, like a piece of ice. There was only a little moon, tangled in the treetops. The torches made yellow-gold circles, and inside them everything was honey-colored. Beyond the torchlight there was only black and white and shimmering streaks of moon-washed silver. Even the blood on his hands was dark instead of scarlet.

A faint jingle of bells whispered in the trees ahead, and then there was a pinprick of light, and then another, as a winding procession snaked its way among the black, gnarled trunks. The leading figures were horned, he saw, not the stag's horns that some of the sun priests wore, but the broad curving horns of cattle. They led another two-wheeled chariot, drawn slowly by a white mare heavy with foal. Her sharp hooves turned up little flurries of snow as she moved, and the cow-horned figures matched their pace to her slow, rolling step. As they came nearer, Nyall saw that they were women, their faces masked by cowhide, their forms black against the snow.

In this light wicker chariot a single slim figure stood, cow-horned also, face hidden beneath the mask, but with a fall of pale hair gleaming in the moonlight. She too was naked, and Nyall saw that there was blood drawn into the Sign of Horns on her breasts, and that a trail of blood dripped from the mask into a dark curve on her shoulder. Like him, she also carried a little bronze axe, blade forward, and a sheaf of grain. Even through the mist of blood and magic she was beautiful, a flawless form that shone milky in the moonlight. Nyall caught his breath beneath the horse mask. Then he realized uncomfortably that the girl beneath the cowhide had an equal view of his own scarred body. He straightened his shoulders.

The white mare pricked her ears and whickered as they approached, then came up to the King Horse to nuzzle at his face. The two women who led her stepped back. They were masked also, but Nyall thought he recognized Gudrun's angular form in one of them. They made the Sign of the Mother over the girl in the chariot and then slipped back into the crowd of women behind them. Valgerd stepped up and drew his wheat sheaf across the girl's body from breasts to belly, and then across Nyall's chest and loins. He took the grain and axe from each and laid them on the flat rock that marked the crossroads. In the two chariots, the Horse Man and the Goddess-as-Virgin gazed at one another through the eye-slits of the masks, and Nyall felt himself stirring. He was unsettlingly aware of his nakedness before this throng of unknown warriors and women.

A man in the red-roan mask of a war-horse—it must be Arngunn—stepped up and took the girl's hand in his. He led her from the chariot as Lyting bent to let down the step into the car of the King Horse. The Red Horseman laid the girl's hand in Nyall's and then boosted her in a flurry of flying hair and bare feet into the chariot beside him. Nyall caught her to him with one arm and held out a hand as Lyting put the reins of the King Horse into it. The crowd of women drew back before him as he shook out the reins, and Ranvig stepped forward and slapped the King Horse hard on the flank.

They flew like the Elves' Hunt down the track, Nyall's arm tight about the girl's naked body, and one horn of the cow mask grazing his ear, with the knife-wind cold about them. After a while he drew rein and reached behind him in the chariot for the woolen blankets that Lyting had put there.

After drawing a blanket about her, he untied the leather thongs that bound the cow mask to her. He drew it gently from her head and she turned a bloodstained face up to his, which was still hidden behind the stallion mask of the old King Horse.

"Take it off," she whispered.

"That you may be sure what it is you ride with?" He pulled the stallion's mask from his face. She stood looking up at him for a long moment in the white silence, and then reached out for a second blanket and drew it around him.

"So you are real," she said.

Nyall laughed. "You were expecting another horse head under the mask?"

"I don't know," she said. "The women make much talk that the god himself comes in the bridegroom's place at a solstice wedding."

This time he didn't laugh. He knew that it had been in the back of his own mind to wonder what it really was that had ridden in the crook of his arm. "I admit that the gods have been rather thick about our heads of late," he said, "but I am real enough, I promise you."

His hand slipped up and brushed across her breast where the cow's blood had dried stiff and rough to the touch, and she gave a little shiver. "Yes," she said with a ripple in her voice that surprised him, "I see that you are."

He shook out the reins again and they rode on, arms

about each other beneath the woolen blankets, fair head against red one, until they came to a hunter's hut in the heart of the forest. It had been made ready for them, and Nyall unyoked the King Horse and tethered him under a wooden shelter beside a pile of hay. He put an arm around the girl and pushed open the door. The hearth fire was laid ready to light, and a bed of grass and dried herbs was spread with piled hides and a wolfskin blanket in the corner. There was a wooden chest beside it with clean clothes, but now he no longer felt the want of them and crouched, wrapped in his blanket, to strike a flint to the tinder on the hearth.

It took a while to kindle the fire, and when it was burning he turned to see that the girl was curled under her blanket on the spread skins of the bed. There was a bucket of water in the corner and she had washed the blood from her breasts and face in it, so that the skin was white and unmarked and the damp hair hung down pale around it.

Nyall plunged his own head into the bucket to get rid of the clinging feel and scent of the blood and came up shaking like a hound. He dipped the tail of his blanket in it and scrubbed at the blood on his chest and hands. The girl looked at him apprehensively. "I didn't think—" she said. "It is a sacrifice. Perhaps we are supposed to leave the blood—"

"I have done any number of unpleasant things tonight because the priest-kind said to," Nyall said firmly. "But I will not lie with my wife smeared with a horse's blood." The girl sat up, the striped blanket slipping off one damp, white breast. She smiled with a little sideways smile that lit up her face like a May fire. "And in any case," Nyall said, "it is too late now." There was a catch in his voice, and as he knelt and put his arms out for her she held up her own.

It snowed in the night, and the morning sun came through the withy shutters of the hunter's hut as silvered as the moonlight. Fiorgyn stirred under the wolfskin covers and propped herself on one elbow to watch Nyall combing out his red hair by the fire, which he had relit. The hut was warm and he had not bothered to dress. The

red hair fell like a flame down his back. It was hair that
a woman would have bartered her soul with the elf-
folk for, and she had a feeling that he knew it.

"You are as vain as a woman," she said, watching
him comb out the copper-colored fall. "Why do you
bother to bind it up?"

Nyall looked at her over his shoulder, and she gave
him a half-grin and snuggled deeper under the wolfskin.
"If you are not liking me, wife, let you go back to your
father and let him give me back again my twelve cows."
He pulled the flaming hair into three strands and began
to braid it.

Fiorgyn chuckled. "You got me cheap for your twelve
cows, husband. I am remembering that Ingald offered
sixteen."

Nyall swung around to face her, the half-braided hair
falling over the white scars on his chest. "Then say now
why you spoke for me and not Ingald."

"Why, you are four cows the richer than he, for not
having paid them," she said innocently.

"Fiorgyn—" He put a hand out and grasped her wrist.

"Oh, very well." Fiorgyn looked uncomfortable. "It
is only that it sounds foolish. I don't like Ingald."

"Why not? He is a fine warrior."

"When we were children," Fiorgyn said thoughtfully,
"he used to bully anyone he could. It occurred to me that
his wife would be treated no different. And . . . and he
has thief's eyes. He goes sideways to what he wants."
This last was a warning, Nyall thought, a pointed one.

"I will remember." He sat back and finished braiding
his hair.

"Nyall."

It was the first time she had used his name. He stuck
the gold pins home and looked at her.

"You took me to hold my father's war band."

He nodded.

"Was that all?"

"It was . . . then." He thought of the night past, and of
the warning she had just given him. "It may be that it is
not now." He looked at her and smiled, then stirred up
the fire and put more wood on it. Between the firelight
and the sunshine they turned the hunter's hut golden, and

the girl on the bed seemed to lose her silver shimmer and grow golden also. "And me?" Nyall asked her. "You accepted me because I am a chieftain and because I am not Ingald. Was that all?"

"It was then," she repeated his own words. "It does not seem to be so now." She held out her arms, gold-washed in the sunlight, and he slipped into bed beside her again and tangled his long hands in the curtain of her hair.

They rode back to Arngunnshold at noon, dressed in the finery that Ranvig and Lyting had placed in the hunter's hut for them. A trail of oak branches was threaded through the sun-disks on the chariot in token that their first coupling had been made as a gift for the gods and the tribe and not for themselves alone. Nyall's shirt and trousers were of forest green, heavily sewn with gold thread and small bits of amber. Fiorgyn's gown was sun-colored, like a splash of light in snow, and her long hair was braided as befitted a married woman. A cluster of little golden apples chimed and jingled at the end of each braid.

The whole of Arngunnshold turned out at the first shout that the King Horse and chariot were approaching —the chieftain's own household, freemen, thralls, and hounds; Nyall's Companions; and the warriors of the Nicretes who were gathered from their own holds for the war that was coming.

Nyall stepped down from the chariot and, feeling conspicuous, lifted Fiorgyn after him. In some tribes, he knew, the Council hung about the marriage bed in person when a chieftain was wed, but he found the ring of expectant faces and the pointed jokes of his Companions quite enough of a trial. Only Ingald, he saw, stood apart, leaning, with booted ankles crossed and thumbs hooked in his belt, against the forepillar of the hall. His handsome face was completely blank, but there was a look about the eyes that made Nyall remember Fiorgyn's words: thief's eyes, she had said.

He turned Fiorgyn over to her mother and the other women who bustled forward, noting that the small, freckled girl, Saeunn, dodged determinedly past Lyting to get to her mistress. Nyall waved the warriors into the hall with him, and Lyting abandoned his pursuit to bring Nyall a horn of beer and settle himself in his usual place at Nyall's feet. Nyall eyed his young Companion thoughtfully. So the pup began to grow into a hound, did he? He supposed he would have to do something about that. Lyting was too young and too well born to be married off to the first girl whose round backside caught his eye, but it wouldn't do to have him prowling through Fiorgyn's women like a wolf on the hunt.

Nyall pushed the problem to one side. He had more important matters at hand just now, notably Kari and Geir, who had returned the day before while Nyall was twitching impatiently under the hands of the priests, making ready for his wedding. They came into the hall now, their hands full of tally sticks, and knelt down before him to count out the strength of the men and horses he could draw to him in the spring.

"Of our own war band and Arngunn's, you know well enough," Kari said, counting out the notches on two sticks. "The Hermanduri have sworn to Rome, but they will blow with the wind, I think. For the rest, Egil and Sigvat will follow you, and Thrain now."

"Your wedding Arngunn's daughter made a turning point there, I think," Geir said, and Nyall nodded.

"And the other five?" The Nicretes were the main strength of the Black Forest, but he would like the nine lesser clans also if he could get them.

"Sigurd and Mord, yes," Geir said. "Gunnar's no more than a hill bandit with twenty thieves to call warriors, but he'll come if the pickings look good. The same goes for that old fox Runolf. The best reason to have those two is to keep them from looting our cattle when our backs are turned."

"And Jorunn?"

Geir spat with emphasis. "Jorunn doesn't like foreigners, and that means us. He will ally, but only with the Nicretes. Pompous old bastard. He'd have set the dogs on me if I hadn't given him to think twice about it."

Arngunn pulled his cloak about him and leaned toward the fire. "I will go to him," he said, "but it will take a while to get there on a winter trail." It was warm for a winter day, especially with the press of bodies in the hall, but he looked cold, and the blue-veined hands were not steady.

He's old, Nyall thought, with a new sympathy. *Old, and he's been ridden over enough.* "No, old Father," he said aloud. "Jorunnshold is a wild ride at midwinter. It's a young man's trail. Who of your warriors carries the most rank?"

Arngunn didn't protest. He was tired, and he had given over his warriors and his tribe to Nyall. Let him have them, he thought. He was cold. "Ranvig," he said, "and Ingald. And Arni," he added, nodding at a young man with a scarred ear and a flyaway smile who sat perched cross-legged on the end of a bench.

Nyall thought. He knew Arni, and that reckless smile summed up his nature. But still . . . "Ranvig," he said. His eye lit on Ingald and passed by. "And Arni. Go you and . . . reason . . . with Jorunn. Take enough men that he declines to set the dogs on *you.* I will tell you what you may promise him after—" He broke off as a bench crashed back against the wall, sending a little cloud of dust and a trickle of clay chips onto the floor.

Ingald was standing now, his face set and furious. "*I* will ride with Ranvig!"

"No," Nyall said flatly.

"By what right?" Ingald shouted.

"By the right of the war leader!" Nyall slapped his hand hard on the arm of the chair, and half stood, leaning forward. "*I* command the war band, and the war band has sworn to *me*! And if you cannot abide it, Ingald, go out from here, and back to your hold, alone. Or stay with your tribe and obey!"

To be tribeless and alone was a road no man in his right mind would walk. Nyall knew it, and Ingald knew it. Ingald swallowed hard and brought his voice down. "I also have sworn with the war band," he said stiffly. "Why then do you pass me by?"

"You swore unwillingly."

"But I swore. You lay insult on me by sending a babe in my place." He jerked a hand at Arni, who bristled and reached for his knife.

"Stop it!" Nyall was standing now, hands on hips and

his gray eyes wolf-bright in the shadows of the hall. "Ingald, you have a quarrel with Ranvig and a quarrel with me, and to my mind that does not make you the man to send to Jorunn."

"And now a quarrel with me also!" Arni was on his feet too by this time, knife in hand. The rest sat silently, just watching. Nyall could not hold the war band if he couldn't hold these two. It was a test.

"Put up your knife, Arni," Nyall said quietly, "or I will send you back to your nurse instead of to Jorunn. You are like to have worse insult than 'babe' from him."

Arni hesitated and then slid the knife home.

Good. Nyall could knock enough sense into Arni to keep him diplomatic while Ranvig made the treaty with Jorunn. He turned back to Ingald.

"If we wrangle among ourselves, we might as well send our heads on poles to the commander of the Eagles and have done with it. You have a choice, Ingald. Me or the Roman-kind. Decide now."

Ingald fingered the bronze ring at the end of one braid, and his eyes slid away from Nyall's. "I told you. I have sworn." He turned on his heel and stalked roughly through the crowded hall to the door.

Kari watched him go, his brown eyes serious. "Shall I hunt that ferret out of his hole for you?" he whispered.

Nyall dropped into his chair again. "My thanks for your care," he said drily, "but no. He is no oathbreaker yet, and I won't begin with a killing. Especially not that one."

Kari sighed and nodded. He knew Nyall better than most men, perhaps because his own half-blood birth made him no rival for the chieftainship. But Nyall was wrong this time, Kari thought, staring at the empty place where Ingald had sat, and the little drift of clay gouged from the wall. Maybe deadly wrong.

XI

A Springtime War

IN THE BLACK FOREST THE FIRST SIGNS OF THE TURN-
ing season were the swelling leaf buds and the wild
things that came blinking up out of their burrows in the
warming air. Then the snow began to melt in the hill
pastures, and the thin cattle were turned out to forage
with the first show of new grass.

They felt it in the camp of the legion. The heavy cross-
gartered leggings began to come off and so did the extra
cloaks, and they raised their noses to the new smell in the
air. The ground turned to slush, and a sprinkle of snow-
drops lifted their heads by the Dexter Gate only to blacken
again in a late frost. The whole army took a deep breath
and stretched its muscles and set about cleaning a winter's rust from its pilum points.

Correus chased his century out onto the parade ground
for the first open-air drill they'd had in two months. He
was pleasantly surprised when they champed at the bit
like chariot ponies and got it right every step. The long
weeks of turn-and-march in the drill shed had paid off.
The straight scarlet column of another century marched
past, heading out the Praetorian Gate on patrol; with
them, Silvanus, newly promoted to second-in-comand
of the Fourth Cohort, raised his vine staff in greeting.

In the hospital Labienus turned his hacking, sniffling
patients out in the central courtyard to soak up the sun,
and the "on report" list pushed a phalanx of brooms
down the Via Principia, mounding up the winter's trash
and sludge before them. The log road began to creep east
again while the scouts ranged well ahead of it. Of the
Germans there was no sign now, and that was a sign in
itself. In the ragtag huts outside the walls, the entrepreneurs debated—stay one more week while the spring air
made business brisk, or pack up for Argentoratum before

trouble began. The comings and goings of the frontier scouts were watched with interest. They were a disreputable-looking band, and until you saw one washed and in uniform you'd never know him for a Roman. And they were mostly officers, at that. But they could whisper through the forest like a drift of leaves, and live on the land. It was one of these that Correus remembered afterward as marking the start of war.

He wore his hair long and braided like a German's and affected the wolfskin jacket that was a matter of pride with the frontier scouts. He came through the gate on a pony whose shaggy winter coat and matted tail almost obscured its Arab blood, and he gave a casual salute to the stiff and polished sentries who barred his way.

"You look like a bog troll," the gate centurion said disgustedly. "Go and clean up before you see the legate."

"When I want to march about with a pilum up my ass, I'll rejoin a legion," the frontier scout said in an eduated voice. "Step aside."

Two minutes after the scout's appearance in the Principia, three optios erupted through the tent flap, and the cohort commanders and tribunes received an abrupt summons. By midday the whole camp was being pulled down, and everyone knew the Germans were on the move.

Correus had seen a big camp broken before, but not like this. They had a good two days' march to catch the Germans where the frontier scout reported the ground was best for Roman-style fighting, and everything had to be taken with them. They were not so much dismantling the camp as draining it hollow, leaving behind for a home base only the actual fortifications. Everything else was loaded in the baggage train, made as small as possible by burdening the legionaries themselves with their own gear. In the kitchen the head cook sat on a sack of onions grumbling over the provision lists, while the quartermaster quarreled with the armorer and with Labienus's field-hospital crew over the allocation of the wagons. In the centuries, each centurion called his roll and checked off names against the fit-for-duty lists, reporting the tally to his commander, and so upward to the legate. The centurions were the backbone of the army, and they were at work everywhere, like an iron framework that held it all together; checking and rechecking, chewing out malingerers and calming new recruits, gathering their men about them with words of praise and duty.

The couriers to Vindonissa had gone out hours ago and would be back before dark with confirmation from the legate there; in the meantime the machinery of the army rolled on. For Correus, caught up in it, everything burned brightly, like a pitch flame, and the lump of fear in his stomach was acknowledged and then ignored. There was no time for fear, although he knew that the same leaden lump must be riding in the belly of every man in camp, unless he were a fool. *So this was how you got around fear,* he thought with the back of his mind while his optio read off the century's supply lists. You crossed off one task and went on to the next, and not even fear could stand up to the endless tide of details that made it possible to move five thousand men on a day's notice.

Far past nightfall, the torchlit camp scurried like an anthill, but they marched in the morning with the dawn mist swirling around their feet, a winding, deadly column moving down the log road like a spined beast with iron feet. They went in battle order, pilum points bristling above them in the chilly light, with the scarlet of the officers' cloaks making fiery splashes at intervals among them. At the tail of the vanguard, the Eagle-bearer carried the great golden bird before him, as the legate and his tribunes rode behind. Then came the bulk of the legion in a steady tramp that drummed like thunder on the wooden road.

Paulinus, packing his saddlebags, with Tullius beside him, watched them move out. He had orders to get the hell out of there and back to Argentoratum, and he knew that this time he would have to obey. As the tail of the baggage train rumbled past and the rear guard came up in its wake, he thought: *so many friends . . .* So often before he had watched friends march out and wondered which of them would not march back. He shoved the pack buckle home and nodded at Tullius.

"Best we be going."

The forest was lifting its green head to spring, and ferns and blue flowers grew in the damp patches between the rocks. It seemed ironic to Correus that this quickening of of the world could signal the death of men, but his own troops seemed unconcerned by such philosophical considerations. One of them raised his voice in song, a rolling tune the legions marched to, and the rest caught it up, shouting out the chorus. Correus joined in, proud of them as he tramped at their head. They marched as they would fight, and in battle a centurion was a foot soldier like his men.

They camped at midday on an upland slope and dug in. The Germans should still be well to the east, but the legate took no chances that they were not closer. The legion was making slightly short marches to keep the Vindonissa Legion, traveling at a forced-march pace, within reinforcing distance if the scouts' information should prove wrong and the Germans showed themselves before they were expected. They had better not, the legate said, and the frontier scout went over his deductions again, pointing to a herd of scrawny cattle grazing at the far end of the meadow. No tribe would leave its cattle loose where it planned to fight, and no more would they if they expected the legion to be on their trail so soon. The legate nodded thoughtfully and called up a troop of cavalry. They whooped off joyously, and in an hour or two there was beef stew bubbling on the cookfire.

"Nyall's own damn cows," Correus chuckled as he ate. "Now there's justice."

"Actually these pastures are in the Hermanduri's land," Silvanus said.

"I thought they were the only clan that had sworn allegiance to us," Flavius said. The constraint between him and Correus had faded somewhat with the winter and seemed to vanish entirely on the march in the face of coming battle.

Silvanus wiped his bowl out with a piece of bread. "Yes and no," he said. "They swore to us, all right, but I didn't see one man of fighting age in any of the holdings we passed. I think we can eat their cows with a clear conscience."

"When will it come?" Flavius's face was carefully blank, but to Correus, at least, it was plain that he was tense.

"To a fight, you mean?" Silvanus looked cheerful at the prospect. "Tomorrow, maybe, but better the day after when Vindonissa's had a rest. They'll catch up with us by tomorrow midday."

"What are the Germans like as fighters?" Correus asked. "I've had some training in their weapons." He thought gratefully of Forst.

"Fierce enough," Silvanus said. "They paint themselves up like devils to scare the daylights out of you. And they get their licks in now and again." He glanced at the white, healed scar on his sword arm. "But they're death-or-glory boys. They think it a point of honor to be in the front of a charge. Our men, who've had that sort of thing beaten out of them, make better soldiers."

All of which did little to banish the fear of the unknown that lurked at the back of Correus's mind—a fear that ran rampant in his brother's. Maybe only your first battle could banish fear. Or perhaps nothing ever did. It was not a question that Correus wanted to ask Silvanus.

Two mornings later, he buckled on his lorica as the shrill notes of reveille and then the fall-to-arms sang out over the mountain pasture where the army had drawn up. The nervous sensation was unabated—a tight, solid knot at the pit of his stomach—and a hot excitement seemed to run just under the skin. The world looked very sharp and clean-edged as the mist drew off and revealed the bronze and scarlet of the Eighth Augusta and the detachment from Vindonissa, the bulk of that legion, who were spread out along the rise.

Before them, the ground dipped into a flat valley and then climbed again to a second hillcrest. That hill stood empty along the skyline, but they knew well enough what lay behind it—for the scouts who had slipped across the high moor in the night had seen the German campfires. Hundreds of them.

The legate moved along the line with his optios and his Eagle-bearer beside him, speaking to an officer here and there. The tribunes scurried in his wake like chicks behind a hen. They had probably never fought a battle before either, Correus realized. And they weren't soldiers—not really. They hadn't had a centurion's training. They might outrank him, but he was the professional. He straightened his back and took a grip on his pilum staff, and the tight knot unwound just a little.

There was a sharp intake of breath from the man beside him, the standard-bearer of his century, and the bronze disk with "IV" inside a laurel wreath dipped as the soldier's hand slipped on the staff.

"I see them," Correus said quietly, looking where the man was pointing.

All along the hillcrest they stretched, too far away to be more than a black mass of spear points and tossing heads of horses. Something hung in the air, a sound almost too low to hear. It swelled up until it became the ominous rumble of a storm sky. Correus heard the rhythmic clatter of spear shaft on shield, and the chant of voices calling down destruction from German gods.

"Look now, they're tryin' to sing us to death!" someone called out. Another man answered, "Well, it's workin'," before Correus glared them into silence.

The legate gave a signal, and as the booming note of a German war horn rolled over the chanting on the hill, it was met by the high, sweet call of Roman trumpets, and the auxiliaries, the light-armed van of the army, moved into place on the valley floor. Then, with a thunder of hooves and a screeching war cry that set the teeth of every man in the legion on edge, Nyall's war band came pouring down the slope—two thousand horsemen riding bareback with leveled spears, their faces and bodies painted with red clay and charcoal and blue herbal dye so that they looked like a Hell-wind and not men at all. Almost at their heels ran the swiftest of the foot fighters, ready to move in when the onslaught of horsemen broke the legion's line.

The Roman auxiliaries flung their pilums. A few horsemen in the leading edge went down, but the rest still came on. The auxiliaries knelt to meet them, shields tipped up, swords held ready to stab into the bellies of the horses. They took the weight of the charge, and more riders crashed down in the spring grass, and then the trumpets sang again and the auxiliaries were pulling back, circling wide to harry the flanks of the enemy while the heavy-armed troops of the legions moved in.

"Our turn now," Messala Cominius said, and they moved out with the rest to meet the baying horde that streamed down the far hillside. The German horsemen were in the thick of it, and Correus thought he saw Nyall's flaming head behind a green and scarlet shield as an arm drove a spear clean through a legionary shield and the soldier behind it. Then the battle closed in around Correus, becoming a few feet of blood and clashing metal, the screams of men and horses, with the sun riding hot in a pale sky above, and there was no time for anything but to look to his men and to his own life.

They flung their pilums with deadly aim, then stepped forward as one man, and stabbed and stepped up again. When a soldier went down, another took his place, shield locked to the shields beside him, in the formation which gave a meaning to all those days of drill. Roman ranks held long enough to break the momentum of the German charge, and then the battle dissolved into a chaos of individual wars, fought out by cohort and by centuries with the standards swaying above them in the sun. Higher still on the hillcrest, the Eagle of the legion perched on his thunderbolts, and the legate sat calmly on a gray horse, taking stock, directing, and cursing the Emperor's mistrust. With another legion he could simply have rolled over the Germans and there would have *been* no battle. He nodded an order to the bugler beside him and the boy licked his lips and blew hard. The cavalry pulled back and wheeled along the rocky southern edge of the meadow to harry the German flank.

Correus heard the bugle faintly above the din and fury, but all he could see was the naked, screaming warrior before him. He drove his sword upward under a bronze and blue shield, and the man crashed down in the trampled meadow grass. But two more took his place. There was no fear left in Correus now, only a deadly, singing excitement that said stab and push forward, kill or be killed. Stab and push forward. A dun horse reared and crashed down almost on top of him as a legionary rammed his sword into its belly, and the rider scrambled from its back, his sword flashing. Correus moved his shield just in time to send the blade sliding off the iron plates of his lorica. He thrust with his own blade and felt it pierce the breastbone. As the painted figure fell, Correus saw that he was no more than sixteen—a boy just come to manhood. And there was no time to mourn the the wrongness of that death—he was fighting for his life with a snarling blond man with the gold collar of a chieftain and a red shield with a bronze boss shaped like a stag's head. Odd, that he should see that all so clearly.

They were hardly moving now, and the battle began to have the nightmare quality of trying to run through water, while the smell of blood seemed to soak into the ground and the air. Correus realized that his sword hand was wet with blood. He tucked up under his shield and wiped his hand as well as he could on his tunic skirt —the blood would make the hilt slippery. The reserves, he thought. Surely now the legate would bring them in! The Germans had thrown everything they had into a wedge to try to break the legion in two, and it wasn't going to hold much longer.

The legate on his hilltop also saw it and knew it was time. He had to break Nyall's war band or it would break him. They were stronger than he had thought. But —and he smiled a grim little smile—he had something that Nyall hadn't counted on, or the German would never have thrown his whole force at the legion's center that way. The bugler blew again, the trumpets picked it up, and the reserves (mostly the Vindonissa detachment) moved out to shore up the front line. And then from among the trees at the tumbled northern edge of the meadow another trumpet sang out, and two full cohorts poured in a precisely calculated pattern through narrow gaps in the trees to hammer against Nyall's flank. The legate smiled again as the Germans rocked under this counterattack. It was no easy maneuver to take a thousand men in battle order through a close-growing wood, but that was what Roman drills were for. And this one was going to save the Emperor's frontier for him.

The battle was shifting. Correus could feel it as his men surged forward around him, without knowing what it was that had done the trick. Nyall's allied war band was roughly the equal of the legion in number, but the foot fighters who followed the mounted warriors, most armed with only shield and spear, were no match for the heavy-

armored infantry cohorts of the Romans. They buckled
at the flank, and the whole northern wing of the German
host began to fall in on its center. The legion's left flank
swung around behind them and pushed, and if the Roman right flank and cavalry could hold, they would have
the Germans between hammer and anvil.

Nyall, in the thick of the horsemen, saw what was
happening. The strength of the German war band lay in
the weight of its first charge. Boxed in by the mechanical
advance of the legion behind its locked shields, his flanks
would crumble until they went down. He had never
fought a Roman legion in full strength before. The de-
moralized troops of isolated Rhenus forts, caught in the
upheaval of civil war, had been easy pickings. But now
Nyall saw his mistake and knew that it was almost too
late to recover. He pulled his horsemen back and hurled
them at the weaker southern flank of the legion while
the war band fell back behind him.

The Roman southern flank wavered and barely held
under this onslaught, but the war band was fighting in
desperation now, with the bulk of the legion pushing at
its rear. There was a trumpeted order and the standards
of the Eighth and Ninth Cohorts moved above their soldiers' heads in the sunlight, drawing their men after them
to shore up that wavering southern line.

At the southern end of the valley, the ground fell away
into a running slope of tumbled rock and stunted trees,
jagged ground that was dangerous to heavily armed soldiers.

In the end it was that slope that saved the Germans.
They poured along it like mountain goats, their hill-bred
horses keeping their footing where the lumbering troops
of the legion began to stumble. There was a cry as the
commander of the Ninth Cohort and his standard-bearer
went down together, the standard pole snapping under the
hooves of a war-horse. Someone else, a centurion,
snatched the standard from the ground.

"Hold them! To me, and hold them!" the officer
shouted.

Correus heard the shout, and over it the notes of fall-
back-and-regroup. The legate was allowing the Germans
to go, unwilling to break more men on the rocky slide

that ran away downhill into the forest. Correus gathered
his century, moving them back toward the main lines.
Suddenly there was room to breathe as the war band
streamed away. The enemy were foot troops mostly, with
the horsemen giving cover at either side, and their
wounded were borne among them at the center. German
dead lay thick along the valley floor. The legion licked its
own wounds and let them go; time enough to hunt the
living on better ground.

"Ah, Julianus. Still with us, I see."
Correus looked up to see Messala Cominius leaning
a blood-streaked arm on a broken shield. An optio was
trying to bind up with his neck scarf the gash that ran
from wrist to elbow.
Correus inspected himself hesitantly, remembering the
boar hunt when he had been hurt but did not feel it. This
time there were no surprises. "Yes, sir," he said a little
shakily. "But you're wounded. Let me get you back to
Labienus."
"No, no, I'll do well enough," Cominius said, "till—"
He broke off as a gap opened up in the fleeing mass of
Germans on the slope below. "Who's the deaf fool that
did that?" The fall-back-and-regroup had sounded three
times, insistently, but someone had disobeyed, and
charged the retreating war band. Far below them they
could see a broken cohort standard waving at the edge of
the trees with a single bronze century standard beside it,
caught between a knot of some fifteen mounted warriors
and another fifty at their backs. The century had pursued
a group of Germans in vengeance for their dead commander. It should have been an easy one to take—but
they had not allowed for the fact that Nyall of the Semnones rode among that little knot of horsemen, or that
his Companions would turn back for him.
Messala Cominius swore, and his face, under the mud
and sweat, was furious. Now he would have to disobey
orders also, or watch another century slaughtered for no
good reason. He started to lift his shield and yelped. His
arm was useless, and his second-in-command lay dead
somewhere on the valley floor.
"Typhon take their souls, every one!" Cominius gritted

his teeth. "Julianus, take the cohort and go get those fools out of there! Circle around but don't try to fight the whole German army."

Correus nodded and motioned the cohort standard-bearer up beside him. They circled away from the flying tail of the war band, and he hoped to Mithras he could get around through the wreckage of the battlefield and down the far slope in time before the century was cut to pieces.

Cominius, watching them go, hoped so, too. But he knew well enough that his cohort was alone in this. The cavalry and the rest of the right wing were scattered and just beginning to reform, and the remains of the Ninth Cohort were leaderless except for that madman down the slope. So he had sent an untried centurion, still shaking from the effects of his first pitched battle, to haul the fool's ass out of the fire if he could. Cominius didn't even want to think about what the legate was going to have to say about that.

Correus took them over the torn bodies of the dead (later he would be sick, he thought—not now) and down the sloping shelf of rock turned sideways by some ancient upheaval, at as reckless a pace as they could manage. The legate was still perched on his hilltop, and a staff optio was undoubtedly making a beeline between him and Messala Cominius even now, but Correus knew, as Cominius had known, that he would get there too late to call the cohort back. They made the last hundred yards at a stumbling run and threw themselves at the Germans, knocking them back by sheer weight of numbers to let the trapped century draw off. At the back of the press, the smaller group of enemy riders was also caught between the century of the Ninth Cohort and a face of rock that jutted up behind them. The trapped century had locked their shields into a square when the Germans had first encircled them, and if they couldn't move, neither could Nyall and the handful of warriors under the rock face. But now the square was breaking up faster than Correus's men could pull the Germans off their backs.

Correus could hear the clash of swords and the shouted orders of the centurion, but all he could see above the thrashing forms of the horsemen was the silver of the co-

hort standard and the bronze insigne of the century. The
bronze turned in the sun, gleaming and unreadable, but
then as it turned again, he could read it all too clearly.
The sixth century! Flavius's century! It was his brother's
voice that he had heard screaming "Hold them!" above
the chaos. Something ran hot under his skin, and Correus
drove the cohort forward into the plunging horsemen.

"Out! Push out! Break out, damn you!" he shouted to
the faltering men in the square, and they turned with a
last desperate effort as the Eighth Cohort broke the way
open for them.

A mounted warrior came plunging at him, and Correus
swerved away from the deadly hooves as the man beside
him went down screaming under the German's spear.
Correus felt his sword hilt slip from his hand as he fell.
He rolled and came up and caught frantically at the spear
shaft as the warrior leveled it at his breast. It was a
chancy thing, he knew, but his shield wasn't going to
hold under the blow with the weight of horse and rider
behind it, and he was caught tight against his own men
behind him. He slipped his right arm free of his shield,
kicking it under the horse's feet, and swung hard on the
spear shaft with both hands. It caught the warrior in the
eye with the haft end as it came up, and he loosened his
grip for only a second. It was enough. Correus twisted
the spear away and ran the German through the chest
with it as the man came down on top of him.

The horse shrieked and reared, teeth bared and hooves
black in the air above Correus's head. Correus ducked
and caught at the bridle reins, and as the horse came
down he threw himself across its back, the spear still in
his hand. The horse screamed and plunged again, and
Correus hung on with his knees and reached down to pull
its head tight against its shoulder. He couldn't get down
now or the horse would kill him. And he wanted that
horse. He could see above the battle from its back.

It was like fighting a wild thing, with one hand on the
bridle, up close by the enameled ornaments of the bit,
and one hand clutching the spear.

"Look to the commander!" someone shouted, and Correus saw, as the world rocked around him with the stallion's plunging, that the men of his own century were

packed tight about him, as close to the flying hooves as they dared. He quit trying to watch his back and pulled the horse's head hard until it could move only in a circle and then he simply hung on. Slowly, it ceased to fight him, knowing only that the man on its back was not afraid and thus was someone who must be obeyed. Correus, thanking Poseidon Horse-giver for the short memory of the beast, put his heels into its flank and turned it on its own kind, with the men of his cohort attacking behind him.

The German riders were falling back, and now he could see the trapped men of Flavius's century beginning to fight their way out. Behind them, equally desperate, rode Nyall and his men, their horses foam-flecked and running with blood. As Flavius's century began to reform, Nyall rode straight for them with a scream of fury, and Correus saw the front ten soldiers go down under German hooves. Nyall rode at the center, and Correus, breaking clear almost on top of his brother's men, could see his face. It was blood-smeared over the paint, and his knotted hair was coming down in a fall of flame over his shoulders. Except for the paint and a leather loin covering, he was naked. But it was his eyes that Correus saw most clearly. They gleamed like a wolf's eyes at night and the only emotion in them was hate. Nyall drew his spear back from the body of a dead legionary and hurled his roan horse forward again, bringing another man down under its hooves.

"Get him!" Correus screamed. If the legate and Cominius had known that the war leader rode in that knot of horsemen they would have sent the whole legion after him. That was what none of them had bargained for— Nyall himself, yelling like a demon astride the roan horse, and his Companions fighting like furies with a cohort ten times their number instead of fleeing before such odds.

Flavius had known it, from the moment that the Companions had first come riding back against him; known that he had pulled the trap down around his own ears and that if he couldn't kill Nyall, it would be better if he died trying. Splashed with the blood of his own dead men, he was bleeding from wounds in his leg and arm, and weaving on his feet, but he could still see Nyall, red death on a red horse, riding straight for him.

"No!" Correus saw him too, and saw his brother rise from a tangle of armored bodies almost under the red roan's feet, shield dropped low from a wounded arm, and sword raised for a last desperate stroke. Correus kicked the gray forward until it caromed into the roan's shoulder, and he felt Nyall's spear go into his thigh below the leather strips of his harness tunic. He shortened his own spear and then thrust. The roan reared as Nyall jerked back and the spear point punched through the green-and-scarlet shield. Flavius had stumbled to his knees, and as Correus met Nyall's eyes over the broken shield rim, he knew that it was kill Nyall or save his brother and that there was no right choice, and no time to make it. He dropped the reins and swung his right hand down to catch Flavius by the arm.

"Jump!" He pulled him up across the gray's back and spun the horse around as Nyall and the last of his warriors plunged past.

The Companions broke free, and Nyall swept away with them. They flew in a pack down the slope while the cohort and Flavius's weary men watched them go.

"After 'em, sir?" The standard-bearer of the Eighth Cohort kept a respectful distance from the gray horse.

Correus shook his head. "Infantry don't catch horsemen. We did what we came for. Take the cohort back to Cominius, with my compliments." He gave the standard-bearer a tired smile.

Flavius began to slide down from the gray's back.

"You're wounded," Correus said. "Ride."

"No." Flavius dropped to the ground. He was shaking, but his eyes were steady and cold as dark glass. "I'll not ride back in your tender care a second time . . . brother. You should have gone for Nyall, not me." He turned and started up the slope. One of his men respectfully picked up his shield and sword, and another slipped Flavius's arm around his shoulder to ease his wounded leg.

Correus watched his brother walk away, supported between them.

* * *

Flavius's men lied for him and swore to the legate that they had not heard the order to pull back. Flavius denied their tale just as vehemently and took the blame on himself. In the end the legate let him go with little more than a reprimand and a warning to the new commander of the Ninth Cohort to mark him for a hothead and keep his eye on him. With Correus he was somewhat less gentle. Flavius hadn't known what he was doing when he took his century after that little knot of horsemen and thus called down fifty more on his head. Correus had known only too well who it was that he had traded for his brother's life.

"If Centurion Cominius didn't swear he needs you where you are I'd break you back to sixth century for this!" the legate snapped. "As it is, you're off privileges for a month!"

"Yes, sir," Correus said stiffly. A blood-soaked bandage was knotted around his thigh, beneath the healed scar of the old wound.

The legate glared at him. "Is that all you've got to say for yourself?"

"Yes, sir." Nothing else was left, just an empty sickness that was partly Flavius and partly the battle.

"Then why in Mithras's name did you *tell* me that was Nyall you let loose?" the legate exploded.

"I didn't feel I had a choice, sir."

The legate said nothing. It was humid in his tent and he was tired and gritty and wished he could bathe. He glared at Correus again. "This was your first battle, wasn't it?"

"Yes, sir." Again the memory washed over him—dead men, eyes open and staring to the sun.

"All right, you're dismissed."

Correus turned to go.

"Julianus!"

"Yes, sir?"

"Your horse is still tied where you left him. You'd better go water him."

Correus blinked. Antaeus was with Bericus and Nestor and the baggage train, where he had been all day. "The gray, sir? You mean you're *giving* him to me?"

"He has kicked my commander of horse from here to

next Saturnalia, and bitten the cavalry vet," the legate said with acid politeness. "You took him, Julianus; you deal with him."

"I don't get it." Correus sat by the fire and put his head in his hands. It ached, like the rest of him. "Why in Poseidon's name would the legate threaten to break me two centuries and then give me a valuable horse that ought to have gone with the rest of the spoils?"

"Such as they are," Silvanus said, thinking of the broken German bodies they had pulled from the field; poor men mostly, from a poor land. He shook his head and regarded Correus with an expression of elaborate patience. "Because, you thickwit, you are a hero."

"I'm a what?"

"You're a hero. You took command of a cohort when you'd just fought the first battle of your young life, and you saved a whole damn century of fellow citizens. They ought to give you the *corona civica* for it, but they won't."

"I also let Nyall get away."

"And saved another life while you were at it. Your brother's life—and he hardly even likes you! The story's all over camp. We didn't exactly win an unequivocal victory today, and your little stand for glory and the legion has raised morale enough to be worth a whole cohort of reinforcements."

Correus poked at the fire with his vine staff. He'd have to clean it, but he didn't much care.

Silvanus shook his head and his eyes were amused. "You didn't really think that a one-to-one fight with a warrior like Nyall was a sure thing, did you? He'd probably have killed you and got away anyway, with that ring of watchdogs around him. You aren't *that* good, you know."

Correus looked up as the irony sank in. He laughed tiredly. "No, I suppose I'm not."

"I should think not," Silvanus said, "or you *would* have a swelled head. Here, have some wine and quit lashing yourself over it. The legate had to take some notice, but it's not you he's mad at. The only thing that saved Flavius's ass was his owning up to being wrong in disobeying orders to fall back. And that's just because we're short of officers, and his men are too loyal to him to take kindly to a replacement. He's made good *there*, you know."

Correus nodded. "I saw that. They fought well for him."

"Well, it's just as well he's got something to hang on to," Silvanus said brutally, "because the next time it comes to a fight, he's going to be marked for a place at the rear."

Correus was silent, thinking of Flavius's cold eyes as he had turned away from him with his smashed century around him. Why did it have to be Flavius? But he knew why. Flavius had been proving something to himself, or trying to. Something that had to do with Correus, and the boar, and a family name.

"I've lost him," he said finally. "He's gone from me completely now."

"Then let him go," Silvanus said. His voice was unexpectedly gentle. "Your brother is what he is, and I don't suppose he likes it much, either. My friend, if you don't let him go it will tear you both apart."

The dark bond that linked his life to Flavius's seemed to wind around his throat, strangling him. "He's part of me," Correus whispered. "I can't."

Below them in the twilight a black cloud rolled upward from the valley floor. The legion was burning its dead.

They moved out again in three days. The worst wounded, Flavius among them, had been sent back to the hospital at Argentoratum. Correus watched his brother go with relief.

He was grateful that his own wound proved to be minor; he couldn't have faced a month in the hospital with Flavius.

The legate sent for him to interrogate the few Germans they had managed to take alive. He got little enough from the prisoners. They lay shackled together in a guard tent, blank-faced and hopeless, prepared merely to grit their teeth and endure whatever came. One of them even tried to kill Labienus with a knife hidden in his boot when the surgeon came in to see to their wounds.

"Let the bastards bleed, sir," the guard said when he had kicked the German off Labienus and helped the surgeon to his feet.

"I'm a surgeon," Labienus said, panting. "I took an oath to more than the army." The guard shrugged and sat on the prisoner, none too gently, while Labienus dressed his arm.

Correus gave the legate the best estimate of the war band's strength that he had been able to get, and he shook his head when Calpurnius Rufinus pressed him for more details. "I don't think they really know, sir," he said.

The legate wasn't overly surprised. These were merely foot fighters called up by their chiefs. Most had probably never even seen Nyall close up. It was pure chance that the legion had even these, for unless they were hard pressed, the Germans took their wounded and their dead as well. They had even been known to sacrifice a safe retreat to bring their dead away. Nyall was apparently more ruthless—or a better strategist. At any rate, he had learned *one* strategic lesson—he would not meet the legion face to face again in a pitched battle. That meant they were going to have to hunt him down among the hills.

The most severely wounded of the prisoners were executed and the rest sent back under guard to Argentoratum to be sold in the slave market there.

Correus, seeing the bodies of two of the men he had questioned tipped into a common pit with the rest of the German dead, said a brief prayer over them, the only one offered by Rome for the dead of the enemy. Below them in a broken heap he saw a braided knot of gold hair, bloodstained and muddy now, and a face he knew —the boy he had killed himself, the boy who had been a warrior for no more than a year and who had stood beside Nyall and the one-eyed envoy at the meeting with the legate. "Valhalla take them," he whispered, and turned away, saddened.

In their own common grave, the legionary dead had been laid out with the prayers of their comrades and a coin for Charon's passage fee on each eyelid. Pitch had been poured into the trench and brushwood laid on that, and the whole set alight, with the cohort standards and the Eagles of two legions paraded beside them in farewell.

The grave of the German dead lay open to the sun and the wheeling ravens above; and when it was ready, the army pulled back out of sight and waited, hoping that Nyall would try to retrieve his uncovered dead. It was a brutal tactic, but Rome had never forgiven her enemies easily.

Nyall kept clear. The legate never knew (although Correus, remembering the things that Forst had told him, suspected) that Nyall's orders to ignore their dead had very nearly broken the remains of the war band in two.

When it was plain that Nyall would not take the bait, the Romans moved out, leaving the open grave to the ravens and the wolf-folk as a warning. What followed was a mopping-up operation of march and countermarch, night raids and burned villages. Correus stayed with his men, riding the gray war-horse until his leg was healed enough to take a march again. He had given Antaeus into the charge of one of the wagon drivers, for Bericus had gone back to Argentoratum with Flavius. Correus rode the gray simply because no one else could get near him.

The Twenty-second Legion from Moguntiacum caught up with them in camp, and two heavy drafts for the Eighth Augusta and the Vindonissa forces also came in on the second day out. Someone's counsel had finally prevailed in Rome, but Calpurnius Rufinus, who was in overall command of the expedition, noted that the Emperor's trust had not extended to more troops for the Twenty-second, which had played a part in supporting Vitellius's bid for power. Emperor Vespasian deemed it enough of a favor that they had not been cashiered like the rest who had given Vitellius their allegiance.

But the army was up to strength again, and it pushed through the mountains of the Black Forest like an armored beast with three heads, sweeping clean north and eastward to form a new frontier line along the valley of the Nicer River. In their wake they left smoking ruin and the rough-cut beds of new roads to link the Nicer Valley outposts with the old frontier along the Rhenus. What was left of Nyall's war band harried them as they went, striking and retreating through bog and forest, but never willing to waste their strength again in all-out attack on that iron-clad beast.

Calpurnius Rufinus grew daily more irritable under these attacks. With three legions camped along the Nicer, Nyall's attacks were futile, but Rufinus couldn't keep the legions there forever, leaving the rest of the Upper German frontier unguarded. And then on the hottest day of midsummer, the legion caught Nyall almost by accident.

XII

A Traffic in Souls

THE TWENTY-SECOND AND THE VINDONISSA TROOPS WERE hunting to the north and south, and the legate had taken the Eighth Augusta in a predawn attack to break open the last of the German strongholds on the Nicer River, a village on the river bank that the scouts had reported was unusually well-fortified. They broke the timber walls with siege towers, and the Augusta poured in to find the bulk of Nyall's war band massed and readying for a counterattack of their own while the Eighth was still separated from its sister legions.

Nyall had waited too long, bowing to the priests' insistence on a month of sacrifice and prayer for the dead abandoned by him, knowing that his war band would not ride united without it. And the legion's reinforcements had come, fresh troops, tight-wound with a wearisome summer of small wars and no glory. They came through the broken walls in a river of red and bronze, with the weight of a full legion behind them, and caught the war band between its own fortifications and the fast-flowing river.

Correus, back in the line with his men now, took them in behind Messala Cominius, over the outer ditch and past the splintered wreckage of the walls where the siege towers leaned drunkenly and their cargo of archers shot flaming arrows into the roof thatch of German huts. The Germans met them in the gray light, howling behind their shields, but there was no room to charge, and most had not even had time to mount their horses. The legion pushed them back step by step as the flames of the burning hold leaped up around them. Cattle and goats broke free of their pens and ran lowing and terrified between the huts, and the screams of horses could be heard from the burning barn. The Germans fell back and yanked the barn doors open as the roof caved in, scrambling to mount the panic-stricken animals. It was chaos; carnage in the half-light of dawn, gold-tinged by the burning buildings that were made of timber and reeds beneath the plaster. Blood was turned orange by the flames. The women of the hold, most in nightclothes, fought beside their men with daggers or long swords or spears or even kitchen knives. Correus heard with horror the screams of children in the tumult.

When the Germans pulled back, the women and children were hurried through the far gate, or climbed the timber rampart and dropped to the ground below, for a desperate swim across the fast-flowing waters of the Nicer. The warriors had split outside the gate to block the legion from coming around either side of the walls and to keep them from the fugitives in the river. Now, with the last of their people out, they jammed the gate closed, too.

The Eighth Cohort was well inside the hold, and Correus was in the charge that threw itself at the gate. They hit it like a ram, but the opening was narrow and a small force could hold a large one from it for some time.

"Damn!" Messala Cominius pulled himself up on the rampart to look over, then dropped back as a spear sang past his ear. "We've got to break out. Half the German war band is in that lot that's heading for the river!"

The rearguard wings to either side of the holding and

the blockade at the gate would remain steadfast until they died, and if they didn't die soon enough, the rest would escape. The far wall was blazing at the end where a burning cow byre had fallen against it, but it would never burn down in time for the Romans to attack through it. Correus looked where the charred cow byre lay against the timber wall, and something prodded insistently at the back of his mind. Something Forst had said . . . "The horned ones are the creatures of the Goddess. That is why when the dead go back to her, they go by the Horned Gate." The narrow door set in the hold wall beside the cow byre . . . not for living cattle but for dead men, carried past the creatures of the Goddess so that their souls might be known to her.

"Come on!" Correus signaled to Cominius and they raced through the smoking rubble to the byre. A pair of cow's horns was set into the timber at head height, and beneath it, through the smoke, they could just see the outlines of a narrow door. Correus pushed through the smoke, choking, and knocked the latch pin loose. The flames were eating close to it and the wood was hot to the touch, but he put his shield edge against it and pushed. The door swung open. It was narrow, no more than the width of a bier, and the soldiers formed up single file and ran through the spreading flames and thick smoke with their scarves over their faces. They had nearly the whole cohort through, coughing and slapping at sparks that fell from the flaming wall, before the warriors at the main gate saw what was happening and pulled back to face them.

The cohort met them, choking, soot black, and half blinded from the smoke, but standing solid with shields up. All but the last century was through before the wall caved in with a roar of flame that no one could have crossed.

"Hold them!" Cominius shouted. "That's all we have to do, lads—just hold them!"

As the Germans pulled back from the gate and from the right-hand wing outside the walls, the legionaries who had been hammering at them surged through and caught the fleeing war band on the river bank. They tore them to pieces while the Eighth Cohort struggled in the smoke and flames with the warriors who had tried to buy the band's escape with their lives.

In a few minutes it was over, and there was nothing between the blazing hold and the river but the bodies of Germans, smeared with blood in place of the battle marks they had not had time to paint.

Correus and Cominius stumbled with their singed cohort to the river. They knelt on the bank, pouring clear cold water over blistered skin, while fresher troops from the rear roved through the hold like hounds to hunt down survivors.

There were few enough. Most who couldn't flee had burned. A few women who hadn't made it out the gate had killed themselves, and more had drowned in the cold, fast waters of the river. A number of warriors, stronger swimmers, had made it across in the confusion of the final fighting, including some of the rear guard. The legate had no wish to drown his own men in pursuit, and it would take a full day to get a bridge across, by which time the Germans would have disappeared in ones and twos in the hills to the east. The war band was broken, Rufinus thought—let the stragglers go. It wasn't until they put out the flames and cleared the burned fort that he discovered to his utter fury that Nyall was not among the dead. A few bodies were burned beyond recognition, but none was of the right build. It might be that they would pull his drowned body from the bank downriver, but it was infinitely more likely that he was gone away into the eastern hills with the crippled remnants of his army.

It was in no very good mood that the legate went to deal with the survivors.

Correus was crouched on a stool in the field-hospital tent, talking to a gray-haired German with a scarred and pockmarked face. His only garment was a pair of woolen trousers, filthy with mud and ashes, but he wore a gold collar around his neck and the thongs in his braids had once been fine scarlet-dyed leather. He had been found pinned beneath a fallen roof beam. Labienus had cut the trousers away and was wrapping a wet bandage around the burned leg.

"His name is Jorunn," Correus said when the legate came up. Rufinus's face was soot-streaked and his gilded breastplate was covered with wet ash. "It was his holding we burned, and he's not overly talkative, but from what I can pry out of him, they were planning to stage a major raid on the legion soon. Most of the war band was in the hold when we hit it."

The legate nodded. "How many got away?"

Correus repeated the question in German, and Jorunn spat out an answer. "Not enough to trouble the commander of the Eagles on his frontier. Or enough to rebuild my hold."

The legate gave him a hard look, his eyes flinty in the soot. "That would not be permitted, anyway. Your hold is gone, Jorunn, and your people with it, and if you do not like it, you should have thought of that before you allied with the Semnones."

Jorunn spat at him and slapped Labienus's hand away from his burned leg, but the surgeon merely shrugged. He was finished, anyway. Labienus gestured to Correus to hold out his hands and began winding bandages around them.

The legate wiped the spittle from his face with the back of his hand. "That could get you crucified, but I'm thinking you'll like the mines even less. It lasts longer." He nodded to the optio beside him. "Send him to Argentoratum when he can travel."

He was about to move on to the next man when there was a scuffling at the tent flap, and two legionaries struggled through, dragging a woman between them. A tribune named Crassus followed, looking amused, and saluted the legate while the woman kicked and bit at her guards. One of them cuffed her hard across the face and she subsided.

"They found her in the main hall, sir," Crassus said. "She got caught when the roof came down. She tried to burn herself first, and she had a sword. She cut two men before they took it away from her. I thought we should hang on to her. She looks like she'll clean up nicely."

Correus looked curiously at the girl. Her face and arms were filthy, and her gown, which might once have been green, was tattered and blood-soaked. The gold hair that fell past her waist was burned off on one side almost to her ears, and he saw that her gown was burned as well on that side. As the tribune had said, she would be beautiful when she was clean, but what caught at him were her eyes—trapped eyes, like a hunted cat's, under the singed lashes.

Messala Cominius came in just then to have his own burned hands salved, and he also gave the girl an appraising look. The legate studied her, noting the curve of her body under the ruined gown, mentally wiping away the blood and dirt. He nodded.

"Yes. She ought to be worth a fair amount once someone's knocked some manners into her. Labienus, what about those burns?"

The surgeon studied her. The girl was still now, rock still, only the green eyes moving from one face to the other. "They seem to be superficial, sir. They should heal with no mark if they're taken care of."

"Then do so. And put a guard on her to make sure she doesn't try to ruin herself. Or knife you with a scalpel. We'll ship her to Argentoratum when she's healed."

The tribune coughed. "Uh, sir . . . I was thinking. Rather than go to the trouble of sending her to Argentoratum, I'd, uh . . . like to have her. I'll pay a fair price to the spoils chest, of course. Rome price," he added, "more than we could get at Argentoratum."

"No!" Correus was on his feet without thinking. "No, let me have her. I'll—I'll match the tribune's price," he added recklessly. He gave the tribune an urgent look. "You don't really want a woman you can't even speak to, do you?"

"I wasn't planning on discussing philosophy with her," Crassus said. "Now see here—"

Messala Cominius saw that Correus's face was pale and there was something in his eyes that matched the hunted-cat look in the girl's. "Just a moment, sir," he said to the legate. "If it wasn't for Centurion Julianus we wouldn't have got through that back wall in time. I was going to recommend him for some sort of reward. Why not let him have the girl?"

"I have already given Centurion Julianus a valuable horse," the legate said, and Correus thought there was a faint note of sarcasm in his voice. The gray war-horse had kicked the rear wheel off a baggage wagon that morning.

"I would be glad to give the tribune the horse in compensation," Correus said.

The legate chuckled and the tribune's mouth set in a stubborn line. He was tired of the woman he had now, and he outranked this centurion. He outranked Messala Cominius too, if it came to that. "I fancy you'll find my claim the better one, sir," he said loftily, and adjusted the purple sash of office that was knotted neatly around his immaculate breastplate. He had not taken an active part in the fighting.

Perhaps it was that which decided the legate—Calpurnius Rufinus was a career officer himself. "There are other women," he said to the tribune. "You may have your pick of any we have taken—since you're willing to pay Rome price—but I'm going to let Centurion Julianus have this one. Also at Rome price," he added, "since the purchase is disputed."

Correus calculated quickly. It would take all his pay and most of his father's allowance to meet the price, but there wasn't much else to spend it on out there. And the girl wouldn't go to this lofty, bored-looking young tribune, who would sell her off to the men as soon as she, too, began to bore him.

The girl had stood silently between her captors (one of whom had a scratched face and a swollen eye) understanding not a word, but when Correus nodded to them to bring her up to have her burns treated she began to struggle wildly again.

Jorunn lay staring at the ceiling, unmoving. The girl had been one of his wife's waiting women, but his wife was dead, and his son with her, and he didn't care anymore.

"Be still!" Correus snapped at her in German, and she flung her head back and stared at him while the guards twisted both arms behind her. His mother might have looked like that when she was first captured, he thought, and knew suddenly why he had bought her.

"Look you," he said softly, "you belong to me now. I have bought you. Do you understand that?"

She nodded, and her eyes went cold, like a tide pool.

"I won't sell you again, and I won't hurt you. Now will you be still and let the surgeon treat your burns?"

She nodded stiffly at that, then pulled her arms free from the guards and sat on a stool while Labienus eased the burned gown away from her breast and smeared salve on the reddened skin. She knew that the men were watching her, but she never flinched.

Correus wished she didn't have to endure that under the hungry gaze of a room full of men. He turned his back and moved away to the next prisoner, and the legate followed him. Cominius said something to the tribune and he stalked out with Cominius behind him.

When they had finished, Rufinus surveyed the collection of burned and wounded legionaries awaiting treatment. They were watching the girl avidly. "Get her out of here before she starts a riot," the legate said. "And watch yourself." Correus thought he looked amused. "Maybe I should have let that tribune have her. She might have got rid of him for me."

The girl was still huddled on her bench. Correus beckoned to her and she followed him, seemingly resigned now. She still hadn't spoken.

He took her across the camp to the baggage wagons, where a stout woman with hennaed hair, named Rhodope, kept a firm rule over the five cowed whores in her charge. Labienus also had a woman, a round matronly female with a bit of a squint who bullied him like a nurse and kept his tent clean, but Correus thought that Rhodope was better equipped to deal with a woman who had wounded two legionaries with a sword. She also spoke some German.

Rhodope was sitting in front of her tent in the padded armchair that she dragged everywhere with her, crimping an Ethiopian girl's dark hair into stiff waves with a hot iron. She looked up at Correus and smiled. A gold front tooth gave her a barbaric splendor, and her orange hair was startling against an olive complexion. Her voluminous gown of scarlet was trimmed around the bedraggled hem with bright green embroidery. "Correus! Come and sit down and talk to me. I'm tired of these stupid girls." Correus patronized her establishment only infrequently, but he treated the girls well and Rhodope was fond of him.

"Charis, bring the centurion a chair!" she called into the tent.

"No, no," he said. "I have to get back to duty. I came to ask a favor of you."

"Oh?" Rhodope put a last crimp in the girl's hair and the iron smoked with the scent of old hair oil. Rhodope thrust the iron back in the pot of hot coals at her feet and prodded the girl with the toe of her blue sandals. "All right, Leza, go and help Charis with the cleaning. We'll be having callers tonight and they won't pay money to bed down in a pigsty." The Ethiopian girl departed with a pouting look—they had cleaned the tent only last week—and Rhodope settled herself in her chair. "Now, Correus, what is this favor you wish?" She gave the German girl an appraising look.

"This is—" He turned to the girl. "What's your name?" he asked in German.

She stared back at him, holding her torn green gown around her. She was tall—she could look him in the eye. "Freita."

"This is Freita. She comes from the holding we burned out this morning, and she's mine now."

Rhodope looked amused. "It seems I have lost a customer. It also seems to me that I remember you telling me a tale once that you would not own a slave."

"Well, I do now," Correus said. "Shut up, Rhodope, and listen to me."

Rhodope leaned forward with her elbows on her knees. "Very well, I make myself attentive." Her brown eyes were bright and curious.

"I want you to look after her for me until I can make some arrangements. Get her clean and find her something to wear, and keep an eye on her—she may do something stupid."

Rhodope studied the girl. "Probably. She is a fighter, that one."

"And keep her away from your customers," Correus added.

"Of course. And what were you planning to pay me to care for a she-cat who may stick a knife in me?"

They haggled mildly over the price until Rhodope nodded her orange head in agreement. Correus turned to the girl. "You will stay with this woman," he said. "Her name is Rhodope and she will look after you, and you will have some women for company. But you belong to me, not her. You won't have to, uh . . ."

"I can tell what she is," Freita spat at him. "I am not stupid."

"No, I expect you're not." Correus was beginning to feel a little harassed. His distress at the thought of the girl going to that bored-faced tribune was fading before the problem of what he was going to do with her now. He didn't want a mistress—Rhodope's Charis had been a much less complicated solution when his physical urges grew out of bounds. "Yes—well, you only have to live with her, not take up her trade," he said. "I will come back as soon as I can and we will talk." The girl looked as if she'd see him in Hell first.

Rhodope heaved herself up out of her chair. "Come along, child," she said in rough German. "The world will look less black when you have washed and had something to eat."

Correus left her to Rhodope. Any "Venus" stalwart enough to follow an army on campaign could undoubtedly handle one German girl, and Rhodope was legendary. He returned to his century with the pleasant task of informing them that the cohort had earned a commendation from the legate and that there would be a ration of good wine that night and a bonus later when the spoils had been turned to cash.

The camp was in a festival mood. Their losses in the last engagement were few and there was the promise of largesse to come. Nyall had escaped with no more than a fifth of his original war band, counting those who had not been in Jorunnshold when it was attacked, and these latter were now leaderless and lying low if they had any sense. The frontier would stay quiet while the Roman army dug in along the Nicer. The whole of the Black Forest, more than a third of the Agri Decumates, was now in Roman hands, and the new string of forts along the Nicer would make a base from which to bring the rest under control. There were few Germans left to fight for it.

Correus proudly paraded his men before the standards at the evening prayers. He had lost only two men out of a full complement of eighty (brought up to strength by the new drafts from the Emperor), and one of those was in the hospital with a wound that would heal cleanly. The other lay among the dead, and Correus called out his name in the Prayer for the Slain that followed the worship at the Altar of the Standards.

When they were dismissed, Silvanus came hunting him. He had a cloth tied around a cut in his temple, which gave him a rakish look, and there was a light in his eye. His helmet dangled by its strap from one hand.

"Damn thing rubs right on it," he said. "I've got to figure out some way to pad it. The supply train caught up with us just now, and the post was with it. My sister wants me to send her a blond wig from Germany, my mother wants to know if I'm drinking too much, and my father has sent me my allowance, may the gods bless him. Here—this one's yours." He handed Correus a folded sheet of papyrus with a little blue seal.

Correus looked at the handwriting, a round childish scrawl with fancy flourishes. Aemelia. He was going to have to make her stop that, but he couldn't figure out how to write and tell her so without getting caught by Aemelius. Maybe he could write to Julia. Typhon! What a mess!

"You look like a bear that waked up in midwinter," Silvanus said. "What's wrong?"

Correus explained. He probably shouldn't have—Flavius wouldn't like it—but he was feeling beset. He wanted a listening ear that wouldn't blame him for the whole tangle concerning Aemelia.

Silvanus whistled. "No wonder Flavius is so broody."

"I'm not sure Flavius actually knows why the silly girl won't have him," Correus said hopefully.

Silvanus snorted. "Oh, he knows. I'd bet a month's pay he knows. You aren't actually thinking of marrying that girl, are you?"

Correus gave him a harassed look. "Of course I'm not, you fool. What my father would have to say about it aside, she's no more fit to follow the army than a week-old kitten. I could hardly steal Flavius's bride and then leave her with his mother. I'd marry her if I were Flavius, though, and I made the mistake of telling her that when she asked point-blank. Now I'm in trouble."

Silvanus looked thoughtful. "She must be awfully young."

"She is," Correus said shortly.

"Pity. If she'd marry Flavius it might go a long way to patching things up between you two. Well, there's not a lot you can do about it here. Flavius will simply have to shower her with exotic gifts when he gets his leave."

Correus laughed. "A blond wig?"

"Don't remind me. Where am I going to get a blond wig in the middle of a marching camp?"

"What does your sister want with a blond wig, any-way?" Correus asked, looking at Silvanus's barley-colored locks.

"Oh, she's furious because I got the blond hair. Hers is mouse-color. Women! I tell you what, let's go see if the Egyptian's rolled in yet. You need a drink."

Correus shook his head. "I can't. I've got another woman problem to cope with." He told Silvanus about Freita. "I've left her with Rhodope, but I've got to get her a tent from somewhere, and make arrangements about food and I don't know what all. Silvanus, how do I get into these things?"

"I know why you bought that girl," Silvanus said seriously. "Your birth comes back to haunt you, and it always will, so you might as well get used to it."

"Right," Correus said sarcastically. "I won't own a slave because I was born one. So now I buy one, and she's a woman to boot!"

"Well, in this case I'd have bought her myself," Silvanus said. "I know Tribune Crassus, and I wouldn't sell him a dog. You can always let her go."

"No, I can't. She stood and fought with a sword, and I think she's been trained to it. That makes her an enemy soldier in our book, so I can't send her to Nyall even if I knew where he was. And if I send her back to what's left of her tribe, she'll just be rounded up with the rest and sold again."

"Well, find the woman a tent and then come over to the Egyptian's," Silvanus said. "You're going to be needing some Falernian." He tucked his vine staff under his arm and sauntered off, swinging his helmet with the air of a man whose life held no problems more complicated than getting a blond wig.

Correus gave him an exasperated glance (although he really didn't know what Silvanus could have done to help) and set out to haggle with the quartermaster for the purchase of a tent, sub rosa.

It was full dark by the time he presented himself at Rhodope's establishment, and she was doing a lively business. Rhodope's tent was almost as spectacular as the madam herself—a gaudy affair of red and lavender stripes with rugs on the floor and a clutter of small tables supporting incense burners and bronze figures in inspiring poses. The beaded curtains over the draperies that divided the rear of the tent into private cubicles gave it an air of Eastern splendor. It was all very portable. Rhodope could pack statues, girls, and curtains into her brightly painted wagon in less than an hour, to be set up aagin at the next camp. Correus asked her once why she didn't keep a permanent establishment at Augusta Treverorum or one of the other big towns, rather than trooping after a legion in dangerous country. Rhodope had laughed and told him the difference between the prices she could command in a town where her house was one of many and the competition was keen, and the take in a frontier zone where she generally had the field to herself. It added up to a healthy retirement.

"You'll find your girl in there," she said now, pointing to one of the curtained cubicles. "Martia's sick and out of business for a few days, so I've put her in the wagon and given your wench her place."

Correus threaded his way through the crowd of soldiers who were waiting their turn or haggling about the price or merely lounging about and getting in the way. Rhodope was clucking over a wine stain on one of her rugs, and Charis was playing something inexpertly on a cithara. The transparent draperies of her gown more than made up for her lack of musical talent, and she gave Correus a hopeful smile as he passed. He pushed back the blue glass beads and the curtain behind them, and found Freita sitting on a cot bed in a blue-and-yellow gown that he remembered as being one of Martia's. It was too tight across the chest and too big in the hips, and she looked miserable and uncomfortable. A plate of food and a pottery goblet stood untouched on the floor.

"Hello," Correus said, and she looked up at him stonily. "I've found you a tent of your own. We'll set it up tomorrow. And we'll get you some clothes that fit," he said with a smile. He sat on the bed beside her. "You haven't eaten."

"I am not hungry." Her sea-grass eyes looked at him indifferently.

She *was* beautiful, he thought. Her skin was a pale milk color except where the burns showed red on her throat and cheek. They looked well enough under Labienus's salve, hardly blistered at all. Rhodope had cut her singed hair into layers, so that it fell in little waves on that side. But her face was blank, lifeless. She looked like someone had put a blue-and-yellow dress on a temple statue.

Correus sighed. "If you don't eat, you will get sick," he said patiently. "I don't want to have to feed you."

The green eyes flashed, and just for an instant her face came alive. That should have warned him. She reached down for the plate and came up with a knife instead.

Correus struggled with her as the blade ripped into his tunic under the edge of his lorica. He flung himself back on the bed and grabbed at her wrist, turning the knife so that the blade scraped painfully along his skin. His howl of indignation sent Rhodope running in as he smacked the girl across the face with his free hand and twisted her wrist hard. The knife thudded on the rug just as Rhodope jerked the curtains open. Correus kicked it across the floor at her. Outside a curious crowd of faces peered through the open doorway.

"How in Hades did you let her get a knife?" he shouted furiously. The scrape on his belly hurt like fire, and he jerked the girl's arm around behind her roughly.

Rhodope picked up the knife. "It's Martia's. She keeps it under the bed for . . . emergencies. All my girls do. But I told the stupid thing to take it with her."

"All right, get out." He pulled the girl around and sat her down on the bed. "I ought to beat you within an inch off your life!" he said. He was boiling mad, and he took a deep breath, remembering the trapped-cat look he had seen earlier. There was no point in shouting at a hunted thing. "Now look," he said more calmly, "where did you think you were going to go if you killed me in the middle of a Roman camp? Assuming you could even get out of this tent alive, which I doubt."

She was breathing hard, but her face was blank and closed again.

"You told me you weren't stupid," he said. She had relaxed and he let go of her arm. She sat in silence, rubbing the red mark on her wrist. "You'll like belonging to me a lot more than you'll like what will happen to you if you kill a Roman officer," he said bluntly. "Slaves who kill their masters aren't just executed, you know. There are . . . other things that happen first. I ought to know. I was born a slave."

Her eyes flew up at that, startled.

"Now if you will give me your oath to behave and obey me, you will have a place of your own and as much comfort as I can provide in a marching camp. If you don't, I will tie you up and you will stay that way until you do. Make up your mind."

The girl closed her eyes for a moment, apparently thinking. "I will swear," she said when she opened them. Her voice was tired and resigned.

In his own tent Correus stripped off his lorica and tunic to see how much damage the little demon had done. He didn't feel like making explanations to Labienus, so he cleaned the scrape himself with wine, gritting his teeth. He hoped Martia's knife had been clean.

As he picked up his tunic again, Aemelia's letter fell from its folds. He'd forgotten about that. He sighed and sat down at the camp desk to read it.

My dearest Correus,
I am sending this to the post with my page Hyacinthus. He is very loyal to me . . .

I'll bet he is, Correus thought, remembering how the wine steward's boy had fallen over himself staring at Aemelia during Appius's dinner party.

. . . and never gossips. I know that you can't answer because Papa sees everything that comes to me here, so I shall take my comfort by writing to you as often as I can.

Oh, wonderful.

Papa hasn't weakened so far, but I know that your father would if mine did, and your mother has been so very kind. I spoke to her the last time I visited Julia, and she was so much in sympathy. She must have had a very hard life, and she said that marrying a man you cannot love is only another form of slavery. I think all the time about the morning when you kissed me in the rose garden, and I wish that I could be with you now. I hope that you are well and not wounded— I couldn't bear to think of you hurt. I must give this to Hyacinthus now, because Papa will be home soon and then Mama will be looking for him to carry their chairs into the garden.

                              Your devoted Aemelia

Correus crumpled up the letter and flung it across the tent. Damn his mother! And damn Aemelia. He damned Freita as well when he stood up and scraped the cut she'd given him on the edge of the desk.

The next morning his troops were surly with the after-effects of the wine ration and disinclined to work. The legion was beginning construction of a permanent fort on the site of the destroyed Jorunnshold, but first the mess had to be cleared. It was hot work in the muggy summer weather; dirt and ashes stuck to the skin and itched. At the end of the day Correus went with his sweating crew to wash off the grime in the river and then, still in no pleasant mood, set out to put up Freita's tent.

He picked a spot by the baggage wagons where the other officers' slaves were quartered, next to the tent of Verus, Silvanus's sturdy body servant. From his rapidly dwindling purse he gave the man a coin to look after her and make it plain to any man with ideas that she was an officer's woman. Once that was known, she wouldn't be touched. Until then, in the chaotic aftermath of a battle, he wasn't so sure. The manners of the army were never improved by a long campaign.

Verus helped him wrestle the tent into place, and Silvanus appeared and told him, laughing, that as long as he had bought one slave, he might as well break down and buy another—male—and then he wouldn't have to put up tents.

Correus, half buried under the tent's leather folds while he struggled with a pole, made a rude gesture and his friend departed unchastened. When Correus had finished, he brought the gray horse around and tethered him nearby, knee-deep in the meadow grass. The horse snorted and nuzzled at his tunic for the honeycake which Correus occasionally filched from the mess for him.

"Well, you find me tolerable, anyway," he said, rubbing its nose. "It's a pity you couldn't be so fine-mannered with the cavalry commander." It was at that officer's request that he had removed the gray from the cavalry pasture. Correus had been casting about for a name for the beast since he had acquired him and had finally settled on Aeshma, the demon, as appropriate enough. He gave the animal a piece of cake.

Freita was not so friendly when he fetched her from Rhodope's tent, but she didn't try to knife him again. She followed him docilely to the tent and folded her few possessions into a small chest. He had found her a comb and a mirror and two gowns, bought from a sulking Charis, who was more her size than Martia. A rug from his own tent was spread on the dirt floor and there was a bed of straw with a good blanket on top. She looked around her in silence, her body slumped and resigned, her face devoid of all animation. It was that stoic withdrawal that made Correus first exasperated and then angry.

He made her sit down on the rug and began to teach her a few words of Latin; enough to get by on with Verus, and to get a point of Correus's own across: "I belong to Centurion Julianus."

He thought she was going to protest at that, but she repeated the words after him, and the flash of anger in her eyes faded almost as soon as it sparked up. He knew the anger was still there, but it was a brooding thing, a black hate inside, somehow all the worse for being unspoken. Outside she was a statue in a pool of twilight; pale and cold and unreachable. And beautiful. Very beautiful.

The only time she had shown the slightest life since he had saved her from the untender hands of Tribune Crassus was when she had tried to kill him, he thought angrily. He wanted to shake some life into her, anything to make those cold green eyes take notice of him. The letter from Aemelia and the memory of her warm body against his among the roses were stirring in his blood unbidden. The knife score on his belly still hurt, and there was a debt to pay for that, too. He felt his anger rising. He reached out roughly and tore loose the ties at the shoulders of her gown.

She never flinched. She rose, her white face moving up out of the twilight into shadow, and tugged the gown down over her breasts herself. She let it fall to the floor and stood, her body dappled with the shadows, watching him. She had expected no more. Why else would the Roman have bought her?

That wasn't why he had bought her, but Correus, with that cold, white beauty and his own anger singing in his blood together, didn't care anymore. He pushed her down onto the bed under him.

She made no sound, her mind moving somewhere in the dark night outside, while his hands wandered over her body not caring now whether he woke anything in her or not. The scent of her hair was as heady as the summer grass, and the feel of her breasts in his hands, and her hips under his own, washed away everything— everything but a longing that not even red-haired Emer had ever stirred in him. He wanted her. He had wanted

her when he first saw her smeared with blood and ashes,
and he knew it now. It was like making love to a statue,
but he took her anyway, the blood pounding in his head
so hard that he never heard her cry out as he entered
her. It was the only sound she made.

Desire crashed around Correus like waves, and when
it ebbed at last and he lay spent on top of her, he was
soaked with sweat. He lifted his head to look at her before he pulled away, and as he did so, he felt a shudder
go through her like an earthquake. He had done . . .
something wrong . . . something he should have known
about . . . but his mind was clouded, drunken. He turned
over on his side and slept, feeling sad for whatever it was.

In the morning things were all too clear—a vicious
clarity like a jagged edge of broken glass. Freita was
asleep beside him, the exhausted sleep of someone
pushed past endurance, her golden hair tangled with
straw. Correus looked at her despairingly. He had bought
her to save her from this, because *he* once had been a
slave. And then he had thrown her slavery in her face
and taken her himself, perhaps as brutally as Crassus
would have done; not even stopping to ask if she were
virgin. And she had been. When he pulled the blanket
back he saw her thighs were streaked with dried blood.

He dressed without waking her, and left, ashamed of
himself.

XIII

The Road Home

IT WAS TWO DAYS BEFORE CORREUS COULD BRING HIM-
self to go back, and then he went only because he hadn't
left Verus enough money to feed Freita any longer, and
Aeshma had to be moved to fresh grass.

He left his men at their noon meal amid the new ditch

and rampart that were rising on the burned hold, and made his way reluctantly up the grassy rise to the marching camp. The grass was worn and trampled between the new camp and the old, but around it the river valley was green in the sunlight. And just as well, because Aeshma needed it. Correus couldn't afford to keep Freita and stable an extra horse just now, not after the price the legate had demanded. Antaeus, as an officer's mount, was quartered with the cavalry horses, but centurions were only allowed one each on the army's denarius.

Correus picked his way through the hodgepodge between the camp and the outer ditch. He never ceased to be amazed at the number of hangers-on that an army on the march attracted. Every so often, when the legate felt that things were getting out of hand, he would order them out of camp, and they would disappear for a few days. Then, slowly, they would trickle back in again. But mostly the commanders ignored them, as long as they didn't get in the way. It helped keep their troops from running riot among the locals. Now that the Nicer River line was secured, the camp followers would arrive in droves, and a ragtag village, a "vicus," would grow up beside each new fort almost as fast as the fort itself. On a frontier with closely spaced outposts, the vicus behind it was an almost continuous narrow settlement of tradesmen, artisans, and merchants running the length of the frontier road. In the interior of a province the vicus might grow large enough to obtain colonial status, forming the nucleus of a new city when the army moved on. Veterans might be settled there as well, another step in the Romanization of new lands.

At the moment, however, the Eighth Legion's followers were a motley herd of whores and peddlers, and the encampment behind the baggage wagons was a jumble of carts and ragged tents, an instant slum beside the orderly barracks rows of the legionary camp. Between it and the camp were the tents of the legion's servants, privately owned slaves with their masters' horses and hunting dogs. The army servants looked down on the camp followers, patronizing their establishments as their masters did but otherwise keeping themselves snootily aloof, even when the army was under attack and they were forced to huddle with them in the center of the camp proper.

Correus had tethered Aeshma in the grassy stretch that divided the two areas, with few worries that the foot traffic would trample his feed. Passersby gave the gray stallion a wide berth. Now, Correus was much surprised to find that the horse had already been moved from the grazed-over ground to a fresh stretch of grass. Aeshma was cropping contentedly, and beside him stood a slim figure with a fall of gold hair.

Freita looked up as he approached and gave the gray shoulder a pat. Aeshma's hide shone like a sword blade in the sun and Correus saw that she had been brushing him.

"Are you out of your mind?" he snapped, and then changed to German as she looked at him uncomprehendingly. "That horse has nearly killed three people!"

"As you can see, he has not killed me," Freita said practically. "He is a war-horse of my own people, isn't he? I used to train them."

Correus stared.

"It was not thought proper for a woman," she explained, "but the horses like me, and the priest said I had the horse magic, so it was allowed."

Aeshma whickered when he saw him, and Correus rubbed the horse's nose absently. "You must have had more than magic to get near this one. He almost killed *me* at first."

Freita shrugged. "I spoke German to him. And also I am not afraid of him. It was . . . something to do." She put a hand on the horse's mane as if she would cling to him.

The horse was her last link with her own people, Correus thought. "I'm not going to take him away from you," he said more gently, and the girl relaxed. "Since he likes you, you can exercise him for me. I don't have enough time to keep two horses ridden." She could have ridden the gray stallion out of the camp and been gone by now, if she were going to.

Freita's eyes lit up at that. "Truly? If you will let me, I will take him and cut grass for him. This is almost gone."

She was still guarded, but the horse had opened up something in her that he could not. She seemed to bear him no grudge for his treatment of her, but watched him with a stiff resignation when he came near. It must have been no more than she had expected, he thought unhappily.

"Come. He will do well enough for now." He walked back to the tent with her, keeping a careful distance. "You will need money for food and such, and I have brought that."

"Do you trust me?" She gave him a sideways look.

"You gave me your oath. Would you break it?"

"No. I *cannot*," she added. An oath was magic. A broken one followed the breaker like a curse.

"Then I trust you." He wouldn't have trusted a Roman's oath, but a Roman didn't regard his word in such a serious light.

They ducked in under the tent flap and she looked at him warily. He stood on the rug as far away from the bed as he could get. "I only have a few moments," he said. "I have to get back to my men."

The girl seemed to relax again at that, and Correus thought wistfully that when she came out of hiding her face had a fierce, alive sort of beauty that filled the tent, even more compelling than the statue in the shadows had been, and more unreachable; an elf-gold that faded as you touched it.

"Is there . . . anything else that you need?" he asked.

Freita hesitated. "Earrings," she said after a moment.

Correus looked surprised.

"I . . . the holes, you see," she tried to explain. "They close up again if you do not keep earrings in them, and I was not wearing mine when . . . when—"

Correus winced. *When her world fell down around her.* "Yes, I do see, and you shall have them." He thought that she was embarrassed to ask, as if he might think she had given up and would use that bright beauty now to wheedle favors. Or that he might demand favors himself in exchange. A bugle call drifted up from the river. "I must go now," he said, before his instincts could prove her right.

The girl stood at the tent flap to watch him go, a long-legged figure in an iron helmet, and plated like a tortoise with the iron rings of his lorica. He was left-handed. That might be evil; she wasn't sure. Everything about him, from his dark eyes and short-cropped hair to his bare legs, was alien. But of all the people in this place, he was the only one who could understand her speech. That made him the center of her life. Without him she was deaf and mute— abandoned. She turned to look out over the river valley, and the woods and wild berry stands beyond. Familiar lands, but different now, unwelcoming, as if she belonged to them no more. Her own world was gone from her as quickly as a sword point under her chin and a hard hand on her wrist. She had never felt so alone, even when she had thought she was going to die in Jorunn's burning hold.

Freita lay down on the bed and willed herself to sleep.

A hundred riders, and half again as many men on foot, paused on a rise of land, looking backward to where the Moenus lay in a blue loop behind them. A Roman patrol had been on their heels for five days, and their horses were nearly done. The mounts stood with heads low, flanks heaving, and tails matted with thorns and burrs.

"There's no sign of them," Geir said.

Ranvig nodded. "I am thinking they turned back when we crossed the river." His eyes were sunken and his blond braids were almost as matted as his horse's tail. They had neither washed nor eaten a full meal since the battle at Jorunn's holding, sleeping only when they had to, and then only the half of them, while the rest stood guard.

Nyall passed his hand across a five-day growth of beard that itched in the heat. He narrowed his eyes, still looking backward across the river. "No," he said. "They will not come farther." He smiled grimly, a bone-weary smile with little humor in it. "We are not worth the chasing just now."

A rider behind him muttered something, and Ranvig spun his horse around with a snarl, his crooked teeth bared like a dog's. "It was you, Ingald, who urged the priests on to keep us chained in Jorunnshold for a Dead-Sacrifice, because you thought it would give trouble and turn the war band to your own hand! Keep your viper's tongue between your teeth or I'll cut it out!"

Ingald slapped his hand to his knife, and Nyall pulled his own mount around.

"Stop it! Do we ride on, or shall we all go and fight a blood feud on the riverbank until Rome catches up to us?" They backed away from each other reluctantly. "Ranvig, go and tell the others that we will ride another half-day, until we have some cover. And Ingald, I know well whose voice it was that whispered in the priest-kind's ear, and I am not needing Ranvig to fight my battles for me. Best that you remember that."

Nyall turned his horse away to the head of the little band. So many dead, he thought. So many gone to keep those other dead company. *Lyting,* he thought, clenching his hands on the saddle. Lyting, whom he had refused to order home. And now Arngunn . . . Arngunn, who had wavered one time too many and at last listened to the priests. Gudrun, dead beside him, and small, freckled Saeunn drowned in the river. Of the allied chiefs, Egil and Sigvat were gone, and Jorunn, too, he thought. Also, the chief of the Hermanduri had been killed in the first battle, and his people had gone back to Rome afterward.

So few left . . .

Fiorgyn rode at the head of the band with a handful of women and children, and that was a bright spot in his heart. Mord was there also, tied to his horse because he was unconscious. He was badly wounded and they didn't think he would live. There was no priest to tell them for sure.

There might be more in flight. He didn't know. They had split when they crossed the river, to give the Romans more roads to chase down. They would be taking their own trails, with the Semnones among them for guides, riding for Nyallshold. There was nowhere else to go.

And Kari . . . What road had he taken? Before the Roman attack Nyall had sent him with four of the allied chiefs and their warriors to make a diversion that would keep the soldiers from Moguntiacum busy to the north. Had Kari seen the smoke from Jorunnshold? If he had, he would have turned back—but for where? For Jorunnshold, with the Romans waiting for him? Wuotan Father, not for Jorunnshold!

Nyall took a drink from one of the water flasks that

they had filled as they crossed the river, and tried to think. If Kari *had* gone to Jorunnshold . . . Gunnar and Runolf would have dived back in their holes at the first sign of a Roman victory. Thrain and Sigurd? Sigurd would probably stay. Of Thrain he wasn't sure, especially if he learned that Arngunn was dead. Thrain was sister's-son to Arngunn, and that was a strong bond—maybe the only one that had bound him to Nyall. And *Lyting* . . . Nyall pushed Lyting's face back from his mind, but a ghost rode at the empty space on his right hand as it had done since the first battle, when the boy fell. Without the priests and Ingald, Nyall could have bought a better vengeance than this for Lyting. Valgerd could have beaten Jorunn's priests, but Valgerd was an old man, and ill, and he had stayed at Arngunnshold. Now the Romans would catch him as well, and they had no liking for the Free People's priests. Nyall lifted his hands from the saddle and saw that they were shaking.

Fiorgyn, her pale hair dirty with sweat and ashes, came up beside him and laid her own hands on his. "It is time to walk again," she said, and Nyall nodded.

He got down and gave his weary horse to another man. Fiorgyn did the same, and walked beside him through the hot grass, northeastward.

The hand of Rome passed along the Nicer Valley and the forts sprang up behind it—full forts, turf- and timber-built, that would be garrisoned by auxiliary troops when the legions pulled back to winter quarters. This year's cold-weather headquarters would be their home bases on the Rhenus—Argentoratum, Vindonissa, and Moguntiacum.

Correus, knowing that it might be the last time Freita would see this valley, took her riding with him on a day's leave. He rode Antaeus, who needed it—they had been building the new fort for so long that his gold hide was full of frisk and bounce and he curvetted like a chariot pony in the Circus. Freita looked as if she had been born on the gray, he thought, as he watched them fly along the steep uphill track into the forest. The girl's gold hair made a cloud around her face, and she was laughing with pleasure as he caught up with her.

Correus hadn't laid a hand on her since that first disastrous night, and slowly, over the space of a long, touchy month, she had lost some of her stiffness and her wildcat look. Her eyes still had that gone-away look when she thought he wasn't watching, but she had learned a little Latin and seen Tribune Crassus's other woman, and her judgment of Correus was softened as a result. He no longer seemed evil, but was familiar and safe beside the others. She hated him, but he was there, inevitable, a known enemy among the unknown.

They rode on into the stillness of the cool woods, skirting around a grove that Freita told him was sacred and forbidden to men. It had the look of the grove they had stopped in the day he had carried Flavius back to the hospital, and Correus was glad that he had laid that crust of bread on the rock then. He had enough to worry him without a German curse snapping at his heels. At home, he had never believed in curses, but the German forest seemed to bring out the Gaul in him. The Gauls cursed each other regularly, and their gods had a reputation for making it stick. A Gaulish bard could raise hives on a man's face with a mere satire song. Or so they said.

They halted where a little stream bubbled along through a bank of ferns and fat orange slugs came out to air themselves in the damp shade. Freita pulled a canvas sack from her saddlebag and began to pick berries from the bushes that grew above the stream. Correus recognized it with amusement—an army courier pouch. Freita had proved as admirable a scrounger as Tullius once she got her bearings. He laughed and told her so, and she gave him a rare smile. She smiled often enough at Aeshma, or at Silvanus's jokes, or at the cat she had acquired from somewhere—and which Correus had named Baucis before she could give it some name no one could pronounce—but she smiled seldom at him.

There were minnows darting in the clear, cool water, and water bugs skated lazily on the surface; Correus sat down to watch them while Freita picked her berries. When the pouch was full, she brought it to him, and they made a lunch from berries and the barley cake and dried fish he had brought. The German waters were thick with fish, and the legion spread its nets in the rivers with abandon. In overpopulated Rome, fish was a luxury.

When they had finished, she wiped her mouth with berry-stained fingers and stretched out on the loamy stream bank, hands behind her head. She was wearing a rough riding gown of cheap cloth that she had sewn herself. She picked a piece of thorned berry vine from the skirt and flicked it into the water. "When do we leave?" she asked quietly, lying back again to watch the leafy canopy above her.

"In a few days," he said. "I'm sorry."

She shook her head. "There is nothing here now for me. My father is dead, and my mother with him. Or gone to Nyall maybe, but I am thinking not. They were too old to swim that water."

"Freita—"

"Yes, Centurion?"

"I would have sent *you* to Nyall if I could have. If the legate thought we wouldn't meet you again on a battlefield . . ."

She sat up to face him, suspicious, as if there might be a trap somewhere.

"I didn't *want* a slave," Correus said gently. The green gaze remained skeptical, and he tried to explain. "I was born one."

"All things change, Centurion," she said. "I was born a warrior's daughter." She seemed to find the reversal grimly amusing.

"My mother," he went on, not looking at her now, but digging with a twig at the damp lichen on a rock, "was bought by my father on a campaign in Gaul. She was younger than you are, but maybe not so different. She doesn't have a bad life now, I suppose. Lots of pretty things, and my father is a kind enough man. She cajoles him well."

He had taken off his helmet, and she thought that the sharp angles of his face were shadowed by more than the dappled pattern of sunlight falling through the trees.

"Now you follow in his footsteps," she commented.

"No!" The vehemence in his voice startled her.

"Then why?" Freita sat stiffly, head up. Correus was

still digging at the lichen, cutting little roads in it, and he didn't see her.

"It was . . . me, or some other man. I don't think I thought first." He looked at her now, his eyes unhappy. "But I didn't mean to . . . to——"

To lie with me, she thought. Well, she hadn't wanted him to. But to be bought for pity, like a stray . . . Her eyes flashed. "My thanks for your . . . *care* for me, Centurion!" She spun around and stood up.

"Freita——"

She stumbled up the slope to the berry vines and began picking again, so he wouldn't see her face. "It was not necessary. Best that you sell me again."

"No," he said quietly. "You would end up as my mother has. You think you won't, but things . . . wear you down, and after a while there is nothing left. I won't go into eternity with that on my soul. Not when I have come so close to walking that same road myself."

She didn't answer, and finally he got up and put his hands on her shoulders, speaking to the back of her head. She flinched again, but didn't pull away. "You must hate me greatly, I suppose; me and all my kind. But you have no choice. I do own you, whether either of us likes it or not. Learn to live with that for now, and you will go free one day, Freita, when it is possible. I promise you that."

"The Roman-kind have made many promises, and mostly the words blow away in the wind." Her voice was clear and bitter, but she knew that he would not make her that kind of promise. That made things even worse, for she had nothing left to hate; and it was hate that she lived on now. Her shoulders slumped, as if she gave up all at once. "Free . . ." She said the word dully. "I suppose one can learn to bear anything . . . for that."

"I did," he said.

He took his hands from her shoulders, and she turned and followed him back to the horses.

The fort on the Nicer, and its sister forts, were finished at summer's end. The auxiliary garrisons moved in, and the Eighth Legion moved out for Argentoratum and winter quarters.

Freita rode the gray at the rear among the other soldiers' servants, carrying Baucis, complaining in a covered basket, and leading Antaeus. She had made no mention of that last ride in the wood, but Correus saw that the faint, dawning easiness between them was gone. In the weeks of her captivity, Freita had hugged her hatred to her as a balance point in an overturned world. Now he had taken that from her by a kindness, and in return she adopted an aloof kindness of her own. She mended his clothes and took a polishing rag to his lorica like a body servant. When he protested that that was not necessary, she snapped, "At least you will have *some* value for your money!"

Correus, who was beginning to understand, made no further protest. His mouth twisted. It seemed he had the choice of being hated for rape or hated for pity. There was no middle ground. Worse yet, if his conscience spoke loudly for pity, his body had other ideas. She still drew him, waking an aching hunger that he pushed angrily to the back of his mind.

She wore the earrings he had bought her, but steadfastly refused any other adornment, including new clothes, until he finally shouted at her that she was not going back to Argentoratum in a hopsack riding dress or a whore's gown. Thereafter she shrugged irritatingly and wore what he told her to.

The only time they did not rub each other raw was when he taught her Latin. He discovered that she had as quick an ear for speech as he did. It was when she asked him why his German had the accent of the Semnones that it occurred to him that she had lived among them. After that he plied her with so many questions about Nyall and his tribe that she asked sarcastically if he thought the Semnones were going to come leaping out of the bushes like elf-folk to rescue her.

Correus shook his head. "Not to rescue you. And not this soon." She glared at him, but that was all he would say.

The legion made Argentoratum at the start of the fall wine-making, clattering over the Rhenus bridge while the river traffic scooted by below. Freita, used only to the rafts and small dugout craft of the tribes, watched the ships with a wide-eyed curiosity that she tried to hide

from Correus. He saw his men to their barracks and came
back across the bridge to her, while the baggage wagons
and the rear guard were still crossing. With winter supplies being laid in all along its length, the Rhenus was
thicker with traffic than usual, and the dock below the
river gate was mobbed.

He pointed out to Freita the long, lean patrol galleys
with their black eagles spread-winged on crimson sails, and
the fatter bulk of the cargo ships. Roman maritime law
wisely specified that a merchantman must be at least one-
third as wide as it was long, so that the sleeker patrol
craft could outrun them for cargo inspection. Smuggling
was a constant problem, and an enterprising trader in
a fast ship saw no reason to pay Caesar his due if he
could help it. There was also the matter of smuggled
weapons, for which a subject people contemplating rebellion would pay well, especially among the metal-poor
tribes on the German frontier.

On the jetty, sacks of grain were being unloaded from
one ship, and clay amphorae used to transport oil, wine,
and olives were being carried from the hold of a second.
A pile of dried branches lay to one side, to be burned,
and fresh ones would be cut to cushion the return cargo.

Argentoratum had turned out in force to welcome the
legion home, in the hope that a summer's campaign had
raised a thirst for the wares that the marketplace could
offer. A milling crowd of women were also there to welcome back their men, and so was the Argentoratum
magistrate, plump and important in his official robes.
Aeshma began to dance nervously as they came off the
bridge, and Correus took his bridle while he pushed his
way through the crowd. Technically the soldiers were not
allowed to marry while they were in service, but as their
wives and children would be made legitimate on their discharge, few bothered to heed this regulation. Only officers
were allowed to drag women along with them on campaign, at their own expense, and that was frowned upon.
Crassus got away with it because he was a tribune, and
Labienus because his fat and homely woman helped in
the hospital. Freita would have to stay behind when the
legion marched out again in the spring.

Paulinus was waiting for them, lounging in front of the

newly built basilica. Correus greeted him with relief. He
had sent a message ahead to him, hoping that he would
still be at Argentoratum, and asked him to find some sort
of housing in the town for Freita. Something cheap, he
had added in a harassed postscript that had made Paulinus smile. He could imagine what old Calpurnius Rufinus
had stuck him for in payment for his German beauty.
What he couldn't figure out was why his friend had
bought her in the first place, and his freckled nose
twitched with interest as Correus presented the girl to
him. She had a wicker basket on the saddle before her,
from which an infuriated rumbling could be heard.

Paulinus bowed as gravely as he would have to a senator's wife, and greeted her in German while Freita
watched him with her usual suspicion. It certainly wasn't
for a slave that he bought her, Paulinus thought, watching Correus hand her down carefully from Aeshma's back
outside the small timber house near the edge of the town.
And Correus was a career officer. He wasn't likely to
go throwing his heart after a barbarian beauty on a moment's acquaintance. Paulinus remained alert and puzzled.

His curiosity was unabated when Silvanus appeared as
they were inspecting the house—no more than a one-
room hut, really, but plastered inside, and clean enough.
Freita gave Silvanus a cheeky and unslavelike smile in
greeting and chuckled at his description of the riotous indignation of one of his men upon discovering that his
woman had borne, in his absence, a baby that showed
every sign of paternity other than his. Correus watched
this interchange gloomily as the cat twined itself about his
legs.

When Silvanus took his departure, Paulinus followed
him, and after asking the centurion a few direct questions, a certain amount of light began to dawn. Paulinus
turned back to the house with a worried expression, and
Silvanus nodded.

"Damn fool," Silvanus said. "She's not thanking him
for it."

Paulinus doubted that Correus was thanking himself,
either, when they went to the slave market in Argentoratum the next day. Correus's face was white as they

inspected the rows of huddled, miserable figures chained to rings in the floor, most with bare, white-chalked feet marking them as new slaves of foreign birth, their eyes listless in the hot stink of the sale room, or wide and terrified as the slave master dragged them forward for inspection. Buying Freita had been one thing. To buy a slave deliberately from this animal pen was another, but he had no choice. The nightmare logistics of transporting horse, cat, woman, and tent from the Nicer Valley to Argentoratum were still vivid in his mind, and Messala Cominius had told him bluntly that if he didn't buy another slave to cope with his newly acquired encumbrances, he would have to sell them. Reluctantly, Correus agreed.

Now he stood with gritted teeth while the slave master presented his wares for the centurion's inspection.

"Now this one—" He brought a slim, dark youth forward. "This one is a real find, and cheap at the price. He plays the flute and dances, and even speaks some Greek. He has never run away, and is only being sold because his master—for your ear alone, you understand, he is an important man—has found himself in debt. But the centurion may be happy to reap the reward of such improvidence."

"I don't want to be entertained," Correus said shortly, "and I haven't much money. I want someone who can handle a jumpy horse and do some work. No more."

The slave master sighed. The only groom among his wares was a habitual troublemaker, and by law he was marked as such. There were stiff penalties for falsifying a slave's history. He wasn't going to be able to pry much out of this centurion for him. The slave master clapped his hands and one of his men dragged the boy forward.

He was not more than thirteen, with a thin, pinched face and a cap of mousy hair that needed washing. A tag with a sale number was pinned to his ragged tunic and the notation beneath it said simply, "Fugitivus"—a chronic runaway.

"Oh, come now," Paulinus said as the slave master held up the boy's arms to show that they were strong and wiry in spite of his small size. "My friend is looking for

help with his household, not five hundred sesterces' worth
of trouble."

"Five hundred sesterces?" The slave master was horrified, deliberately misunderstanding. "I would have to
charge much more than that for a strong boy like this."

"He'd be expensive at any price," Paulinus said.

The boy's eyes shifted between them, sullen and wary.
So far life had shown him no great kindness, and there
was no reason to think that this dark-eyed centurion offered hope of anything more than another master who
would beat him.

"Just a minute," Correus said. "Come here." The
slave boy sidled up to him. "You know horses?"

"Yes," the boy muttered, amending it belatedly to
"Yes, lord," as the slave master kicked him.

"And like them better than men, I expect," Correus
said. "Why did you run away?"

"Because I was frightened. I was not so old then as I
am now," he added pathetically.

"Was that the only time?"

The boy looked at Correus. The centurion didn't seem
to be going to hit him. "No."

"And the next time?"

"Because they beat me, to make sure that I wouldn't
run away."

Correus turned to the slave master. "I will give you
seven hundred fifty sesterces for him and not a penny
more."

"But, lord—" The slave master spread his grubby
hands wide in the gesture of a man much misunderstood.
"It is not possible. I have spent that much on his keep
alone."

Correus looked at the boy's thin arms. "I doubt it.
Have you had any other offers for him?"

"There is a lady, lord, who needs a small dancing boy
to fill her troupe. She comes this very afternoon to see
him," he added triumphantly.

Correus turned away. "Good. Then you may sell him
to her."

Even under his chains, the boy moved as if tensed for
flight.

"Lord, wait! Perhaps—a thousand sesterces, only because I have so great a respect for our defenders here. For you, only a thousand."

"I haven't got a thousand. Eight hundred. No more." His expression said plainly that he would go no higher.

The slave master sighed. The lady was mythical, as Correus knew. "Very well," he said grumpily. "Eight hundred." He hoped the brat ran away the first day.

Paulinus's expression said that he considered that prospect only too likely.

The slave master struck the chains from the boy's leg, and Correus bent down and looked the child in the eye. "Now then. You belong to me, and I do not beat people. You will have enough to eat and a decent place to sleep, and a household and a very troublesome horse to look after. Probably more troublesome than you are. So you will have to be more grown up than you really are, and there will be no more running away. Is this all very clear?"

The boy nodded, obviously reserving judgment.

"Very well, then." Correus turned away without waiting to see that the boy followed him.

Paulinus trailed behind them, watching his friend's straight back and the ragged urchin scrambling suddenly after him. One day Correus would learn that such was the way of the world, and cease to break his heart over it.

They made their way through the bustling marketplace and then down a dusty side street with the boy still hurrying to match Correus's brisk military stride. Freita was kneeling by the hearth combing out her wet hair when they came through the door. She peered up through its damp curtain, looked at the boy, and burst into laughter.

"So you . . . you have bought me a protector . . . to guard me from bandits, no doubt!" She stood up, shaking her hair back and towering over the boy like a statue of Juno beside a midget.

"Shut up," Correus said good-humoredly, pleased enough to see her lose some of her stiffness with him.

The boy bristled. It was plain that he spoke some German. "Is this blond witch yours also, lord?"

"She is," Correus said, trying not to laugh as Freita

regarded the child indignantly. "And you will refer to her as 'mistress' or 'my lady' or she will turn you over her knee. Now what is your name?"

"It doesn't matter," the boy said, still glaring at Freita. "They always give me a new one. The last one was just 'Servus,' " he said, his mouth twisting.

"Why?"

"They don't think my name is *suitable*." He was plainly quoting.

"What is it?"

"Julius. But it *is* my name, truly."

"An ancient name of much distinction, and highly *un*-suitable," Correus agreed. "But if that is your name, that is what you are to be called. And this lady is called Freita, but not by you."

"And what is it that I am to do here, lord?"

"See to the house, and the horse stabled at the back, and run errands and whatever else the lady wishes. And she will not laugh at you anymore"—he gave Freita a steely glance—"if you will not call her a witch again."

"Very well. If *you* say I mustn't."

"I do," Correus assured him solemnly.

Paulinus had retired to a chair in the corner and appeared to be having hysterics. Freita caught his eye and relented.

"Come along, O my protector." She pointed at the little alcove which was curtained off at one end of the room. A trail of wet footprints still ran from the curtain to the seat by the hearth.

"Where?" Julius dug in his heels with dawning suspicion.

"Yes," Correus said, divining her intentions. "Definitely a bath. You may buy a new tunic afterward," he added as Julius howled in protest.

Freita trapped one grimy hand in hers. "I can carry you, you know." She pulled him, still fighting, back behind the curtain and stripped him ruthlessly, but her face softened as she saw the still-raw scars on his back.

"Who did this to you?"

"I don't remember," Julius said sullenly. "They all do."

Freita glanced at the curtain with an odd expression. "This one won't," she said. "And I'll not laugh anymore, either."

XIV

Harvestnight

A STRUGGLING BAND OF HORSEMEN MADE ITS WAY ALONG a forest trail where fallen leaves rustled golden under their feet. They were lean, grim-faced men who rode with backs slumped and hands fallen low, as if they had only the strength to keep themselves in the saddle, and no more. As they wound out of the wood and into a clearing at the foot of a hill, a child playing in the leaves alongside the track jumped up and ran for the walled holding that stood ahead on the hillcrest.

They were no more than halfway to the holding when the log gates swung open and a crowd of men and women came hurrying down the track to meet them. The lead rider raised his dark head and pushed his weary horse forward. His blue-and-green shield thumped against his knee where his arm hung loose at his side, and he straightened it carefully.

"I'll take that, lord," a small boy panted, outdistancing the rest to hurl himself practically under the horse's feet. Kari nodded and handed the shield to him, and the boy clutched it to himself importantly, chattering as he trotted alongside the horse: "We had given up looking for you, and the chieftain almost made the Death Song. Are you truly all right, and have you brought your harp back with you?"

"That will do, youngling." Kari slipped from his horse as Nyall came up beside them. "Yes, I have brought her, and if you give my shield to a friend, you may carry her, very carefully, to the hall for me." He handed the boy the deerskin harp bag from his back. "And bring the other boys to see to my men."

The boy ran off and Kari turned slowly to Nyall. The chieftain's eyes were pinched and worried, older than they had been.

"He's right," Nyall said. "We nearly keened you." He put out a hand and gripped Kari's arm hard. "Brother, I am glad to have you back."

"I was not . . . sure that I would find you, either," Kari said. They stood and looked at each other for a long moment before they turned and walked together through the gate.

The stumbling horses and their weary riders followed, and the women of the hold clustered around them, faces alight or bereft as each searched the horsemen for the face that mattered most. Nyall's mother, Morgian, sent thralls scurrying for food and to take the horses. They were all her people to care for now, the Black Forest men as well as the Semnone warriors, but she looked for no one among them. The face that she wanted would not ride home.

Nyall drew Kari away with him into his own chambers, and shouted for someone to bring food.

Fiorgyn came herself with it, hot thick stew and beer from the last year's brewing. She settled herself like a cat in the rushes beside her husband's chair, and watched Kari with relief while he ate. Of them all, she thought, it was Kari that Nyall feared most to lose.

"That was good." Kari put the bowl on the floor and one of Nyall's hounds slunk forward to lick it. "I can't remember when we've had a decent meal."

Nyall nodded, remembering their own nightmare trek from Jorunnshold. At least Kari had not had to watch women and babies die, he thought. But he had gone through something bad enough, Nyall knew. The harper's thin face was flushed and the sunken dark eyes had an unnatural brightness.

"What happened?"

"We . . . saw the fire," Kari said. "So we pulled around and rode back, but it was too late. Everything was burning."

"You didn't attack—?"

Kari shook his head. "No. There was . . . no point. It was lost already. And Gunnar and Runolf drew off as soon as they saw what had happened. They will be back in their holds by now," he said, "no doubt telling the Roman-kind they had nothing to do with any of it. We . . . we crossed the river without being seen, and rode." His face was bleak and Nyall knew that it must have cost him something to leave that burning hold behind.

"The Romans were out hunting," Kari went on. "We dodged them but we found . . . bodies. We buried what we found." He broke off and ran a hand over his face. The flush was gone and he was pale now and sweating.

"What is it?" Fiorgyn looked at him sharply.

"Bad water," Kari said. He shook his head as if to clear it. "The Romans fouled it, I think. I . . . should have known they would."

"You are ill," Fiorgyn said. "I will get the priests."

"No. No . . . it is almost gone now. We had to ride on anyway, and some died of it, but we are mostly all right now."

"Are you sure?" Nyall said. "We have . . . something of a surplus of priests at the moment."

"Valgerd is here," Fiorgyn explained. "He came in two days ago with his beard full of twigs like a woods hermit, and all he will say is that he had a vision and so came away before the Romans reached my father's hold. I think it must have been a message sent by the priests' drums. We are glad to have him—he is a very great man —but he and Asuin sit and glower at each other, and argue about signs in the sky and the proper time to gather herbs, until Morgian is afraid they will put a curse on each other."

"Then I shall do without their potions," Kari said, "lest they kill me trying to outdo each other. I saw Geir as we came in. Who else rode with you?"

Nyall gave him the total, and Kari grimaced as he came to Ingald's name.

"So the gods spared his thief's hide and took your kin," he said to Fiorgyn. "Lady, I am sorry."

Fiorgyn nodded her thanks. "Perhaps they saw more use for my father in Valhalla," she said sadly.

"Mord was with us," Nyall went on, laying a hand on

her shoulder. "But he died on the trail. Arni came in behind us. He must have tracked us like a hound—there
were none of our men with him, only some of Jorunn's
and Mord's."

Kari gave Nyall his own tally. Sigurd and his men had
stuck with him, and so had Thrain, after some debate.
It was likely that he would stay now that he knew Fiorgyn, who was kin to him, still lived. Nyall mentally re-
counted the survivors. Too few for a war band, and too
many to feed. "We will have to split them up before snowfall," he said. "The hold won't support them all. I'll try
to sort them out after they have slept."

The sun was dropping and a thrall came in to light the
fire in the stone hearth. Fiorgyn gave him the empty bowl
to take away and told him to send blankets and bed-
straw to the main hall.

"We've been giving the warriors holdings left empty
by our own dead," Nyall said. "With luck they will marry
the widows."

Kari nodded. There were too many widows. Best that
they go to new husbands if they could. And best that the
Black Forest warriors become Semnones, and so come
under Nyall's rule. There would be no way to judge their
disputes otherwise, and make the judgment stick. And
the chieftain who couldn't keep order soon found a
Council looking down his throat.

Kari went away to the Companions' chamber to sleep,
and Morgian, having seen to the others, tapped on the
doorpost and came in to sit by the fire with Nyall and
Fiorgyn. She still mourned Lyting, Nyall knew, but he
thought she had forgiven him for his death. Morgian had
welcomed Fiorgyn, bereft of her own mother, with love.
Fiorgyn returned it with a whole heart. She had loved
her mother, but Gudrun, shrewd and practical by nature,
had put so much of herself into holding her uncertain
husband's chieftainship for him, that there was little left
over for tenderness. A soft bosom to weep on and a
sweet, clear voice that could sing away her nightmares
were new to Fiorgyn.

Morgian looked concerned at what Kari had said about
the bad water, and his refusal to have the priests pester-
ing after him. "If he is still fevered in the morning, or any

of them are, he will drink their potions and like it," she said. "But Nyall, you must send Valgerd to another hold soon. Two high priests under one roof draw more attention from the gods than we really need."

"I'm going to send him with Arni," Nyall said. "Mord and Jorunn's men who rode with Arni have asked my permission to swear to him, so that will give him enough followers to take holding with, and Valgerd may put a little caution into his young brain."

Morgian picked up a stick and poked thoughtfully at the fire, making its glow ripple along the stones on the hearth front. "Ingald also needs ... occupation."

"Ingald's occupation has always been with the rumor that runs in the marketplace!" Fiorgyn said. "Let him out of your sight and he'll make trouble!"

Nyall looked at them both and thought a moment before saying: "He is of the chieftain's Kindred of your tribe, Fiorgyn. If I let Arni and Ranvig take holding and keep Ingald here to dance attendance on me, he will have a right to make trouble. Mother, I want to give Lyting's holding to Ranvig." He waited to see her reaction.

Morgian spread her hands in her lap and looked at them. "It is going to ruin now that it is masterless. Yes, better that Ranvig have it."

"There is another holding empty close by," Nyall went on. "We will put Ingald there, and let Ranvig play watchdog."

"They will fight and steal each other's cattle," Morgian said.

"But I will know what Ingald's doing, won't I? *And* I will have put no insult on him."

Morgian nodded, and Fiorgyn also, though reluctantly. Morgian understood why Nyall refused to fight with a man he had already bested in the matter of his wife and the command of the war band—it would seem a jealousy, as if he feared Ingald. Fiorgyn found that harder to understand.

"That will give him a place in Council," she said. Any lord with a holding of his own, and warriors and peasant folk under him, was entitled to a voting voice in the Council. Younger men who were still holdless, or warriors sworn to a lord, could also speak their mind, but the final vote rested with the landed lords.

"He has a right to it," Nyall said stubbornly.

"Your own Semnone lords are calling for a Council already," Morgian said. "There is some question over the rights of the newcomers."

"I feel like a nursemaid with a pack of children," Nyall said. "What they mean is, they are worried about their own rights. Well, we'll thrash it all out when Kari's men have had time to rest."

It was almost a month before Nyall could call his Council. The bad water had taken a greater toll than Kari admitted, and when Morgian went to look at him the next morning, she drew in a sharp breath and sent for Asuin and Valgerd both.

The fever was back, and a wasting sickness of the stomach with it. After that one meal of stew and beer the night before, Kari could keep nothing more down. The two priests put their quarrels aside and worked together in a healers' truce so amicably that Morgian said that if Kari lived, his sickness would have been worth it. But she was very much afraid that he wouldn't, and it was plain that the priests were worried, too. There were others sick as well, but Kari was the worst.

"I think that he got here on nothing but strength of will," Asuin said, coming out of the Companions' chamber with a barely touched bowl and the deerskin bag, embroidered with the healing signs, that held his herbs and potions. "There is nothing left but his will." He gave his things to the boy who served him and pulled a chair to the hearth. The day was turning gray and there was a wet feel of rain in the air.

"The others grow better," Nyall said, then, almost pleading, "why not Kari?"

"He is half-Roman, chieftain," said the boy, an apprentice priest and full of his own knowledge. "It may be that the gods show their hand against him."

Nyall's eyes flashed and Asuin cuffed the boy into silence. "Do not be thinking that you know the gods' minds so well! If Kari's half-blood has any bearing here it will be to his good. They are a strong people, the Roman-kind, not in size but in force of will. They hang on like fighting dogs. That is how Kari came back to us at all, lord," he went on to Nyall. "He brought the others in on his will alone, I am thinking, and he has drained himself doing it. You know well that it takes more strength to command than to follow."

"Indeed it shows the gods' favor that he is here at all," Valgerd put in. "So perhaps the Lady Eir guards him still. Did she not lift the sickness from me, when it was time to go from Arngunnshold?"

"Yours is the sickness of age," Asuin said, the truce temporarily forgotten, "and an easier thing to lift than bad water in the stomach." He was younger than Valgerd, his beard still a light brown clay color. Age equated with wisdom among the priest-kind, and Asuin combated Valgerd's advantage in this by a show of earthly medical knowledge.

Nyall left them arguing, while Morgian made soothing, peaceful noises, and he went to sit by Kari's bed.

They fought the chills and the burning fever that ran their alternating courses through Kari's restless, shaking body for more than three weeks, while the others grew well. Nyall sat beside the bed until he was bleary-eyed, deaf to the priests' urgings to leave. Fiorgyn finally persuaded him to get some sleep, promising that she would sit with Kari herself, or bring Morgian to do so, until Nyall came back.

Nyall slept restlessly himself, amid bad dreams of Lyting in an open grave, and Kari's dark, half-Roman face strangely overlaid with an iron Roman helmet, and the Roman centurion who spoke Semnones' German suddenly sprouting a Semnone beard and mustache. And then they straightened themselves out again, and Kari's face was familiar again behind his brown mustache—Kari never wore a beard, perhaps because Nyall did not—and the Roman had his helmet on again. Nyall awoke sweating, and with something vague about half-blood chasing its tail in the back of his mind. The Roman centurion was half-blood also, he thought. You took one blood or the other, he thought, and became that . . . but somewhere in the depth of things, the other blood still ran.

He stood up, feeling in the rushes for the soft indoor
boots that he had left by the bed—itself a pile of rushes
and straw threaded through with sweet herbs and covered with soft, worked deerhides and a blanket of bearskin. He had fallen into bed without undressing. He
rebraided his hair and pinned it up; outside the hall he
took an icy splash in a beer vat of water. In his chamber, a thrall lit the fire and straightened out the rucked-up
bed. He brought the chieftain clean clothes and scurried
away with the dirty ones. There must be a washing today,
Nyall thought. The women were making a lot of bustle
in the great hall, and he could hear the splashing of the
washtubs being filled outside with water from the rain
vats that stood in the open court. It was morning, and it
had been morning when Fiorgyn had made him go and
sleep. He must have slept the day around. He shouted for
a thrall to bring him food to the Companions' chamber,
and went to sit by Kari again.

The Companions had risen already, and the chamber
was empty except for Fiorgyn and the priests by the bed-
side and Kari's still figure, cold and sweating now in damp
bedclothes. When they had finished with their potions,
the priests called in a thrall, who changed the bedclothes,
and Nyall sat down again to his vigil.

He sat, sometimes holding Kari's hand in his when he
grew restless, sometimes just watching the dark, sunken
eyes and the chalky face, while the business of the hold
went on all around, unnoticed.

Morgian came once to tell him that the Council lords
grew demanding, but Nyall just shook his head and never
took his eyes from Kari's. She shrugged and went about
her work again. The fall rains would come heavily
soon, and after them the snow, and Nyallshold made busy
in preparation. The chambers were swept of their old rushes
and fresh ones were laid down, and there was still the
last of the autumn brewing to be done, and the stacked
hay in the fields to be brought into the barns. Morgian,
Fiorgyn, and their women, in rough gowns with aprons
tied over them and their sleeves rolled up, worked in
the hall and over the drying ovens in the smokehouse.
The men rode after meat, returning at dusk with wild
boar or a red deer carcass slung from the carrying poles.

The meat was dried or smoked, and the hides would be scraped, stretched, and tanned; the bones and horns were saved for knife handles, combs, and other implements, and the entrails were thrown to the hound pack. Nothing would be wasted.

The red coats of the cattle were already growing shaggy with the cold as they were driven in from the pastures, and the weaker ones, not worth feeding through the winter, were slaughtered. The horse herds were brought into the barns and the sheep into folds near the hold where the tribe could stand guard over the midwinter lambing.

Every building in the hold was aired and scrubbed from rafters to floorboards, and the herbs and onions and garlic hanging to dry in the still-room gave off a pungent scent. The harvest tribute from each lord came in to the chieftain's hold, and with it came such lords of the tribe as were not there already for the Harvest Feast that marked the ending of the year. A place had to be found for all, with their wives and thralls and dogs; and those who were feuding had to be kept well apart.

Through it all, Kari slept or more often thrashed restlessly on the bed, sometimes singing to himself feverishly jumbled snatches of Hero Songs or songs of the battles of the gods. Once, he sat up and looked frantically for his harp and would not be quieted until Nyall put it in his hands. Occasionally Fiorgyn came away from her work, her pale braids wound into a crown on her head to be out of the way, to sit with Kari and make her husband sleep; but for the most part it was Nyall who kept watch, day after day, shaking off even Geir when that old councilor tried to reason with him.

Finally, on the third day before Harvest Feast, with the hold crowded with quarrelsome guests and two blood feuds already sparked by sheer boredom, Kari opened his eyes and seemed to see not the dark things that prey on a fevered mind, but Nyall's face above him in the firelight, almost as haggard as his own.

"Have you been here . . . all this time?" he whispered, and Nyall nodded. Kari smiled and closed his eyes again, at last in quiet sleep, and Nyall got up and staggered to his bed to sleep also.

He called Council for two days later, nearly a month after Kari had come in. Kari was also awake now, and Valgerd and Asuin had nodded their heads in agreement, saying that the sickness had passed. The Council would be on the day of Harvestnight—propitious enough if a chieftain wanted an excuse to cut a Council short once his orders had been given. Harvestnight marked the end of the old year, when the herds had been gathered in, and the tribe gave thanks for the stored harvest that would sustain it through the dead time to come. On Harvestnight, folk paid a wary homage to the dead of mankind, who might come to warm themselves at the feast fire on this one night when Hellgate stood open at the joining of the year. It was ill luck to talk of living matters on a night when the dead, or worse things that might come out of Hellgate, could hear and decide to take a hand in them. For that reason, when the feast began at sundown, the Council must end.

It was plain, when Nyall came out into the courtyard with Geir beside him, that he had waited too long to call the Council. Ranvig and Ingald were arguing with each other under the carved dragon's head on the roof tree, and both glared at him out of sheer temper as he passed. Fiorgyn was talking in a low voice to Thrain, while Sigurd, who had renewed an old enmity with him over some long-gone cattle raid, was working off his temper in a boys' game of ball in the field. Arni was perched happily enough on the stone wall of the well, mending a bridle strap, but the glowering looks being accorded him by two of the Semnone lords indicated that he too had found time to pick a quarrel. Valgerd and Asuin, their truce abandoned with their patient's recovery, were standing over a terrified thrall with a rush basket of river herbs, debating whether or not he had cut them properly.

Matters proved little better in the Council. Nyall strode in, his green tunic and trousers freshly cleaned and his flaming hair washed and neatly braided and pinned. Kari came beside him, his thin form wrapped in a blanket, to sit in Lyting's old place. It was raining, and the cold and wet came in through the withy shutters and down the smoke hole to make the fire smoke and spit. Almost before their chieftain was seated, the Council lords were on their feet, each trying to yell above the others.

Nyall sighed, gripped the oaken arms of the chair where he sat on piled deerhides, and began to sort through the complaints. He assigned empty holds to new masters from among the chieftains and Kindred of the newcomers, and although the Semnone lords spat like cats and shifted in their seats, it was finally, grudgingly, agreed that the Black Forest men must be taken into the tribe and this was the best way to do it. A man who had once been chieftain or chieftain's kin in his own tribe must be a lord in his own right. Taking holding under another tribe's chieftain was hard enough to swallow.

When he had finally wrested agreement for that much, Nyall assigned the Black Forest warriors among the new lords, taking into account those who had been sworn to certain lords before, as well as those leaderless ones, such as Arni's group, who had asked permission to swear to one new lord in particular.

And then the debates began. Each holder, new and old, shouted to be heard over the rest and over the thunder that was booming above the hold, while the dogs added their howls to each new thunderclap. If an adopted lord of the tribe was killed, did it carry the same blood-price as a birthright lord? And what about existing feuds between hold and hold—did the new lord make good his predecessor's quarrel? And if not, what recompense to the other aggrieved party? And what of marriage, and of daughters sent to wed new holders? Did blood-right apply? And what of dead holders' widows, dead holders' sons? What rights there?

Slowly, and with much dispute, Nyall sorted the questions out, giving each an answer, some anticipated, some thought out in haste, and every single one argued with from all sides by anyone who could think of anything to say.

After that came the peace-making, the settlement of quarrels and lawsuits arisen since the last Council, done amid the usual protests that the chieftain did not have the right to intervene unless he was requested to. Fortunately, someone involved in the tangle could generally be found to make that request, and once the chieftain was asked to decide, his judgment was final. It was all done amid much shouting and banging of tables while Asuin thumped his staff and shouted for order.

Finally, when the last judgment had been made and the Council lords were glaring balefully at each other, but were quiet, Nyall stood up, put hands on his hips, and glared at them all himself.

"We are the Free People!" he said with a fine, cutting scorn in his voice. "We make a Council and spend it arguing over precedence and cattle-rights, while the Romans build their eagle-forts in the lands we have lost!"

They sat up and looked at him. These other matters were important, as important as war with the Roman-kind, maybe more. They touched on a man's honor.

"We cannot raid the Roman-kind again until spring," pointed out Hauk, a square-faced lord with heavy bull's shoulders, whose holding lay to the east on the edge of the Semnone lands.

"We do not 'raid' the Roman-kind again at all," Nyall said flatly, and they stared at him again. "We make a war, a Roman war. I have been thinking while the Council has been quarreling, and now I will tell you what I have thought, and for this there will be no argument!"

There were mutterings. Argument was always the privilege of the Council.

"Silence and hear me!" Nyall's gray eyes were dangerous. "The rights of the Free People will be the death of the Free People if they do not learn to use them wisely! The commander of the Eagles said to me that he commanded soldiers, not warriors, and there was much in what he said. It is why he beat us. He had an army that marched when he gave the word, while *my* war band hid their heads in their cloaks for a full month because a priest and a few warriors of our *allies*"—he spat out the word—"made large talk and were listened to!"

"Not by all of us!" Ranvig jumped up, his bright, slightly askew eyes fixed on Ingald, whose own anger was rising.

"By enough of you," Nyall said grimly. "Ranvig, I know your loyalties, sit down."

"The dead must be—" Ingald said.

"Those dead are still unburied!" Thrain snapped. He

had a thin face with a healing scar on one cheek, and a look of Fiorgyn about him. "*I* listened to that talk, and it cost me my land!"

Hauk nodded, but another lord, Koll, shook his head dubiously. "Let the chieftain explain to me," he said gruffly, drawing bushy gray brows together in a frown. "I am thinking that I do not understand where this talk is going."

"It is simple," Nyall said. "We must stand together against the Romans, or go down, divided, as the Gauls did. So unless you are liking the idea of that, this time *I will be obeyed!* There will be no more *alliances* and no priests telling me when I may or may not make war. And no man will answer to any other man but me."

"Plain enough," Koll said. "Tell me this, young chieftain, before I swear this obedience—*can* we conquer Rome?"

"No," Nyall said flatly. "We cannot. But we can make it so great a trouble for Rome to conquer *us* that we are not worth the effort of it."

"How do we know Rome *will* try to conquer us?" Ingald asked quietly.

After a moment of heavy silence, Nyall said, "They will come. If not next year, the year after. Would you wait and see? And when they come what will you do? Maybe throw rocks at them on the doorstep?"

There was a murmuring of agreement to that, especially from the Black Forest lords. Ingald, seeing how the wind blew, said nothing further. He lounged forward on the table, chin in hand, his handsome face devoid of any expression but polite attention. Ranvig, who possessed no such subtlety, turned toward him to speak, but Kari, wrapped in his blanket by the chieftain's chair, caught Ranvig's eye and shook his head slightly.

"You have heard my thinking," Nyall said. "Does anyone wish to make challenge to it?" His voice was soft, but there was a tinge of menace in it that was well noted. "If so, do it now. Because I will kill the man who does it on the war trail."

No one moved. Kari held his breath. Then Koll stood up and said: "I vote with the chieftain."

"And I." Hauk heaved his bull shoulders up out of his

seat, a giant of a man dwarfing even the big men beside him.

"I also!" Ranvig leaped up lightly, followed by Arni, Thrain, and Sigurd.

Kari let out his breath slowly as the rest followed— one-eyed Geir; Steinvar, the lean, scarred holder from the south; and the landed lords of the Companions' troop, Svan, Starkad, Asgrim, and Gilli the Lame, who fought better with a limp than most men with two good legs. Ingald gave his vote also, and Valgerd and Asuin solemnly swore obedience with their hands clasped on the sun-disks of their staffs. Kari pushed his blanket back and stood, still weaving a little on his feet, to add his voice. He drew a snort of amusement from Geir, who was keeping track of the vote with his tally sticks. Kari would have ridden through Hellgate and back if Nyall had asked it.

Nyall stood with thumbs hooked in his belt, rocking lightly on his heels and watching until the last lord had spoken. Then he sat back in his chair, strong hands on the oaken arms, and looked each man in the eye. "You have sworn to keep your peace with me in this. So. Now I say that you will also keep it with each other. When we make Council again in spring, it will be a Council of War, and there will be no feuds and grievances to settle, and no dead men to make the war band one spear lighter. That you understand this law clearly, I tell you now that I will put curse on the man who breaks it."

They eyed Nyall with a wary respect at that; even Asuin was impressed. The chieftain's curse was stronger even than a priest's curse; and it killed always—the man who was cursed, and sometimes also the chieftain who had set it. The last chieftain who had invoked that curse was only in ancient Hero Songs, but that did not lighten its strength.

"So," Nyall said into their silence, while the rain poured down outside and the fire spat in protest, "it is done. There will be a gathering at midwinter, for those who are not snow-held, and a Council at first thaw. Now let us leave the hall to the thralls."

The smell of roasting meat had begun to drift in on the wet wind, and there was a scurrying of footsteps and voices outside the doors as thralls waited with trestle ta-

bles and armloads of green branches to begin decking the
hall for Harvestnight as soon as the lords had gone.

Nyall paused for a brief, quiet talk with Geir and Kari,
and then made his way to his own chamber where he
flopped wearily down in a chair and watched his wife's
woman dress her hair.

"That will do, Hallgerd," Fiorgyn said, waving the girl
away as she knotted the last of the little gold balls into the
ends of Fiorgyn's braids and held a bronze mirror up for
her mistress to see. "Go and make ready yourself."

Hallgerd pattered away and Fiorgyn pulled her chair
around to face her husband. She looked very bright in her
Harvestnight finery, with a gold collar glowing against her
pale braids, and gold bands on her arms. Her gown was
of three shades of blue, pale at the top, and deepen-
ing in wide bands to the midnight-colored hem. It was a
rare pattern, difficult to dye, and it had been part of Nyall's bride-gift to her. The hem was sewn with twining
vines in gold thread with the berries picked out in red.
She rested her blue-slippered feet on the warm hearthstone and looked at her husband thoughtfully.

"And have you whistled your hounds to order?" she
asked.

"Yes," Nyall said, "but I carried a large whip to do it."
He tugged off his boots and began to pull the laces from
his trousers. His Harvestnight clothes lay spread on the
bearskin blanket on the bed.

"And my people?"

"The lords are all hold-settled, and their men with
them. That was the easiest part. For the rest, they are
oath-sworn not to question my commands by so much as
a whisper—there will be no repeat of Jorunnshold this
spring." He flung his boots and trousers into a corner for
a thrall to pick up. "And I have put threat of the chieftain's curse on them that they are not to raid each other
this winter."

Fiorgyn's sky-colored eyes narrowed. "They will not
bide still all winter. They will raid in other tribes' land."

Nyall chuckled from beneath the folds of his shirt as
he pulled it off over his head. "And that will make the
other tribes . . . amenable, when Geir takes the green
branch to their chieftains."

Nyall threw the shirt in the corner with the rest and stretched, naked, by the fire, turning his hands outward with a crack of knuckles.

"Do the Council lords know this?"

"No," Nyall said. "They don't need to. It is enough that they will be hunting where I wish them to."

Fiorgyn nodded. He looked pleased with himself. He had maneuvered his Council with a ruthlessness that would have done credit to a Roman. And when Nyall had used their raids to hammer the other tribes of the Suevi into agreement with an alliance, and told his own lords that now they couldn't raid there anymore, either—it would be too late for them to argue with him. Then they would have two months, she thought, penned in and restless, to turn all their energies to thinking about what they were going to do to the Romans. Sufficient time to build up a good fury, though short enough not to break peace before Nyall was ready. Suddenly she laughed. She began to see how a man so young had held the greatest tribe of the Suevi to his hand. And now he would call the rest to him also. Fiorgyn's face turned thoughtful again.

"Why did you not tell your Council that you intend to make alliance?" she asked. "Surely they will see the need for it if they are not fools?"

Nyall began to dress, not in his usual forest-green color, but in a shirt and trousers of autumn russet, like his hair, with a gold embroidery running like fire around the hem and sleeves. "They are not fools, and they will see the need when they have thought of it." His face was more sober now. "It was plain enough that we hadn't the men to make war properly, even before Jorunnshold. I underestimated the Roman-kind. It is not a mistake I will be making again."

She watched him quietly, hands in her lap, and he came unexpectedly, shirt and trousers still in his hand, to sit in the clean rushes beside her.

"Fiorgyn, I am tired." He leaned his back against her knee while she ran her hands over his bare shoulders, rubbing the tension from them and from the nape of his neck where the bright hair ran upward into the warrior's knot on the right-hand side. "I am tired with fighting the Roman-kind and my own kind as well. I did not tell them of the need for alliance because they need to learn a lesson: that *I* command. *I* rule. You cannot fight a war from a Council chamber. That is something your father never learned."

"Why do you think I asked to be given to you?" Fiorgyn said quietly. "It also occurs to me that if your own lords have no say in this alliance, it will make it easier for the other chieftains to swallow their pride and come oath-bound to you. It is not exactly alliance that you want, is it? You want complete obedience."

Nyall twisted his head around to look at her over his shoulder. "You are no fool either, are you? No, wise one, the others also will come oath-bound, and for that I put a little fear in them first. I learned that from Jorunn. May the gods take his prideful soul to Valhalla, anyway." He shifted his shoulders and Fiorgyn's hands slipped over them, down across his bare, scarred chest. He caught them in his own, and looked up at her, his head still twisted sideways like an owl. "Tell me, was that the *only* reason you asked for me?"

It was an old joke between them now and she bent to kiss him, but stood up before he could pull her down on the floor with him. She chuckled at his obvious intent and dropped his clothes in his lap over the evidence.

"Go and dress before we make ourselves late for the feast."

He thought about saying that he didn't care, but she called a thrall in to help him dress and watched with a wicked little smile on her face as the thrall retrieved his boots from the corner and brushed the dust from the russet shirt. Nyall stood docilely while his cloak was pinned on with the huge amber-studded pin. Then, as they paced side by side up the hall to the High Table, he put his arm around her waist and whispered something in her ear that made her blush and laugh.

The hall was now ablaze with torchlight and hung with pine branches; the withy shutters were pulled close against the rain and whatever else might be about on the night of the dead. The storm howled in the courtyard, but inside it was warm and comforting. The men and women came running through the rain from the buildings that ringed the yard, hurrying into the welcoming safety

of human companionship. They shook off by the fire and
made their way to their places at the tables that ran the
whole length of the hall. The thralls came around with
food and beer, and strong, sweet mead was ladled into
pitchers from the vats in the storehouse.

The walls were hung not only with pine branches, but
with wheat sheaves, onions, sweet herbs, and the few
fruits that grew in these parts. (It was bad country for
orchards, although the Romans had begun to cultivate
grapes in terraced vineyards on their side of the
Rhenus.) When they had eaten and wiped the hot fat
from their hands in the rushes on the floor, the pitchers
went around again, and laughter and tall tales flowed
with it, as did a new kind of hunger, born of the heady
harvest mead on a night when all things were possible.
Harvestnight was an older festival than even the solstice
gatherings, and it honored an older god—Frey, lord of
fruitfulness and increase, who lay with the Goddess in
her winter form to quicken the seed that would make
the land green again in spring.

Kari took up his harp and began to make music, not
a battle music now, but a song of joining and new be-
ginnings. The men and women of the tribe, carried on
the music and the need to shut out the dead that battered with the rain against the shutters, drew closer together. Nyall gazed at his wife. She dropped her eyes,
but he could tell that the Harvestnight magic was running in her blood, too. He also saw that Kari, lost in his
music with his dark eyes closed and his thin hands rippling on the harp strings, was oblivious to the girl
Hallgerd who had crept up to sit in the rushes at his feet.
He nudged Fiorgyn and pointed, and she smiled.

Kari began to sing the Song of Frey's Wooing. The
men of the tribe, with their arms around their women,
settled themselves to listen. The man who could read
was rare, and in any case the runic script was for magic,
not for stories. The only tie they had to the lives of the
gods and the history of their people was a skald's songs.
Kari had learned to fit Gaulish harp music to the old
songs, and to new ones of his own devising.

The tale was familiar, but they listened intently nonetheless, perhaps gaining in persistence from the example

of Frey's servant Skirnir, the Bright One, sent to woo the giant's cold daughter Gerda, in his master's stead. First he offered her the eleven golden apples of immortality, then the magic arm ring, Draupnir, which produced eight rings like itself on every ninth night. These were scorned, and Skirnir resorted to threats. He would cut off her head and her father's too, to set them on poles at the gates of Asgard. Gerda spat at him. A giant's daughter had no fear of gods. Skirnir fell back on curses: Gerda would waste away and her flesh become evil to all men. She would lust after monsters. At that she relented finally and agreed to wed the longing Frey who had seen her when he looked out over the world from Wuotan's throne. In nine nights she would meet him and lie with him in the windless barley field.

The song ended with Frey's lament at the delay, and a sad acceptance of the great price he had paid for his bride:

> One night is long and three are longer;
> How can I endure for nine?
> Often a month has seemed to me shorter
> Than the thrice three nights I pine.

Frey had won his bride, but lost his magic sword to Skirnir as the price of his silver-tongued wooing. And at the last battle of the gods, at Ragnarok, the price would come home to him. There was always a price.

Kari drew a last note from the harp strings, and as it died away there was a murmur of approval and calls for other favorites. Kari waited until the commotion died down and then took up another song, also the Song of Frey, the golden lord who danced in the sun and rain while the fields swelled where his feet had touched. Still unnoticed, Hallgerd snuggled against Kari's knee, and Nyall began to laugh.

A few couples were slipping from the hall now, hand in hand, for their beds in the guest chambers, or for the warm straw of the stables. Thrain had pulled the young widow of his new holding close to him, and she seemed content enough; even Morgian felt the magic of Harvest-night as she lifted her still unlined face to smile at

Steinvar's lean, scarred one as it bent above her. In the ordinary way, the Germans counted the passions of men and women strictly—a matter for marriage and alliance and not to be taken lightly. But things done on Harvest-night were the god's affairs and never questioned after-ward. It was as well, Nyall thought, looking at a hall too full of women, even though many of the lords had left their own behind them in their holds. There were too many women in the aftermath of war. It was not right that they should always walk lonely.

He saw Arni pull a girl with a fall of red-gold hair into his arms. Astrid, Steinvar's daughter—if that went well it would be a good match, he thought with half his mind, while the other half made him lay his hand on his wife's arm with a new urgency.

Fiorgyn set down the mead pot she had been drinking from, and before she rose she whispered something in Kari's ear as his song ended.

Kari blinked, looked down at Hallgerd cuddled close against his knee, and opened his eyes wide in surprise, while the chieftain and his wife laughed and made their way with arms entwined through the revelers in the hall.

XV

The Lyxian Horse

"WHEN I HIRED THIS HOUSE," CORREUS SAID, LOOKING AT Freita across the hearth, "it was not with the intention of providing an inn for my layabout friends."

He had come to have her mend a torn tunic for him and had found the hut (now transformed into three rooms, for Freita had curtained off a second cubicle at the far end for young Julius) full to overflowing. Paulinus and Silvanus were both lounging by the fire on a couch Correus had never seen before, while Tullius sat cross-legged on the floor teaching Julius to cheat at dice.

Even Flavius was there, in a folding camp chair, with his slim legs stretched out to the fire. Freita, with all the airs of a gracious hostess, was plying them with honeycakes and sweet spiced wine from a pot that steamed aromatically in the hot ash at the edge of the hearth.

Paulinus and Silvanus looked up from the couch and moved to make room for him.

"Where did this couch come from?" Correus asked suspiciously.

"I brought it," Paulinus said, seeming a little embarrassed. "Thought the place, uh . . . looked a little bare."

"My thanks," Correus said. He looked at Flavius. "Greetings to you, brother." *And what in the name of Hades was he doing here?*

"And I have brought wine," Flavius said. "My contribution to domestic felicity." Correus and Freita shot him a simultaneous glance of irritation, and he rose to go, lazily. "My thanks for the hospitality . . . lady." He gave the title a slight emphasis. "It has been most . . . interesting to make your acquaintance."

Flavius picked up his helmet and strolled off, leaving Correus restraining his temper. Flavius had been patently curious ever since Correus had brought his oddly assorted household back to Argentoratum, but the constraint between the two brothers had left his curiosity little scope. Correus wasn't sure now whether Flavius was trying to make friends, or had come merely to annoy him. Or possibly he was there to gather enough information for a really inflammatory letter to their father. Well, Flavius had better keep his curious hands off Freita, Correus found himself thinking. Then, seeing the look Freita was giving Flavius as he went out the door, he decided that Freita would see to that herself.

"Sorry about that," Silvanus said. "He, uh . . . attached himself."

"Limpetlike," Paulinus agreed. "Sit down, Correus, and stop scowling. We came to see how Freita was, and there wasn't any way to discourage Flavius without being rude."

Freita spoke for the first time, and Correus saw now that she had put on one of her new gowns for the occasion. "I thought perhaps you wouldn't have minded if

I was rude," she said, "but I don't know the right Latin words. Centurion Silvanus has promised to teach me," she added with such a demure expression that Correus laughed and took the chair vacated by his brother. "Julius took him to see Aeshma," she added. "I think he was hoping he'd get kicked, but the wretched beast *liked* him."

"Flavius has what you Germans call horse magic," Correus said. "He always has. Why didn't *you* like him?"

"I am not a horse," Freita said. "And he doesn't like *you*."

Correus blinked at her in surprise. "I would have thought that would be a recommendation," he murmured.

Silvanus seemed to feel that a change of subject was in order. "It's a pity you can't turn that beast loose on Gallus," he said idly, referring to the legion's horsemaster. "The old devil palmed off those two nags he gave you and Flavius on another pair of babes in the wood this morning. One of them's posted to my cohort, and his beast stopped dead still in the middle of parade and refused to move. The poor man did everything but get down and kick it in the ass, and the damn horse just stood there like a dairy cow chewing its cud. His men were practically rolling on the ground. He cried on my shoulder about it afterward."

Correus's ears pricked up. "Is the beast back in the stables now?"

"Oh yes," Silvanus said, chuckling. "He took him back after parade and threatened to beat Gallus to a bloody pulp unless he gave him another one. But the man's a laughingstock now."

"Can't have that," Correus said. "It'll ruin our reputation." His dark eyes were bright, and a wicked little light had begun to dance in them. He couldn't do much about Flavius, but there was one debt he could pay off. "Lucius, are you acquainted with Horsemaster Gallus?"

"No, I'm not," Paulinus said. He looked at Correus with suspicion.

"How providential," Correus said. He poured some of the hot spiced wine into Flavius's empty cup and reached for the wooden tray of honeycakes balanced on the hearth edge beside it.

Horsemaster Gallus was taking his ease in the shed that was used as a cavalry tack room. He had come to regard this as his private office; here he was screened from any passing official eyes who might want him to do some work. He looked up in the manner of a man interrupted while thinking great thoughts when the tall centurion poked his aquiline face around the doorpost. The face was vaguely familiar, but he found himself unable to place it immediately. Gallus had the cavalryman's dislike of the regular legions, overlaid by the professional malingerer's dislike for officers in general. He avoided them where possible, and contented himself with annoying them where it was not.

"Horsemaster Gallus?"

"Yes, sir?" Gallus's bowed legs were stretched comfortably out on a hay bale in front of him. He swung them off reluctantly and saluted, since the centurion seemed to be expecting it.

"Oh, sit down, Horsemaster, by all means," Correus said, making himself comfortable on the bale.

"Thank you, sir." Gallus's bright eyes regarded him curiously. "What can I do for you, sir?"

"I am told that you are in charge of acquiring remounts as necessary," Correus said. "And of selling off the animals no longer fit for use?"

"Yes, sir, that I am," said Gallus, striving to figure out what was going on. There was also a matter of requisition slips and properly signed forms from the cavalry commandant's office, but he saw no need to mention them.

"Excellent," Correus said. "I want to buy one of your mounts."

"Well, sir, it's not that simple." Gallus mentally ticked over his secret stock of signed sale permits.

"Oh, I think you'd be willing to part with this one," Correus said with a smile. "He wrecked a whole cohort parade this morning. And I'd be willing to give you—I mean give the army—a good price for him."

Gallus grew more perplexed. The centurion's slight

swagger and lazy speech fairly screamed of a good family, and money. Gallus knew him from somewhere, he was sure.

"I had him for a personal mount for a month or so," Correus said.

Gallus gave him a wary look, the memory of his visit from the nag's most recent rider still fresh in his mind.

"He's a bit of a plug," Correus said in a friendly, soothing voice, "but the fact is, the beast saved my life—shied and took off into the brush like the Furies were after him. Turned out later there was a whacking great viper coiled up in the rocks, and the thing would have had me in the leg if it weren't for that horse. After this morning, he's sure to be sold off, and I'd like to return the favor if I can. Hate to see him go for dog's meat."

Gallus began to relax, the scent of sesterces strong in the wind. "Well, sir, as I said, it's not all that easy. We don't generally sell 'em off except in lots."

"I'm sure I could make it worth your while," Correus said. "I want that horse. Made a thanks-vow to Poseidon after he saved my skin for me," he added, his expression pleasant and not overly intelligent.

"Well . . ." Gallus said dubiously.

"Say five hundred sesterces?" Correus suggested.

Gallus hesitated. The horse wasn't worth three hundred, and the cavalry commandant would be on his tail to sell him as soon as he'd had his own tail chewed by the camp commander for that wrecked parade. "I dunno, sir. The commander mightn't like it. Like I said, we sell 'em off in lots, and there's a batch ready to go out now. I need that one to make up ten—that's the smallest lot the dealers'll bother with."

"Well, then, say eight hundred," Correus said, with the air of a man to whom money is a small matter. "I'm going to send him back to my father's farm," he improvised, "as a present for my sister. So you won't get in any trouble."

Gallus felt that the gods had finally smiled on him. "Well, sir, I'd have to pay the dealer some—to take a short lot, you know. Maybe for nine hundred . . ." He didn't think even this idiot would go higher than that.

Correus smiled. "You drive a hard bargain, Horsemaster. But of course I appreciate your position. Very well, nine hundred it is. I'll just give it to you now, to seal the bargain, and I'll send my boy around for him in a day or so, when I've made the arrangements." He took a pouch from the front of his uniform tunic and counted out a stack of coins. "Have him cleaned up for me, will you? Girls like their beasts to look pretty. And you won't mind giving me a bill of sale, of course, just to make it all legal."

Gallus delved into a chest and produced a sale permit, which he duly inscribed with the figure of nine hundred sesterces. Correus departed and Gallus sat down again, counting ecstatically on his fingers. If he turned in a duplicate sale permit for three hundred, the army would think itself overpaid.

Gallus spent a pleasant evening listing the things a man could do with six hundred sesterces, and in the morning he had the nag trotted out and set a stable-hand to performing such beautification as was possible on so unprepossessing a beast. He wondered if the centurion would change his mind when he saw him again, but decided that it didn't matter. He had the nine hundred sesterces, and the centurion had a silly vow to Poseidon Horse-father, who was probably laughing hard enough to flood Atlantis again.

An exclamation and a pair of raised voices from the stables outside drew him from this pleasant reverie, and Gallus ambled out to see what was going on.

The cavalry stablehand was brushing the dun nag's coat and swearing at a sandy-haired youth in a plain civilian tunic, while the latter clambered about under the beast's splayed feet, peering at the half-moon brand on the inside of one mud-colored haunch.

"Here, now," Gallus said, adjusting his uniform tunic, regrettably devoid of the cavalry scale he was supposed to be wearing over it. "What do you think you're doing?"

"Gettin' in the way, sir," the stableman said in aggrieved tones. "Bargin' in like—here, what do you think you're doin'?" The sandy-haired man was inspecting the dun nag's ears and clucking to himself over the cavalry crop that had been given its straggling mane.

"Let's see your pass," Gallus said.

"Pass be damned," the other man said. "Where'd you get this horse?"

"He's a cavalry horse," Gallus said acidly, "*as* you've no doubt noticed by now."

"You mean you don't know what—" The man broke off, and an expression of obvious guile passed over his freckled face.

"Don't know what?" Gallus shot out one callused hand, unexpectedly strong, and gripped him by the wrist. The young man wore a plain buff linen tunic of good cloth and a silver band pushed up high on his arm under the tunic sleeve. It was a warmish day for fall, and his thin, bony feet were bare of sandals. Someone's slave, and a high-up one at that. Gallus narrowed his eyes, puzzled and alert. "Don't know what?" he repeated.

"Why, don't you know where he came from?" the sandy-haired slave said. "Don't you keep records?"

"We aren't a stud farm," Gallus said. "He was bought in Nero's day." He nodded at the brand on the outer flank: N IMP. "I wasn't around then to take his pedigree," he added with elaborate sarcasm.

"Couldn't have if you'd wanted to," the slave murmured. "Look here, will you sell him?"

Gallus stared at the ungainly dun form, from heavy head to turned-in hocks. Two fools in two days, and both for the same horse. It was most unfair. "If you're looking for a good mount, lad, I've got just the thing," he said hopefully. "Prime stock, but just a bit past cavalry work." Anyone who would want to buy this nag wouldn't be too choosy.

"No, you fool," the slave said, exasperated. "*This* horse. And it's not for me, it's for my master."

Gallus started to protest that the horse was no longer his, and then thought better of it. "Well, you see, I've had an offer for him already, from an officer at the fort here. Couldn't sell him out from under him, you know."

The slave blinked in surprise. "*He* couldn't use him. Do you mean to tell me you really don't know what you've got here?"

"No, I don't," Gallus said, "and you're going to tell me, or I'll have you thrown out of here!" The stablehand had ceased work and was watching the exchange with curiosity. Gallus glanced at him and then jerked his head at the tack-room door. "Get in here."

The slave followed him obediently and sat down on the hay bale previously occupied by Correus. "Now," Gallus said. "Start talking."

"My master will meet any price you've had offered," the slave said abruptly.

"You're authorized to speak for him?" Gallus inquired with great irony.

"Of course," the slave replied. "I am steward of the household. Do I look like a vine tender? Now, how much have you been offered?"

"Will you tell me why you want him!" Gallus looked as if he were ready to burst with irritation, and the slave sighed.

"Very well. Have you ever been in Lyxia?"

"Where in Hades is Lyxia?"

"In Asia. Just a little bit of a country tucked in below Pergamum."

"Never heard of it."

"You wouldn't have." The slave made it plain that this lack of education was only to be expected. "It's not big enough to be worth anything. Everybody who comes along has conquered it, from the Greeks on, and the Lyxians go along as they always have. They aren't interested in anything much except their temple, and as long as they get to worship their god the way they want to, they don't care who they pay their taxes to."

"What about the horse?"

"I'm getting there," the slave said. He seemed prepared to run through the history and culture of Lyxia first, however. "They've got an odd religion. Really nothing else like it anywhere. They keep a special herd of horses, just for their god."

"That's nothing new," Gallus said. "So do the Germans and half the barbarians in Britain."

"Not to sacrifice." The slave looked horrified. "They dance. Every year at midsummer, the horses dance for their god."

Gallus snorted. "*That* beast? He's got the gait of an ox and a mouth like an iron ingot. He couldn't dance if you put strings on him."

"Well, of course not," the slave said patiently. "I don't expect there's anyone in the Empire trained to give the right commands, outside of Lyxia. Except for my master. But this one's been trained, all right. They don't give 'em that half-moon brand until they've passed their training."

"If these horses are so fabulous, how come we don't import 'em?" Gallus asked suspiciously.

"The Lyxians won't teach anyone but their priests to ride 'em," the slave said. "And they don't look like much to anyone who doesn't know what he's looking for. Lyxian ceremonies are secret."

"And I suppose your master's one of these Lyxian horse priests?"

"Oh no. They never leave their temple—it's a city in itself, really. But we are very well traveled, and my master made friends there years ago, with one of their priests. He'll pay anything you like for that horse."

Gallus found greed outweighing his good sense. "Well now, to tell the truth, that horse is promised. The centurion took quite a fancy to him. Offered a thousand sesterces."

"A thousand?" The slave looked appalled. He twitched the folds of his tunic into place primly. "A Lyxian temple horse is priceless."

"Priceless?"

"Well . . . in Lyxia, of course." The slave seemed to feel that he had said too much. "Here, of course . . . well, there's no one but my master that he'd be any use to."

Gallus's eyes were beady now, and he rubbed his hands together. "He was worth a thousand to the centurion. Of course, we hadn't *exactly* struck a bargain yet. He might go higher."

The slave thought a moment. "My master will give you fifteen hundred."

"For a Lyxian temple horse?" It was Gallus's turn to look appalled. "And in any case, I couldn't sell him out from under the other gentleman. It wouldn't be right."

"I thought you said no bargain had been struck?"

"Well, we did have sort of an understanding. . . ."

"In that case, it's not likely he'd go above a thousand, is it? Look here, my master will give you two thousand,

and not a copper more. The horse is worth a lot to him, but you haven't much market for it here, you know. No one else can ride him. The commands are all in Lyxian, and there's a special way of sitting him to make him dance. That's why they seem so awkward when anyone who's not trained rides them. They're bred for the temple dance, and it takes a different set of muscles. I can't think how a Lyxian temple horse ended up in the cavalry," he added. "He must have been stolen by some fool who didn't know what he had. Two thousand, Horsemaster. Even my master won't go higher than that."

Gallus counted mentally, and a dream of retirement in the sunny East, with a nice little harem and a house with marble floors, rose up before him, superimposed on hay bales and bridle bits. He had already put by a good sum, acquired one way and another, and this could make all the difference. He couldn't resist the temptation to try to pry another five hundred out of this windfall sitting before him. When, after a bit of haggling, he got it, he increased the horizon of his dreams a little further. It was fortunate, he thought, as they shook hands on the bargain, that it had been the slave and not the master who had happened by as the horse was being groomed. He might not have got as good a price from the master.

The slave departed to fetch the money, and Gallus sat down to concoct a story for the centurion who would appear in a few days to find his horse gone. He would have to give him back his nine hundred sesterces, he thought sadly. But after giving the army the three hundred he had listed on the duplicate sale ticket, he would have twenty-two hundred left. A house with marble floors . . . and maybe a little pool to sit by in the evenings. . . . He told the stablehand to put the Lyxian horse in a loose box and gave the dun flanks a fond pat. He settled himself in his office again to await the return of the man who had so fortunately traveled in far-off Lyxia.

"Ah, Horsemaster." A tall, angular form poked its head around the door and Gallus awoke from his dream in a hurry. The centurion! He wasn't supposed to be back for two days.

"I've come for my horse," Correus said pleasantly.

Gallus thought fast, congratulating himself on having had the good sense to have the horse put out of sight. He launched into the explanation apologetically, and with much bemoaning of the stupidity of the under-horsemaster who had sold the beast off without asking— Gallus had only just found out, but it had been bought for a riding horse and would have a good master, and that was what the centurion had wanted after all, was it not? And here was his nine hundred sesterces back, of course.

The centurion proved unexpectedly stubborn. "That's my horse," he said flatly. "I bought him."

"Indeed, sir, and I am most dreadfully sorry. The man has been disciplined, of course." Gallus saluted several times and pushed the stack of coins at Correus.

Correus pushed them back. "I want my horse." He waved the bill of sale under Gallus's nose.

"But, sir, as I have explained—"

"Perhaps he hasn't been taken off yet," Correus said. "I'll just have a look."

"No, wait! I assure you, sir—last night, it was." Gallus pushed the sesterces at him again.

"I want my horse," Correus repeated stubbornly. "He's my horse. I bought him." Obviously a man with a one-track mind. "You'll have to get him back."

"But I can't, sir." Gallus peered anxiously past his shoulder, hoping the sandy-haired slave would take his time returning. "He's . . . uh, he's been sent out of the Province already. Most unfortunate. Now, sir—"

Correus appeared to have grown roots. "I want my horse," he said again, peering down at Gallus from under his helmet with a threatening eye.

"Perhaps . . . a hundred sesterces more . . . for your trouble, sir?" Gallus could hear voices outside now.

"I wrote my sister, telling her I was sending her a special horse," Correus said. "Am I supposed to send her a hundred sesterces instead?"

"Two hundred," Gallus said. He rummaged in his own purse. "You could buy her a fine horse for eleven hundred, sir."

"I want *that* horse," the centurion said stolidly. He stood in the doorway, blocking Gallus's view.

Gallus frantically worked sums in his mind. Twenty-two hundred profit from the second buyer, as opposed to six hundred from this one. That left . . . sixteen hundred, in difference. Minus the two hundred he had already offered. Fourteen hundred . . . he could afford a little more to get rid of this ass before the second buyer came back. "Why don't we sit down and talk, sir?" He tried to edge him away from the door.

"I want my horse," the centurion said again, maddeningly. He leaned against the doorpost and seemed inclined to stay there.

Gallus could hear voices clearly now. Inquiring voices, one of them familiar: the young slave's. He fished in his purse again. "Four hundred, sir," he said desperately. "Because of all the trouble. Please, sir, it wasn't my fault, truly. And four hundred's all the fool got for him. I can't give you more. And I don't know *how* I'll square it with the commander. Come out of my pay, I expect," he added dismally.

Correus appeared to relent. "Well, it's your own fault, you know, Horsemaster. Let it be a lesson to you to keep better watch on your men in future. An officer is responsible for his men's actions as well as his own," he added pompously.

"Yes, sir," Gallus said. "You're quite right." He pushed the nine hundred sesterces at Correus again and breathed a sigh of relief when he accepted them.

Correus tucked the money in a pouch and stood expectantly. Gallus counted out another four hundred from his own purse, hardly feeling a pang at the parting so long as he could also part with this pigheaded fool before someone brought the Lyxian horse out again.

Correus accepted the money gravely and made much business of stowing it away in his pouch, while Gallus danced with impatience. Finally Correus allowed himself to be hustled out into the stableyard. He strolled leisurely to the end of the stable row with the horsemaster beside him.

"Remember, Horsemaster," he said gravely in parting, "a good soldier always takes responsibility for his . . . mistakes."

Wiping his brow, Gallus watched Correus amble

away. The voices could be heard from behind the stable row, quite loudly now, and he hurried in their direction, cutting through a side passage into the rear courtyard.

The Lyxian temple horse stood apparently asleep in the sunny courtyard, the dun hide twitching only enough to shake off the cloud of flies that buzzed around it. The sandy-haired slave stood beside it, while a tall, blond centurion leaned against the open door of the loose box and howled with laughter.

"Lyxian temple horse!" he spluttered. He clutched his helmet to his stomach and bent over it.

Gallus felt a horrible suspicion creep over him. "It's . . . not a Lyxian temple horse?"

"Hell, no!" The centurion wiped his eyes with the back of his hand. "That's a nag!"

Gallus turned on the slave with an awful eye, and the slave backed away.

"But the half-moon brand," he protested, and prudently put the centurion between himself and the horsemaster.

The centurion looked at the horse again. It was still asleep. It swayed slightly, appeared about to fall over, and opened its eyes with a snort. The centurion let out another whoop of laughter. "Not a waxing moon," he said to the abashed slave. "A waning moon! Like the horsemaster's fortunes, I fear!"

Correus took Paulinus and Silvanus to dinner at the best inn in Argentoratum with the horsemaster's money. They took Freita with them, and her green eyes were wide and dancing as they regaled her with the tale of the horsemaster's downfall.

"Oh, Lord! I wish you could have seen his face!" Silvanus said. "And the poor man who had that nag on parade spotted Gallus this morning and yelled, 'Hey Gallus, you want to sell a horse?' and a whole cavalry troop practically fell off their horses laughing. We won't have any trouble with Gallus for a while!"

Freita chuckled, but her face developed a thoughtful look as she bit into a pastry with spiced meat folded inside it. "This is good," she announced. "I will learn to make this. But you three are like it—most unexpected inside."

"How do you mean?" Silvanus asked.

"I think she means our operation on poor Gallus," Correus said. "It gives you a new view on Rome, perhaps?"

"Mmm," Freita said through a mouthful of pastry. It never ceased to amaze Correus how much she could eat and still stay slim. A Roman girl would have been as fat as a pretty pig on half of what Freita ate. But she rode Aeshma every day, and when she wasn't riding, he had learned from Julius, she walked—a restless prowling that was half sightseeing, he thought, and half the pacing of a caged cat. She seemed cheerful enough tonight, however, as she washed her pastry down with sweet watered wine, and tried to explain. "It puzzles me . . . surprises me? I am not sure of the word I want. One day you are putting much time and thought into a boy's prank, and the next you are a . . . a fighting machine, marching your men back and forth, and all the rest has gone away inside that helmet as if it had never been there."

Correus said, "Well, I'm not a fighting machine. No one here is."

"I always thought that Rome was."

"There's some truth in that," Paulinus murmured. "Let us say that Rome strives to appear so, in her provinces." He picked up an apple and began to peel it with his knife.

Freita watched the spiral of red peel uncoiling. "I seem to be thinking in terms of food tonight. Maybe because this also is new to me." She waved a hand at the array of dishes—pastries and iced cakes, olives, pickled eggs, and a plate of sliced beef in *garum*, the fish sauce the Romans seemed to pour over everything. She nodded at the apple. "I've never seen Rome without its skin on before. And mostly it's been a skin of iron plates."

"We sound like lobsters," Silvanus said. "We're not so different underneath."

"Different enough," Freita said.

"We're a standing army," Correus said. "We have no farms and herds to go back to after a battle. We go to winter quarters instead and twitch with boredom till spring."

"And when you get too bored, you set snares for the horsemaster?"

"That was a debt to pay," Correus said. "I rode that plug for two months and got blisters on my behind with every step. Besides, if Gallus hadn't been greedy and tried to cheat me, it wouldn't have worked."

Freita pushed a tendril of hair back from her face. Correus noticed for the first time she had piled it on top of her head, Roman-fashion. It gave her an odd look. She also appeared to be watching him, he thought, as if he also had suddenly changed form.

"Did you ever find your sister her blond wig?" he asked Silvanus, beginning to feel uncomfortable under Freita's scrutiny.

"Yes, but I didn't tell her where I got it," Silvanus said with a laugh. "Rhodope had one—Leza had bought it, and Rhodope took one look and said that not even her hair looked that ridiculous, and took it away from her. She had to give the girl two new gowns to make her shut up about it."

"What do Roman women look like?" Freita asked suddenly.

"Well, not like Rhodope, if that's what you're thinking," Silvanus said. "Not respectable ladies. They look like . . . oh, like the legate's wife." Calpurnius Rufinus had recently brought his family out to the frontier to be with him. His wife was army-bred herself, and took better than most to the Spartan conditions. She was a brisk, practical woman with a fondness for jewelry, which was, as she said, the only luxury that was really portable.

Freita recalled the legate's lady as she had seen her in the market square. "She paints her face," she said.

"Roman ladies believe in giving their faces as much help as possible," Paulinus said.

"Would I be prettier if I painted my face?" Freita asked.

Correus couldn't think of a safe answer to that, but Silvanus had no such qualms. He studied her carefully, wide cheekbones narrowing to a small chin, white skin, and grass-green eyes, darker now in the lamplight. It was a cat's face, and not a house cat either; a mountain panther.

"Well," he said, apparently giving the matter some thought, "you're a big woman—tall, and your shoulders are broad. You wouldn't want to overdo it. Your skin's too good to powder. Our ladies put white stuff on theirs to make it look like yours. But your lashes are too pale —they get lost. You might darken them, and put some red on your mouth. A rose color, nothing too dark. And a little green on your eyelids would bring out the color of your eyes."

Freita burst out laughing. "Thank you, Centurion. I believe I will. How do you know so much about ladies' paints?"

"He has a sister," Correus and Paulinus said together.

"Three sisters," Silvanus said. "And a mother who was the reigning beauty of Neapolis. I was the youngest. I think my father encouraged an army career because he was afraid I'd grow up to be a hairdresser."

Correus suspected that Silvanus's knowledge of feminine adornment also stemmed from the fact that he generally kept a mistress somewhere. His love life was uncomplicated, and revolving. Correus hinted as much, and Silvanus grinned at him.

"Yes, but I don't generally tell 'em how to dress. I find they don't much care for that."

"Well, you may tell me," Freita said. "If I am going to live here—and it seems I must—" She shot a glance at Correus. "I won't go about looking like a freak. A—a barbarian." She took another drink of her wine, and Correus remembered uneasily that Germans didn't drink much wine. She wouldn't be used to it. He tipped some water from the pitcher into her wine cup. Unobtrusively, he hoped.

Freita gave him a look and put her hand over the top of her cup. She turned back to Silvanus. "Anything else, Centurion?"

"Well," Silvanus said seriously, "if you won't be insulted . . . Don't let Correus buy you any more gowns with all those drapes and flutters in front. Your breasts are too big."

Correus half-expected her to toss the cup, wine and

all, at Silvanus, but she didn't. She gazed down at her breasts thoughtfully, with an expression that made Correus bite his lip to keep from laughing. Then she looked up at Silvanus with a giggle and a small hiccup, and said, "I think you're right, Centurion."

Oh, Lord, Correus thought, *she is drunk.* Then he decided to let well enough alone. She was having a good time. He just wished she were having a good time with *him.* It did occur to him, though, that her interest in Roman ladies and their fashions might stem from a chance remark that morning that he and Flavius were going home on leave while the army was idle for the winter. If the frontier stayed quiet, of course. There was always that if. He wondered if she were drunk enough to talk about her people without being made unhappy.

"What do German ladies wear?" he asked, edging into the subject carefully.

Freita thought. "Bright colors. Roman clothes always look pale to me. Sometimes two or three colors together. A woman wears her hair loose until she marries. Then she braids it." She put her hands to her Roman-style hair. "I am not used to this. It feels like it's falling down. The Semnone *men* knot their hair this way," she added. "But at the side. Our men only braid theirs." She studied the three of them. "Your short hair still seems odd to me. Among my people it means a man is disgraced. Nyall Sigmundson had a man's hair cut for going to sleep on guard."

"That's right," Paulinus said. "You were with Nyall, weren't you?" His eyes grew interested.

A little shadow flicked across her face, and Correus wished he had kept quiet, but she answered calmly enough. "I was at Jorunnshold, lord. Is that right? Lord? I don't know what to call you."

"Lucius will do."

Correus called him Lucius, but his servant didn't, and the servant was a free man, Freita had learned. "Is that proper?" she asked.

Paulinus smiled at her. "No, not really. But call me that, anyway."

"Very well, Lucius." She had trouble pronouncing it. "What is he like, this Nyall?" Paulinus asked.

"He is . . . a very great man. If he were a Roman, he would be a Caesar, I think."

"What will he do now?" Paulinus asked. "If he lives, of course."

Freita gave him a long look. "Oh, he lives, Lucius. He is too . . . ruthless not to live. What he will do, I suppose, depends on how many of my people also live." She reached for her wine cup again, and Correus didn't try to stop her. Damn Paulinus and his prying. And damn himself for starting it. He knew very well that he had had the same tactic in mind. A fine trio of Romans they were—they got a homesick girl drunk and tried to make her betray her people.

Freita unnerved him by apparently reading his mind. "Don't worry, Centurion," she said drily. "I don't know enough to help you. Or hurt Nyall."

Paulinus changed the subject adroitly. He had already heard what he wanted to. "It is the nature of the historian to be curious," he said lightly. "Since you also are curious about us, I'll send Tullius around with some of my sketches of Rome—drawings of the City, I mean. You can see what we have built. It might help to explain us a little."

"It is so different from this city?"

"*Roma Dea*, Argentoratum's not a city," Silvanus said. "It's a hovel."

Freita looked around the inn's dining chamber—a tiled floor with a small mosaic of fish in a circle, walls painted in bright colors by a provincial artist, oil lamps suspended from bronze chains, a pool with a small fountain that gurgled from a stone conch shell . . . alien magnificence. And Rome was . . . what compared to this? Yet another side to the Roman-kind . . . another look under the skin. Builders of things . . . straight roads and great cities. She stared into her wine cup, as if something about the Romans might come up from its depths.

"Frightening, aren't we?" Correus said gently. "If it's any comfort, the Germans frighten *us*."

She looked up and laughed at him gently. "You mean Nyall frightens you. He ought to, Centurion. He ought to."

They walked back through the moonlit streets of

Argentoratum, with the fallen dry leaves scudding before them in the wind. It came down from the mountains with a smell of snow in it.

"The Frost-Folks' breath," Freita said, lifting her face to it. "Wolf winter. It will seem odd not to worry about the lambing this year."

Correus moved closer and put his cloak around her. "You can worry about Julius instead," he said. "The little devil stole three apples off the grocer's cart yesterday and I had to pay his way out of it."

Freita laughed again and didn't seem to notice his arm around her. "He won't do it again," she said. "It's only that we didn't tell him *not* to."

Paulinus and Silvanus had dropped a few paces behind, and Paulinus looked at them thoughtfully. "D'you know," he said quietly, "if they could just forget who they are, they'd do well enough."

Silvanus shook his head. "Easier to make that nag into a Lyxian temple horse, I expect."

XVI

The Arena

THE WATCHER IN THE WOODS CREPT CLOSER, SILENTLY, then crouched in the shadows to watch the men sent here to watch him. The dawn light had begun to run silver along the meadow he had passed through, but here in the black woods the dying fire still glowed red in the darkness. The men sleeping around it began to stir, and he waited patiently until they should wake. Men who were surprised often came up with a dagger in hand.

"Well, here's a piece of luck," Messala Cominius said as Correus turned through the door of his office and saluted. "We've got our very own spy. Came in this morning with two of the frontier scouts. The legate's compliments, and would you go and speak German at him?"

Correus groaned. "I'm due for leave, sir. Don't tell me he's going to cancel it. We're almost packed."

"Depends on what our spy has to say, I expect," Cominius said. "I didn't know you were so anxious for three months in your brother's company."

"I had hoped it might mend some fences," Correus said.

Cominius nodded. "Understandable. Well, I'll do what I can, but we need our frontier scouts out sticking their long noses in the Germans' business, not hanging around camp playing interpreter when there are others like yourself who speak German." There was no question of using a native interpreter; not if the legate really had latched on to a spy out of Nyallshold.

The German proved to be a Black Forest man, disgruntled with his people's losses to the Romans and chafing under the Semnones' rule. His name was Ingald.

"Look you, Commander," the German said as Correus translated, "you want peace on your frontier, and I want my lands back. I would sooner hold them under Rome than not at all." He smiled, a pleasant open smile. "I am a practical man."

Legate Rufinus snorted. "Your lands?"

"I would have been chieftain after Arngunn," Ingald said. "I am of the Kindred of the Nicretes. Give me my tribe again and the overlordship of the other tribes, and I will hold your frontier for you."

"Three of those tribes have already sworn to Rome," the legate said. "And the others are . . . not troublesome to us just now."

"Sworn and unsworn and sworn again," the German said shrewdly. "Gunnar and Runolf would swear to the Dark Ones if it would gain them six gold pieces each. And the Hermanduri will go with the stronger force, as ever."

"And that is Rome," the legate said. "Frankly I don't see much use for you." The German had already confirmed the one vital point, he thought: Nyall had got out of Jorunnshold alive. Rufinus's expression registered studied disinterest.

"What if Nyall should take the war trail again?" the German said.

The legate became more disinterested than ever. "Will he?" he inquired politely, arranging the loops of his purple sash of office to his satisfaction. "And with whose warriors?"

The German hesitated. "Not as yet," he said at last, smoothly. "But without me, how will you be knowing when?"

"I doubt this man knows, either," Correus added to the legate in Latin, when he had finished translating. "If I were Nyall I wouldn't tell this one what time I was going to eat dinner."

Calpurnius Rufinus gave the German a long, hard look from beneath his eagle-crested helmet, until the German's handsome, smiling face lost some of its blandness. The legate didn't like traitors, even those on the other side; but Rome made use of what fell to her hand. "Just so," he said. "Without you I won't be knowing. And that makes you useful to me in Nyallshold at the moment. If Nyall doesn't have you killed, and you bring me something worth the hearing, *then* we will talk about your lands."

The German seemed about to protest, but after a long look at Calpurnius Rufinus's face, he closed his mouth again. The legate's meaning had been plain in his voice even without the translation, and having his words repeated in a Semnone accent gave them a double edge of menace. If he didn't get the legate what he wanted, the commander of the Eagles wouldn't hesitate to sell him where it would do the most good: back into the Semnones' hands, to turn Nyall suspicious of *all* his men. And he would do it as ruthlessly as he himself had been prepared to sell Nyall. He had hold of a sword by the blade now, he thought. It might still be turned where he wanted it, but he would need to move carefully. His face grew blank and pleasant again as he gave the commander his agreement.

The legate spat on the wooden floor when the German had been escorted out. "I want a bath," he said, and stalked to the doorway.

Correus watched him, surprised. There was something

in the German's smooth, handsome face that had made
him feel unclean also, but somehow he hadn't expected the
legate to react the same way.

Calpurnius Rufinus turned back at the doorway. "Yes,
I use 'em, Centurion, but I don't like 'em. Go and take
your leave. I doubt he'll come out of his hole again until
spring."

Correus didn't mention the interview to Freita when he
went to the house to leave her money to see her and Julius through his absence. He would have liked to ask her
what she thought. Freita seemed a good judge of men.
Except, he corrected himself ruefully, for her blindness to
his own qualities. But even in a Roman gown, poring over
Paulinus's ink drawings of that shining, marble city, she
was still a German, and she had known Nyall. He had a
feeling that anyone who had known Nyall would love or
hate him, with not much space in between. "I don't know
enough to help you, or hurt Nyall," she had said. Best to
see that this remained the case with him as well.

She was sitting in the chair with her slippered feet on
the hearthstone. Lying on a couch made her go to sleep,
she said. The sheaf of Paulinus's drawings was spread out
in her lap, and she was biting at the nail of one finger,
while Julius, with a patronizing air, pointed out the buildings to her.

"That's the Basilica Julia, where the law courts are.
And that one's the Temple of the Divine Claudius."

"How do you know so much about Rome, young one?"
Correus asked.

"I was born there," Julius said.

"How did you end up in Germany?" Correus realized a
little guiltily that he had never even bothered to ask the
boy where he came from.

"There's not a lot to do in Rome for my kind," Julius
said. "Except wait for the grain dole and the free games.
And drink in between times. I expect the price my father
got for me let him drink a few months longer. It's killed
him by now, most like," he added with an acid tinge in
his voice. He was clean, his hair cut properly, and his
pointed face had lost the fear that Correus had first seen
in it. He looked much as he must have before he had

been sold, Correus thought. Julius was a street urchin, a true child of the City, wary and suspicious, but ready to make the most of anything the Fates should see fit to pass his way. Old beyond their years, the street children made bad slaves, he remembered someone saying. Flavius, he thought.

Julius seemed to read his thoughts. "I haven't run away yet, have I?" he asked defiantly. "I wouldn't either, if you took me to Rome with you." A hopeful look, which Correus thought for a moment was mirrored in Freita's face.

"No, I don't expect you would, but I can't do it," he said firmly. "I need you here to look after things." To look after Freita, whom Correus certainly couldn't take with him. He had a brief mental vision of himself arriving home, trailing his ill-assorted household after him. He might be his own master in the army, but in Rome he was Appius's son.

"How do you know *I* won't run away while you're gone?" Freita inquired.

"Because you don't have any place to go," he said, and then feeling that he had been brutal, he sat down on the floor by her chair and took her hands in his. She was still wearing her hair pinned up, he saw, and noticed also with some amusement that she had altered the gown she had worn to the inn into a plainer style. "Look, child, don't do anything foolish. I can't go if I spend the whole time worrying about you, and I must go. My father expects it."

"You love him, don't you?" she said. "Even after— Julius, go and feed Aeshma, please. Give him some grain. I rode him hard today."

Julius departed, with an inquisitive backward glance, and Freita turned back to Correus. She didn't pull her hands away, but let them rest in his. The cat leaped into her lap with a soft purr, scattering the drawings, and Correus moved one hand to scratch its ears.

"Yes, I do love him," he said. "Even after a childhood as a slave, if that's what you mean. My father did everything he could for me. More than most would have done."

"I suppose slavery seems not so terrible if you are born to it," Freita said.

"Wrong," he said. He turned away from her to look into the fire. It had snowed that morning, the first snow of winter, and the air was clammy. "I doubt I'll ever outrun mine."

"Oh, yes. I was forgetting why you bought me." She pulled her hands away, and he caught them back.

"Freita, don't. Whatever my reason for buying you, I thought we had become friends in a way. Don't back off from me again." His dark eyes were serious, and she looked at them warily. The cat butted its head against his hand impatiently, and he absently scratched the gray ears, still holding Freita's green tide-pool eyes with his. He could drown in those eyes . . . easily. He put his hand in the gold hair and pulled her head down to his and kissed her. She never moved. It was the first time he had touched her since that night in the tent when he had been half drunk with anger and fatigue; all the longing she had stirred in him then blazed up again like a fire. He pulled back, shaken, and stood up.

Then he was gone. Freita sat watching as the door swung shut. After a while she got up and tried to explain to Julius that it wasn't that the centurion didn't trust him . . . that wasn't the trouble. . . .

They rode out an hour later through the powder of new snow—Correus, Flavius, and Paulinus, who had decided only that morning to accompany them. Business in Rome, Paulinus said briefly, and Correus thought again of the Imperial Post permit, and the bland-faced man of the Nicretes he had questioned in the legate's office in the Principia. Bericus and Tullius rode behind them, leaving Dog howling indignantly in a kennel in Argentoratum.

They went by road this time, traveling light and moving fast. It was more than eight hundred miles to Rome, and an officer could use up his long leave just getting there if he were too particular about his comfort on the way. The road skirted along the Rhenus, dived through a short tunnel, and emerged at Augusta Raurica, the oldest of the Rhenus settlements and the upriver terminus for the Rhenus fleet. From there they turned southward over the windy rock-cut Alpine pass that led south to Mediolanum and thence to Genua and the Via Aurelia to Rome. Paulinus produced another invaluable permit that got them

rooms in the Imperial way stations a day's march apart
along the pass. Correus and Flavius looked at their friend
with raised eyebrows, but kept quiet and enjoyed their
good fortune. They had been bitten by bedbugs and had
slept with one hand on their packs and the other on their
daggers when staying in the common inns between Rome
and the Rhenus a year ago.

The road was well traveled by couriers, troops, and
civilians hastening to outrun the coming winter before the
passes would be closed with snow. Correus had drawn
Freita a rough map of the Empire and its roads, and she
had opened her green eyes wide in patent disbelief. He
wished he could have brought her with him to see the
stone-paved road that snaked its way across mountains
that had once been thought an impassable barrier. Banked
at each turn, the road was wide enough for wheeled traffic
to pass, and the milestones spelled out the distance to cities on its route, with the name of the legion that had built
it and the emperor who had commanded it. Roman roads
and the soldiers who laid their stones built the Roman
Empire. Drawing Antaeus up at the height of the pass to
see the road spilling away behind and before him, Correus
thought the road might explain Romans to Freita better
than most things could.

Flavius shouted to him to move, it was getting dark; and
he turned Antaeus's head down the switchback slope. It
was snowing again, lightly but steadily, and ahead the
light of a way station shone warmly. He prodded Antaeus
with his heel, the road forgotten save as a means to dinner
and, if they were lucky, a bath.

The journey took them the best part of a month, although once out of the mountains and into the Po Valley
above Mediolanum the road was straight and fast and the
weather warmer. Winter came later and with a gentler
hand to Italy than to the forests of the Rhenus or the
ragged peaks of the Alps. Correus was grateful for the
presence of Paulinus and his hulking servant, cheerful
travelers both. He had been dreading a month's close
company with his brother, and the companionship of the
others seemed to draw Flavius out of his brooding silence.
Or perhaps it was the prospect of a stay in Rome. Flavius
loved Rome and was at home in the City in a way in

which Correus would never be. The crowds, the smell, the festivals, and the games were excitement to him, a heady pleasure after a year on the frontier. For Correus, somehow, it was the frontier that had become home. Only Appius Julianus drew him to Rome again.

For both, the journey home was pure tedium, a month in the saddle with nothing to do but watch the road roll out ahead of them. Even the countryside was drab and bare with the beginning of winter.

They arrived in the City tired, travel-stained, and screaming from boredom. They stopped at an inn called the Shield and Pilum, with a centurion's helmet painted on the signboard, on the theory that if it catered to army officers it probably wouldn't be overpriced. They took two rooms, one for Paulinus and Tullius, and one for Correus and Flavius, with a bed on the floor for Bericus. The rooms were comfortable enough, with floors of plain stone, overlaid with bright rugs in an outlandish pattern, probably brought by the innkeeper from wherever it was that he had served his military tour. The beds were straw-stuffed but smelled fresh and seemed to be free of any unwelcome occupants. A plump girl with a cheerful face and a grubby apron brought them jugs of water to wash in. She looked the two brothers up and down in obvious admiration, and made it quite plain that should either of them require company for the night, hers was available.

The invitation was repeated as they finished a meal of hot stew and bread in the dining hall.

"My dear fellow," Flavius said gravely when she had cleared away the bowls and disappeared into the kitchen with a wriggle of her backside, "don't let me stand in your way."

"On the contrary," Correus said, equally solemn, "I feel sure that it is you she longs for. I wouldn't dream of interfering."

"Or we could always send her Bericus," Flavius murmured. "He doesn't get much fun." He tilted his head back to catch the reaction of Bericus, who stood behind his master's chair.

Poor Bericus looked so appalled that both brothers chuckled and assured him that they would do no such thing. Correus and Flavius went up to bed in reasonable charity with each other. They planned to sleep as long as possible and then spend a day or two doing the town and shaking the frontier out of their brains before they pushed on for their father's estate.

Tullius, who had been watching this exchange, rose quietly and prowled off into the kitchen, where he met with a good reception. The girl would have preferred one of the handsome centurions who looked so much alike (or even both of them), but Tullius was, after all, one of her own kind. He might even pay her more.

Paulinus left his servant to his own devices and took himself off to his own room to write in his private journal before he slept. There had been little chance in the crowded way stations on the road, and there were things he wished to set down while they were still fresh in his mind.

A wearisome journey, but still the best and fastest road to the City from any place of power. Germany becomes more unmanageable by the minute. Sending more troops there would threaten Vespasian's security by strengthening commanders on the Rhenus, and the Senate wants peace at home. Not enough troops on the Rhenus, and that river will go up in fire again. The Emperor picks his commanders carefully, but there's always a doubt. No man wears his ambition branded on his forehead. Even my friend Correus, who is so loyal that he frets himself half into a fever if any two loyalties conflict, is beginning to understand the power that the command of armed men brings with it. And power breeds temptation, even for those loyal to the Emperor. The feeling that an emperor is blundering has provoked good men to rebellion before. Vespasian himself, for instance. In this case, though, I don't think Vespasian has much choice but to reinforce the Rhenus, and someone, it seems, has told him so—someone with a louder voice than mine. New detachments came through this summer, while I sat in Argentoratum counting cracks in the plaster. Legate Rufinus was most forceful in his wish for my absence. Occasionally lying low becomes a necessity.

Odd letter from my revered uncle on the heels of

those reinforcements. He had personally delivered the letters I sent on to Appius. Correus has invited me to spend part of my stay here in his father's house, and I think I will. Tomorrow I dine with Uncle Gentilius, a polite round of sparring and innuendo. Following another appointment in the morning with the man in charge. In between I will take in the games with Correus and Flavius. Not my idea of entertainment as a rule, and Correus does not wish to go either, but he is going anyway because his brother wants to and he is still trying to be friends. Have the suspicion that Correus would prefer to haul off and slug Flavius, which wouldn't solve anything but would certainly relieve his feelings. I shall attend in my dual role of nursemaid and peacemaker, and take along my sketchbook. I have a lovely satirical painting in mind, composed of the vulpine faces of the crowd encircling the tiny figures of the poor doomed souls below. Nasty, so I shan't show it to Correus's Freita, who is only just beginning to like us. When we get back to the frontier I am going to paint something on the walls of that dreary little house for her. That's no occupation for a gentleman, my uncle Gentilius would say, but so few of my occupations are.

Paulinus sighed and laid down his pen. He locked the journal away and took a clean tunic and a toga from his pack. He spread them out on Tullius's bed (he doubted it would be occupied tonight) to let the wrinkles shake out. He had other clothes at his uncle's house, but he didn't much want to run into Gentilius until his confidential morning appointment was concluded.

Correus and Flavius made a leisurely breakfast at the Shield and Pilum, and then lounged in the inn's small garden, making army small talk with the proprietor. They awaited Paulinus's return. He had apparently risen with the birds. He strolled in shortly, his freckled face and thin form looking older than usual in the purple-bordered folds of a carefully draped toga. Correus, remembering his own struggles with that garment, was grateful for the comparative simplicity of parade uniform, distinguished now by the silver Valorous Conduct torque that hung against the gilded scale, just beneath the centurion's insigne. That had come after Jorunnshold, and Correus wouldn't have traded a senatorial toga for it.

It was not a festival day, but games of one sort or another could generally be found somewhere in Rome. A gladiatorial show was scheduled for the Theater of Pompey, and Flavius's eyes were bright and excited. The theater was reasonably crowded—as young Julius had said, there was little enough to do in that teeming city. Not enough honest work to go around, Correus thought, watching the avid faces. Free bread and free games kept an unstable population quiet, and gave them a chance to feel at one with their betters—the senatorial and equestrian boxes were also full. The crowd chattered among themselves and bought sausages and hot drinks to take off the winter chill. It looked like rain, and the canopy had been stretched out to shield the tiers of seats from any downpour. A troupe of acrobats was tumbling about in the freshly raked sand, largely ignored by their audience. The crowd was waiting for the real thing.

The Emperor was not in attendance today, and the main box was occupied by the sponsor, a City official with a harassed expression who conferred with the arena master every few minutes, then clapped his hands finally in irritation when he saw the crowd begin to grow restless. A horn sounded and the acrobats cartwheeled out. The gladiators came up from the gates under the stands, blinking in the sudden light, and saluted the sponsor with the cocky bravado that delighted the crowd. A favorite gladiator could grow rich from the presents flung his way by his admirers. A woman in the next box, curled up comfortably on cushions with a box of sweets, flung a silver bracelet at one of the men. He picked it up on his sword point with a swagger and a rakish bow of thanks. Then a shower of coins and flowers rained down around them, as the crowd cheered its pets. These were the professionals, the men of the gladiators' schools, who, if no one wanted to pay for a fight to the death, might even live to get their wooden

sword—the token of freedom. There were twenty pairs
scheduled to fight today, net-and-trident men against
sword-and-shield; Samnites with short swords against
Thracians with scimitars. Some had been prisoners of
war, some had been sold into the arena, others condemned there. A few were gentlemen's sons, fallen into
debt and with no friends who thought them worth sav-
ing. The night before, they had been honored at a banquet held less for their benefit than for that of the
admirers who came to rub shoulders with their favorites,
and for the gamblers who looked them over with an eye
to the odds. Now the gladiators came to make good
their reputations, or to die.

Behind the trained gladiators of the schools came
other, less valuable bodies, and these were the surely
doomed ones: prisoners sent to die in droves at the
hands of others similarly condemned, or to be torn
apart by the fangs and horns of caged beasts whose
furious screaming could be heard from the pens under
the arena. Correus found himself studying his brother's
eager face; then he watched Paulinus's impassive one,
bent over a sketchbook with a piece of charcoal,
drawing quick, vicious portraits from the crowd. . . .
Paulinus was looking anywhere except at those doomed
faces below him: frightened faces or resigned, some
glassy-eyed and staring stupidly. These last, knowing
themselves without hope, had used the banquet to drink
themselves into numbness.

The grim parade made the circuit of the half-circle
floor and disappeared again, the arena "mercuries"
prodding the laggards on their way. Two remained behind—a net-and-trident man and a sword-and-shield
opponent. The arena master looked toward the sponsor,
who nodded and let a handkerchief fall from one
plump hand. The games had begun. The sword-and-
shield man circled the other warily. The net-and-trident
fighter wore only a loincloth and shin greaves, while
the swordsman was helmeted and heavily armed behind his shield—but none of his equipment would do
any good if he let himself be caught in that flying net.
Betting usually ran heavily on the net-and-trident. The
first combat proved true to form. The net flew out and

the sword-and-shield man thrashed in it like a caught bird, while the crowd screamed "Habet! Habet!" The sword came out through the net awkwardly and slashed at the net-man's legs. It caught him on the ankle just below the greave and drew blood, and the net-man thrust his trident down, pinning the other's sword arm to the sand. The net-man bowed to the sponsor, and then to the cheering crowd that was shouting for his opponents blood. The net-man gravely asked leave to spare him, and they cheered him again, while the fallen fighter in the net lay motionless, accepting his fate. That also was part of the game.

The sponsor appeared to consult the crowd and the Vestal Virgins in their private box, then graciously turned a white hand upward. The net-man jerked the trident out of the sand and the fallen gladiator rose, stumbling a little as the pain of his lacerated arm hit him. One of the mercuries took a step forward with the iron hook they used to drag the dead or badly wounded away, and the net-man hissed something at him. The mercury backed off again and the sword-man managed to salute and walk to the gates. The net-man walked beside him, carefully avoiding touching him—a gladiator left the arena on his feet or on the mercuries' hooks; there was no in-between. But something in the set of the net-man's shoulders made Correus wonder if they were friends . . . and what would have happened if the sponsor had bought a death fight.

The mercuries raked the sand out, sprinkling some fresh sand over the blood. Flavius beckoned a passing food seller over and brought a plate of sausages.

He settled back, munching sausages, eyes bright as the horns signaled the next fight—two pairs, Samnites and Thracians, with the victors to fight each other. Besides the trumpet player, a trio of musicians on curving horns and a movable water organ made incongruous accompaniment to the battle, while the arena master hovered to one side shouting instructions at his charges. Their faces were hidden under gilded, elaborately decorated helmets with grillwork that came clear over the face, like cavalry parade helmets. It must make it hard, Correus thought, not to be able to see your opponent's eyes, and then he decided perhaps it was better not to see his face at all if he was a man you had eaten bread with the night before. The fight began.

"Marvelous style," Flavius said. "Look at that one, with the Thracian shield. He's going to get him! *Marvelous* style! They're wasting him, so early in the show!"

The Thracian got his curved sword in under the Samnite's guard and hacked at the back of his leg, hamstringing him. The Samnite went down with a crash of shield and armor, and his helmet broke open and rolled away. Correus saw that it was the man who had caught the silver bracelet in the opening parade, the crowd's favorite.

Flavius chuckled. "I told you. Someone's going to get a beating for that. Look at our sponsor—he's seething."

The sponsor, an aedile who wanted to be a praetor, and was counting on a popular series of games to pave the way, glowered furiously at the arena master while the crowd shouted for the fallen man's blood, the woman who had thrown him the bracelet shrieking as loud as anyone. He was a favorite, but he had fallen too quickly, and they turned on him like Furies. They were angry now, and an angry crowd was dangerous. The Chief Vestal gave the sponsor a long look and a minute flick of her eyebrow, and stretched out a white hand, palm down. The aedile echoed the gesture. The Samnite had been doomed as soon as he was hamstrung. It was a wound that healed badly and rendered a man unfit for further arena work. The aedile would have had to pay the cost of losing him anyway. The Thracian fighter struck the man through the throat while the crowd cursed him for a sham and a coward as he died. The mercuries, dressed as the godly messenger and guide of the dead, dragged the still-twitching body away with iron hooks, leaving a broad scarlet smear across the sand, while the music played on, harshly triumphant.

I'm going to be sick, Correus thought. *I'm going to disgrace myself.* He bit hard on his lower lip and willed his nausea to subside. A case of battle shakes was one thing; but no one got sick in a nice safe box in the arena. *He* was the freak, Correus thought, not Flavius and all these other people, not even Appius, who disliked the games but could sit through them without throwing up. It wasn't just the death or the blood, he thought; there was a certain uncomfortable excitement in that, and his mouth twisted as he admitted as much to himself. It was his slave days, pursuing him even here. There, but for the grace of the gods and Appius Julianus, might be Correus. The mercuries raked clean sand across the sticky smear of blood, erasing the last trace of the man who had been Rome's pet a moment ago. And it was the crowd; by letting that blood-spawned excitement touch him, he became part of it, part of a mindless, faceless thing that fed on fear. And it was easy, so easy, to let that happen. He looked at his brother with a new understanding. Flavius couldn't help himself. The blood and that hot, choking excitement stirred something in him, something that was better left dormant . . . something insidious, that touched the soul. Seneca, the philosopher who had been a friend of Appius's, had said that watching the games ate away a man's soul, and rotted it. Correus closed his eyes, willing the smell of blood and the harsh, exultant music away.

He wasn't sure how long he sat that way while the battles fought themselves out to a shrieking climax on the hot sand below him . . . but it was long enough for Paulinus to elbow him sharply.

"Stop it!" Paulinus hissed. "You wanted to come, you fool. And there are people here who know you!"

Correus knew what he meant. His position was tenuous anyway, because of his birth. A public display of revulsion at the games could brand him as a radical and sink a career before it was started. He opened his eyes and stared at the arena, while Flavius gave him an ironic look.

"A mite squeamish for a man who's supposed to be a soldier, aren't you, brother?"

Correus didn't bother to deny it. They often knew what the other was thinking. It was part of that bond that held them so unwillingly together. "It's a different war," he said, tight-lipped, and turned his eyes back again to the sand.

The combats of skill had ended, and the crowd pelted its favorites again with coins and jewelry as they made their final parade, managing a swagger and flourish even now, despite the mild dose of opium the arena physician would have given the wounded ones to get them on their feet again. There were more intimate gifts as well, discreetly sealed notes delivered by some lady's page, and tucked into an upturned gilded helmet carried jauntily under one arm. Fear, pain, mourning for the dead—all were hidden. The crowd would have none of those, and it was the crowd that would call out life or death the next time they fought.

Then they were gone, and the crowd settled back with a little expectant shiver. Now. Now was the time of slaughter. The condemned came out through the dark doorway beneath the stands: the murderers, the thieves, the religious misfits, driven by hot irons and whips, most of them armed with unfamiliar weapons, or no weapons at all. The crowd licked its lips.

They fought blindfolded with spears, or tied together in threes, or unarmed on horses shod with iron spiked shoes, and they fought badly, comically, while the crowd howled with glee. And when the dead had been pulled away, and the victors stood weaving and terrified in the bloody sand, the beasts were let loose. Lions and bears and wild boars, starved into madness.

Correus was never sure when it was he ceased to watch, deliberately shifting his eyes out of focus so that the arena below became a blur and the screams were the faraway sounds of nightmare. Flavius caught his breath beside him and leaned forward, gripping the stone railing of the box, carried on a blood-tide of fear and a hot, pounding excitement that was overpowering. Paulinus watched them both with the uncanny feeling that he was seeing not two men, but one, and each was a shadow cast by the other. They were too drawn into whatever private land they walked to notice him, and he took up his charcoal and began to draw them: Correus, unfocused eyes gazing into nothing, aquiline features and sharp-angled brow blank as granite, hair ruffled slightly in a wind that smelled of blood; hands, unknowingly twisting and twisting at the silver torque that hung against the golden parade scale. And beside him, a dark-side mirror image, Flavius . . . eyes bright and glittering, mouth slightly open . . . avid, eager, lost in the blood.

XVII

The Outcast

INGALD WATCHED THE RIDERS STREAMING IN; A HALF-
dozen of them this time, warriors all, with their gray-
haired chief at the center. The horses snorted and blew
out clouds of steam as they were reined in; the riders were
heavily cloaked against a chilly wind with a promise of
snow in it. There was snow on the ground already, from a
recent fall, and the man who tried to outrun winter from
hold to hold at this time of year had serious business in
mind. Since he had learned of the first of these visitors to
Nyallshold, Ingald had made it *his* business to be in and
around the chieftain's hall as much as possible—with
Ranvig snapping at his heels like a herd dog. It was almost
midwinter, and any Semnone lords whose trails were not
snow-choked would be gathering in Nyallshold for the
solstice.

Fiorgyn and her women came out of the great hall with
cups of mead to greet the guests as thralls saw to the
horses. At the sight of Ingald lounging near the gates,
Fiorgyn shot him an unpleasant look. He turned away
with a smile, back to the guest house. If he got the
chance, he was going to show that lordly bitch a thing or
two, but she was a small matter now. With Rome behind
him, he wouldn't need Fiorgyn. But without Rome . . . the
wind drove through the open court in an icy blast, and
Ingald shivered in spite of himself, remembering the Roman commander's cold look.

In the great hall, Ranvig spat in the rushes on the floor
of the Companions' chamber and voiced his own opinions
in a tone of sheer fury, while Kari mocked him gently
with the opening harp notes of a Hero Tale.

"You—you have known Nyall all his life—" Ranvig
motioned with his oddly set eyes at the partition that di-

vided the Companions' chamber from the main hall. Low voices could be heard through the withy and plaster. "Cannot *you* make him see?"

"He sees," Kari said. He ran his hands idly along the strings now, a thoughtful whisper of sound. "He is not chieftain of the Semnones—and I am thinking maybe of the Confederation of the Suevi by now—for nothing. But he has this notion that we should be fighting Rome and not each other."

"Then he had best put Ingald's head on a pole!" Ranvig snapped. "What is the use of bending the Suevi chiefs to his hand, and leaving Ingald to carry tales all winter to our own lords?"

"What sort of tales?"

Ranvig's crooked face was still furious. "That Rome cannot be beaten. That Rome is not so bad a master when a tribe once puts its head in the yoke. That the lands-across-the-river grow prosperous under Rome's hand. Those tales! Is that enough?"

"More than enough for me," Kari said. "But I am not the chieftain."

Ranvig picked up a frayed bridle strap that someone had begun to mend, and turned it in his hands. "Would you want to be?"

"I am half-blood," Kari said. "I couldn't be."

"So is Nyall," Ranvig said, surprised. "I did not think that was a law with the Semnones."

"Nyall's half is Gaul, and they are kin to us. My half is Roman." Kari raised his dark brows expressively. "That makes all the difference. There was even some talk that I should not take my spear with the other boys of the tribe when the time came—my parents were old when I was born, and both dead by then—but Nyall's father, the old chief, spoke for me."

Ranvig returned doggedly to his first question. "If you were not a Roman woman's son . . . if you were of the Kindred . . . would you wish to be chieftain?"

"No." Kari, who had stretched himself out on the straw of one of the beds, raised himself up on an elbow and looked at Ranvig. "Why are you asking?"

Ranvig fished among the jumble on the table for a bronze rivet and began to mend the bridle strap. "Because

I would not either, even if I were still hunting in my own lands. Although I might have tried to keep it from Ingald. As it is . . ."

"As it is?" Kari prompted him.

"As it is, I am Semnone now, I and Arni and the rest. I have a holding as rich as the one I left, and a better chieftain, and there is a girl in my hold I may marry. I am content. But Ingald is not. And he will not be until he has the chieftainship that he thinks Nyall has taken from him."

"And the woman?" Kari said, remembering the night that Nyall had asked Arngunn for Fiorgyn.

"He would take her if he could, from spite," Ranvig said, "but that is a matter of pride only. The other is a . . . a hunger. I would rather see my lands stay in Rome's hands than go to Ingald."

"If he is that hungry, he may have an eye to the Free Lands as well," Kari commented.

Ranvig blinked. "Even if he brought Nyall down, would the Council stand for a chief who was not Semnone-born?"

"No. Not if the Council still had any power." Kari's dark face suddenly looked very Roman in the fading light.

There was the sharp sound of Ranvig's indrawn breath. "If Ingald goes that road, he'll cut his own throat, but he'll take us all with him. Kari, I am going to kill him."

"No!"

"Try to stop me."

Kari sat up slowly. "Wait. Wait until after the Gathering, and see what Nyall will do."

"Nyall has already taken Ingald's woman and his chieftainship, and he will do no more. Isn't that what you were trying to tell me?"

"It may be that Nyall's mind can be changed and he will deal with Ingald," Kari said. "Wait and see. If you kill Ingald yourself without cause, you'll start a blood feud and we can't afford one now. Ingald has made friends, and his holding is loyal to him."

Ranvig tossed the bridle on the table and swung

around to face Kari. There was a cold light in his eyes.
"And if the chieftain does *not* change his mind?"

Kari's face was equally set and cold. "Then I will
help you kill Ingald. But wait until after the Gathering. And until the chieftains of the Suevi have gone."

Ranvig nodded and rose. "Very well. I will be remembering that." He flicked a hand at the bridle he
had been mending, and Kari saw that Ranvig's fingers
were long, and all of approximately the same length.
There was some tale among the thralls that the Lord
Ranvig had the elves' blood in him. He gave Kari a
smile, crooked teeth in a crooked mouth, but oddly
pleasant. "My apologies to whoever owns this. I meant
no harm in handling his property."

Kari smiled back. "It is my bridle, as it happens. My
thanks for the mending."

Ranvig pulled back the curtains at the far end of the
chamber, which opened not onto the main hall but into
a corridor, and nodded in greeting as he passed a girl
who came in with her arms full of tallow lights.

She had on a yellow dress that glowed like a spring
buttercup as she lit one of the tallow dips at the fire
and set it onto a nail in the wall. She smiled shyly when
she saw Kari, and he got up and kissed her, partly because it seemed to be the thing to do after lying with
her at Harvestnight, and partly because she looked so
warm in the cold twilight.

Kari had ridden in from his own holding for the
Gathering only that morning and hadn't seen Hallgerd
since Harvestnight. She snuggled against him happily.
He should marry her, he thought, if Fiorgyn would let
him have her. He took a deep breath of the soft smell
of her hair. He remembered Ranvig's words: ". . . and
a girl in my hold I may marry." Odd how many of the
men seemed suddenly to be thinking of marrying. With
a war band forming for the spring thaw, the desire to
leave something of yourself behind was very strong, he
thought, feeling the girl's soft shape against his shirt.

"They are almost through, I think," Hallgerd whispered. "The chieftain and Geir One-Eye and the stran-
ger lord. They have gone away into the chieftain's
chambers, and my lady with them, so the thralls can

put the tables up. There are too many feasts," she added in a vexed voice, "and someone always makes blood-trouble at them."

"Well, they won't tonight," Kari said, "with the chieftain's curse hanging over their heads."

"No," Hallgerd said disgustedly, "they will think up some other mischief instead."

Kari remembered the chieftain's curse and winced. If he helped Ranvig kill Ingald, Nyall would never invoke that curse on him, he knew. He probably wouldn't call it down on Ranvig, either. But showing that restraint would lessen the threat to the others and do Nyall's hold on the tribe no good. If Ranvig and he did kill Ingald, he thought swiftly, they weren't going to be able to admit it. Then Nyall could curse the "hand unknown," but it would be awkward if no one fell down dead. And more unpleasant still if someone did. Kari twitched in spite of himself. His Roman half did not much believe in curses, and he privately thought that Ranvig was more than a match for any curse demon that Hell chose to send after him. But still, you never knew. And he had never lied to Nyall. . . .

"They are itchy as an old pig," Hallgerd was saying, "and behaving like boys in a fight. My brother and Starkad decided to have a snow race without clearing the track. Starkad's horse broke both its front legs, and now they are furious with each other. They were rolling in the snow and pummeling each other because the threat of the chieftain's curse wouldn't let them fight with knives. I am sick to death of men!" she added, and glared at him.

Kari dragged his mind back to what Hallgerd was saying. Her brother was Gilli the Lame, who had had the temperament of a fighting cock ever since a childhood illness had left him with a short leg. He had compensated—in much the same fashion that Kari had for his harp-playing and his Romanness—by thrashing anyone who looked sideways at him; but Gilli was a year or two younger than Kari, and it hadn't worn off yet. Kari chuckled. "The chieftain is right. They need badly to learn discipline. Nyall will give them other things to think of soon enough."

"Another war!" Hallgerd's eyes flashed. "Another time of killing, and them maybe never coming back again at all!"

Her mouth began to tremble and Kari put both his arms around her. "Are you frightened, sweet?" he asked softly.

"Of course I'm frightened," Hallgerd snapped. "And you would be too if you had any sense." She turned her back to him in the circle of his arms, fighting back tears.

Kari sighed and rubbed his face against her loose hair. "I am," he whispered. "I have more sense than you think." She nodded her head and leaned back against his chest. He held her close for a long time, trying to put her soft form between himself and Ranvig's demanding face and Ingald's bland, infuriating one.

Fiorgyn stood, sleeves rolled up and hands on hips, surveying the great hall and thinking, as Hallgerd had, that there were too many feasts. Too much mead, too much bragging, too many chances to get on each other's nerves in a winter of enforced idleness. Four thralls came in, stamping and shaking the snow from their boots, dragging the heavy yule log to the hearth. A group of girls followed them, their arms laden with fir branches, giggling among themselves as they stood precariously on benches atop tables to hang the branches from the support pillars of the hall. There was an extra chair at the High Table for Hoskuld, the visiting Suevi chieftain, and a wooden, bronze-bound chest beside Nyall's chair with a gilded, enameled horse bridle in it —the guest-gift intended for Hoskuld. It was a particularly rich one and would necessitate the giving of gifts of almost equal magnificence to their own lords as well. Gift-giving was a complicated ritual with many facets of subtlety involved. In the past, loss of face over a gift given or received had started feuds and even wars. Fiorgyn and Nyall picked their solstice gifts with a care that would have done credit to a pair of skilled ambassadors. Something was needed to take the sting from Hoskuld's forced oath.

Fiorgyn pushed back the stray hairs from her forehead as she remembered Hoskuld's weathered face glowering at Nyall beside the hearth fire in their chambers. Hoskuld hadn't liked going oath-sworn to a Semnone chieftain barely out of his teens, but he had done it, as the rest of the Suevi chiefs had. Nyall and Fiorgyn together had painted a picture of the Roman-kind that was quite clear, and quite unpleasant, and stated flatly that this time they would not fight another chieftain's battle for him. The rest of the Confederacy of the Suevi could join with the Semnones and keep their lands clear of Rome, or they could take their chances on their own.

"While your lords raid my cattle in the meantime," Hoskuld had snarled.

"They are forbidden to raid each other," Nyall said, as if that much should be obvious. "We are first in Rome's path, and I want no feuds to distract them from fighting the Roman-kind."

"Well, they will have feuds with my lords if yours do not keep to their own hunting runs," Hoskuld said.

"They grow restless," Fiorgyn said gently. "Not even my husband can chain them entirely." With a deft hand, she poured a cup of winter mead and passed it to Hoskuld.

"Feuds with your lords will be no threat to our unity if you have not joined us in this," Nyall pointed out.

"And if we do join?"

"The Semnones do not raid an oath-sworn ally."

Hoskuld gave him a black look. The Semnones were the greatest of the Suevi Confederation, equal in numbers to all the rest put together. "And how if we join together against the Semnones instead?" he suggested.

"Then we will all be quite busy fighting each other," Fiorgyn said. "And when we have done, we will look up to find our walls pulled down, and a Roman fort built out of them. If you are still alive you may spend a peaceful old age asking the commander of the Eagles at what time it is proper to eat and spit and piss. And never again will you call your tribe your own."

"Strong words from a woman," Hoskuld said resentfully.

"I am a chieftain's daughter and a chieftain's wife,

and a woman of the Free People. Do I speak an untruth, Hoskuld?"

He watched them sitting side by side before him, golden head by red one, both young enough to be his grandchildren. Yet there was something in their eyes that was old and implacable. Hoskuld did not know Rome save by reputation, but these two knew Rome . . . knew Rome well enough to take a dangerous way of forcing an alliance with him as a last resort. Hoskuld leaned back in his chair, his face impassive, and let his thoughts run. The Semnones' chieftain played a dangerous game, indeed. If Nyall was willing to do that, it was likely that he had reason. Rome . . . Rome was a new world, come out of nowhere, a wrong thing, a bad wind that changed old ways and old loyalties. If Nyall could see a way to push it back across the Rhenus again, then Nyall was the man to follow.

Hoskuld breathed in slowly, choosing his words to guard his dignity. "Very well. I will ally. I will even swear to you, Nyall. There must be only one war leader in this, or you will never hold the alliance together. But there are conditions."

"Of course." Nyall's voice was smooth and polite, conciliatory. He leaned forward as they began to work the conditions out, and Fiorgyn rose and slipped from the room.

"One year wed at the solstice, are you not?" a pleasant voice said behind her. "Dreaming, then?"

Fiorgyn jerked her mind out of her thoughts of Hoskuld and spun around to see Ingald leaning, smiling, against a pillar.

"What are you doing here?"

Ingald waved a lazy hand at the scurrying thralls. "Admiring the yule log. And wondering what new affairs of state rode in with that old grandfather this afternoon."

" 'That old grandfather' is the chieftain of his tribe, and a greater man than you are, Ingald," Fiorgyn said in an exasperated voice. "And if you cannot be civil, then go home again to your own hold. I don't have time for you!"

"You might make time," Ingald suggested. He couldn't resist prodding her. "Eventually you might have to."

"Eventually my horse might sing," Fiorgyn snapped. "I warn you, Ingald, make trouble tonight, and even Nyall's patience will wear out."

Ingald's hand shot out and grabbed her by the wrist. "Patience! Look you, lady, I speak nothing that is not truth. Why should I sit by and see our chieftain lead us into a war that's never going to be won? Have you ever thought, just once, of what Rome has to offer?"

Fiorgyn's free hand slapped down on her dagger hilt and the blade was in her hand in a second. She brought it down on Ingald's hand and he jerked back, dropping her wrist and letting out an angry howl. He clutched his bleeding hand, and she brought the knife up again.

"Touch me, Ingald, and I'll kill you. Someone should have done it by now." She took a step toward him.

There were running feet in the corridor and suddenly the room was very full of people. The thralls shrank back against the platform where the High Table stood, and made themselves small.

Ingald felt his heart pounding. The she-demon had been about to kill him whether he touched her or not.

"Fiorgyn!" Nyall grabbed her by the shoulders, looked her over quickly, and spun around to face Ingald. "What have you done to my wife?"

Ingald swallowed hard and put on his blank, pleasant look. He held out his bleeding hand ruefully. "I . . . ran into the lady's knife when I happened to speak of Rome." He looked around him carefully. He had a good audience now . . . better maybe than at a Council. "There was . . . no offense intended. Perhaps the chieftain should keep his she-wolf better leashed."

Fiorgyn still held the knife and her blue eyes were blazing. Nyall took it gently from her hand and slipped it into the sheath at her belt. "Can't I even trust you?" he hissed, low enough so that no one else could hear him.

"You ought to!" she hissed back.

Hoskuld had followed Nyall and was looking at Ingald thoughtfully, while Ranvig, Kari, Hallgerd, Morgian, and anyone else who happened to be within earshot came crowding around them.

"And what is it that you had to say about Rome," Hoskuld asked, "that got you such an answer?"

There was a murmur of agreement from the warriors in the hall. "Let him speak!" someone shouted, and Kari and Ranvig exchanged a grim look, while Morgian came up and put an arm around Fiorgyn, who shook it off, saying, "I am well enough." She was still furious. If no one had come in, she might have been able to kill Ingald, and claim her honor as the reason.

"Speak, Ingald," Nyall said. "There is no man in this tribe who may not speak his mind . . . once." The implication was clear, and Ingald searched quickly for the right words.

"We are of the same tribe, Fiorgyn Arngunn's-daughter and I," he said. "We know well enough what Rome does, when Rome conquers in a war. And Rome has more legions than those we have seen. It is in my mind, lord, that if Rome spoke truth about not going beyond the Black Forest lands, perhaps there need *be* no war. Are we so sure we can win one?"

"When has Rome ever spoken truth?" Fiorgyn said. "Or you either, Ingald?"

"Lady—" Ingald was placating. "Those lands are lost to us now, you and me. Why chance on losing our adopted lands as well?"

"Do not be speaking to me as if you and I were one blood, Ingald!" Fiorgyn snapped. "I am no kin to you!"

"We were . . . once."

"I am Semnone now. You also took an oath," she added disgustedly. "Or are you forgetting that so soon?"

"He forgets much," Kari said quietly. "This was not his tale as I heard it."

Nyall's gray eyes were acquiring a dangerous glint, and he swung around to face Kari. "And what have you heard, brother harper?"

Kari nodded to Ranvig, who stepped forward. "What he heard, he heard from me, lord. It is not a tale my *tribesman*"—he spat out the word with plain dislike—"would tell to the chieftain's harper. There is talk in the wind that Rome makes a just master and makes her client chieftains rich. That we fight a lost cause, when Rome could bring us peace and many cattle and southern wines and such like." Ranvig swung his off-center gaze around to rest on Ingald. "Talk that perhaps the Semnones need a new chieftain who can see this."

There was a stirring among the warriors, and some, who had plainly been listening to such talk, jerked their heads up cautiously.

"Talk in the wind?" Nyall said. His words dropped like ice chips. "And which of you has listened to this talk, and grown dreamy with thoughts of Roman wine and marble houses to strut about in like tame cats?" They shifted their feet uncomfortably. In a winter-bound hold where the snow blew in under doors and rations of dried meat and stale barley turned to sawdust in the stomach, Ingald's picture of life as a Roman subject had looked warm and promising. In sight of Nyall's cold eyes, colder than snow, things looked somehow different.

"Better you think of life with a Roman thrall ring, and a warm corner in a Gaulish tin mine!" Nyall shouted, his voice raised furiously now. "Who would be chief in my place and learn what it is that Rome offers him? You, Hauk? Gilli? You, Steinvar?"

There was silence, heavy and pregnant like the eye of a bad storm, and Fiorgyn bit her lip. They would lose Hoskuld, and the rest of the Suevi, if Nyall couldn't hold his own tribe to him.

"No one?" Nyall said, quietly now. "Not one?" His hand rested very lightly on his dagger hilt and his feet were braced wide apart, while his hair made a flaming crown above his face. It would take more courage than any of them had—and they were fighters—to face down the chieftain in that mood.

"Then why do you run like puppies to the first man who whistles and offers you a box of elves' gold, that turns into serpents by sunlight?" Kari said. "You are fools."

"No!" Ingald said suddenly, trying to draw them back to him. "We are fools if we do not think twice about fighting Rome! Fight Rome and we will all end our days in a thrall ring!"

"Not you, Ingald," Ranvig said. "Yours are going to end somewhat sooner."

"Ranvig!"

Ranvig turned to Nyall, his face set. "Even now? You cannot let *this* pass!"

"This is my decision, Ranvig," Nyall said. "Bide still."

"Then you had best make it, lord of the Semnones," Hoskuld said. He pushed his gray bulk up beside the younger chieftain and gave him a plain look. "I am oath-sworn," he said. "Oath-sworn to you only, not to any other chief this tribe may call up. And to you only on conditions. Meet them or I break the alliance."

"I can't kill him," Nyall said, and he thought he saw Ingald relax just a little. One of the conditions he had made with Hoskuld was that the oath held only so long as Nyall could keep unity in his war band. Divided they could not stand against the Romans, and Hoskuld had made it plain that he would go back to his hold and hope that Rome would not venture that far east, before he would put his men in a war band that couldn't move as one. Now he was obviously prepared to make good that threat.

"I can't kill him," Nyall said again. "I put the chieftain's curse on my warriors to keep the peace with each other. I will not break it merely because I am chieftain."

"Then you break your war band," Hoskuld said, "and this one will not need to do it for you." He gestured contemptuously at Ingald.

"Neither do I break my word," Nyall said.

Hoskuld grunted something that might have been agreement and hooked his thumbs in his belt, waiting.

Nyall said, "Ingald, come up to me and keep your tongue still."

Ingald hesitated, and Ranvig took the opportunity to give him a shove. It was plain that Ranvig wished there had been a knife in it. Ingald staggered a little and halted before Nyall, his bland look slipping now and his eyes angry.

"Lords of the Semnones, Council of the Semnones, hear me." Nyall pitched his voice to reach the farthest end of the hall. "From this day's sundown, Ingald is no more of the Semnones."

There was a sharp-drawn breath from every man in the hall, and Ingald's face went white. To be tribeless, outcast, was worse than death. For the tribeless man,

there was no hold to go to, no refuge, no protection, and all men were foes. The tribe meant survival. Ingald rocked on his feet a little and Hoskuld watched him with a certain grim sympathy. Better for the fool if the chieftain had killed him.

"Ingald, you are landless," Nyall said ruthlessly, "you will not return to what was once your hold, nor will you come again into these lands. You may take with you your shield and spear, and one horse from the common herd, and you will be given one week's food for your trail."

"My sword?" Ingald whispered. The sword was a warrior's weapon, to lose it a disgrace.

"No. It may be that you will find another one, if you live long enough, but you will not ride out of my hold carrying a sword." Nyall turned to the tribal lords, to Fiorgyn and Morgian, and to Asuin the priest, who had come in to stand at the back of the hall. "Does anyone protest my judgment?" The square lines of his jaw were set tight, and it was plain that the question was only a formality. "Kari. Steinvar. Starkad. Take him and see that he rides out before sundown." Nyall took Fiorgyn by the arm and stalked to the door that opened by the High Table, the thralls melting out of his way.

Steinvar and Starkad took Ingald by the arms. He went, face set and unreadable, but his arms and shoulders were stiff, like a man barely in control. Ranvig started to follow and Kari shook his head at him.

"No. Let this serve. I've seen Nyall in this mood. He's mad enough to curse you now if you disobey him."

"He'll go to the Romans," Ranvig said.

Kari shrugged. "Let him. If he gets that far, they may kill him for us. He doesn't know anything useful enough to tell them, except that we may fight them. They probably suspect that already." He looked toward the open doorway. "It's midwinter, Ranvig. What chance do you give him?"

In their chamber, Fiorgyn stood silently, watching Nyall. He let go her arm and took a deep breath. "I ought to beat you," he said finally, tonelessly.

Fiorgyn made an angry noise. "You may try! I would

have put my knife in him if you hadn't come in, and you should have done it yourself a year ago! You are a chieftain, a great man, a leader of men! And Ingald is a blind spot with you! What is Ingald to you but a thief and a danger?"

Nyall slumped down in a chair and stared at the fire. "He is . . . a doubt. A voice that may be right after all. Everything that I have done has taken something from Ingald. You . . . the lordship of the Nicretes . . . his home hills. I came lordlywise into the Black Forest saying we must fight the Romans, and we came near to losing everything. How can I kill Ingald and not wonder afterward if it was because he spoke the truth?"

"Ingald speaks what will serve Ingald!"

"Does that make it untrue?" Nyall whispered.

"Nyall . . ."

"So many dead," he went on dully, eyes lost in the fire. "And more dead this spring. And all just to make us too big a nuisance for Rome to swallow . . . all just to push them beyond the Rhenus and hold them there . . . to spend year after year just holding them. Rome has pushed into the Free Lands before, and always they have been driven back, but only that. Never conquered."

She knelt down and put her hands on his shoulders and dug her fingers in hard through the woolen shirt. "Then we hold them, if that is all we can do. We hold them. We must."

His eyes were clouded and unhappy, but they drew back from the fire finally and focused on her. "Yes, we must." His voice was older than Geir's or Steinvar's, too old for his face and body, too old for everything but the look in his eyes. "And I have sent Ingald to his death for speaking the things I won't admit to thinking. Fiorgyn, I am tired."

She dropped her hands from his shoulders and sat back, holding out her arms to him. He slipped from his chair and knelt beside her among the rushes on the floor while she put her arms around him and held him tightly. After a moment he lifted his own arms and pulled her close, but over her shoulder he was still watching the fire.

* * *

Outside in the courtyard, Kari followed Steinvar and
Starkad through the trampled snow to the barns. Together they set Ingald on a horse, gave him his spear
and blue-painted shield, and a saddlebag of dried meat
and hard barley cake. He looked down at them with a
cold, white face, but didn't speak. They would not have
answered him. Steinvar dragged open the heavy outer
gates of the hold and raised one lean, scarred arm in
a silent gesture. The snow-covered road wound away
down the hill before him, and dark clouds had begun to
bank up above it. Ingald hesitated and Kari brought
his hand down hard on the horse's rump. The animal
leaped forward and suddenly Ingald dug in his heels
and took the road at a gallop, snow flying up under the
horse's hooves. They stood in the gate and watched him
go, westward into the falling sun and the black clouds.
It was like watching a ghost ride away.

XVIII

Home Leave

"MY DEAR BOY!" APPIUS JULIANUS PUT HIS ARMS AROUND
his tall son (a shade taller than his father now—Correus
had grown) and held him close for a moment, then stood
back and looked him up and down, noting the way his
lorica and leather harness skirt sat upon him with the
rightness of usage. His eye lit with satisfaction on the
Valorous Conduct torque, then traveled again to Correus's
face.

Appius had already greeted Flavius with affection,
but it was uncomfortably plain, Paulinus thought,
watching them, that it was Correus whose presence
called up that joyful light in the old general's eyes. That
much was probably equally plain to the Lady Antonia,
although nothing escaped her well-bred countenance

but polite welcome. Only when she put her arms around Flavius did her expression change, to the sharp, protective love of a mother tiger.

Paulinus noted the dark, pleasant-faced girl beside her—the sister, Julia, no doubt—who greeted the brothers with indiscriminate affection, admired their uniforms and new military bearing, and smiled shyly at Paulinus as he was introduced.

"What did you bring me?" she demanded, returning her attention to her brothers and linking an arm with each.

"A severed head to put on a pole outside your window, like the German girls get," Flavius said, giving her a horrible leer. When Julia looked suitably revolted, he relented and took out a silk bag with a pair of gold eardrops in it, worked in German style. Correus gave her the necklace to match them—hammered gold twisted into spirals through which two hunting dogs chased a deer.

Julia put them on and peered into the atrium pool to admire herself until Antonia told her to get up off the floor and remember she was a young lady.

"They're splendid!" Julia announced, dusting off her gown. "Every girl I know is going to be broken-hearted!"

"Most becoming," Paulinus agreed gravely. "I think you're lucky it wasn't the horse."

"Horse?" Julia gave him a puzzled look, and so the story of the Lyxian temple horse was retold.

Appius Julianus was greatly amused, and Lady Antonia looked blank and seemed to feel that a great deal of effort that could have been better employed elsewhere had been put in on a joke. She excused herself with a gracious smile, saying that she had an appointment with the cook, but would see them all again at dinner.

"Correus, dear, you should go and see your mother," she added gently, and departed.

Appius was still wiping his eyes. "She's quite right," he chuckled. "Helva's expecting you, and I have estate business to talk over with Flavius." He nodded at Paulinus. "If you can put up with my daughter's youth-

ful company, I'll have her show you the gardens before
it gets dark."

"I should be delighted, sir," Paulinus said politely, as
Julia shot her father a quelling glance for his aspersion
on her maturity. "Don't mind your father, child," he
said with a certain amount of sympathy. "My uncle
Gentilius treats me in much the same fashion."

Paulinus caught a muffled snort of something that
might have been laughter from his host as the study
door closed behind him, but Julia merely smiled at him,
an expression which transformed her mother's handsome features into something approaching real beauty
in the daughter. Paulinus noticed it with pleasure.

"I suppose I'll have to get used to it," Julia said. "Being the youngest is always like that, and it's worse now
with my brothers in the army. Papa was saying last
night what a pleasure it would be to see army scarlet at
the table again, and looked at me as if I ought to have
been a boy. I bore him, I expect," she added philo-
sophically.

"Why?" Paulinus held the door open as they stepped
out into the colonnade.

It was chilly and Julia paused to adjust her light
woolen wrap. "He needs someone to talk army with."

Paulinus chuckled. "And you don't speak army?"

"Not very well. Though I've tried to learn for Papa's
sake."

"There *are* other things of importance in the world
besides the army, whatever your papa and your brother
Correus may think to the contrary."

"Not in this house," Julia said with a trace of humor
in her voice. "The garden doesn't look like much right
now." She eyed the mulched-up beds dubiously.
"Everything's laid down under straw, but we'll go and
admire the roses so we can tell Mama you did."

*And so we will stay out of the way while Correus vis-
its his socially unacceptable mother and the old general
tries to decide if Flavius is going to make it in the army
or not,* Paulinus thought. "I shall imagine them in full
bloom," he said solemnly, looking at the geometrically
arranged beds of pruned-back sticks.

Julia gave him a curious look. He was an unprepossessing figure—slightly built, with a freckled face and ears that stuck out a bit, but there was something . . . knowledgeable in his face. "Did you really dress up as someone's slave to trick that man about the horse?" she asked.

"Certainly," Paulinus said. "I haven't had so much fun in years."

"But . . . you're a gentleman. How could you pass yourself off as a slave?"

"My dignity's not as high as you seem to think."

"Oh, no, I didn't mean that. But how did you get him to believe you? You're obviously *not* one. I mean, you could put a field slave's clothes on Flavius, and he'd just look like someone dressed up for Saturnalia night."

Paulinus thought of all the other things he'd passed himself off as from time to time. "I'm a frustrated actor, I suppose," he said mildly. He unwrapped his toga and drew its folds up over his head. He pinched a withered bloom, missed by the gardner, from one of the rosebushes, and held it out to her—

"The flower of the lotus, mistress—imported direct from the Nile. It cures all manner of ills. A boon to those afflicted with baldness and female troubles, and all nervous disorders. Just two denarius, mistress, to bring these great powers to all sufferers at home."

His voice had a marked Egyptian accent and the singsong tone of the street markets. His eyes were squinted and slightly crossed, his expression importunate. Julia began to giggle.

"For you, mistress, *one* denarius," he went on insistently, trotting beside her and thrusting the flower at her. "Just one denarius for the lady with the bright eyes. I'm a poor man, mistress, but for you, one denarius."

Julia laughed. "Yes, I see."

Paulinus gave her the rose with a flourish and reassembled his dignity and the folds of his toga. "It's all in what you *think* you are."

They had reached the end of the rose garden and Julia laid the flower at the feet of Athena's statue. "I never thought of that. Can you make yourself anyone you want to?"

"Sweet Aphrodite, who's that?" Paulinus was staring across Athena's courtyard at the colonnade that ran along the upper servants' wing of the house. Correus was strolling along it arm in arm with the most stunningly beautiful woman Paulinus had ever seen.

Julia made a little clicking sound with her tongue that was somehow reminiscent of the Lady Antonia. "That is Correus's mother. I suppose you know about her. She's been the most awful nuisance all day, and I just don't want to talk to her. Come and admire the trellis with me."

Paulinus followed and gave Julia an inquiring look.

"It's Correus's coming home," she said. "Ever since Papa adopted him, Helva's been so . . . well, set up about it, there's just no living with her, and that puts Mama in a temper, which puts Papa in a temper."

"How trying for all of you," Paulinus commented. "Especially for Correus."

"Well, yes, I suppose so. I hadn't looked at it that way."

"There are generally about eight sides to everything, I find," Paulinus said. "I knew a woman in Judaea like that. With one innocent-sounding sentence, she could wreak more havoc than a whole houseful of ordinary people. She was someone's mistress too, and unfortunately he was very high up."

"Have you been in Judaea, too?"

"I've been in most parts of the Empire," Paulinus said. "And a few places we haven't got to yet. I'm writing a modern history, you see, and I believe in sticking my nose into things firsthand."

"How wonderful!" Julia sat down on a bench under the trellis and sighed. "I've never been anywhere."

"Bored?" Paulinus asked. She was a nice child, he thought, and undoubtedly had been given a back place to her brothers.

"Yes." Julia put her elbows on her knees and looked up at him, chin in hand. "It's very dull being respectable, I think. Helva's had a much more interesting life than I have."

"You wouldn't want to trade places with her," Paulinus said, remembering what Correus had told him.

"And be someone's mistress? Certainly not." Julia giggled. "I'd never get the chance. But I would like to . . . see things." Her face was eager, curious. An inquiring face, ready to go out and take stock of the world. She probably wasn't going to get much opportunity, he thought. The adventure in Appius Julianus's household was confined to its male members. They'd marry her off to some up-and-coming career soldier whom she'd see once a year when he came home on leave to be bored and patronizing with her. It seemed a pity.

"I expect I'll be married soon," she said, echoing his own thought. "It'll be better when I have a house of my own to run."

Don't count on it, he wanted to say, but that seemed cruel. "Who are you going to marry?" he asked.

"Oh, a soldier," she said. "I can't imagine Papa not picking a soldier." It was obvious that the prospective bridegroom was still hypothetical at this point.

"And you'll let Papa do the picking?"

"I'll have to," she said. "*I* never get to meet anyone. Anyway, I trust Papa. He picked a wonderful girl for Flavius. My best friend. Only——" She stopped.

"Never mind," Paulinus said. "I know about that. Again, poor Correus."

"Why poor Correus?"

"Use your head." He found himself speaking to her as if she were a much younger child. Or an old acquaintance. "He can't do anything about her. Not honorably, and probably not any other way. And to have the girl insisting on mooning after him is an embarrassment."

"Aemelia's very determined," Julia said admiringly. "She says she'll die an old maid if they won't give in."

Across the garden, Helva was telling Correus much the same thing.

"The poor child hasn't forgotten you a bit," she was saying, apparently oblivious of the seething expression on her son's face. She had on a gown of deep rose, exactly the color that she had painted her lips, and wore a fluttering woolen mantle, two shades darker, embroidered in fanciful black butterflies at the ends. She walked with the studied carelessness of a woman who knows that her appearance is flawless.

"You'll see for yourself," Helva went on. "Correus, dear, if you would only *try,* I honestly think your father might come around." She tapped the Valorous Conduct torque with one delicate finger. "How clever of you to have won that just in time to please your father."

"There was nothing 'clever' about it," Correus said irritably. "And I didn't win it to convince father to give me Flavius's bride, so will you please just let it drop?"

Helva patted his hand with ostentatious deference. "Well, of course, dear, if that's what you want. Come and tell me about the army." She sighed reminiscently. "Appius always used to tell me about the army. Of course, I never understood half of it, but I always used to listen. It gave him so much pleasure."

In spite of himself Correus chuckled at her frankness, and began to tell her about the Rhenus frontier.

Dinner was . . . interesting. That was the only word Correus could think of that covered everything. Paulinus and Appius seemed to be trying to find out something from each other, but Correus couldn't tell what, and he wasn't dead sure they knew, either. There were a good many names dropped, some famous, some that Correus had never heard before. He had the feeling that they brought out each name like a piece on a game board and set it there to see the other's reaction.

Flavius carried on most of his conversation with his mother, filling her in on the news since his last letter and restraining himself admirably from any comment on his half-brother's household at Argentoratum. That Flavius *had* mentioned it to his father, Correus was certain, but so had he himself in a letter. There wasn't anything wrong with it; he just didn't care to figure as the center of dining-table jokes. Tonight, however, on his home ground, Flavius seemed less inclined to dig at his half-brother. He leaned across the corner of the table and laid a hand on his mother's.

"Lovely to shake the bog out of my hair and see you again, love." He smiled at her affectionately.

"And my cook, no doubt," Antonia said in teasing tones, and smiled back at him.

The cook had given his all for their homecoming dinner, and Flavius happily took a bite of custard. "Eggs," he said. "And cream. Glorious. I shall eat until they have to put new rivets in my lorica."

"Can they do that?" Julia asked curiously.

"Not very easily," Correus said. "Simpler to chase us around the parade ground until we sweat it off."

"Would they really?"

"They'd love to," he said, thinking of Drillmaster Mucius. "Fortunately there's no amount of weight that you could put on in a month that two weeks of army cooking wouldn't take off again."

"I wouldn't be too sure," Julia said, watching them eat ravenously. "What *do* they feed you in Germany?"

"Swill."

"Pine cones."

"Fish heads."

"Mud pies."

"In other words, plain but serviceable food, child," Appius said with a smile. "In any case, it seems to have agreed with you two. You both look remarkably fit."

"It's the uniforms," Julia said irrepressibly. "Tell me, sir"—she honored Paulinus with the courtesy due an older gentleman and he smiled ruefully to himself—"is that the sort of fare *you* had on the frontier?"

"Well, not exactly," Paulinus said. "A civilian has more options."

"He has a servant that steals chickens," Correus explained.

When the slaves began to clear the table, the ladies rose and left the men to their wine. It was time Julia was in bed, Antonia said firmly, and she herself had a full day tomorrow. Paulinus had always found it odd that a woman with hundreds of slaves could find the running of her household a full-time occupation, but his own mother always had, and obviously Lady Antonia did. He supposed that just seeing that the slaves kept working was work in itself. Julia gave Paulinus a smile—less shy now—as they left, and he smiled back at her. A thoroughly nice child.

When the ladies had left them, the wine steward's boy

brought up more wine, and the men settled down to talk about the Rhenus frontier again. His host might have welcomed a retirement from active service, Paulinus thought—unlike many generals, Appius had retired voluntarily—but it was plain that the army still held the closest place to his heart.

When he had gleaned as much information as his sons could supply, Appius in turn gave them his own advice on the handling of men and the tactics of emergency. Their year's campaign gave his words new meaning. Paulinus maintained an expression of polite interest, watched the mosaic lobsters scuttle across the floor, and kept both ears open wide.

"As you have both discovered by now," Appius was saying, "you won't always have some commander above you to say when to jump, or how far. Plenty of fast decisions by junior officers have won battles." *Or lost them.* But he didn't say that, thinking of Flavius's unhappy description of his trapped century in his first real battle. The boy had been so transparently worried his father was going to be angry with him that Appius hadn't found the heart to be. Flavius had leaped gratefully, and with a plainly genuine interest, into discussing affairs of the estate, Appius's spurious reason for their private conversation. *He must learn to command,* Appius thought dismally. *He's got to. And he's my son, so why can't he?* Correus had learned it, but there wasn't Persephone's chance in Hades of Flavius learning anything from Correus, even if Correus were willing to teach him—and now he wasn't sure about that, either. But he was sure he had made a mistake when he forced that promise from Correus. On that disturbing thought, he changed the subject.

For politeness' sake, he asked Paulinus if he wished for company that night, and if there was a particular girl he fancied—if she was the agreeable sort, he would arrange it.

Paulinus declined, equally politely. He wasn't inclined toward casual lovemaking unless the girl really took his breath away. It didn't seem tactful to say that the only woman in Appius's household who had done that was Correus's mother. And even if her position were different, he thought, remembering Correus's story and Julia's comments, he'd as soon bed a barracuda. Appius Julianus must be a singularly strong-minded man to handle Helva.

No similar offer was made to Flavius and Correus. They would know where to find a girl if they wanted one.

Paulinus seemed perfectly content to talk provincial politics with Appius for the rest of the evening, so Correus excused himself to go and pay his respects to Thais and any other of his old tutors as were still awake in the servants' wing. After a moment Flavius followed him.

Thais was placidly setting neat stitches in a piece of green silk for the hem of 'one of Julia's gowns—an embroidered border of red apples. She set it aside when she saw them in the doorway and tried to hug them both at once. She came barely up to their collarbones, and they laughed and scooped her up in a chair formed of their interlocked hands and carried her triumphantly around the room.

"Put me down, Master Flavius, Master Correus, do! What Philippos would say if he saw you—"

"He'd be right scandalized," a voice said from the corner, "but can you see old Philippos coming into your chambers at this time o' night? That'd twist his dignity even more." The voice spoke with obvious affection, and Correus looked over his shoulder to find Forst sitting on a stool, his large, callused hands delicately sorting embroidery silks into varying shades of red and peach. Correus set Thais down with a bit of a thump, smacked her on the bottom, and then stood docilely while she boxed his ears in return. He tried not to look surprised. Bereft of someone to mother, Thais had apparently picked on the unlikely person of the German, and Forst seemed to be blossoming remarkably under this treatment. At any rate, his Latin had.

The German stood up to make his obeisance to Correus and Flavius, then arranged the silks carefully in Thais's workbox. He kissed her on the cheek. "I'll be off now, Granny. You'll be wanting to talk, and I want to have a look at that new mare that's near foaling."

When they had told Thais the latest news and allowed her to exclaim over how much they had grown and to ply them with honeycakes that she had sent a maid scurrying off to the kitchen for, Correus strolled down to the horse barns for want of anything else to do. Alan and Diulius and the weapons master, Sabinus, would probably be in bed. He could see them in the morning. It was a fine night for winter, crisp and cold with a black glassy sky strewn with stars. A faint odor of manure and warm horse drifted up from the barns, familiar and homey.

There was a lamp hanging from a peg by one of the loose boxes, and inside Correus found Forst, flat out in the straw with a laboring chestnut mare whose breath came in heaving gasps as she struggled to push the foal out. Forst's arms were slick and bloody to the shoulder and he was breathing heavily.

"It's her first," he said, looking up as Correus's shadow fell across the straw. "I had to turn it, but I think we're all right now."

As he spoke, the red mare gave one last shuddering contraction and two tiny hooves poked out. Forst gave them a gentle tug as Correus knelt down by the mare's head and told her softly what a fine lady she was. Her foam-flecked head subsided a little under his soothing hands, and after a moment a small wet nose followed the front hooves, and then the foal slid suddenly out into the straw.

The mare scrabbled with her forelegs to shift herself around and sniff at her offspring, while Forst pulled the afterbirth away and Correus cleared the mucus out of the foal's nose and mouth and rubbed the small body down with a feedsack. He was black, with four white boots and a white splash down his nose, as if someone had dribbled paint on it. The mare heaved herself to her feet and nuzzled gently at the colt, blowing her breath out her nose in an encouraging sound. After a few minutes the colt gathered his spidery legs under him and lurched to his feet, uncertainly, like a man on stilts. But he made unerringly for the mare's swollen teats and in another minute he was sucking away, his stubby brush of a tail switching briskly back and forth.

Correus and Forst stood in the loose-box door and regarded him with satisfaction.

"Thank you," Forst said. "I thought she might foal tonight and I didn't want to stir up Alan if I could help it. He's been ill, and he needs to sleep."

"Nothing serious, I hope?"

"Just age." Forst smiled. "And the notion that he could go chase down a loose horse in a rainstorm and not pay for it."

There was something odd about Forst . . . different. For a moment Correus couldn't put his finger on it, and then he realized that it was the fact that Forst was *not* sounding different. He spoke like a ten years' servant on the estate, not the new-captured, rebellious fighter that Correus remembered.

Forst caught the master's son looking at him strangely, and he shrugged his shoulders. "It pays to . . . adapt, lord, I find." He pulled the bottom half of the loose-box door closed and leaned on it to watch the colt. "He'll do well enough now. He's one of Orion's get and they're all as tough as bears from the day they're foaled."

"Forst—" The coiled knot of pale hair at the side of his head, the bristling mustache, the carefully clipped beard were all still at odds with the matter-of-fact Latin voice. The last time Correus had seen that knotted hair was over the edge of a painted shield, with a spear behind it.

"Lord?"

"Forst, are you all right here now? I've been fighting your own folk for the last year, you know. Would you rather I went away?"

Forst sighed and some of the careful glaze slipped away. "No, lord. As I told you, I learn to adapt. Mostly that's been Granny Thais. It's none so bad, having someone to . . . cosset you. I near died of loneliness before old Granny took me under her wing." Forst paused and Correus realized with a slight shock that Forst was not much older than he was.

"No, lord," Forst said again, "don't go. If you can spare the time, tell me how it is with my people."

Correus turned a pair of empty feed buckets upside down on the wooden aisle that ran the length of the barn between the double row of loose boxes and, for the third time that day, began to explain the chancy war on the Rhenus frontier that year.

Forst listened in silence, but as Correus spoke, the layers of Thais's "cosseting" slipped away one by one until the man who crouched on the upturned feed bucket merged slowly into the grim warrior who had given Correus his first taste of fighting a German long sword. Forst's adaptation to Rome ran only deep enough to preserve his sanity; no deeper.

They talked until the faint, deceitful light of false dawn began to show outside the stable doorway, and then they walked up the frostbitten road to the great house together while the chestnut mare and the black colt snored softly, curled around each other in the warm straw of the loose box.

In the morning, Correus paid his duty to Sabinus, declined a session on the practice field on the grounds that he had fought more than he wanted to lately, and went off to find Alan and Diulius and the horses.

Alan was still in bed and Antonia herself was applying a hot poultice to his chest. Correus told him about the red mare's foal—a colt, and maybe even good enough to keep for breeding—and gave him the polished wooden riding crop with the white horsetail end that he had bought in the Argentoratum market.

Diulius he found schooling a new chariot pair around the track. He speedily sweet-talked the chariot master into letting him try them out. It was all very uncomplicated, he thought, pulling off his helmet and letting the wind whip his hair back while Diulius scowled at him from across the training track. He needed a few uncomplicated pleasures before he coped with the complication that was even now awaiting him at the house—Aemelia, come ostensibly to visit Julia, encouraged by her father to spend some time with Flavius, and threatened by her father with horrible consequences if she so much as batted an eyelash at Correus.

Aemelia . . . Correus stood in his chamber and peered into the plain wood-framed mirror that hung on one wall. A trio of plump ladies in improbably diaphanous gowns cavorted around the frame, painted into the plaster on the wall; they gave him the come-hither over bare, dimpled shoulders. He had ducked in the back gate and soaked off the smell of hot horse in the baths. He then scurried for his own room, avoiding the chatting quartet who could be seen through the atrium doorway, soaking up the winter sun and the heat which ran through the hypocaust channels under the floor. He was going to have to come out sometime, he thought disgustedly. He couldn't spend the next month hiding under the bed frame like a turtle. Aemelia had looked cheerful and polite, making small talk with Julia, Paulinus, and Flavius, but she had been craning her pretty head around like an owl, all too plainly looking for someone—and that someone was Correus.

He regarded his aquiline reflection in the mirror and pulled the neck of his scarlet tunic straight, knotting his scarf carefully above it. The tunic was freshly cleaned and pressed by Antonia's admirable staff, and his belt buckle gleamed with new polish, setting off the insigne of the Eighth Augusta. Correus felt like putting his armor on, to give him a helmet to hide under. He picked up a fine-toothed bone comb and began trying to make his hair lie flat. It needed cutting. He would have to have Appius's barber do something with it before he left, or Messala Cominius would trot him off to the legionary barbers and they would shave his head for him, so as not to have to bother again for six months.

He laid the comb down and peered at himself in the mirror. What in Aphrodite's name did the girl want with him? He looked enough like Flavius to be his twin. So why him and not Flavius? Correus thought of a few of the reasons why he could want Aemelia, if he gave them half a chance—beginning with the soft warm feel of her body pressed up to his in the rose garden. It would be so easy to want Aemelia . . . Correus made a face at himself in the mirror and thought that he should have gone and woken up red-haired Emer last night. That would have taken the edge off his unwillingly amorous mood. It was a shame he couldn't have brought Freita home with him. That would disillusion Aemelia in a hurry, since she would be incapable of imagining any other reason for his having bought the woman except the obvious one.

Freita . . . Correus sat down on the bed and put his head in his hands, which made his hair stand up on end again. Typhon take the woman! He missed her. She might even have been able to give him some idea of how to cope with Aemelia. Freita had a way of seeing through people to their core. He cursed again as the thought of Freita set a chain of unwelcome emotions running through him. Not even the presence of Aemelia could stir him as the mere thought of the pale German witch did. He flung himself down on the bed, feeling sulky and childish. He would take a nap, and maybe when he woke up, Aemelia would be gone and Emer would be handy. But he didn't sleep, and every time the darkness came close it dissolved into a pair of sea-green eyes and a cloud of gold hair.

He managed to avoid Aemelia for that day, and a night spent in red-haired Emer's arms took the edge off his physical craving. But it did precious little for the rest of his troubles, and his frame of mind was not improved when Appius requested his presence in the study a few days later.

Trotting gloomily and obediently along the colonnade toward his father's private lair, Correus winced as he caught sight of Aemelia and Antonia in earnest conversation in the atrium. He had returned home from a grim and bloody campaign feeling that now he was a man, and childhood only a distant, misty memory of innocent days that would never come again. But the longer he spent in his father's presence, the more the blood and the high, fierce mood that was the frontier washed away, until now he would not have been surprised if some figure of authority suddenly appeared before him to order him off to school and ask him what he thought he was doing dressed up as an army officer. Maturity, it seemed, was relative.

Antonia, in the atrium, was trying to pound much the same thought into her prospective daughter-in-law's head.

"My dear child . . ." Antonia schooled her face into its usual placid, well-bred expression, but with difficulty. "Have you ever had a career soldier in your family?"

"Well, certainly. My uncle and—"

"That you were old enough to take notice of?" Antonia pursued.

"Well, no . . ."

"I thought not. Well, I have. I even followed the legion with Appius for a year because I thought it was my duty; but I couldn't bear it, and you couldn't bear it, and no woman in her right mind could bear it."

"I could bear it . . . with the man I love," Aemelia said bravely.

"You don't know what you're talking about," Antonia said in a voice that was not unkind, but her eyes were heavy. "Flavius can give you an estate and servants and the . . . the life you know . . . to make a home for him to come back to."

"Correus—"

"Correus can give you a mud hut on the frontier. And —and his mistress underfoot. He has one, did you know that?"

"He wouldn't, if he had me," Aemelia said with certainty.

Antonia bit her lip. She was damned if she would go into the question of marital duty with a girl not yet sixteen; how could she explain about sleeping with a man who had neither shaved nor bathed for weeks, and who woke up in the middle of the night, sweating and shouting orders to a nonexistent cohort.

"Have you ever seen a wounded soldier?" Antonia asked grimly.

"Well, of course."

"No, I don't mean passed one in the road. I mean, have you ever seen a man with a wound that's old and rotten and stinks of infection? A man that *you* have to treat because the only surgeon available is out there somewhere on the field, treating *your* man's soldiers, because your man told him to? A man who wants to climb into bed with you with a suppurating wound that smells like a sewer? A man who may die in your arms?"

Aemelia blanched, but she bit her lip and said, "I wouldn't care."

"Aemelia . . . child, listen to me. That is what you would have with Correus. Not a comfortable home, and a husband coming back to recuperate, with an estate physician to look after him. No. You'd have a hovel, a tent— and your handsome officer coming back in pieces, dripping blood, filthy. And what happens to you if he dies out there, and leaves you out there, with no one . . . and no place to go?"

"I wouldn't care," Aemelia said again, but she looked a little green. "I should want to be with him. I wouldn't care," she repeated.

Antonia lost her head. Not only for Flavius, her beloved Flavius, who *wanted* this pigheaded little moron, but for Aemelia, who didn't know what she was talking about, who could no more stand up to a year on the frontier than she could sprout wings and fly. "Well, Correus would care," she said. "He's not my son, but he's Appius's, and the army is bred into him blood-deep, bone-deep, deeper than any woman is ever going to get. If he scuttled his career by making a dishonorable marriage, he'd never forgive you."

Antonia turned on her heel and left, her sandals making a cold little whisper along the tile, and Aemelia put her head down on her arms and began to cry.

Helva, passing through the atrium a few minutes later, found her thus and sank down on the tile beside her chair and put her arms around her.

"My poor child, don't cry." Helva cuddled the shaking body to hers and ran a soothing hand over Aemelia's dark curls. "There, then, you're all right now. What is it?"

Aemelia turned and buried her head in Helva's shoulder. "It's Lady Antonia. She doesn't . . . she said the most awful things about the army . . . and Correus . . . and . . ."

"It's never easy, is it?" Helva said. "Women are never . . . never given the chance . . . Oh, dear Aphrodite, what I would not have given for the chance to marry a man for love!" She bowed her pale head down onto Aemelia's lap and began to weep softly.

"Correus," Appius Julianus was saying, his eyes not meeting his son's and apparently counting the cracks in the plain buff plaster of his study wall, "you are going to have to do something about your mother."

"What?" Correus gave his father a harried look and sank a few inches deeper into his chair.

"Your mother," Appius said, keeping his voice bland and noncommittal, as if Helva were a leaking roof he felt constrained to remind his steward about. "For the past year she has gone about being tragic and noble and bemoaning her own lost youth every time she comes within earshot of young Aemelia, who is, I regret to say, a very susceptible girl."

Correus groaned.

"Precisely. I have managed to keep Helva in line since before you were born," Appius said thoughtfully, "but she has finally hit on a cause from which nothing is going to sway her, short of sending her away, which, since I have adopted my son by her, is unthinkable. However," he looked his son in the eye, "now that you and Flavius are at home again, if somebody else doesn't make her behave, I am very much afraid that Antonia is going to do it, and I don't think I want to be around for that."

"Mithras, no, sir!" The prospect of an all-out war between his mother and Lady Antonia promised all the amusement of an eruption of Mount Aetna. Correus shuddered. "I'll talk to her."

"Thank you," Appius said. "I feel sure that you can make her see reason. Failing which, I am afraid you are going to have to speak rather brutally to Aemelia instead."

Correus stood up. "I'll deal with Mother," he said grimly.

When Correus made his appearance in the atrium some two hours later, Aemelia had already called for her litter-bearers and gone home—not overly surprising after Correus had stalked in following his conversation with his father and said, "Mother, I want to talk to you, I'm sure Lady Aemelia will excuse us." He had taken Helva by the arm and had dragged her bodily into the next room, where they had quarreled furiously.

Paulinus and Julia were ensconced in the atrium now, over the warmest part of the floor like a pair of cats, and Paulinus was teaching Julia to play latrunculi. Correus was still too irritated to be curious at his friend's preference for his baby sister's company.

"You look like Donar Hammerer on a bad day," Paulinus said.

"I feel more like the hammered," Correus said, flinging

himself down in a chair. "I've been . . . uh, talking to my mother. I expect you could hear us," he added. "They could probably hear us in Egypt."

Julia looked up from the game board. "Aemelia heard you."

"Great. Glorious. Purely wonderful. I suppose she also heard my mother call me an ungrateful, unfeeling son who was going to drive her to the grave?"

Julia nodded. "She was very upset for you."

"*Upset* for me? Why in Hades isn't she mad at me? That would be more to the point!"

"She thinks you're being noble," Julia said. "Are you?" She was beginning to look uncertain.

"No!" Correus shouted. "Typhon take her, *and* my mother, and *your* mother, and—women!" He glared at her, hurled himself out of his chair again, and disappeared into the garden, where it was raining.

"He'll get wet." Julia looked after him dubiously.

"Do him good," Paulinus said. "You know, that would be a ghastly match. Aemelia should thank Juno she *can't* marry him."

Julia looked at him shyly. "I'm going to tell her that. I always thought I knew what *I* wanted, too."

Paulinus gave her a thoughtful look, reached out to move a piece on the game board, and then put his hand over Julia's instead.

Correus spent a highly unpleasant week telling himself that, having finally shouted his mother into an unwilling silence, there was no need to talk to Aemelia as well, though he knew that only an oaf would leave again without seeing her. He was wondering if he was going to have to go to her and hope her father didn't set the dogs on him, when she finally reappeared for a visit with Julia. Correus told Julia flatly to go bill and coo with Paulinus (it had finally dawned on him that his friend seemed to have grown roots to his sister's side) and he was lying in wait for Aemelia when she appeared.

"Correus—"

"Now listen to me," he said firmly, taking her damp cloak and handing it to a slave to dry before she could say anything. "We haven't got much time, and I don't want to make you unhappy. But you've simply got to think about marrying Flavius—or someone else—and stop thinking about me."

"They can't force me," she said, holding her chin up.

"No, and you can't marry me, either," he said harshly. "If things were different . . . well, things would be different, but they're not. I don't want to hurt you, and I don't want my brother hurt, either. And I can't take much more of this," he added.

"You can't—"

"No, I can't. Now look here—" He was beginning to feel exasperated and Aemelia was looking at him oddly. "I'm not some fairy-tale hero who can come and sweep you away. I'm the adopted son of a slave, with a very tenuous position in the world. And if you don't realize that, I do!" He paused, got a grip on himself, and took her by the shoulders. He kissed her on the forehead. "You're a sweet child. Now for all our sakes, marry my brother."

Correus left her, still staring after him, white-faced, and bumped into Flavius in the doorway. "Go talk to her," he growled, not even trying to keep his voice pleasant. "Read her poetry. Kiss her hand. I'm going riding."

Flavius glared after him, his mouth set in a tight line, and then turned slowly to Aemelia, who was now huddled in a chair. Flavius sighed and pulled another chair up beside her. She turned to him, tears rolling down her cheeks, and he wiped them away gently with the back of his hand.

"You'd do better to have me, child," Flavius said softly. "You see, there's one thing you haven't thought about."

Aemelia looked at him blankly.

"I love you," Flavius said, and she could read the truth of that in his face. "And Correus doesn't."

It was raining, a dark storm-rain with thunder in it, and the dripping courier waited impatiently at the outer door until his hammering should rouse someone in the sleeping household to come and let him in.

Old Philippos, the steward, in his night tunic with a cloak pulled about him wrong way out, and a lamp in his hand, grumbled his way across the cold marble floor. The furnace had been allowed to go out, a blatant piece of negligence.

"I'm coming, I'm coming. Stop that racket, can't you?" Philippos unbarred the door and pulled it open. "What do you think you're doing raising the house at this hour?"

The courier stepped past him and stood dripping in the doorway. "Orders. And I didn't ride all this way in the rain to stand here nattering with you." He held out two tablets closed with scarlet seals.

Philippos raised the lamp and squinted at them. He had been Appius's steward long enough to recognize military orders. The courier held them out, inscription topmost. "Flavius Appius Julianus and . . . uh, Correus Appius Julianus," he said. "These came into our camp tonight and the commandant chased me out here with 'em right off." He wore a Praetorian Guards uniform under his wet cloak.

"They had another week of leave left," Philippos said.

"Tell that to the Germans," the courier said. "Not that I know anything, mind, but the dispatch rider said these came down from the Rhenus with a 'priority' on 'em. Looks like they've got their hands full up there."

XIX

A Face by Torchlight

"WHAT'S GONE WRONG?" JULIA TURNED A TROUBLED FACE to Paulinus as a slave hurried past them, dragging her brothers' kits behind him to the door. Flavius could be heard in the distance shouting to Bericus to see if the horses were saddled.

Paulinus, also in riding clothes, put an arm around Julia and sighed. "It looks like the spring campaign is going to start earlier than we thought. I'm afraid I saw it coming."

"But why are you going with them? You aren't in the army."

Paulinus gave a snort of amusement. "It seems I might as well be. I got some orders of my own this morning."

"Lucius, you're dodging me."

Paulinus sighed again and looked embarrassed. "I know I am. You can talk to your father about it after we've gone, and I expect he'll explain what he can."

"Papa?"

"Yes. I . . . er, had a talk with him this morning. I meant to talk to you first, but . . . things came up."

"A talk about what?" Julia prodded him.

"A talk about us," Paulinus said. He gave her a hesitant look. "I know I'm not what you had in mind, but . . . well, frankly, you didn't strike me as a possibility either, at first. But now . . . well, it seemed like the right thing to do," he finished lamely.

"Lucius!" Julia flung her arms around him and he staggered back. "And he agreed?"

"Well, I'm glad to see you do." Paulinus smiled and looked relieved. He was a wealthy man with no necessity to marry for wealth, and in fact he had a good many reasons *not* to marry at all. He wanted a wife who wanted *him*. "Yes, he agreed. We don't quite see eye to eye on some points, but we have a healthy respect for each other." He didn't add that he had ceased to hedge with Appius over exactly what it was that he did for the Emperor . . . and made a promise not to involve Julia in it. Paulinus had also stated flatly that if the Emperor wanted to hold the Rhenus he had better put all the men and money into Germany that he could, and the Senate had better like it. Paulinus had already said as much to the Emperor himself, of course, but Vespasian collected opinions the way he collected spies. The more voices that spoke as one on the subject, the better.

He wrapped his arms around Julia. These were things he would have to tell her, and she had enough brains to cope with them, he thought with satisfaction. But not while she was living under her father's roof.

"Lucius." Julia's voice dragged him back to the pre-

sent. "You haven't even kissed me," she said firmly, and
so he did.

The household turned out to watch them ride away, a
more tense farewell than they had made nearly two years
ago. There was war in the air, and this time they had a
harsher destination than a training camp at Rome. Aemelia and her parents were there as well, on Appius's
invitation, and Aemelia saw sadly that it was Flavius,
not Correus, who turned to look back over his shoulder
as he rode away.

Julia took her by the arm. "Come to my room with
me," she whispered. "I've got something to tell you."

Aemelia looked unhappily down the tree-lined road
at the diminishing figures of the riders moving along it,
and Julia changed her mind. Her own news would keep.
"I was wrong about Correus and you," she said firmly.
"Aemelia, Lucius says . . ."

Correus and the others drew rein at the foot of the
great natural barrier that divided Italy from Gaul and
Germany to the north, and they gave a gloomy eye to the
roadway that snaked its way up into the Alpine passes.

"Damnation," Flavius muttered from the muffling folds
of his cloak. Real thaw had not yet fully come to these
high peaks, and the view ahead offered an unpromising
journey. A courier riding light on a hill-bred pony was
one thing. Five heavily laden horses were another.

"We could have stayed out our leave and not lost any
time," Flavius grumbled. "What do you suppose has got
old Rufinus in such a tearing hurry?"

"What do *you* suppose?" Correus said. "Somebody
saw a German under his bed, I expect."

"More likely the Rhenus has had an early thaw," Paulinus said. "In which case they're probably seeing Germans coming through the windows by now."

Correus thought of the German spy he had inter-
viewed for the legate at the start of winter. Something
there, maybe. He put his heel to Antaeus's flank, almost
eagerly. Germans he could cope with; better than he had
coped with the problems left two weeks behind him in
his father's house.

* * *

Paulinus had been right about the early thaw. Weather along the Rhenus had taken a freak turn and spread a warm hand unseasonably early over the hills of the Agri Decumates. And Calpurnius Rufinus now knew three things. Nyall would fight; Nyall had dragged the rest of the Suevi into an alliance with him; and Rufinus's spy had been thrown out of Nyallshold on his ear. Which left one important thing the legate didn't know—just when Nyall would fight, and where. Calpurnius Rufinus recalled every man away on leave and ordered commanders of the other Rhenus garrisons to do likewise.

Weapons drill and route marches through the muddy slush stepped up with each day the weather held clear. Patrol galleys whisked along the river with supply ships and transports lumbering in their wake, and the Argentoratum fortress was thick with a changing parade of frontier scouts and couriers. The common legionary groused about the weather while his centurion stood by to see that every last speck of winter rust came off his pilum point.

The Argentoratum marketplace was full of bustle and rumor. Julius prowled among its stalls on a daily shopping excursion, but the best source of information was Rhodope, whose establishment he visited secretly. Freita, he felt certain, would place a whorehouse off limits if she thought of it, but Rhodope knew eveything almost as soon as it happened. Julius took Rhodope small posies of wild flowers and was allowed to sit amid the oriental splendor and listen. He was at Rhodope's when he heard that everyone on leave had been recalled.

"It's war," he told Freita. "And the centurion's coming back!" He dumped an armload of firewood on the hearth and turned to see how the lady was going to take that.

Freita looked up from her loom, one hand arrested in midair as the shuttle fell to her lap. "Are you sure?"

"He's been recalled. They all have."

"But war?" War with her own kind.

Julius gave her a patient look. "They don't send courier riders over the pass in this weather for nothing. What else would it be, an invitation to dinner?"

Freita lifted her hands to the loom and then let them

fall back in her lap, all the while staring past the half-finished cloth toward the door as if she expected Correus to come walking through it on the heels of Julius's news.

"Better hurry up with that cloak you're making if you want it to be a surprise," he said, and she opened her mouth to answer that it wasn't a cloak, but he was gone, catching up the water bucket that hung on a peg by the door.

Freita pushed her stool back from the loom and stood up, eying the red cloth on it. Originally, it was to be a saddle blanket for Aeshma, a bright one to set off his gray hide, but somehow it had kept getting bigger. She supposed it really was a cloak for Correus.

War . . . war with her people. Or at any rate war with Nyall and such of her tribe as had not drowned or burned or been sold, she corrected herself with an acid taste in her mouth. War with Nyall, who would have learned from last year's losses . . . who might win this time. She opened the door and stood leaning against the post, looking out across the dusty street to the scrubby wood that lay at the edge of the civilian town. Beyond it lay the ploughed land of the settlement, grain and vineyards, and the cabbage patches that Nyall Sigmundson had spoken of so scathingly. War . . . war to take her out of this strange place with strange straight streets and stone houses that were blind and windowless outside and full of unexpected gardens inside, with pictures of gods on the walls. Away from the great gray fort that loomed above her, and the red-uniformed sentries that paced its walls. Away from the Roman-kind, leaving them dead behind her as they once had left her kin dead at Jorunnshold. Dead. A picture of Correus, dead in that fortress with blood on his face, rose up, and she brushed her hand across her eyes to push the vision away.

The picture stayed with her, stubbornly . . . Correus, eyes open and sightless, with a broken helmet beside him and blood in his hair.

No! Freita backed away and closed the door, and other memories came crowding in instead. Correus bringing Julius home, another stray to make a set with

her and Aeshma . . . Correus dozing by the fire with
the cat in his lap, or just watching her brush her hair
. . . sitting up half the night inventing a breed of horse
that didn't exist . . . his lips against hers, and the feel
of his body shaking because he wanted her and
wouldn't take her because of what he had done once
before. . . .

Julius came back with the water and a queer look on
his street-urchin face. "I hadn't thought," he said. "It's
not our side you'll be cheering for, is it? If your Nyall
wins this one, you can be shed of us, me and the centurion. . . ." He dumped the water in the kettle on
the hearth. "You can go home to your people, like
you've been wanting to."

Freita turned slowly to look at him. If Nyall won
she could go back to her own kind and leave this half-
year dead behind her, but not as if it had never been
. . . not with Correus also dead behind her. "No," she
said. "No . . . it's too late now." She lay down on the
bed in her curtained corner of the room and began to
cry.

The men on leave were streaming back into Argentoratum, mixed with yet more reinforcements that somebody had miraculously sent from somewhere. In thanks
for the troops, Calpurnius Rufinus prayed for a long
life for the Emperor and for whoever had given the
Emperor an opinion that echoed his own endless dispatches.

Rufinus smiled a wolfish smile and settled his eagle-
crested helmet on his head. "I'll give Vespasian his money's worth."

Paulinus had other business and went his own way
with Tullius when they reached Augusta Raurica. Correus and Flavius reluctantly left their horses there with
Bericus and caught a ride downriver with a patrol ship.
They were in familiar territory now, and they spent
much of the trip pumping the galley's master for news
rather than watching the still-leafless vineyards of the
Rhenus slide by.

"There's more traffic on this damn river than at the
Forum in Rome," the captain said disgustedly, as the gal-

ley backed its oars and slowed to avoid ramming an overloaded supply ship wallowing its way downriver ahead of them. The Rhenus was beginning to rise with the melting snow from the mountains, and the current was swift and tricky.

Correus leaned on the bow rail, listening to the changing hammer strokes from the rowing deck below as the galley maneuvered carefully and then shot past the supply ship in a clear stretch. The Rhenus road running along the bank on his left was also thick with traffic. To the right, the hills of the Black Forest rose dark and misty, but less ominous now, crisscrossed with log roads and heavily patrolled. As they neared Argentoratum Bridge, a cavalry patrol clattered across and into the wood, their fish-scale armor rippling in the cold sun. Correus had an uncanny sense of homecoming.

The galley backed around and bumped gently against the mossy bulwarks of the jetty; her passengers trotted down the boarding plank, among them Correus, Flavius, and two young tribunes newly posted to the Eighth Augusta. The brothers threaded their way through the crowd —on the other side a ship was unloading quarried stone for road repairs—and the mountain of baggage that the tribunes seemed to have brought with them.

"Nice present for old Rufinus," Flavius said as he and his brother, carrying most of their kits on their backs, turned at the river gate to lift a hand in farewell to the galley's captain. He waved back and cast an irritated glance at the tribunes, who stood with lordly indifference in the middle of the jetty while seamen wrestled a succession of trunks and boxes up from the hold.

"They'll be needin' a whole mule cart just to get around," the sentry at the river gate said, watching the tribunes. "I'd best send someone to help with that or them sailors'll leave it sittin' on the jetty just to spite 'em. Ah well, they'll tone down when they've been out here a bit," he added, not unkindly, and Correus and Flavius chuckled with the indulgence of career men with a heavy year's campaign behind them.

When they had reported their presence in the Principia, the optio checked their names off and told Correus to report back in the morning because the legate wanted to see him. "Something to do with that tame German of his," the optio added, "so don't keep him waiting, mind." Junior centurions, even veteran ones, rated very low on a headquarters optio's list of those in power.

"I shall sleep on the doorstep," Correus assured him solemnly. He went off to look for a bath and his commander. Messala Cominius—in that order. He was putting off telling Julius and Freita that he was back. This new war, although not unexpected, put a new perspective on things regarding Freita. He was going to go out and kill her tribesmen, and that was not going to cast him, or the army, in any favorable light in her eyes.

He spent as much time as he could soaking and getting the news from the other bathers. The news was mostly rumor and speculation, but there was a heady excitement in the air, which Correus could sense even in Messala Cominius when he tracked him down at catapult practice. The catapults were still tricky after a wet winter, and Cominius had two centuries, one of them Correus's, at work adjusting the skeins and lobbing stones into the open ground to the south of the fort. An eight-man patrol stood on the edges of the target to keep any traffic well clear. A group of small boys from the town stood behind them, wide-eyed as the stones came hurtling down.

Correus took over his own century, mostly to have something to do, and was pleased to discover that his second-in-command had kept them in good order over the winter.

"They're shaping up very well," Correus said as the catapult was drawn back in and the canvas covering lashed down. "Any problems?"

"Well, not to speak of, sir. Except for Quintus."

"Quintus?" Correus remembered Quintus plainly. A barracks lawyer and a drunk, when he could find anything to get drunk on. A parade-ground nuisance. And an excellent soldier in the field, once he had something to fight besides the army. "What's he done now?" he asked.

"Three days unlawful absence, sir," the second officer said. "With extra punishment for slugging a sentry on his way back into camp. He's in the guardhouse now."

"Typhon take him," Correus said. "Did he have a reason to go, or did he just get bored?"

"Well, he's got a woman in the town, sir. She was pregnant and overdue, and having a hard time of it, and he took off to stay with her."

"Well, why didn't he just ask for leave? We aren't on campaign—he'd have got it."

"He did, sir," the second said, "but he was already on report for missing parade, so they turned him down."

"So the damn fool just took off?" Correus tried to think of the best way to tackle Cominius on this. Unlawful absence was serious, but he wanted Quintus back in the ranks before they marched.

"He forged a pass," the second said, and laughed suddenly. "With your name on it, so of course he had to wait for someone on sentry duty who wouldn't know you were on leave. I asked him why you, and he said, real patient-like, as if I was a fool kid, that your hand was the easiest to copy."

"Thank you," Correus said. "I shall remember that. I suppose I had better go and talk to him. Did he come back of his own accord?"

"Yes, but by that time they were looking for him, and the sentry grabbed him, so Quintus punched his nose for him."

"And in three days, no one thought to search his woman's house?"

"Well, the town watch did. But like I said, the girl was in a bad way. It's my belief the commander of the watch knew where he was, and let him bide until he was sure the girl and the baby were all right."

Correus sighed. "All right, I'll see what I can do. Go and tell him to start behaving like a Vestal Virgin, and I'll plead his case with the commander in the morning. I suppose they've stopped his pay for this. Has the girl got any money?"

The second shook his head. "I doubt it, sir. Quintus gets his pay stopped a lot."

Correus fished in his tunic. "Here. Make sure she's got enough to eat, and then go see Quintus. Maybe that'll tone him down some."

A bugle call sang out through the dusk, and the usual unpalatable smell that signified dinner drifted on the evening air. Correus went and had a meal in the mess, and then a drink with Silvanus, whom he regaled with the tale of Paulinus's unexpected courtship of Julia. And then, unable to come up with any other delays, he put on his cloak and went out through the landward gate to announce his return to Freita.

It was full dark now, the night lit only by an occasional window or by the gold rectangle of an open doorway. The firefly lanterns of the watch making its rounds glittered in the distance. Correus could hear the click-click of their nailed sandals crossing the paved square of the town basilica, fading into a thudding tramp as they passed on into Argentoratum's unpaved streets. Nearby, a door swung open to the sound of irate feminine voices, and a legionary stumbled out into the street. He picked up his helmet, dusted it off, and shouted something back.

An indignant voice yelled after him, "You want it twice, you pay twice!"

Correus recognized Rhodope's scolding and drew back into the shadow of a silent house to watch.

Charis stood in the doorway beside her employer, a blanket clutched around her and her hair disheveled. "It wasn't my fault you couldn't do anything!" she shouted. "Next time don't come here drunk. I gave you *plenty* of time—I don't have all night, you know!" There was a hoot of laughter from the house, and the legionary fled.

Rhodope slammed the door behind him, and Correus doubled over in the dusty street, laughing silently. When he had recovered, he went on, ambling slowly and watching the moon bob up over the distant trees. Finally, and reluctantly, he came to the shabby little house on the outskirts of Argentoratum. He had asked Silvanus to keep an eye on Freita in his absence, and over wine in Silvanus's quarters had inquired how she was, but the other centurion had merely shrugged and said that she did all right. But she was . . . well, quiet, lately.

"Since there's been talk of war?"

"No, ever since you left." Silvanus looked as if he might say something more, and then changed his mind. "Here, have some more wine. The Egyptian's best." If his friend were a little drunk, Silvanus thought, it might help.

At his knock, Correus heard the bar being lifted from

the door. It swung slowly open and Freita stood there, a
kitchen knife in one hand and her green eyes open wide.

"I hope that's not for me," Correus said mildly.

"No." She looked around for someplace to put the
knife and set it on the edge of the hearth. "I . . . I
wasn't sure it was you . . . although I thought . . ." She
looked unsettled and pushed stray tendrils of hair back
from her face. Her hair never stayed pinned up very well.

"Where's Julius?"

"I . . . I told him he might go night-fishing with some of
the other boys. It is dull for him here with only me, and
besides, he heard at the fort that you had come back,
and told me . . . and I . . ." Her voice trailed off
uncertainly.

Correus stepped in and looked around. The house was
lamplit, and somehow neater than he remembered.
"Where did the loom come from?"

"Julius and I built it," Freita said proudly. "I saved
enough of the money you left us to have the wood cut at
the mill. I . . . I thought maybe you wouldn't mind."

There was an almost-finished piece of cloth on it, he
saw—of a bright military scarlet. He started to ask her
what it was for, but something in her face told him that
maybe he shouldn't.

"Freita—"

"Yes, Centurion?"

"Don't call me that!" he said. It came out harsher than
he intended, and she gave him a queer look.

"What should I call you?"

"You call Paulinus by his name," he said. "And Silvanus even, sometimes."

"Lucius is a friend."

"And what am I?"

"I . . . don't know," she said. "Slaves don't call masters by their names."

"I didn't buy you for a slave," he said bluntly. "And
don't stiffen up on me like a plaster statue, again."

Freita sighed. She picked up a stick and poked at the
fire. The stick was charred through at one end and broke
off, sending up a little red shower of sparks. "This . . .
isn't turning out the way I meant it to."

Correus was growing more puzzled by the minute.

Maybe it was Silvanus's wine, but he didn't think so. "Why did you send Julius away?" he asked.

Freita fidgeted with the fire some more. "I didn't want him here when you came home," she said finally. The fire flared up under her prodding and settled back again with a red glow that turned her hair to an autumn-leaf color. She had on her best gown, he noticed suddenly, and a faint rosy wash on her cheeks and lips that must be paint, because the rest of her face was pale. There was a fine green shadow along her eyelids that gave her eyes a sea-mist translucence. She dropped the stick into the fire and turned to look him full in the face. "I am glad you are come home," she whispered.

She was plainly uncomfortable, and Correus wondered what was going on behind those sea-mist eyes.

"You don't trust me, do you?" she said, unnervingly.

"Am I that transparent?"

"I don't need magic to read your thoughts. We have never trusted each other, have we?"

"Should I now? With a war coming, my people against yours, and me in the middle of it, and you saying you're glad to see me?" He wondered if perhaps that kitchen knife was for him, after all. "Have you suddenly come to care for Rome so much?"

"Not Rome," Freita said. "If Nyall Sigmundson wins this war, he will burn the Rhenus from one end to the other, and I could ride with him and take a fine, bloody revenge for my people. I thought about that. And then I dreamed about it," she went on shakily. "And then I knew that the price for that is one that I can't pay anymore."

He stood looking at her for a moment, beginning to understand, and was startled by the sharp stab of happiness that went through him. After another moment she lifted her hands and whispered his name, just once. And then she was in his arms, with her face against his shoulder. He held her, dazed, thinking that it had been for him—the painted face, the absence of Julius, the nervousness . . . all that for him, and with no knife at the end of it . . . only for him.

"Freita," he whispered, brushing his mouth against her hair and the white curve of her neck. She stirred in his arms and the old longing washed over him, deeper,

stronger than anything that Aemelia's childish prettiness
had ever stirred in him. He kissed her full on the lips,
long and urgently, forcing his restless body to wait until
hers should wake under his hands. Never again would he
take Freita the way he had taken her the first time.

He felt her grow tense, not with fear this time, and
bent and scooped her up in his arms, staggering a little
with her weight—she was as tall as he was, and big-
boned. He ducked under the curtain that screened her
end of the room and laid her on the bed, kicking off his
sandals. The pins had slipped from her hair and it spread
out about her in a pale cloud, washed to silver by the
shadows. She rolled into his arms as he lay down beside
her and they fumbled awkwardly with his tunic and the
clasps of her gown, laughing one moment and kissing the
next, while Correus hoped that Julius's fish were biting
well that night.

He sat up and threw their clothes on the floor. The
light that came in around the curtain, and the moonlight
slipping through the shutters of the one high window
dappled their skin like zebras, and the blanket was warm
and scratchy under him. He rolled over on his back, letting her hands explore his hard, scarred body, and saw
that hers bore old scars too, as well as the slightly darker
patch on throat and breast that was the healed burn. Jorunnshold was not the first time that Freita had fought for
her tribe, he thought, tracing the flat white line that ran
from thigh to knee. A cavalryman's scar, that one. He
reached out and cupped one breast, while his other hand
slid up past the old scar and slipped between her thighs.
She wriggled with pleasure and wrapped her arms around
him. Strong arms. This was a woman like himself, a
woman who faced reality with a knife in her hand. An
army outpost would hold no terrors for Freita.

He moved his hand experimentally, and she opened
her legs willingly to let him in, but he hung above her
for just a moment, catching her eyes with his. Nothing
between them would ever be the same after this night,
and he had to know with a certainty why she was doing
this. The green eyes looked back at him, blazing up like
fire in an emerald. She whispered his name as she pulled
him down to her and arched her back as he entered her.

Then she wrapped her long legs around him, setting free all the hunger she had raised in him. They rolled together on the rough blankets of the bed, until in the outer room the fire sank down to embers, and the oil lamp sputtered and went out.

Afterward they lay entwined, spent, each unwilling to let the other go. Finally Correus sat up and pulled the blanket from under him, drawing it up over them both. Freita sighed and snuggled her head into the hollow of his shoulder. She said, quite distinctly in her careful Latin, "This it is that I trade my freedom for."

"Heart of my heart, you *are* free." Correus drew his hand across her face. "I will draw up the papers tomorrow."

"No." Freita propped herself up on one elbow. "No, it doesn't matter now." She didn't add that it hadn't mattered since she had seen that horrible, haunting vision of him lying blood-covered in a ruined fort. She had realized then that her heart lay where she would not willingly have put it, but it was there all the same, and the rest of her would follow it. But a death-vision is not something to tell a man who goes to fight a war. "No," she said. "Let it bide until we are gone from here. There will be a new posting for you soon, won't there? Silvanus says so. The commander of the Eagles here will not like it if you free me, and I do not mind—now."

"No!" Correus remembered the coming war. It slammed into his mind like a fist. "We'll do it secretly, but it has to be done." He rolled off the bed and pulled the curtain back. "There must be something here to write on."

"Why?" Freita sat up in bed with the blanket clutched around her.

"I may be killed," he said, rummaging in a storage chest in the main room. "They'd send you back to my family." He scrabbled among the chest's contents and found pen and ink.

"Would that be so bad?"

"Yes," he said shortly. "With manumission papers at least you'd have a fighting chance, depending on how much damage Nyall had done, and what mood they were in. But you'd have a chance. Damn it, there must be a piece of papyrus somewhere!"

"Correus, stop it!" There was something in his taut face that totally unnerved her. "You are not going to be killed," she said, thinking again of that nightmare vision. She had never had the Sight; please the gods it had not come upon her now. She got out of bed and laid a hand on his shoulder. "Correus, you need witnesses. If you insist, we'll do it in the morning, but stop making a mess of that chest."

He scrabbled along the bottom of the chest anyway. She had suddenly become very precious to him, too precious to take a chance with. But there was no papyrus there, not even a wooden tablet, and he began to replace the strewn contents. "Tomorrow," he said shakily. "Tomorrow. Silvanus and Paulinus. No, Paulinus won't be here yet. Damn!"

His face was strained, the bones standing out in high relief, and she tugged on his hand to draw him back into the bed. Then he exclaimed:

"Flavius! Yes, Flavius, and he'll swear . . . I did my damnedest to give him what *he* wanted, he can . . ."

His voice was still shaking, and she pulled him up close against her. She had never seen him like this, and it frightened her, even as his fear for her sounded a small triumphant note at the back of her mind. "Sleep," she whispered, and stroked his back gently. Eventually his eyes fell closed and his breathing deepened, regular and contented, and he slept, with his face in her hair.

He awoke restless and still worried, and would not be satisfied until he had found his brother and Silvanus and dragged them out of bed before reveille.

Silvanus came willingly enough when Correus told him what he wanted, and Flavius came grumpily, rubbing the sleep from his eyes. The manumission papers were made out and signed four times, one copy for each of them. Correus was taking no chances. Silvanus looked pleased, and Flavius amused, as they signed the papers. Flavius had no high opinion of Freita ("impudent and stubborn" was the kindest remark he had ever made) and Correus suspected that Freita's views were similarly

unflattering. But still, Flavius would swear to the validity
of the papers. Maybe more willingly with Correus dead
than alive, Correus thought, watching his brother walk
away back toward the fort.

The bugle shriek of reveille split the morning air, and
Correus pulled Freita to him and kissed her before he
made his own way back toward Argentoratum and his
appointment with the legate and the legate's tame German.

Freita looked after him, wistful and content with nine-
tenths of her being. The other tenth wondered at Silvanus's parting comment, made low-voiced to Correus in
the doorway: "He'll cooperate, and if I were you I
wouldn't worry overmuch about the ethics of it. Nyall
threw him out at midwinter. He's more than grateful to
be ours now."

There was something more afoot than a clash of armies, and Correus hadn't told her. She shrugged her
shoulders finally, and picked up her market basket,
leaving Julius still asleep after his night's adventure. There
was no reason why Correus should tell her. Later, when
he was posted to a place that was not also her homeland,
then he would tell her such things.

She prowled the market square, delighted to find spring
veal in the butcher's stall, and bought enough to make a
stew. She crossed the square to rummage among the
bales in a fabric merchant's tent. She wanted enough gold
thread to work a border on the nearly finished cloak, a
domestic occupation to drive the thought of war away.
They would have two weeks at least, she thought. Two
weeks to make the most of. But the fabric merchant held
up his hands in apology. He knew the sort of thread the
lady wanted, but he had none. Perhaps with the next
shipment.

She was about to retrace her steps when she caught
sight of two laden pack ponies, blowing and slobbering
greedily in the stone trough at the center of the square.
A short, wiry man in hillman's clothes stood beside them,
splashing his face with water. Freita recognized him—
Beorn, a northman of no known tribe (outcast, some
said) who made his living trading from hold to hold on
both sides of the Rhenus. Beorn paid no attention to

frontiers, and since he went his own way peaceably, the Romans let him alone. Freita turned and trotted over. You never knew what Beorn might have in his packs; he traded for other goods as often as for silver, and his yearly route took him no one ever quite knew where.

"As it chances, pretty lady," Beorn said, giving her a smile, "I have just such a thing by me, just waiting for some officer's lady to come by wanting it."

In her Roman gown and piled-up hair, it was plain that he didn't recognize her, and Freita sighed with relief. She would as soon make no explanations. She haggled him down on the price a bit and went home with the gold thread tucked in her basket, feeling pleased with herself. She could give Correus the cloak before the legion marched out. Having something of her by him might bring him back safe again.

It wasn't until the stew was made and bubbling in an iron stand over the banked-up fire that she wiped her hands on her apron and glanced out the open window to see that it was nearly dusk. If she was going to exercise Aeshma, she would have to be quick about it. She pulled on the old gown that she kept for riding, wincing as her aching muscles protested. She was stiff and sore from last night's lovemaking, and she wanted to work the knotted muscles loose. Correus would come to her again that night. He hadn't said so, but she knew he would.

"You aren't going out now," Julius said as she put her hand on the door.

"I won't be gone long."

"You'll get into trouble and the centurion will blame me for it," Julius protested.

She was in too good a mood to fight with him. She took the knife from its rack by the wooden table that served as a cutting board, and slipped it unsheathed through her belt. "I was taking care of myself before you were out of your cradle, little man," she told him, and was gone out the door before he could protest.

Julius shrugged and sat down by the hearth to mind the stew. He knew a superior force when he met one. Any robber who tangled with that witch would probably get what he deserved.

Freita saddled Aeshma and slipped the bridle on while

he danced expectantly about the shed. "Be still, you fool!" She buckled the bridle and pulled the shed door open, and the gray horse trotted out at her side, head lifted to the interesting smells of dusk. She swung herself into the saddle and turned him toward the town and the river road. It was heavily patrolled, especially after dark —a nice safe place for an evening gallop.

Her sore thighs strained as they gripped Aeshma's wide back, but after half a mile she let him break into a canter, and then a full gallop, on the grass bordering the road. Aeshma snorted and stretched his legs out, bucking a little every now and then out of sheer high spirits, and Freita settled down to hold on, with the cold night wind singing past her head.

She pulled him up after a few miles, as the dusk dropped into true dark, and turned him back toward the fort, pleased to find that her legs no longer ached. It was a starry night, full of the scent of new grass and awakening land, and she rode happily, lost in her own thoughts, until the face of a man she knew leaped up from a pool of light in the fortress gateway with a clarity that made her drag sharply on Aeshma's reins. The man stood near another face, infinitely familiar, and she swerved Aeshma hard around into the shadows of the deserted market square. Correus's voice came softly, instantly recognizable in the still night, with another voice, a ghost voice, blown on a ghost wind out of a burning hold. They were too intent on their talk to notice the soft thud of hooves in the dirt beyond them; Freita drew rein and sat shaking in the darkness as the meaning of her chance encounter grew clear.

"We'll give you an escort as far as our own lines," Correus said, "but we'll have to lie well back, and I doubt you'll see us. If Nyall's men spot us, you won't live long enough to tell him your tale."

"I rode from Nyallshold at midwinter," the other man said. His voice came to Freita like a cold hand down the back of her neck. "I can ride back again without a nursemaid."

"I'm glad to hear it," Correus said drily. "Across the Nicer, you'll be on your own."

"It wouldn't hurt if they could manage to chase me across," the German said. "For the look of it."

"That can be arranged."

The German smiled, a surface smile, clear-eyed, like a snake's. "We understand each other well, then."

"I wouldn't bet on it," Correus said shortly. "We'll start you off in about four days—these things take time to arrange. In the meantime, keep to yourself. And have a drink on the Emperor." He fished in his tunic and spun a silver coin into the dirt at the other man's feet. "Never say Rome doesn't pay for her work." He turned back through the gates and the German shrugged and picked up the coin.

He walked purposefully toward the wineshops and other businesses of the night across the empty square, and Freita's fingers slid along the knife hilt at her belt. He was going to pass right by her. If Aeshma kept still she could kill him . . . so easily. She knew that bland, smiling face. She had seen it at Jorunnshold, digging away at Nyall Sigmundson's chieftainship. His name was Ingald, and he had pushed the priest-kind into calling a month's Dead Sacrifice, until the Romans burned the hold over their heads.

He came closer, and Silvanus's words came back to her: "Nyall threw him out at midwinter . . . he's ours now." *Ours . . . Correus's . . .* She could kill him so easily. But what was she now? She also had turned her back on her people. *I had no choice,* her mind cried out. But this wasn't war, it was treachery. Ingald was almost upon her, and her hand twitched on her knife, and that awful picture of Correus lying in his own blood rose up before her. She yanked on Aeshma's reins and spun him around into the darkness, while the German whirled around behind her, his hand on his own knife, peering into the night.

Treachery! her mind shrieked at her as she rode away. *You sell your own kind for the love of a man!* She slowed Aeshma, her heart pounding, and tried to think. If she turned from her own kind completely, might not her gods turn from *her,* and take away the one thing she wanted? She bit her lip, half sobbing, torn between two loyalties, and terrified that whatever she did might give truth to

those dark visions. She should have listened to Julius and
stayed and stirred her pots by the fire; then she would
never have seen Ingald's thief's face, and Correus's grim
expression as he used him to trap Nyall. But she had seen
them, and there was no place to run to. She sat, clutching
the horned front-plate of the saddle, while Aeshma fidgeted under her, restless for his stall and his dinner.
Slowly, Freita made up her mind. She put her heels to
Aeshma's flanks, turning him from the road home, out
toward the clearing just to the west of town, where Beorn
the trader was camped. Beorn would want money, but
she had a hidden gold ring that she had put in her gown
when the Roman soldiers closed in around her at Jorunnshold. And she had never told Correus about it, first
because she had thought that it might buy her escape
someday, and later because she didn't want to tell him
that. But it would be enough for Beorn, and she could
bring it to him in the morning while Julius slept.

The small glow of a banked campfire showed through
the night, and she took a deep breath and pushed
Aeshma forward. She would do what she could for her
people, as long as it had no knife in it. And maybe her
gods would understand.

Behind her, another horse trotted by soft-footed in the
wet road. The rider drew rein as he caught sight of a pale
head bent over the fire beside Beorn's.

Correus's German girl, Flavius thought. He shrugged
and rode on. If she was running away from his brother
now that she was freed, it might be for the best in the long
run.

XX

Spies and Allies

HALLGERD CAME DOWN THE STEPS OF THE HALL WITH
an apron full of grain, shooing the birds before her. "Go,"
she said firmly. "Back where you belong." She flung the
grain ahead of her into the far end of the timber-
fenced yard where she was trying to persuade the fowl to
stay. Before she had been wed to Kari and begun to
sweep some housekeeping notions into his bachelor hold,
they had been practically living in the hall.

The chickens clucked and began to fight for the grain,
while a fat duck with a comet's tail of ducklings behind
her quacked importantly and waddled to Hallgerd's feet,
waggling her tail feathers. Hallgerd gave her some grain
of her own. It kept her from terrorizing the chickens out
of theirs. "Greedy bird," she said, watching her dabble
her beak alternately in the grain and the muddy pond.
"I'll make you into a dinner, see if I don't." She wiped
her hands on her apron and marched back to the house
to stir up the kitchen thralls. Kari would be wanting to
eat.

Coming up the hill from the horse barn, Kari watched
her affectionately. She was a brisk, busy little person, and
he couldn't think now why he had waited to wed her until
she had practically suggested it herself. It had been unsettling at first to have his slovenly, peaceful hold turned
upside down and swept out, but a man grew used to lit
fires and properly cooked food in a hurry.

Hallgerd was in the kitchen doing something to barley
cakes on a griddle at the smoking fire when he came in,
and she smiled at him over her shoulder, pulling her
sandy blond braids out of the way as she reached across
the fire to poke at a pot that hung on a hook at the back

of the firepit. The pot steamed appetizingly, and Kari leaned his head over it and sniffed.

Hallgerd shooed him away much as she had shooed the chickens. "It will be ready in a few minutes. Go and wash." She kissed him, her face flushed from the fire. "Bring the lord something to drink," she said to the thrall who was scrubbing off the wooden table, "and then you may eat. Rake the cookfire out afterward and clean it," she added. "It must be a year since it was cleaned."

The thrall departed, grumbling under his breath, to draw a pitcher of beer from the vat in the storeroom. The new mistress had been ordering things scrubbed, the hold's thralls included, ever since the lord had brought her home. He hadn't been so thoroughly washed since he was born. Likely it would give him a cold.

When they had eaten, Hallgerd drew Kari's arm through hers. "Come and see what I have been doing." She led him into the yard behind the main house where a plot of land had been ploughed up and a thrall was setting out young herbs, searched out and dug up from the mountain meadows by Hallgerd herself. A sheet of netting strung on thin poles encircled it, with a second stretched across the top. The duck stood looking wistfully through the mesh at the young greens.

"You'll set a finer table than the chieftain's," Kari said, and Hallgerd looked proud. "You've been very busy, child."

"It is nice, being mistress in my own hold," Hallgerd said. "And that reminds me—" She led him around the house again and out to where the main gates had been drawn open. Kari's holding stood on a hillcrest, within a heavy timber palisade that provided shelter and protection for his people when necessary. In peaceable times the hold's folk occupied the cluster of thatched huts that lay between the foot of the hill and the stream that snaked by beyond. Hallgerd pointed to the two endmost huts. "We had some damage from that last storm," she said, "and I've told them to see to mending it before the rains hit again. Mostly they never think to bother until the water's pouring in through the roof." She turned with compressed lips to nod at another hut. "Old Asvald's been beating his wife again. This time he has nearly broken her ribs."

"I'll put a stop to that," Kari said. "Send someone to fetch him up here before I go out to the cattle."

Hallgerd nodded. "And it is time to make liniment again. I have a recipe for wound salve that Asuin the priest gave me. I will need some of the women to help."

The sun was full up now, with the first hint of spring warmth. A pack of children tumbled about in a running ball game among the huts. Kari and Hallgerd leaned arm in arm in the hold gateway to watch them, and Hallgerd sighed. It was pleasant to stand here together, talking of small domestic things. She would enjoy it while she could. Soon enough a message would come from the chieftain, and Kari and all the men of fighting age would go away to the hosting and she would be left with the women, to try to do their own work and the men's, and wait for them to come back—the ones who did come back. She leaned her head against Kari's neck. Another war . . . there was always another war.

Ranvig's wife was alone when the rider came, pushing his horse hard up the track to the holding, bearing the same message that he had brought to Kari and every other lord between here and Nyallshold.

"My husband is in the high pasture," she said. "I will send for him. In the meantime, they will give you something to eat in the kitchen. You have had a long ride."

"Thank you, lady, that I have."

When he had gone, she beat her fist in frustration on the carded wool in her lap. Like Hallgerd, she had known war was coming, but the knowledge did little to ease her as she sat cursing the Romans, an implacable menace, frightening and unknown, who were armor-plated like beetles and carried better weapons than her own people could forge. Lyting, her half-brother, had ridden away to fight the Romans at the chieftain's call, and he had not come home. Now Ranvig would go, and the hold would be masterless again, and she would be alone.

She sent a thrall to fetch the lord home and sat down to wait for him, the wool forgotten in her lap. She was praying for something, for anything, to keep him from this hosting. If the gods would break her husband's leg for him, she would give them anything they asked.

Fiorgyn watched the last of the chieftain's riders returning to Nyallshold and set off to deal with the coming war in her own fashion. The Semnone lords and their warriors would be hard on the riders' heels, and after them the allied chieftains of the Suevi. The war bands would make a camp for themselves, but lords and chiefs would have to be given hospitality at Nyallshold, fed and housed, and given gifts, while seniority and group commands were decided. The chiefs would be bringing Nyall gifts, and the gods only knew what form *they* would take. One chieftain had brought him a woman, and after he had gone home again, Fiorgyn, with fire in her eye, demanded that Nyall give her away. Nyall laughed and said he couldn't because the man would be insulted; but in any case he wasn't going to do anything with her. Fiorgyn replied darkly that you never knew, and that after this hosting he could give her away, or marry her to someone, and if he didn't she was going to have an accident.

It was still a sore point with them, but a minor one compared to another quarrel that had been raging for three days between the chieftain and his lady.

"I forbid it!" Nyall shouted when she broached the subject again in their chamber. "And I am not going to talk about it again!"

"I am a chief's daughter," Fiorgyn said stubbornly. She faced him, arms crossed.

Nyall sighed. That declaration usually preceded a statement on which Fiorgyn would give no ground.

"I was trained as a warrior, the same as any woman in your own tribe, against the day when we might be needed. I *will* go with this hosting, and if you forbid it, I will put on trousers and walk with the spearmen to shame you!"

"Fiorgyn!" He took her by the shoulders none too gently. "I will lock you up," he threatened.

She beat her fists against his chest. "And send for that . . . that creature, I suppose."

"What in Donar's name has the woman got to do with it?"

Fiorgyn pulled away and stood rubbing her shoulders where his fingers had left an imprint. "I don't know," she admitted, "except that she makes me angry, too. You have given me no reason why I shouldn't go."

"I forbid it."

"That is not a reason. I am not one of your thralls."

"If you were, I would have sold you for an unruly nuisance." She glared at him. "Very well," he said, "the women do not take up their spears except in great need. They are the future of the tribe, and if we must risk that, there is no point in fighting the Romans at all. That is a reason."

"I am not asking you to call out the women. Only that *I* ride with you. So it is not a reason."

"You might be with child."

"I am not."

"Can you be sure?"

"No, of course I'm not sure. Anything is possible."

"There. That is your reason."

"I might be with child? I might fall off a cliff and die tomorrow! The gods might come down from the sky and slay all the Romans for you. 'Might' is no reason."

"Fiorgyn, stop arguing with me!" Nyall ran a hand across his forehead, which was beginning to ache. "I won't risk you. With child or without child. I can't command the war band if I'm worried about you. I can't order a wing into the Romans' spears, knowing that you're riding with it. And if I can't do that, we'll lose. If I were not chieftain, it would be different. I would have no decisions to make. But I do, and I can't play favorites, and I can't say for certain that I wouldn't if you were there. I can't even *look* to the others as if I might. How long do you think I could hold the war band together if they suspected me of that?"

Fiorgyn's face was pale and defeated. She sat down slowly by the cold hearth. "Yes . . . I suppose that is a reason."

He sat beside her and put one arm around her shoulders. "I am sorry."

"Tell me one thing. If you were not chieftain, would you take me with you?"

"Yes." He was silent for a moment, trying to remember a time when he had *not* been chieftain, when everything he did was not touched by it. "I wouldn't want to, for fear for you, but if *you* wanted it, I would take you. I think I would be glad I had, in the end."

She leaned against him and they sat together for a long while. Soon there would be no time for this.

"I am cold," Fiorgyn said at last. She shivered. "Why is this fire not lit?"

"Because you have been too busy arguing with me," Nyall said, "to see to your duties—wife."

"I will send that woman to do it," Fiorgyn said. "She might as well be useful. After you have gone," she added thoughtfully.

Fiorgyn's prediction proved true. From the moment that the first of the allied chieftains of the Suevi rode in with his lords about him and his war band trailing out behind, Nyallshold erupted into the madness of a fair day, only on a scale a thousand times greater. Every guest chamber was filled to overflowing, and even the barns were emptied and their walls hung with rugs. Such spare furniture as could be scrounged from the storerooms was moved in to make them habitable. The Companions crowded themselves willingly into the dormitory chamber that normally housed only those unmarried and holdless men who lived in the chieftain's hall year round. They were a close-knit group and proud of it. But the rest of the Semnone lords expected to be received with no such disregard for dignity. They inspected their quarters and compared them suspiciously to each other's and those of the allied chieftains' lords until Morgian developed a permanent harassed expression. Fiorgyn suggested tartly that perhaps they should build a new hold just for the lords' benefit.

Each lord and chieftain's war band pitched its own camp outside the hold walls until a great city of tents stretched away in all directions. It was the greatest hosting ever made by the tribes of the Free Lands, and it was awesome.

Nyall stood on the walkway that ran around the inner side of the hold walls, looking down thoughtfully at the endless confusion of tents and wagons and rope corrals, while a hundred different shouts and commands melded together into an unceasing billow of sound from the chaos below. If he could hold them together, he could pull the Romans' fortresses down stone by stone and dance in the ruins by summer's end. If. Then he thought of the recent message that had come by the hand of Beorn the trader. He narrowed his eyes to follow the track running westward from Nyallshold toward the Nicer River.

"What are you watching for?" Kari said, as he and Ranvig clambered up the ladder to a place on the walkway beside him. Kari counted on his fingers. "The last of the western holds rode in yesterday. Is there someone else?"

"A visitor, maybe," Nyall said. "Where is Beorn the trader?"

"Gone away to the west, to the Cherusci, he said. I'm thinking he found us too well armed for his taste. Beorn wants no trouble with the Romans."

Beorn must have been well paid for bringing that message, then. Beorn offered a fair price for his goods, but he never gave anything away free. A horseman was coming—four days behind Beorn, but riding faster. It would be soon then . . . or not at all. Because in three days, the war host would be on the move.

As the dawn mist swirled along the valley floor, the camps of the Suevi were already moving. The fires glowed palely in the half-light and went out as they were doused and trod into wet cinders. The tents were already down, the animals fed and watered. The warriors stood or crouched in the wet grass, making a meal of dried fish and bread, while their lords waited for the signal that would come from the chieftains meeting in the hold.

Nyall stood before the great hall in riding dress, booted and cloaked, with his red hair showing fiery in the first light. Around him stood the eight allied chieftains of the Suevi, old fighters all, and northmen most of them, bred to an even harsher land than Nyall's. They were kin to one another, and kin to the tribes of the lands-across-the-river if you went back far enough. But it was a kinship that had never prevented a ceaseless warring among themselves. The Confederation of the Suevi had been one nation in name only, until now. Now they had a common cause to unite them as kinship had not: Rome. Roman forts in the Black Forest were too close to the Semnones and to the four tribes directly to their north. And for the four other tribes whose lands lay more northerly still, these five were too close and too strong to deny. It was an uneasy alliance of shifting power and frequent quarrels, held together only by the iron will of the chieftain of the Semnones. Without Nyall, the war bands would be more likely to turn on each other than put any fear into Rome.

Nyall knew, and the chieftains knew, and the Companions knew. They shadowed him like hounds wherever he went, and now they sat lounging on the steps of the great hall while he went over the war trail for the final time.

"We will cross the mountains here." He drew with his dagger in the dirt. "And then southward this way, and a second crossing here."

"That's the longer march," one of the chieftains objected, and Nyall explained it again, patiently, but with an edge in his voice.

"They are the best crossings for many men and wagons. The best water. And the best trail into the mountains of the Black Forest. Also, I think the Romans will be looking for us to the northward, because this trail will take us through the Hermanduri's lands, and they have spun around like a weathercock and sworn to Rome again."

"Then we will have to fight them to get through. And maybe be caught between them and the Romans," Hoskuld, another chief, objected.

"I doubt it," Nyall said. "The Hermanduri are poor fighters. I'd rather Rome had them than us. They have grown fat cuddling up to Rome, and we will need somewhere to forage."

Hoskuld laughed and one or two of the other lined faces split into a grin. "So we'll forage among the Hermanduri. Nice of Rome to plant them there."

"A fat herd, for our culling," Nyall said. "Rome has beaten them into loyalty again, but not even the Caesar can beat any fight into them. They've been Rome's sheep too long. From there we will split and hit their new forts on the Nicer with a smaller band to tie down the southern legion, so—" He leaned forward to draw three more lines, branching south, west, and northwest. Suddenly there was a commotion at the gates.

The Companions stiffened and Hoskuld's eyes widened as two of Nyall's men staggered in, dragging a third between them. Nyall stood up slowly and faced them, and Hoskuld felt the hair on the back of his neck rise. He wouldn't want the Semnone chieftain's gray eyes fixed on him with that look. Hoskuld was a man who feared few things, but there was death and worse on Nyall's face.

They flung Ingald into the damp earth at Nyall's feet, and he raised his head slowly, wiping the mud from his mouth.

"So you lived," Nyall said.

"Aye, I lived, Nyall Sigmundson." Lined and stretched taut, Ingald's face had lost some of its blandness. "Barely, but I lived."

"Then you should not have come back where you are forbidden," Nyall said. He nodded to the Companions. "Take him and kill him."

Arni and Ranvig rode with the Companions now, and Ranvig was on his feet before the others, with Kari a half-step behind him.

"No!" Ingald said. He pulled himself up and stepped back, his face exhausted.

"No?" Nyall said. His voice had a deadly disinterest in it. "You have a death mark here, Ingald. You knew that."

"Wait," Ingald whispered. "Kill me if you must, but wait until I have spoken. I wouldn't have ridden here with death on my heels, and death waiting, without a reason."

"Death on your heels? Nothing but Hell's folk could drive a man back to put his head on a pole, Ingald, and no man outruns Hell's folk."

"The Romans. I rode a half-day ahead of the Romans

all the way across the Nicer. And in fear of your men after that." He staggered a little. "May I sit down?"

"Certainly," Nyall said, but made no move to have a chair brought.

Ingald's eyes flashed for a moment, and then the look was gone. He sank back down in the dirt where he had fallen, and sat on his heels. "When I left here, I went west, back across the Nicer into my own lands." He looked up at Nyall. "You know the kind of journey I will have made, chieftain—at midwinter."

"Your journey is your own," Nyall said. "You do not belong to us anymore."

"No. So I went back to my own hills, thinking to find some shelter there. And there was . . . nothing. Burned and ruined holds. And . . . bones. I slept one night with rats where Argunn's cattle byre had stood. The walls had fallen in, but it was not quite burned through, and there was room to get out of the snow. I even got a fire going." He gave a short laugh. "Ironic, that. But there were dogs gone wild, prowling through the ruins, and they hadn't learned to fight the wolf-kind for the wild game yet, most of them. We were meat, my horse and I. I rode out the next day . . . to the fort on the river."

"Jackal to jackal," Ranvig said.

"I had nowhere else to go. You do not know what it means . . . to be tribeless."

Nyall watched him carefully as he spoke. The dark shadow on Ingald's face when he spoke of that was truthful enough, he thought. "You made your own fate," he said. "All this gives me as yet no reason not to kill you. I know well enough what the Romans have made of the Black Forest."

"Yes," Ingald said. "You would be knowing. It is not to tell you that that I came for. I . . . lived by the fort on the river for a time. Working at whatever would buy bread. I am a warrior of the Nicretes, and I pruned vines for a fat Gaul in a Roman gown! And other worse things. But there is always talk in these towns by the Romans' forts. And an outcast laborer hears many things, because no one thinks him worth the noticing."

The other chieftains were watching curiously, and Hoskuld explained Ingald's banishment in a low voice.

"It would take a lot to bring him back here, I'm thinking."

"Best we listen then," the chieftain of the Anglii said,
hooking his thumbs in the sword belt that was strapped
over his fur riding jacket. "Anything that bears on Rome
interests me just now."

"A man with no tribe has little enough to occupy him
at night," Ingald said. "I used to get drunk when I could.
And I used to watch the soldiers from the fort on the
river. There was one wineshop they went to and I would
drink there and watch them, and listen as they would
talk. I learned a little Latin. Not much, but enough—
they use our names for places mostly, and twist them to
fit their own tongue. And I came to think that you had
been right in one thing—Rome is not a master the Free
People could live with. And that I had been right in the
other—they are strong, stronger than you would think
such little men could be, and their cohorts move like one
man with a thousand legs. I watched them march on
their parade ground. They are a . . . a machine. And
there is no nation on earth that can beat them when they
are ready to make war—"

"Did you come back to say that?" Nyall interrupted.

"No. I think you are wrong to fight with Rome, and
these"—he gestured at the silent circle of men—"are
wrong to follow you, but my hatred of you does not ex-
tend to my people. Since you are going to fight anyway, I
came to tell you how you may have a chance to beat
them—as Armin of the Cherusci did—when they are
unwary."

"You are so great a strategist?" Nyall asked softly. He
saw out of the corner of his eye that Fiorgyn had come
out of the hall and was standing behind the Companions on the step. "Or did Wuotan's ravens come flying
down to whisper in your ear?"

"I told you," Ingald said. "I listened to much talk,
and finally something worth the hearing. Two officers,
and one of them drunker than I—his fellow kept trying
to quiet him, but he had too much wine in him to
listen—talked of his marching orders. He was to go
out the next morning with a patrol to scout for the best
place to camp in a certain valley, and the legion would

go out after him and wait for the legion from the fort that is downriver. It is beyond the Nicer by the third big bend of the river the Romans call Moenus, and if you go now, you can wait a little back from it until they come, and catch them with their camp unbuilt and with the second legion still on the road."

"You risked death to tell me this, Ingald?"

"Aye. I told you, I do not want my people slaughtered."

"Surprise will give us the advantage," the chieftain of the Anglii said.

Hoskuld shook his head dubiously. "I have seen this one before. I would think long before I let him tell me the best road to a battle."

"You are wise," Fiorgyn said from behind them. "I have known this man longer than any of you, and I say he lies. I don't know why, but he lies!"

"I think the reason is obvious," Kari said. He looked at Ranvig. "You said he would go to the Romans."

"I went to the Roman's town to *live!*" Ingald snapped. "You left me little enough chance to do that elsewhere!"

"An exile has the right to live where he can," another chieftain nodded. "And he risked everything to come back."

"I doubt he had much choice," Nyall said. "Those who serve Rome find it dangerous to refuse their work."

"You can't know that," the chieftain said. He was the Varini's lord, the least willing of the allies.

Nyall ignored him. He looked Ingald up and down, and Ingald half stood, as if to back away. "You're between two pits, Ingald. The commander of the Eagles and me. But you should have played him false, not me. You were seen, Ingald, seen in the gates of the fort on the river, selling out your own kind to a Roman."

Ingald's face paled, but he steadied himself. "You lie! You have no spies in the Roman fort."

Nyall smiled, a thin wolf-smile with no charm in it. "It seems I have. One who saw your thief's face at Jorunnshold. She's a Roman thrall now, and she remembers you well, Ingald."

Ingald recalled the hooves that had cantered away from him in the dark, and he clenched his teeth. "It's a lie," he said again. "No one could have got clear of the Romans to bring you this tale."

"You claim to have done so," Nyall pointed out. "And that I believe even less. She sent me a message with Beorn the trader, who travels free with the Romans' blessing."

The others were watching tensely now, eyes moving from Nyall to Ingald and back. Too much rode on this, on who lied—Ingald, Nyall, or a captured thrall.

"She's the one who plays you false!" Ingald said desperately. "If she's the Romans' thrall, she will have done as she was bid."

"By sending a message four days *before* the Romans knew you had gone?" Nyall inquired. There was a murmur of talk among the other chieftains, and the Companions quietly laid their hands on their sword hilts. Nyall's voice was calm . . . quiet, implacable, the voice of death.

Ingald was backing away, half crouched. There was a white flash in the dawn sun and he had a sword in his hand. Kari and Ranvig were on their feet, and the two men who had brought Ingald in came running from their post at the gates. Ingald looked around him, trapped. If he could kill Nyall, the other chieftains might save him from the Companions long enough to hear him out. Ingald lunged at Nyall.

Nyall had his own sword out and he knocked Ingald's blade away with it. "Get back!" he shouted to the others. "This is between us now!"

The other chieftains moved a prudent distance away, but the Companions stood on the steps, twitching like a leashed hound pack.

"Let be," Fiorgyn whispered, as Kari shifted his feet. "He won't thank you if you disobey him."

"If Ingald kills him, the war is over before it's started," Kari said desperately. "If he's even wounded—"

"Look at them," Fiorgyn said. She gestured to the semicircle where the eight northern chieftains stood, watching silently, considering . . . "If you fall on Ingald in a pack, he'll lose them. And then where's your war?"

"She's right," Ranvig said unexpectedly. "Kari, let be."

None of them mentioned any other reason for putting another sword in, such as love. A man's fight was a man's honor; not even a spear brother or a wife would interfere. But they stood together, the three of them, each reaching out a hand to the others, while Nyall and Ingald circled each other and the sun came full up over the hold.

Ingald was a fighter, a vicious one; he had fear on his side, and the desperation of a man who has nothing to lose. He came in again hard, dodging out of the way of Nyall's swinging blade, and slashed at Nyall's neck.

Neither man had a shield. Nyall flung himself back, away from the downstroke, and rolled. He came up again in a crouch and his sword sliced in an arc at Ingald's legs, then flew up fast to parry as Ingald struck and moved in. They were too close now for a long sword to maneuver, and they drew their daggers almost together, each with his eyes on the eyes of the other.

The sound of running feet and a murmur of voices welled around them, as every person in the hold came thrusting into the circle of bodies that ringed the struggle. They watched with caught breath when they saw that it was the chieftain fighting. Morgian came through the doors of the hall and stopped, leaning against the door-frame with her hand to her mouth.

Nyall and Ingald fought on in that silent circle, oblivious of anything but this dance of death. Nyall thrust Ingald's dagger away with the hilt end of his sword and stabbed with his own dagger, left-handed. They were dressed for cold riding, and Nyall's cloak swirled around him. He could feel it tangling his dagger hand, making the blow awkward. Ingald pulled back with a yelp of pain and only a shallow gash across his chest.

It was enough to throw Ingald off for one split second, and Nyall swung his sword, driving him back farther. He jumped back himself then, and before Ingald could close in, Nyall had ripped the pin from his cloak and caught the end in his left hand, wrapped around his dagger hilt.

Ingald moved warily, eyes wavering between that

snaking cloak and Nyall's cold eyes. He could feel the warm blood seeping down his shirtfront.

"What did the commander of the Eagles offer you?" Nyall whispered. "Argunn's burned lands—or mine?"

"What I was robbed of!" Ingald snarled. His face was taut now, alive, the expressionless mask stripped away. "It's little matter to me which robbers I make truce with! Semnone wolves are cut from the same hide as the Roman-kind!"

"And neither runs tame to your hand, do they? A dog should think of that, Ingald, before he barks at a wolf!" Nyall's sword flashed down, a shining, deadly sweep, and as Ingald raised his to block it, the cloak whipped out between his feet, catching him across his right ankle as the left foot came down on the end of it.

Ingald stumbled, and as he went down he saw the pale fire of a sword blade with the sun on it. It took him through the throat.

Nyall pulled the blade free and flung it down in the dirt, while Ingald's body lay and twitched in the blood that poured from his mouth and throat and soaked through the pale braids into the ground.

Nyall stood looking down until the blood ceased to flow and the body quivered and was still. He turned to the two men who had brought Ingald in. "Take him out again and bury him," he said. They lifted the body, and he added softly, "Tell Valgerd the priest to come and make the prayers over him."

There was a shifting of the crowd as if they'd awakened suddenly and begun to look about them. Morgian let her breath out in a half-sob and her women clustered about her. Fiorgyn, Kari, and Ranvig unclenched their hands from each other's and exchanged glances shakily.

Arni heaved himself to his feet. He looked down to find his hands shaking and felt older by a year. The eight allied chieftains hadn't moved, but there was low-voiced talk snapping back and forth among them. Something more was going to come of this killing.

Nyall murmured some vague apology to the chieftains and stumbled into the hall, then out through the back passage to the storeroom. He found a vat of water and stuck his head in it, coming up coughing and choking.

He sat down hard on a sack of grain and leaned back against the wall, clenching and unclenching his hands until the faraway feel that clouded everything began to fade. The storeroom came slowly into focus: stacked boxes and sacks on the dirt floor, and strings of dried herbs and onions turning slowly in a light breath of air. Last year's onions, shriveled, and sprouting green tops. A mouse scuttled out, sat up on its haunches at the sight of him, and dived under a sack in the corner. Nyall stood up and took a deep breath, then went slowly back out to whatever was going to happen now.

In the courtyard, Kari, his dark half-Roman face standing out like some exotic plant in a cabbage row, was talking vehemently with the northern chieftains. They appeared to have split into two camps: Hoskuld of the Suarines and three others to one side, the chieftain of the Varini and two more to the other, with the lord of the Anglii wavering somewhere in the middle.

"You have no cause for oath-breaking," Hoskuld was saying stubbornly. "It was a clean death and long in the coming, and we know more than we did before."

"And so do the Romans," the chieftain of the Varini said. "I say that changes things. It was Nyall Sigmundson's own man who sold us to the Romans. Let Nyall Sigmundson pay the price."

Damn you, Nyall thought. *You've only been looking for a reason to back off. Break your oath and you'll pay for it.* "Undoubtedly the Romans know our numbers now," he said aloud, trying to keep his temper. "But we know that they do, which is none so bad. And we know where they'll wait for us, which is better."

"If he lied to us, as you say," the chieftain of the Anglii said, "then the Romans are readying a trap."

"Certainly it's a trap. But still, we know where they're waiting. In fact, I think I know exactly. We rode over that country all last year."

"Much confidence!" the Varini chieftain snapped, and the two chieftains beside him added their voices in agreement. "You would stake your life on it?"

"I'm going to," Nyall said. "We will change our road and come through the pass above the Moenus—behind them."

"No!" the Varini said. "They will have their full strength there, and it will likely be more than we counted on since your man has told them our own numbers!"

"You seem to be forgetting," Nyall said menacingly, "that you are oath-sworn, you and all the rest, to this hosting. And that *I* command!"

"There was no oath to overlook treachery!"

"Whose treachery? Ingald's—who is dead by *my* hand —or yours?"

The chieftain of the Varini turned on him, face furious and eyes oddly aloof. "You insult me. And that dead fool's talk has changed things. I withdraw my oath," he said deliberately. He took a step backward, and the two chieftains beside him moved with him. They were the three northernmost of the allies. Nyall knew what they were thinking: if Rome's army was greater than he had thought, and ready for them, and the German army grew somewhat smaller . . . why then, Rome would win. It was very simple. And there would be no more Semnones, which was maybe better to these chiefs than there being no Rome, which had never come as far as the northern lands.

It was too late to renegotiate, to spend another week on threats and promises. Nyall looked the three over coldly. "Go back to your northern holds and sit in them. And if the gods have not rotted you for being forsworn, then when we have beaten the Romans for you without your help, we will come and kill you ourselves."

"If you live."

"You had better pray that I do not." He turned to the chieftain of the Anglii. "And you? Do you break faith, too? I want to be very clear whose holds we will burn, my war band and I, when we are done."

The Anglii lord wavered, and the Varini chieftain shot him a contemptuous look. But of the four northern tribes, it was the Anglii who lay closest to the five southern ones . . . closest to vengeance. And the Semnones might win, which would give him the chance to expand his lands greatly when Nyall took an avenging war band north. He thought long and hard. "The Anglii stay," he said finally.

The three defecting chieftains turned and marched through the gates, and after a while their wagons and men could be seen moving away from the rest, their out-riders headed for the northern track that ran up the valley. Nyall let them go unmolested; there was no sense in losing more men now. If the gods had not marked them for death as oath-breakers, it could be taken care of by mortal hands when the Romans had been killed.

"I don't much like leaving them loose in our land with our backs turned," Kari said dubiously.

"They have eaten at my table," Nyall said. "They won't attack our women. Not until they're sure we won't come back. All the same, we'll give them three days to be sure. Track them."

Kari nodded and signaled to two of the Companions.

Ranvig, who had come up behind them, flashed Nyall a crooked smile with real amusement in it. "And in the meantime, we give the Romans a little more time to set-tle in and wait, and maybe begin to get edgy?"

Nyall smiled back for the first time that day, some of the harsh lines leaving his face. "It is in my mind that we have made the best of the exchange. I am rid of three unstable tribes, and now I know where the Roman wolf is laired. Ingald served me in the end, after all."

"And how do we flush the wolf?"

"We go in the rear door and put a spear through his back."

Kari nodded and twisted the gold ring he wore. It had been his Roman mother's, and her father had given it to her to play with on the day his legion had gone to talk peace with Armin of the Cherusci, and had not come back.

XXI

The Battle on the Hill

CORREUS SAT ON A CAMP BED, POLISHING HIS GREAVES.
They didn't need polishing, but he had to have something
to do. The army was split into two camps, tucked away
in the hills above the Moenus River at the eastern end
where the water tumbled down from the high ground
into the winding valley. The Twenty-second Legion
Primigenia from Moguntiacum lurked across the river in
the second camp, and the Vindonissa Legion had been
left to patrol the Rhenus. All were fully up to strength,
with heavy cavalry auxiliaries attached. Here they sat,
waiting, and Correus found he had more time to think
than he wanted.

His life had made a sudden unsettling shift with the
introduction of Freita into it. Unsettling, but right. The
gods took a hand most unexpectedly, it seemed. And
then, just when all he really wanted to do was lie with
Freita and make love, he had to pick up a pilum and
march off to defend the Emperor's frontier for him.
And if the legate's tame German didn't succeed in the
plan to trap Nyall, very likely Correus would get killed
doing it. Then Freita, who didn't *want* to go back to her
people now, might have to go, and possibly carrying a
half-Roman baby. Correus knew enough about the Germans by now to know that would be a disgrace. Damn!
He resisted the temptation to fling the greave across the
tent, and got up and began to pace, though there wasn't
much room for it. Junior centurions' tents were not very
spacious.

Too many farewells, he thought, too soon, and too
quickly made. Flavius's pathetic good-bye to Aemelia,
with his heart in his eyes and the marriage not yet settled. Paulinus's farewell to Julia . . . a happy one that,

361

and Paulinus was in Argentoratum, not out here waiting
to fight a war. But Correus had deduced enough about
his friend's non-literary activities to know that Lucius
Paulinus would probably never have a safe day in his
life. And then his own leave-taking from Freita . . .

They had been given only a few weeks, and they had
used every spare moment urgently, desperately, as if it
were all they would ever have. Freita had been waiting
for him when he got there on the next night after his
homecoming, and his heart had turned over at the mere
sight of her. Julius was again conspicuously absent, and
Freita, when questioned, said primly that she had sent
him to sleep in the stables.

Correus laughed. "We need a bigger house." He knelt
down by her chair and rubbed his face against her hair.
"My heart, are you glad to see me?"

She put her arms around him. "Heart of my life, yes,"
she whispered. Her hands shook slightly, and he wondered if it was entirely for him. There was something
troubled in her voice.

"Is there something wrong?"

She shook her head. "No."

He pulled her closer. That last interview with the German spy had left a bad taste in his mouth, and he wanted
to wash it away. They held one another for a long moment, stroking each other gently. He felt her shake again,
and this time he was almost sure it was for him. He stood
up, looking down into her eyes, and held out his hands.

"Come."

On the bed she rolled into his arms as if she had always belonged there, and they began to play, exploring
each other by the light of the lamp.

"Don't do that," she giggled.

"Why? Doesn't it feel good? It's supposed to."

"Yes, oh yes . . . But it makes me feel wanton as a
wild sow."

"That's a good way to feel."

"Yes. Do it again."

"There. Now touch me. See, I am not so frightening."

"No, not now. How does it feel?"

"Like Paradise." He groaned. "Dear gods, I want you so."

"I am yours."

Her legs slipped apart for him, and he caressed the soft pale hair and the insides of her thighs, marveling at the whiteness of her skin and the beauty of her body. Her full breasts were pink-tipped in the lamplight and he ran his hands across them lightly for the pleasure of feeling the nipples tighten at his touch. He brushed his lips across the white skin of her belly and she looked up at him shyly.

"I have heard of a thing that Roman ladies sometimes do," she whispered, "and I thought . . . if it would give you pleasure . . . that I would try it."

"Anything you do would give me pleasure."

She slid down on the bed until her head was in his lap, and gently, experimentally, she took him in her mouth.

"Oh, sweet Mother!" he whispered.

He knotted his hands in her hair and lay there, letting that wonderful feeling wash over him. After a while he guided her gently away and she tipped her head back to smile up at him, touching him with the tip of her forefinger.

"Did you like it?"

"I liked it," he said, his voice husky.

She fell back slowly into the blankets, her white legs spread to take him in. And she was beautiful, so beautiful. . . .

Correus ran his hands through his hair with a rueful expression. That was nothing for a man in a marching camp to think about, with only the hairy company of the eighty legionaries under his command. Not if he didn't want to lie awake all night. But he missed her . . . Mithras, how he missed her! They had divided the little time left to them between rides through a countryside suddenly turned lovely under the light hand of spring, and the bed in the timber house on the edge of town. Julius had begun to sleep in the stables of his own accord, but his expression made it plain that he found the master's overwhelming infatuation with Freita (who was good enough in her way, of course, but still a woman) an unnecessary development. Correus suspected that Paulinus and Silvanus were also beginning to be worried about him, but he didn't care. Freita represented something that had never touched his life before—a woman who was friend and lover both. His lovemaking developed a caring and a depth that were new to him, and he was fascinated to learn the things that pleased her. In turn, she responded with a wholehearted passion that left him awed and grateful.

Flavius also took note of the situation, with raised eyebrows and a shrug of his shoulders that said plainly: like to like, slave to slave. Correus found that he didn't much care about that, either. Flavius was unimportant to him in the face of this wonderful, glorious discovery. The few weeks before he marched out were a springtime idyll, marred only by the fact that, with his newfound sensitivity to Freita, he could tell that something troubled her. He had not spoiled the idyll by asking what it was. She would tell him when she was ready, or maybe never. It didn't matter. She loved him and he her. *That* was what mattered.

It had ended too soon, of course. They had marched out, and the legion had taken control of his life again. And now they were on either side of the Moenus Valley like two jaws of a trap, waiting for Nyall to put his head into it. That was how Paulinus had stated it when he had heard, in his usual mysterious fashion, of the German spy sent back to Nyall with a Roman patrol hard on his heels; a patrol that had been careful not to catch him.

Paulinus had ridden into Argentoratum with Tullius, and settled into the best room of the best inn to observe the campaign for his *History*—and whatever else he observed things for. Coming into the house to catch a few precious hours with Freita two days after Paulinus's arrival, Correus had found the rough sketch of a mural now adorning one of the shabby plastered walls. Lucius was painting it for her, Freita had told him proudly as Correus inspected the charcoal outline of a plump Bacchus, comically drunk, with a meal of roast pheasant at his feet. A pair of fat wolf puppies had come out of the forest and were stealing the pheasant off the plate while Bacchus tipped his wine cup, unknowing. There was something familiar in Bacchus's face that Correus finally recognized as the face of Paulinus himself.

He was relieved that Paulinus was in Argentoratum, and had drawn up yet a fifth set of Freita's manumission papers and given them to him. Feeling a little embarrassed and theatrical, he also made his will, and gave Paulinus that, too. If anyone could insure that his wishes were carried out, it would be Paulinus. Freita must have enough money to have some choices about her future if he were killed. He hadn't much to leave her, but Correus knew without even asking that Paulinus would add to it if necessary, and that Freita would accept it from him.

Correus sat down on the camp bed and stared at his helmet and lorica stacked in the corner of the tent. It had never really occurred to him before that he might be killed, mostly because that was a reality that a soldier took for granted and there was little point in worrying about it. But now there was Freita, and parting with her was unbearable.

And that was no way for a soldier to think. That was what *got* you killed, more often than not. A thought to put from one's mind—fast. There was a soft rustling on the tent flap outside and he looked up, grateful for the interruption.

"Yes, what is it?"

A legionary stuck his head in past the flap. Quintus, released from the guardhouse on Correus's fervent plea to Cominius that he "needed that mutinous bastard" and on his promise that Quintus would straighten up as soon as they were on the march.

"The men are turned in, sir. And the watchword for tonight is 'Patience.'"

"How appropriate," Correus said. "I trust you are exercising the same."

"Yes, sir," Quintus said. "You squared me with the cohort commander, and don't think I'm not grateful. My woman and me, we named the babe Julianus, sir. I'm hoping as that's all right."

"Thank you," Correus said gravely. "I'm flattered."

Quintus saluted smartly and withdrew. Correus

smiled. Quintus never got into trouble when there was a fight brewing. It was the boredom of drills and parade that set him to making a pest of himself. Correus shucked off his outer tunic and put out the lamp. If the men were turned in for the night, it was time he turned in also, or he would be groggy when the sentries came to wake him in the morning. The legate had ordered no bugle calls. Their presence in the hills above the river valley was intended as a surprise, and bugle notes carried too far to be safe.

A stirring ran through the camp that pulled Correus out of sleep before the sentry could get to his tent. He sat up quickly in the half-dark and groped for his tunic and sandals and the cloak that served as an extra blanket on the bed. He jerked the tunic over his head and tried to shake the sleep out of his eyes. He slung on the new cloak—it had been Freita's parting gift to him. The sandal laces were stiff and hard to fasten in the damp air, and he kicked them aside and stumbled barefoot out into the misty light.

Half the camp was awake and shaking the other half into consciousness. Correus pushed through the flap of the eight-man tent next to his and laid his hand on the shoulder of his sleeping optio. The man sat up instantly, his hand reaching for the sword that lay with his gear beside the bed. His eyes focused on Correus and he sprang to attention.

"Turn 'em out," Correus said. "I think we've got company." He looked anxiously into the dimness northward where the valley of the Moenus lay hidden under a thigh-deep mist, obscuring the pale waters of the river and the track that ran along its southern bank. There was no movement to be seen except for the oddly amputated shapes of a cavalry troop returning from their night's patrol. The horses appeared as legless bodies floating in the belly-high mist, and they moved in orderly formation with no sense of urgency to them.

Puzzled, Correus swung around. Suddenly, out of the hazy light to the southwest, he saw it—the pale flower of a beacon fire in the far distance.

"Something's gone wrong," Cominius said, appearing

beside him, buckling the straps of his lorica as he went. He stood, eyes narrowed, trying to gauge the distance of the beacon. As they watched, it went out.

"That's been burning no more than ten minutes," Cominius said. "It's gone out too soon! Form your men up for parade, fast!"

Correus dived back into his tent and struggled into his sandals and harness skirt, and then his lorica, tucking his scarf in for padding under the neck edges. Abandoning his search for a comb, he ran fingers through his hair, then put on his greaves and his helmet. He reappeared, tying the strap under his chin, as his men were falling into line beside their tents. The same was happening all over the camp, and Correus could see Legate Rufinus with his staff and a crowd of senior officers around him.

They stood in formation, waiting, as the mist began to burn away and the sun spread a wash of pale gold over the hillside.

"What is it, sir?" the optio whispered.

"I don't know," Correus whispered back, but he thought he did. That beacon meant trouble, and the fact it had been extinguished almost as soon as it was lit likely meant bad trouble. But where was it? He thought it was one of the Nicer River forts, and if it was, it meant that Nyall had not taken the bait. It also meant that a fort and all its men, and maybe the whole Nicer line, were gone, while they sat here over an empty trap, doing nothing.

The legate and his staff were thrashing out much the same line of thought.

"No," Calpurnius Rufinus said. "We aren't stirring a step until I find out what in Hades has happened."

"The scouts went out as soon as we saw the beacon," said the primus pilus, commander of the First Cohort. "Has our spy sold himself over to Nyall again, do you think, sir?"

"Anything is possible," the legate said. "But no, I don't think so or I wouldn't have used him. He was damn near dead when he came to us. Too near to be faking it, and he had Nyall to thank for that. Besides, Nyall wouldn't give him what he wanted, and he had an eye to be chieftain, that one."

" 'Had,' sir?"

"I don't suppose he's still alive," the legate said grimly.

"Then what happened?" Messala Cominius asked.

"Nyall didn't buy his story," the legate said. "I think we can take that as evident, Centurion."

"Yes, sir. But why not?"

The legate hitched his gilded breastplate to a more comfortable angle on his shoulders, and sighed. "Wood-elves, Centurion. Nyall's spy put the finger on our spy, or something like that. It's a question I'll consider when I don't have more pressing matters—such as an army of Germans that's where it's not supposed to be."

"Yes, sir." Cominius decided that further questions would be inadvisable.

"What I would more like to know," the legate said thoughtfully, "is how much talking our man did before he died."

The primus pilus nodded. A man about to be killed might well try to buy his life with the truth. "He didn't have much to tell, did he, sir? We kept him in the dark as far as possible."

"Anything it occurred to him to tell would be too much," the legate said. "I want the legion ready to march on a two-minute notice, and I want a report from those scouts. And I want my breakfast. You will find me in my tent when the scouts come in, which had better be soon."

There was a crash of salutes and the officers eyed his retreating back warily. "For the gods' sake, someone see that he gets breakfast," the primus pilus said.

There wasn't long to wait. The only scout to survive came back with a white face to say that they had stuck their heads over a hillcrest and found the whole damned German war band looking back at them, and the gods must have had their eye on him that day because every other man of the party was dead before he could reach cover. The Germans had seen them and hunted them down. How they'd missed him, he'd never know. He shook violently and threw up, and added apologetically that he'd been sitting in a tree when they'd cut a scout's throat right under him. They'd done other things to him, too. The scout looked as if he were going to be sick again.

The attack had come not at the Nicer River forts, but at the one signal outpost beyond, and the Germans had wiped it out because they had been seen. One man must have managed to get the beacon lit and kept it going until they came up the tower and killed him.

"When this is over," Rufinus said, "I'll build a temple for the man who lit that fire."

The camp was moving like an anthill now, purpose in every step. The wagons were loaded and ready to move out or backward according to how the battle went. The whole legion was formed up and ready with the cohort and century standards marking each unit; the cavalry auxiliaries were mounted and drawn up on the wings. The men chewed a hasty breakfast of barley cake and made last-minute adjustments to armor and weapons at the same time. The Twenty-second Primigenia, alerted by Rufinus's signalmen, was pouring down the far side of the river valley to the ford, while the legate watched their progress anxiously. The planned ambush had turned into a trap for its makers, with the Twenty-second Legion caught on the north bank of the Moenus and Nyall marching on them from the south.

The ford was narrow and the Twenty-second was taking a long time to cross. They had originally been intended to keep Nyall from crossing, and their auxiliaries were heavy with archers. If Rufinus took the Eighth Augusta out immediately to meet Nyall, he would risk outdistancing the Twenty-second. If he did not, he would be forced to fight with a river at his back, as Nyall had done at Jorunnshold. He paced and thought hard for a moment and then motioned to his aides. They would hold the ground they had, a wide plateau that sloped away easily enough on either side for the Twenty-second to come up on their wings. It fell away steeply to the south, where Nyall would be forced to attack.

"At least he'll have to come uphill at us," Calpurnius Rufinus thought grimly.

Correus began to feel the familiar knot in his stomach that meant a fight coming. He could see Flavius's century, drawn up with the rest under the Ninth Cohort standard to his right, and he raised a hand to his brother, but Flavius, eyes straight ahead on the backs of the light troops who would be the first to move, didn't see him.

"Commander's compliments, sir, and you're wanted," an optio said to Correus.

Messala Cominius gathered his five junior centurions around him and explained things bluntly. "We're the lucky ones in the place of honor. Middle of the advance line, and we'd better hold it, because it's none too easy to swim in armor. Wait for the third trumpet, and then fall back into the line behind you. We're going to try to knock the bastards back down the hill and roll 'em into a ball, but not until we've got the Twenty-second with us. Comments, gentlemen?"

"Uh, caltrops, sir?" Correus said. "Their front line's going to be mounted."

The commander nodded and turned to his optio. "As Julianus suggests. Kindly make it so." He looked at Correus. "You have a promising career, Centurion, provided you live."

Correus and the others saluted and turned back to their men. As he took his place beside his own optio and his standard-bearer, Correus felt the ground begin to quiver, the stirring of the earth that only a massed army on the march could make. *This is it,* he thought. *This is our last chance to beat Nyall, or we're going to lose this province.*

A trumpet sounded and the light armed troops in the front moved out through a concealing scrub of trees to meet the first charge. It was frustrating, Correus thought, standing there with nothing to see but trees, knowing that beyond them the battle was joined and that soon they too would split ranks through those trees to confront whatever was on the other side. A signalman in the top branches waved his hand and the legate nodded. The trumpet sang again and the Seventh, Eighth, and Ninth cohorts moved at a trot through the screen of trees. Behind them in the low valley, the last of the Twenty-second Legion splashed its way through the shallow ford.

The skirmishers had slowed the war band's leading edge with a rain of pilums and then pulled back, leaving the sloping ground strewn with caltrops—four-pointed iron barbs that always landed point-up, and were death to horses.

Nyall's horsemen were on the caltrops before they could draw rein, and Correus saw a number of riders leap from their fallen horses, some going down under the hooves of the horses behind them. Then, unexpectedly, the rest swept away to the flanks and the foot fighters came pouring up the hill. The battle was joined in earnest, and the whole world narrowed down to the space of his one century and the ground it was commanded to hold as Correus locked his shield into the familiar slot at the left-hand end of his line. Behind and to either side of him were the rest of his cohort and the other two cohorts that were the center of the legate's strategy. For Correus now, there was only the shield line and his century standard over his head, and the screaming, half-naked warriors who hurled themselves against it. Everything else had vanished behind the curtain of blood and dust and the screams of fallen horses.

"Now! Throw!" The pilums hurtled away, and then shields were locked close, the front-rank shields before them and the others overhead as Nyall's war band swarmed around them. It was a closed formation designed only to hold ground, and Correus could feel the men's impatience, dug in behind their shields, rocking under the weight of Nyall's charge.

Nyall, astride his red roan horse in the rear, watched with satisfaction. The chieftain of the Anglii thumped his fist on his saddle and spoke urgently, and Nyall shook his head. Those Roman shields would break soon under the sheer force of numbers, and then his restive warriors would have their chance. The man who threw himself onto the enemy's spears might die bravely and ride away to Valhalla, but he won no wars. Nyall had threatened and cajoled his lords into a grudging acceptance of this fact, and now he had his best warriors, the flower of his army, where he wanted them, held back for the right time, while the lower-ranking foot fighters cut the first openings in the enemy's lines. It was a Roman tactic to fight a Roman.

*   *   *

The battle line rocked and swayed as the Romans fought a desperate defense. Flavius, locked into the shield line with his own century, felt his throat constrict with the claustrophobic sense of being bricked in behind those shields. A straight charge would be more endurable, even if it ended on a German spear, he thought, and his cohort commander's brusque instructions rang in his ears: "We hold until the third trumpet. Hold and nothing more, and the first man who pulls any death-or-glory stuff on me is a dead man."

And then, the memory of past mistakes plain on his face, the commander had put Flavius's century dead center of the cohort, insulated on four sides by the locked shields of the others. There would be no chance to disobey.

The sun was full up now and it was hot pressed close together behind the shield line. The air was beginning to smell like blood. Correus's hands were damp with sweat, and he tightened his grip on his sword. A German spear punched through the shield of the man beside him and pulled it away, and the man went down with a second spear through his breast. Correus stabbed upward with his short sword as the Germans hit the gap in his line. He rocked with the weight as he caught a German warrior under the man's shield edge and the German fell forward onto him.

"Close up!" he shouted, and a soldier from the rear ranks moved into the gap. More men were going down all along the line now. If the third trumpet didn't come soon, it would be too late. The cohort's second-in-command was dead, and his century was struggling frantically to close their shields where the German advance had torn a ragged hole in their ranks.

"Hold, damn it!" Messala Cominius yelled. "Hold them!"

All along the slope, the front line was beginning to waver. And then they heard the third trumpet, a high, sweet note above the shrieking of the battle, and Cominius shouted "Now!" The ranks broke open and stumbled backward up the hill, as the Germans hurled themselves after them, screaming in pursuit.

Correus and his century fell back in the carefully drilled pattern that looked like a random retreat—but wasn't. It was heavy going all the same, even though his heart pounded with relief at being out from behind that shield wall, and moving. A spear sang past him and someone shouted, "Look to the commander!" Staggering up the last of the slope, they almost fell over Cominius, sprawled on the ground with gritted teeth, pulling a spear from his thigh while his men stood above him, shields locked again now in a frantic defense.

"Get him up!" Correus shouted.

Two of Correus's men got their arms under Cominius and heaved him to his feet. "Take it," Cominius panted. "The cohort—it's yours," and Correus saw with horror that the cohort's third centurion was dead at his feet.

There was no time for orders, but Correus knew clearly what had to be done. The men carrying Cominius turned and ran, with the commander stumbling between them, and Correus pulled the Eighth Cohort around him and back up the hill, increasing the speed of their flight with every hundred paces. Behind them, the war host bayed like a pack of wolves, foot fighters and horsemen thundering up the hill, reddened spear points raised aloft in triumph.

"Now by Wuotan's sword, we fight!" the chieftain of the Anglii shouted.

Nyall gathered his reins in his shield hand and settled his spear with the other. "Yes, now we fight, but you will keep to the orders I've given."

"There is no honor in that! A chieftain *leads* his war band!"

The German footmen were closing fast on the fleeing cohorts. "Our vassals will have the honor," another man shouted, "and we will be fools and cowards!"

"You *are* fools!" Nyall shouted back, his face furious. "That isn't their whole force. There are reserves behind those trees, and maybe on the flanks!"

But the retreat seemed to be becoming a rout; the Romans were apparently driven back on their own reserves, and Nyall couldn't hold his chieftains. Even Hoskuld, fire in his eye, gripped his spear and dug his heels into his horse's flank. There was glory only in the forefront of a charge, and disgrace behind, and honor had a louder voice than obedience.

"No!" Nyall grabbed at the Anglii chieftain's bridle and the man snarled and spun his horse away.

"We've waited long enough! Now we take the Romans' heads our own way!"

They poured up the hill, howling for blood, blood to wash away the disgrace of being held behind, and even the flankers pulled in and followed them, to cut down fleeing Romans and take a fine red revenge for the slaughtered folk of Jorunnshold.

Then a fourth trumpet sounded, and the Twenty-second Legion came around the left slope of the hill at a dead run. The front ranks flung their pilums and knelt down as the rear ranks came through to throw theirs, and German riders and foot fighters went down together in a chaos of splintered shields and speared horses. The Twenty-second locked shields and came on, opened ranks to throw the second volley, and closed again as they hit the Germans' left flank with a crash. The flank turned to fight, but buckled in on the center, and the Twenty-second drew its swords as one man, stabbed, closed ranks, and advanced again through the crumpled dead and abandoned shields of the Germans. As many warriors had lost their shields as had died in that terrible volley of pilums. The soft iron heads were heavy and bent when they struck, and a shield with that weight embedded in it was uncontrollable. The archers of the Twenty-second spread out on the wing uphill and sent flight after flight over their own men's heads and into the German flank.

In the German center the charge began to lose its momentum as the weakened flank fell back, jamming them together. The Eighth Legion opened its ranks for the fleeing cohorts and closed behind them with a snap of shields. There was no pretense of retreat now. The German advance, battle order abandoned in their reckless pursuit, and the flank pushed back on the center, broke at the crest of the hill under another murderous rain of pilums.

Correus, his breath coming in gasps as he pulled the

Eighth Cohort together around him in the rear, could hear the shouted orders as the Eighth Legion and the Twenty-second pushed relentlessly at the German war host and the Germans screamed and fought back with sword and spear, struggling to hold the sloping ground. He took a deep breath and nodded to the two other centurions left to the cohort.

"Now. Hook on to the right between our lads and the Twenty-second—and push."

The Seventh and Ninth Cohorts were on either side of them, the seeming chaos of the retreat now vanished utterly and each man of each century back in his accustomed slot. It was the shield of the legions, Correus thought as they moved into the line again—that parade-ground formation drilled and drilled into them until they could have done it blind.

Then there was no time to think about anything but stab and advance, stab and advance, struggling to push the Germans slowly in on their own center, while the Twenty-second Legion tore an ever greater hole in the broken left flank. The cohort standard rode above the dust and blood at his side. His cohort now, if only for this battle.

Correus stabbed desperately as a screaming German, his blond hair flying and his sword blade red to the hilt, seemed to rise up out of the ground before him. The German, aiming for the left side, the shield side, met Correus's sword instead and went down at his feet. There was blood everywhere . . . blood on their hands, blood on the ground. The Germans were jammed hopelessly together, the horsemen riding down their own men, and only the front ranks were able to fight back. Even the long spears were only encumbrance at close quarters, and the rear ranks were packed too tightly to use them. Correus thought he saw Nyall in the thick of it, on a plunging roan, desperately shouting orders that went unheard. Then the German left broke completely and he lost sight of Nyall as the cohort surged down the hill, trampling the German dead under their feet.

The Roman left and center began to move forward too, and the trumpets sounded for the final time. It was the centurions' war now. Wherever there was a space, they led their men into it, hacking open great gaps in the German front, driving their short swords in against helpless spearmen. The German riders were sword-armed, but they were scattered among the foot troops. The Romans tucked their shields over their heads and cut the riders' horses out from under them. The German lines gave way completely, but it was impossible to retreat in the massed chaos that had been Nyall's battle line.

"Primigenia!"

"Augusta!"

The Romans came in for the kill, screaming the names of their legions for a war cry.

By midday it was ended. There was nothing left but German dead . . . dead men and dead horses stacked three deep in a tangle of broken shields, useless spears still in their hands. The few that had escaped had fled with the Roman cavalry on their tails to hunt them down in twos and threes among the hills. By the time the legate called off the pursuit, the only movement on the hillside was the slow, black circling of carrion birds above the field. Of the Romans, the dead numbered three hundred. Of the war band that was to have broken Rome's hold on the Rhenus, ten thousand.

XXII

End and Beginning

CALPURNIUS RUFINUS SAT WEARILY ON HIS HORSE WITH the legate of the Twenty-second Primigenia beside him and looked out over the battlefield.

"Rome will never go beyond the Agri Decumates," he said. "Nyall succeeded in that at least. I wonder if it was worth it to him, in the end."

"So many dead," the legate of the Twenty-second

said. "For something that might never have happened."

"Don't deceive yourself, my friend. If Barbarian Germany had been easy pickings, we would have picked it long ago. No, we'd have gone beyond, no matter what I swore to Nyall, if we could have. But we've only half-consolidated the Agri Decumates, and there are more tribes than the Suevi beyond it. They'd fight too, and eventually they'd learn what Nyall was beginning to. If you fight barbarians too often, you end by teaching your enemy how to make war. If we'd faced disciplined troops today . . ."

The legate of the Twenty-second nodded. It could have gone the other way—easily. "Still, the Emperor has begun to trust us here," he said. "At least he gave us the reinforcement we asked for."

Rufinus shook his head. "It would take the Lower German legions joined to ours to hold the frontier if we went beyond the Agri Decumates, and he'll never give us that."

"'Too many legions too close to Rome—'" the other said, plainly quoting.

"'—breed too much temptation,'" Rufinus finished. "It's Rome's fear of the strength of her own army that really sets Rome's limits in Germany." He looked down at the endless wave of dead that stretched away over the hillside. "Nyall's shade can have that to laugh at, if he can find the heart."

Correus sat on a flat rock with his knees drawn up under his chin, watching the burial party in the flat land below as they tumbled the stiffening bodies into row after row of common graves. *They are destroyed,* he thought. A whole nation gone, for one man's refusal to treat with Rome. And Rome had not even attacked them. It had been Rome's mere presence here that had sparked this carnage. Correus shuddered. He felt like a leper.

He was putting off telling the legate that they had not been able to find Nyall's body. As the most junior of those who knew the Semnone chieftain by sight, Correus had drawn that grisly duty and had known better than to protest. The legate wanted Nyall's corpse to

hammer home a point to the other tribes whose lands
bordered on the Agri Decumates—unpleasant, but necessary. But that had proved impossible. He was there,
of course, but there were ten thousand dead, many
mangled beyond recognition. At last, Correus had given
up. He had found four that could be identified fairly
certainly from their wealth of gold jewelry as chieftains
of the Suevi. There had been old men and boys in their
teens, and even a few women, and one dark-faced man
with a Roman centurion's twenty-year ring on his hand.
They had puzzled greatly over that before they had
tipped him into the pit with the rest.

Now, sickened by an endless parade of corpses, Correus didn't want to talk to the legate or anyone else. He
took his helmet off and set it on the ground beside him,
letting the clean breeze wash over his face.

"Are you all right, sir?"

He looked up. It was Quintus, black with dirt and
with a piece of bloody rag tied around his thigh. "Yes,
thank you." His eyes focused on the rag. "Are you
hurt? You should be in the hospital."

"It's only a scratch, sir. Surgeon's got worse to deal
with first."

Correus turned his face back toward the rows of
open graves, and Quintus stood at his shoulder, also
watching. "And the men?" Correus asked finally. The
Roman losses had been light, but most of them had
come from the Seventh, Eighth, and Ninth cohorts.

"We lost near a hundred, sir," Quintus said sadly,
and Correus grimaced. Nearly one man in five. "The
commander's still with us, though," Quintus said. "He
was in the hospital tent, swearing a blue streak while
they washed his leg out with vinegar. He sent me to
find you."

Correus nodded. "And the other cohorts? The Seventh and Ninth?"

"Near as bad, sir, and more wounded, same as us.
Your brother's all right," he added. "I thought you'd
want to know."

"Thank you, Quintus." The breeze stirred up and it
felt cold and clammy. "It was good of you to find out."

He should get up, he knew, and report to Cominius and the legate, and find Flavius.

The sun was low and the dying light caught him full in the face. Quintus peered at him. "You don't look so good, sir. Sit there until you get your breath, like." He went on. "I damn near started to report to your brother, you look so much alike, until I saw it wasn't you. Would you be twins, sir?"

"We don't even have the same mother."

Quintus whistled. "The old man's influence must have been strong."

In the hospital tent, Messala Cominius lay with his leg propped up on a cot and glared at the junior surgeon, Lucanus, as he pinned a clean bandage around it. "That will do," he said as Lucanus pushed the last pin home. "I'm not an Egyptian mummy. Now get lost." He looked up at Correus. "You look like a sewer rat."

"A graveyard rat," Correus said shortly, and explained his recent task.

Cominius winced. "No wonder you look sick. Sit down, Julianus, if you can find a place."

Correus looked around but nothing offered itself, so he sat on the dirt floor.

"You did a good job," Cominius said. "I've recommended you for promotion to cohort rank."

Correus blinked. "Cohort rank?"

"You'll serve out the rest of this season as my second until a new posting comes through. And I'm going to have to promote at least one junior centurion from the ranks. Have you got any suggestions?"

Correus took a deep breath. "Quintus, sir."

"Quintus?"

"Yes, sir. He . . . he only makes trouble when he's got nothing to do," Correus explained.

Cominius snorted. "Very well, I'll consider it. Now get out of here. Go report to Rufinus and then go to bed. Get the men settled first," he added. "They're your joy until they let me out of here."

Correus stood up and saluted numbly. Cohort rank . . . Tomorrow it would probably seem real. Tonight he had to go count dead bodies for the legate.

* * *

When the full moon was up, three men crept from a cleft in the rocks and lifted a fourth man after them by thighs and shoulders onto a makeshift litter fashioned from a cloak lashed to two spears. They set off down a narrow track through the trees that was little more than a deer trail. The moon came through the light cover of new leaves and illuminated their faces: pale, blood-stained, with the look of the hunted.

The man on the litter moaned, and the one who walked beside him put out a hand to quiet him.

"Kari?"

The man beside him laid a hand on his shoulder, but didn't speak.

"Kari!" The man on the litter tried to sit up.

Ranvig pushed Nyall back as gently as he could. "Here, brother," he lied in a soft whisper, and the wounded man grew quiet.

The man who carried the front poles of the litter spoke to Ranvig over his shoulder. "Where are we going, lord?"

"North."

"Aye, lord, but where is there to go?"

They might make Nyallshold before they were caught, but he doubted it. "I don't know," Ranvig said. "Just . . . north."

They trudged wearily along the track. Tomorrow they would have to eat, Ranvig thought, and Nyall's wounds would have to be cleaned again. That and staying hidden were the things to worry about. If they made it . . . then he would tell Nyall that he had lied to him.

My dearest Julia,

Things are very quiet now. The German war band that was threatening the frontier is beaten. Massacred would probably be a better word, but I will spare you the description I had from your brother Correus. If you're going to live with me, my sweet, you'll have to get used to being in the thick of such things, but I see no reason to start you off quite so grimly. Your brothers are both well, and although they didn't exactly win the battle single-handedly, they were both in the worst part of it and came off with honors. Correus has been promoted to second-in-command of his cohort, and the word is that he will have a cohort of his own by the end of the year. Flavius has been promoted also, to third centurion of his cohort—like Correus's, a battle-field promotion. And very commendable. We lost four centurions and over two hundred men from a three-cohort advance line. The army's losses overall were minimal, but if you happen to be one of them, I don't expect that's much comfort. At any rate, your brothers are both paying for their promotions by breaking in the new recruits sent out to bring those cohorts up to strength. Centurion Silvanus, whom I may have mentioned to you, is also among the living and has just got a posting to his own cohort command. We are giving him a royal send-off tonight (I have taken to following the legion about once more, and the legate kindly tolerates my presence—until things start getting hot again, at least) so I will finish this letter to you before I get too drunk to write. Tullius sends his regards and asks "if Little Miss will bring her servants with her." I strongly suspect him of having designs on your maid, so you are warned.

My dearest girl, I cannot tell you how much I want you with me. I shall be back in Rome by the end of this season's campaign, and shall return bearing bride-gifts and, I hope, a marriage contract. My lawyers have been communing with your father's lawyers like a pack of diplomats drawing up a treaty, and they keep sending me lengthy letters full of settlements and entails and exclusions, until I finally wrote and said I only wanted to get married, not set up a national constitution. I told them to settle half of what I have on you now, and the other half in the event of my death, and they wrote back and said what about divorce, and what about children? I wrote back and said there *weren't* any children, and we could always amend those things later. But it didn't do any good. I suppose the lawyers will settle it to suit them and then we can get married. If you ever divorce me, I shan't care anyway.

My darling Julia, I cannot tell you how much I want

to marry you. How unexpected it was to find you. How
much I love you . . .

Julia fell over a potted tree in the atrium, reading the
letter as she went, then fixed ecstatic eyes on her father.
"I've had a letter from Lucius, and Correus and Flavius
are *both* promoted, and he's just as tired of lawyers as I
am! Papa, *when* can I get married?"

"You shouldn't be receiving letters without our knowledge," Antonia said, "even from Lucius." But her heart
wasn't in it. It was such a good match and, incredibly,
Julia seemed to be in love with him. Most girls never had
that, she thought sadly.

"Promoted?" Helva looked up from a piece of embroidery. "But you didn't tell me," she said, turning her blue
eyes on Appius. "Surely he has written to you about it?"

"Not everyone reads their letters in public," Antonia
said tartly, and appeared about to do battle. "Julia, go to
bed."

"But, Mama—"

"But how nice that Flavius has been promoted, too,"
Helva said demurely, "especially now that poor little
Aemelia has been made to agree to a marriage."

Appius retreated to his study.

It was a golden season, all that summer. Correus, in
the pleasant haze of a coming cohort command, shook off
the horrors of his grisly battlefield search and set about
knocking into line the new recruits of the Eighth Cohort
of the Eighth Legion Augusta before Messala Cominius
was finally let loose from Labienus's watchful eye. Anset
the Egyptian and Rhodope and her girls made their appearance as soon as the coast was clear, and when Silvanus's posting came through they gave him a party with
Anset's wine in Rhodope's opulent tent. And if the question of how Nyall had learned that Ingald had sold him
away for a promise of Rome's favor crossed Correus's
mind now and again, he put it away from him. Nyall
and his tribe were dead and buried, and it didn't matter.
Knowing Nyall's spy wouldn't bring back the men of his
cohort over whose pyre he had made the death prayer as
the legate himself had put the torch to the pitch-soaked

wood. This was now, and he was among the living, with a cohort command to come, and a girl to go home to.

In the meantime they were at work strengthening the Nicer Valley forts and laying a permanent roadway between them. Flavius had a letter from Aemelia tucked in his tunic—a little stilted and possibly dictated by her mother, but written in her own hand all the same. In the face of that happiness, when the picture of Correus's German girl by Beorn's fire rose once or twice in Flavius's mind, he pushed it away.

And the road moved on. At any other time the howling boredom of cutting turf and digging endless miles of ditch would have driven them mad, but after the slaughter of Nyall's army and the brutal mopping up that had followed, the hard labor of building roads and camps was a pleasure and a release. In the face of all this fortification, the other tribes beyond the Agri Decumates were sitting quietly in their halls and signing treaties with Rome, while from the Hermanduri and the rest of the southeastern half of the Agri Decumates there was only shining good behavior.

The army even found time to do some permanent building at Aquae, just east of the Rhenus in the Black Forest, where a natural hot spring bubbled from the ground. The waters were said to be medicinal, and the civilian population of the Rhenus towns, assured of the district's pacification, began to make the trek to Aquae to soak away whatever ailed them in the bubbling pools. It wouldn't be long, Correus thought, watching a stout matron descending from a traveling carriage with two cowed-looking daughters in her wake, before the eastern bank of the Rhenus was as Roman as the west.

Labienus let Messala Cominius go back to duty in a month, and he took the cohort over from Correus, leaning on his staff whenever his leg pained him. Correus was glad to see Cominius up again, but only the promise of a cohort of his own made it bearable to give back the command. By the end of summer, Correus's desire for peace and quiet was finally wearing thin, as was his enchantment with ditch-digging. A nice land, the Rhenus, when it wasn't winter, but he would be gone from here soon, and he felt he was only marking time. When the

Eighth Augusta was finally ready to march back to Argentoratum at the start of fall, he was pacing like a caged wolf.

He reported in, saw his century settled in barracks, and gave them a short lecture on the evils of too much celebration their first night in town. They would have a whole winter of regular leaves, he said firmly, if they would kindly contain their exuberance now. On the heels of these pious remarks, he pitched his greaves and marching kit into a corner of the central room of his quarters and sprinted for the landward gate, still in his helmet and lorica. He dived through with a word to the sentries and then slowed his pace to a walk as the townsfolk in the market eyed him with curiosity. A Roman officer didn't cavort through the marketplace like a schoolboy on holiday, he told himself sternly, but there was a bounce in his walk all the same. It was almost evening, the air gold and slightly hazy, with the smell of cookfires in it, and the trees were going red and yellow. He felt good. He was home.

He had seen Freita for just a moment in the crowd that had turned out to cheer the legion home, and now she would be waiting for him.

The lamps were lit and light came invitingly through the unshuttered windows. The gray cat was asleep on the steps, and four kittens were wrestling in the path. There were flowers growing beside it now.

The kittens teamed up and began trying to catch a bug, and Correus watched them for a moment, uncomfortably. Amid the ending of so many lives, he had forgotten the possibility of a new one. Was that what had worried Freita in the spring?

"Welcome home."

The door was open and Freita stood there, smiling at him. He took the steps at a jump and pulled her into his arms, drew her inside, and closed the door.

"Take that thing off," she said, and he laughed and began to undo the straps of his lorica.

"I see the household has multiplied," he said, feeling awkward now. "Are there any other surprises?"

Correus had set his helmet on the floor beside his lorica and she caught him eyeing her waistline thoughtfully.

She started to laugh. "No, I have no surprises for you. I wouldn't mind, but that is a thing for the Mother to send, or not send, I suppose."

He put his arms around her again and smiled. "I wouldn't mind either, but it might be awkward just now. Freita, I'm to have a cohort command—I don't even know where yet."

He had known what her reply would be, but he had not expected the vehemence with which she said, burying her face against his neck, "Anywhere, Correus! Just get me out of Germany, please!"

"Wait a minute." He pulled away from her gently and saw that her green eyes were bright and troubled, and her face was pale, not its usual milky color, but a dead, chalky pale. "Freita, what is it?"

She shook her head. "Tell me . . . about the battle. Not the killing . . . but . . . but how it came. Tell me that first."

"All right." He lay down on the couch with his chin in his hand, while she took her usual spot in the chair by the hearth. He began to tell her, starting with the German spy, which was a subject he was never overly proud of, and going on to the trap they had laid in the hills above the Moenus. It was not the conversation he had envisioned for the first hour of his homecoming, but she wanted to know. . . .

Freita listened silently, staring down at her hands in her lap. Correus told her of Nyall's unexpected march from the south and the hasty river crossing by the Twenty-second Legion, the desperate stand by the advance guard, and the slaughter that followed. He painted a plain picture, bloody and factual, and by the time he was through, he thought he knew what was wrong.

"Nyall couldn't hold his warriors, not against disciplined troops," he said, gently now. "Not even when we were surprised. The spy didn't make much difference in the end."

"It made a difference to your own cohort."

His cohort . . . almost a hundred men gone, the worst loss in the legion. *His* men. "Yes. It tore it apart."

"I asked the gods for you," Freita whispered. "I didn't think to ask for your men."

"Freita, look at me."

She raised her head. She was crying, but she made no sound.

"You saw me with the German, didn't you?"

"He was at Jorunnshold," she said bleakly. "He made trouble there, too."

"And you warned Nyall, didn't you?" His voice was harsh.

She nodded. "They are my people. And so are you. I didn't know what to do. I can't be a German, and love you. And I can't be a Roman for you, not here. And now I've lost you both." She sat up straight, as if the tears belonged to someone else. "Bargains with the gods have a way of turning out like that. I should have known."

No! It wasn't fair. It wasn't even *right*. His heart ached for the men he'd lost but he reached out and pulled her from the chair and held her. "I love you," he said firmly. "If you don't hold your people's death against me, how can I hold my people's losses against you?"

She began to cry at that, out loud now, choking sobs that shook her whole body, and he just sat and held her. So many dead. But one lived with death . . . lived with it, and went on. Finally the sobbing subsided and he lay down on the couch and pulled her down with him, and she huddled in his arms.

"Were you weeping for me or for your people?" he whispered.

"Both," she whispered back.

He nodded. "I, too."

She raised her head and traced a finger along his eyelids, surprised to see his tears.

She put her arms around his neck, and they lay and held each other for a long time. Julius poked his head in the door, eager to welcome the master home, but they didn't see him. He backed out again, and then his face brightened. Argentoratum was in festival tonight, the streets thronging and lamplight spilling from every doorway. And he wouldn't be missed until dawn.

Finally Correus lifted his head and propped himself up on one elbow. He drew a finger along Freita's cheek and she opened her eyes.

"Now," he said firmly. "We talk."

Freita nodded. Her green eyes had dark smudges under them and her face looked exhausted. He realized that she must have been tormenting herself with this since the night she had seen the legate's spy. Worse since the legion had marched out. And probably worse still since she had known he was coming home.

"A double loyalty is no easy thing to carry," he said. "I ought to know."

"Your brother?" she whispered.

Correus nodded. "I had a choice once. Of killing Nyall or pulling my brother out alive. An oath to the army, or a promise to my father."

She closed her eyes for a moment. "I thought I could never make you understand. I thought I'd lost you."

"No. A decision like that, and no time to make it in— as much as I'm thinking that if you hadn't warned Nyall, my men might be alive, I've thought that if I had let Flavius go, and killed Nyall when I could, there might be many more men still living."

"With all the time in the world to think it out, would you do differently now?"

"I don't know. Likely not. Would you?"

She shook her head. "No." She was looking somewhere over his shoulder, but now she brought her eyes back to his. "Hindsight doesn't seem to help much, does it? Is that promise to your father still binding?"

"Yes."

"It's as well then, I think, this new posting. Correus, you cannot live forever in your brother's shadow, and he in yours. The sooner you are apart, the better."

"And the sooner you are out of Germany, the better."

"You'll never be able to trust me here, will you?"

He smiled. "I long ago gave up expecting a knife in my back. But I wouldn't be able to tell you things, and I need that. I never had someone to talk to before. Freita, I want you out of Germany for your own sake. If anyone else ever finds out who warned Nyall . . ." His face was worried. "My heart, I'd fight the army for you—but I wouldn't win."

She put a hand to his lips. "When I thought you wouldn't want me, I didn't care. Now . . . understand me, Correus. My loyalty is to you, not to Rome. It may never be to Rome, although I will try. But except for you, and your men because *you* care for them, I can't mourn your legion's losses. Silvanus, Lucius, that troublesome Julius. Those, yes, are friends. Maybe other Romans too, when I know them. But Rome . . . no. Not now, maybe never. I'm not a Roman, Correus, and I may never be. I love *one* Roman, not your so-great Empire. You must realize that."

"You got yourself in trouble, when you fell in love with me, didn't you?" he said.

She smiled at him now, a sideways smile that was almost a grin, cheeky and unrepentant. "I've always been in trouble. They sent me to wait on Jorunn's lady so she could beat it out of me, but it didn't work." Her mood changed abruptly, and she sighed. "Now I've got you in trouble, too."

Correus bent down and kissed her. "Don't flatter yourself, witch. I've been in trouble since my father adopted me. And I love you. That makes all the difference."

Freita wrapped her arms around his neck. "What does it mean, a cohort command?"

"A lot. Almost five hundred men under me. Senior officer's rank. More pay—enough to afford a decent house. A frontier-fort command even. In some provinces they split the legions up, or post legionary officers to camp commandant in auxiliary forts. I—there's no way to tell."

"And you don't even know where they'll send you?"

"There's a lot of Empire," he said cheerfully. "Half the world. Do you mind?"

Freita took a deep breath. "Not if you don't," she said.

"I wouldn't mind anyplace as long as you were there," he assured her solemnly.

And as long as you were still with your Eagles, she thought. Did they matter more than she did? That was a question only a fool would ask. He loved her. He would not be whole without her now. And he would end by going maimed and lacking all his life if some fool forced him to a choice that could not be made. She felt his hands begin to slide across the front of her gown and pushed herself contentedly against them. . . .

*   *   *

The knocking on the door grew more insistent, and Correus dragged himself up out of the depths of their lovemaking as out of sleep. Where was Julius? Oh. He would hardly come in with the master and mistress making love in the middle of the room. Correus fumbled for his cloak and wrapped it around him as he dragged the door open, then stood blinking at the resplendent optio on the steps.

"What is it?"

"Centurion Julianus?" The optio's face was carefully arranged in an expressionless military stare, but Correus thought his mouth twitched.

"Yes?"

"From the legate, sir. Orders, sir." The optio saluted smartly.

Correus attempted to salute in return and gave it up as the cloak showed signs of slipping. He took the sealed tablet and nodded at the optio. "Thank you. That will be all."

The optio saluted again, made a precise half-turn, and stepped off down the path.

Freita had relit one of the lamps. Correus stood beside it and turned the tablet over in his hands, two thin wax leaves sealed with red cord and the scarlet Imperial Seal. His orders . . . his cohort command. His ticket to whatever he could make of it . . . and of himself.

He took a deep breath and snapped the seal open with his fingernail. *Legio II Augusta . . . Britannia.*

An unknown province on the far edge of the world. Agricola had served there, he remembered. A place where a man could make a name for himself. He looked at Freita and then back at the orders. As good a place as any to start—for the two of them.

Glossary

aedile Roman political official in charge of games, the markets, various public archives

Aesculapius god of healing

Agri Decumates the lands between the Rhine and the Danube

Ahriman Persian personification of evil

amphora large, narrow-necked jar used to store and transport wine and food

Aphrodite goddess of love

Apollo sun god

Aquae Baden-Baden

Arachne Lydian maiden who was changed to a spider for bragging to Athena about her weaving skill

arena any theater in which gladiatorial combats and spectacles were held; generally an open-air amphitheater

Argentoratum Strasbourg

Atalanta beautiful maiden who agreed to marry only the man who could outrun her in a footrace; the successful suitor won her by dropping three golden apples given him by Aphrodite along the course, delaying Atalanta, who stopped to pick them up

Athena virgin goddess of wisdom and power

atrium the central room of a Roman house

Augusta Raurica Kaiser-Augst (a locality between Basel and Rheinfelden)

Augusta Treverorum Trier

auxiliaries cavalry, light troops, bowmen, etc., recruited from the provinces; term applied to all units other than the legions; officers were Roman, men received Roman citizenship upon their discharge

Bacchus god of wine

caltrops four-pronged iron spikes thrown on the ground to hinder the enemy

Castor and Pollux twin sons of Leda, devoted to each other even in death.

Centuriate collective term for the centurions of the Roman Army

century a unit of eighty men; six centuries made a cohort

Ceres goddess of grain and harvest

cohort six centuries; ten cohorts made up a legion

corona civica oak-leaf crown awarded to a soldier who saved the life of a fellow citizen

cuirass close-fitting body armor covering the torso

Cybele Asian form of Earth Mother

Danuvius the Danube River

decurion officer of cavalry or auxiliaries

denarius Roman silver coin valued at one twenty-fifth of the standard gold coin, the aureus; four sesterces equaled one denarius; at this time a legionary's pay was 225 denarii a year, a centurion's between 3,750 and 15,000

dexter right-hand

Donar German god of thunder, protector of men

Eagle the standard of a legion

Eagles the Roman legions

Eir German goddess of healing

Flora goddess of flowers and spring

Frey German god of fruitfulness and harvest, patron of marriage

Furies avenging goddesses

games gladiatorial combats, wild-beast shows, and other spectacles put on for the public amusement

Genua Genoa

German gods The gods mentioned in this book are listed individually.

Germany

  Upper Germany the west bank of the Upper Rhine and parts of modern France and Switzerland

  Lower Germany the west bank of the Lower Rhine and modern Netherlands

  Barbarian Germany (or the Free Lands) Germany east of the Rhine and north of the Danube

Gorgons three frightful sisters whose look turns the beholder to stone

greaves lower leg armor

Hades   lord of the underworld; also the name of the underworld itself

Hel   German goddess of the underworld

Hephaestus   lame god of the forge

Hercules   hero god famed for great feats of strength

hortator   on a trireme, one who sets time for the oar strokes with a mallet

hypocaust   Roman hot-air heating system

Isis   Earth Mother in her Egyptian form

Juno   wife of Jupiter, goddess of marriage and childbirth

Jupiter   Roman name of Zeus, all-powerful father of the gods, protector of Rome

latrunculi   Roman board game

legate   commander of a legion

legionary   the enlisted man of the legions; he was a Roman citizen

lorica   body armor of several types; at this time the legions were beginning to change from mail to segmented plates

magistrate   civil official of a Roman provincial town

Mediolanum   Milan

Mercury   messenger of the gods and guide of the dead into the underworld; also an arena attendant who dragged away dead bodies

Mithras   Persian god of light and truth, mediator between man and the supreme god

Moenus   the Main River

Moesia   Serbia and Bulgaria

Moguntiacum   Mainz

the Mother   Earth Mother in any of her many forms

Neapolis   Naples

net-and-trident   a form of gladiatorial combat in which the gladiator was armed with a three-pronged spear and a net with which to entangle his opponent

Nicer   the Neckar River

optio   second-in-command and general aide assigned to all officers

Pan   god of woodlands and horned beasts

Pannonia   parts of Austria, Hungary, and Yugoslavia south and west of the Danube

Persephone   maiden abducted by Hades to become his

wife; doomed to spend six months of each year in the underworld

Picts barbarian tribe of northern Britain, called Picti or Painted Ones from their custom of all-over tattooing

pilum Roman military javelin

Poseidon sea god and god of horses

praetor Roman political official, a legal magistrate appointed to courts in Rome and the provinces

Praetorian Guard the home guard of Rome, the elite of the army, and the personal bodyguard of the Emperor

prefect commander of an army camp; in a legionary base, he would command in the absence of the legate.

Priapus god of gardens and fertility

primus pilus commander of the First Cohort; in the field, second-in-command of a legion

Principia headquarters building in a Roman fort

quaestor Roman political official in charge of financial affairs; the first step in the career ladder

Rhenus the Rhine River

Roma Dea goddess personification of the City of Rome

Roman gods In addition to their own gods, the Romans imported cults from almost all the peoples with whom they came in contact. The Greek pantheon was almost entirely reflected in the Roman one, and Romans tended to use their names interchangeably. Gods mentioned in this book are listed individually.

Saturnalia Roman winter festival when slaves impersonated their masters and vice versa

sesterce bronze coin worth one-fourth of a denarius

Sign of Horns invoking the Horned God (similar to Pan) to ward off evil

Sirens sea nymphs whose songs charm sailors to their death

spina central divider on a chariot track

strigil instrument used to scrape the skin clean before bathing

Tartarus lowest level of the underworld

torque neck ornament, worn by Roman soldiers on the chest as a decoration

tribune officer of a legion, generally a young man serving a short term before beginning a political career

trireme galley with three banks of oars

Tritons male sea gods, half fish, half human
Typhon fire-breathing monster and creator of hurricanes, said to have a hundred heads and terrible voices
Valhalla German paradise for the souls of slain heroes
Venus Roman name of Aphrodite
Vesta goddess of the hearth
Vestal Virgins priestesses of Vesta, supposed to be incorruptible
Via Praetoria one of the main roads of a Roman camp, leading to the Principia and to the Praetorium, the commander's private quarters
Via Principalis the main lateral road of a Roman camp
vicus the civil settlement outside a Roman fort
Vindonissa Windisch
vine staff a centurion's staff of office; literally a cane cut from vine wood
watch troops patrolling a civil settlement
Wuotan German chief of all the gods; sky god; god of light, war, and knowledge, giver of life breath to men

Author's Note

My first encounter with the Romans was as the people who produced Julius Caesar, the man who produced the interminable *Commentaries* through which I waded reluctantly in high school Latin class. Then in college I met the Romans once more, through the eyes of a gifted teacher and such historical novelists as Robert Graves, author of *I, Claudius*. My ensuing love affair with Rome is now twelve years old and shows no sign of abating.

Suddenly the Romans were people, men and women struggling, even as you and I, in a time of civil conflict, unstable government, expanding boundaries, and all the ills of "civilization"—inflation, unemployment, racial prejudice, and overpopulation. What struck me most about the Romans, I think, was their resemblance to the British Empire and to America as we grew to a world power. Rome was the force of progress—not always right, but well-intentioned more often than not; struggling to do her best first for her own people and then for her conquered provinces; cruelly barbaric in some ways, enlightened and just in others; trying to keep pace with her own expansion and the march of progress, which can sometimes be deplored, but rarely turned back.

The Romans are ourselves, our origins. They gave us much of our form of government and our code of ethics. In Rome at her height, science and art reached a peak that was not to come again for more than a thousand years. And in the Romans our own triumphs and mistakes are uncannily mirrored.

In view of my fascination with all things Roman, when Lyle Kenyon Engel of Book Creations offered me the chance to do a series set in Rome, I leaped at it, the more so as the series, as he conceived it, was to be something never done before—a series to take the reader not only into the legions of Rome, but into its families. The series, as Lyle envisaged it, would draw its characters from among the men who were the backbone of the Roman Army at the height of its strength, but also from among their wives and sons and daughters, their lovers and their slaves; from merchants, senators, and tarts; from all the infinite variety that was Rome. And it would have for a setting not only the harsh country of the frontier, but the homes these professional soldiers returned to, the amusements they sought, and the farms they dreamed of retiring to at the end of their service.

"Wherever the Roman conquers, there he dwells." So said Seneca, in an apt summation of the Roman conquest. Rome's soldiers settled in the provinces they conquered, they married native women and raised Roman sons with half-British or half-German blood to follow them in the army. And gradually the provinces became as Roman as the City that stood at the heart of things. They must have looked at the City of Rome, these Romans born and bred on the frontier, much as the British in India looked homeward to England. You will find Roman ruins from Britain to Africa, ruins that once were houses and temples and law courts. The series, as Lyle and I discussed it, would people those ruins with the men and women who had walked in them when they were new. It was a challenge no writer could resist.

The Centurions, we hoped, would catch up the reader in the loves, triumphs, and despairs of one family, set against the gold-and-scarlet glory that was Rome in the days of her Empire, in the same way in which John Jakes's brilliant historical series *The Kent Family Chronicles* painted the lives of the Kents against the turbulent backdrop of the foundation of America, or Roberta Gellis's *Roselynde Chronicles* opened a window onto the world of a Norman-English family in the dangerous reigns of Richard and John. With the aid of Lyle Engel, who is a master of exciting action and plot, and in my opinion one of the most brilliant minds at work in the field of historical fiction today, *The Centurions* will follow our two half-brothers, one slave-born, one heir by birthright to all the privileges of an ancient family, through their own rivalries, loves and losses, and those of their wives and lovers, friends and enemies, seeing Rome both as she looked to the Romans, and as the strange and alien force that she appeared to be to the "barbarian" tribes she conquered. For a historical novelist, it is the ultimate challenge, and one which I am grateful to have the chance to tackle. I hope that I have succeeded in this, the first book of *The Centurions*.

THE CENTURIONS
VOLUME II
COHORT COMMANDER

THE ROMAN ARMY of the Eagles stand poised on their borders tensed to unleash the power to tame the Britons of the western frontier—treacherous, mysterious tribals, painted like fiends from hell, bright with paint and clay, their long hair hung loose behind them, an invitation to each Roman to take his head if he could.

The Romans, driven by the glory of marching where no civilized man had ventured before, build their network of roads in an ever-tightening network around the Britons. The success of their campaign hinges on one man with a terrible secret, Flavius Appius Julianus, a chained and mutilated prisoner. The tribals and the Romans race against time: Will Flavius reveal the secret to the barbarians before the Roman spy can locate the fortress to rescue—or, if necessary, kill him. That spy, who has lived and worked among the Britons, is Flavius's brother, Correus Appius Julianus.

Driven by desperation, the tribal kings struggle without scruples against their invaders, creating events in which all men must test their inner strength and courage, or wither and die. The magnificent Bendigeid, king of the dark and powerful Silures, orders the sacrifice of any man or woman whose death will prolong the life of his tribe—even when it becomes apparent that the death will be his own; Cadal, stately king of the Ordovices, ruthlessly ignores pleas for alliances, calling down the utter destruction of rival tribes; the Old One, queen of the matriarchal Dark People, ancient dwellers of the primeval hollow hills, must repay the Romans a life debt; and Gruffyd, king of the desperate Demetae, sends an assassin bearing a Silure knife to kill the Roman governor, but instead the blade plunges deep into Correus's beloved Freita.

Vulnerable, bereft, numbed by Freita's death, Correus's most menacing adversary is the exotic and beautiful princess Ygerna, Silure priestess and Goddess-on-Earth. Held hostage by the Roman governor, she is befriended by Correus, who has been ordered to protect and defend her against the tribals who seek her death. It is Ygerna who presents Correus with his greatest challenge, demanding him as a man and a lover. He is forced to assume a role more difficult than that of a spy, cohort commander, soldier, or centurion—that of taking a woman into his frozen heart.

Set against the battle for Britain, the eruption of Mount Vesuvius, and the destruction of Pompeii, CENTURIONS II: COHORT COMMANDER carries on the legacy of the half brothers whose lives and loves are inextricably intertwined. THE CENTURIONS is the latest successful series produced by the creator of the KENT FAMILY CHRONICLES, WAGONS WEST, THE AUSTRALIANS, and the AMERICAN PATRIOT Series.

Ballantine presents another series from
the producers of *The Kent Family Chronicles*
and *Wagons West*...

THE
AMERICAN
PATRIOT
SERIES